THE DIXIE DEVIL

BOOK 2 IN THE CIVIL WAR SERIES

DOUG PETERSON

'Shea Books

For Kristen and Ingrid

DOUG PETERSON'S
CIVIL WAR SERIES

Book 1: The Lincoln League

The story of John Scobell, the first African-American spy, operating deep within Confederate lines during the Civil War. Based on a true story.

Book 2: The Dixie Devil

André Cailloux is the forgotten first black hero of the American Civil War. This is the story of André and his wife, Felicie, as they try to survive in the turbulent world of New Orleans.

OTHER NOVELS BY DOUG PETERSON

Underground Railroad Series

Book 1: The Vanishing Woman

Ellen and William Craft escaped when Ellen posed as a white man, while her husband pretended to be her slave. A true story.

Book 2: The Disappearing Man

Henry "Box" Brown mailed himself to freedom. He shipped himself in a box from Richmond to Philadelphia. A true story.

Book 3: The Tubman Train

Harriet Tubman's name is legendary, but most people do not know her complete story. *The Tubman Train* is one of the first novels to tackle her remarkable life.

The Puzzle People

A suspense novel that spans the rise and fall of the Berlin Wall. Inspired by real events.

THE DIXIE DEVIL

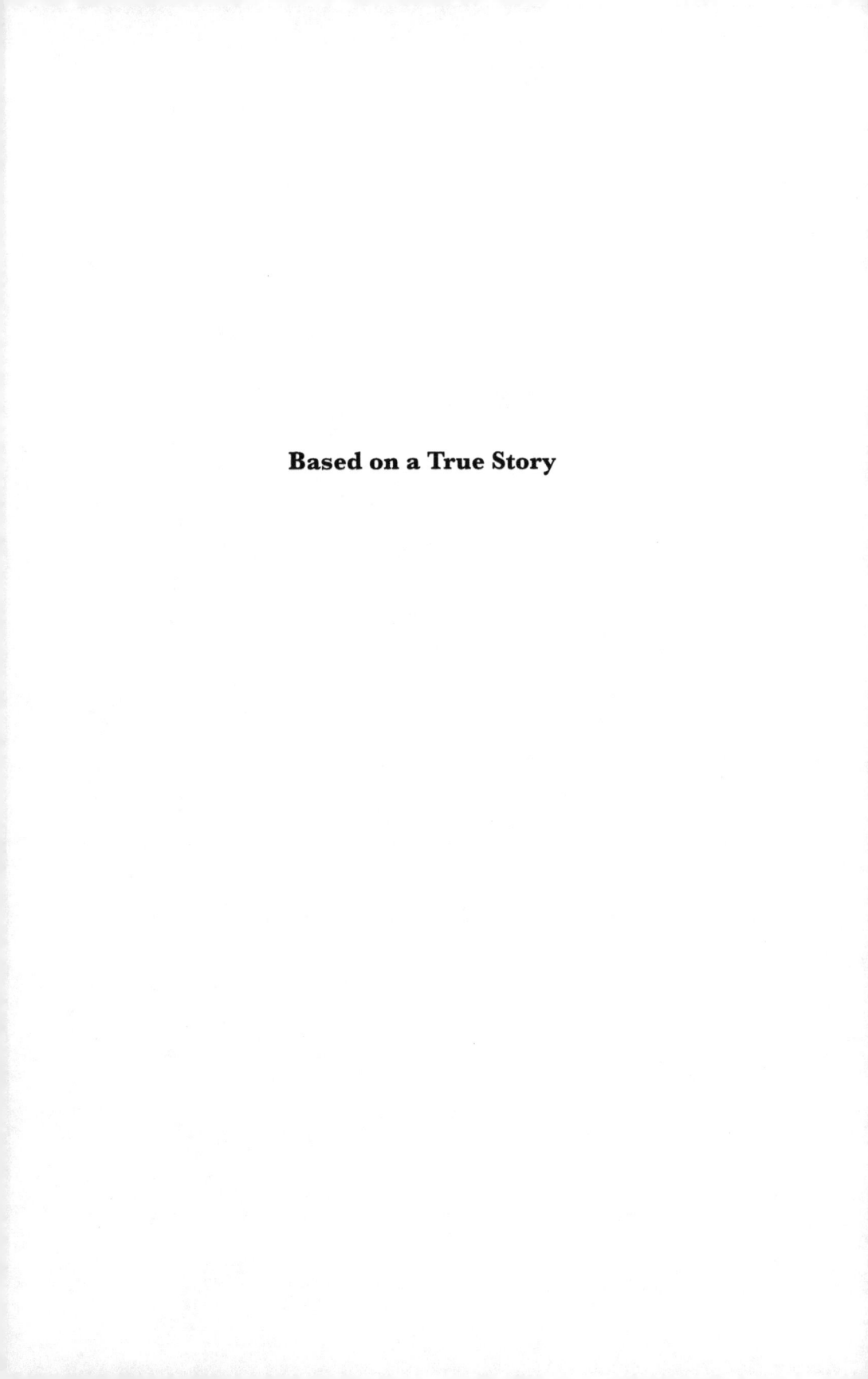

Based on a True Story

"Beauty is mysterious as well as terrible. God and devil are fighting there, and the battlefield is the heart of man."

— Fyodor Dostoevsky

PART I

PARADISE LOST

"He that falls into sin is a man;
That grieves at it, is a saint;
That boasteth of it, is a devil."

— Thomas Fuller

"Fierce as ten furies, terrible as hell...
Satan was now at hand."

— *Paradise Lost*, Book ii, Line 666

1
_____

F elicie Cailloux stood transfixed, listening to the bell echoing
from Christ's Church. As it tolled through New Orleans like a
dirge, she imagined people in town suddenly stopping in place—a
city of statues, everyone carefully counting the chimes.

One...two...three...

Twelve bells.

"Que Dieu nous vienne en aide," Felicie said to herself.

Twelve bells signaled that the Union fleet had broken past the
forts protecting New Orleans. Felicie tossed aside her cleaning rag
and barged from the detached kitchen, the _cuisine d'été_ just outside
their four-bay Creole cottage on Baronne Street. She made for the
house as their back door was thrown open with a bang.

"The Yankees are attacking!" Eugene, her fourteen-year-old son,
stood in the doorway with his hands on his hips, grinning as he
announced the news, for he had a boy's obsession with war.

His two sisters squeezed past him, with the youngest bursting

3

into tears as she made a beeline for her mother. Felicie crouched and opened her arms for Odile.

Wrapping her in an embrace, she shot a look only a mother could give. "Eugene, you're upsetting your sister."

"I'm not upset," said eleven-year-old Athalie, even though Felicie was obviously talking about four-year-old Odile.

Felicie hurried her three children into the house as if a hurricane were bearing down on the city. That's when the faint thud of artillery filled the air. The cannon fire sounded too far away, too muffled to be striking New Orleans, but like any approaching storm, it would only get louder.

Eugene rushed to the front casement window, threw it open, and stuck out his head as if expecting to see a line of blue-clad soldiers streaming into New Orleans. "*Maman*, I see smoke!"

Odile broke into a fresh flurry of tears.

"Eugene, please keep your thoughts inside your head! You do not need to be saying everything you think and see."

"But *Maman*, don't you wanna know what's happening? Papa is out there," Athalie said, squeezing beside her brother and leaning out the open window. The noise was building in the streets. People were shouting. Some screaming. Doors slamming.

Papa is out there.

Felicie didn't need the reminder. As a first lieutenant in the Native Guards, her husband André was doing who knew what to keep order in New Orleans. The Native Guards, a local militia unit made up entirely of free men of color, had not yet seen any action in the war, thank God, but was that about to change?

As if to answer her question, pounding thundered across the city, reminding her of tribal war drums. These were not the rat-a-tat-tat of Anglo instruments, the kind carried into battle. These were African drums, an urgent rhythm that increased the cadence of her own heart, and she had to rein in her panic. She wondered if the Union fleet would dare to bombard Confederate New Orleans, the largest city in the South.

"Grandmama!" Odile shot from Felicie's arms to her grand-mother, Feliciana, who had just rushed through the front door. Feli-cie's mother, whose nickname was Ana, broke into a broad smile, only reserved for her grandchildren—rarely for Felicie.

"Eugene says the city is being attacked." Odile stared into her grandmother's face, searching for reassurance.

"New Orleans is *not* being attacked, Little One," said Grand-mama Ana. "You are safe with me."

Felicie strode past her mother and opened the front door. The streets were clamorous and chaotic. She bit her lips as a mob of men moved down the avenue in a bristling unit. Hunger stalked the city, and a hungry populace can be dangerous.

"Bastien, come inside!" she commanded, waving her arm.

Bastien was Felicie's forty-six-year-old half-brother. Although he was three years older than her, his mind was that of a child. Bastien lived next door with their mother, Ana, and was a constant reminder of their mother's former existence as the concubine of a white man, a sugar planter from Jefferson Parish. Ana had three children with three different fathers.

Bastien turned and smiled at his half-sister, laughing. But he obeyed, as he usually did, and strolled into the house, grinning as if it were his birthday. Everyone was safely together, except for her husband and their oldest son, twenty-three-year-old Jean Louis, who lived a little farther down on Baronne Street.

"I am going to find out what is happening with Jean Louis." Felicie gathered her shawl, giving her mother a questioning look. "Would you watch the children?"

With rosary beads in hand as they often were, Ana nodded slowly, her smile vanishing the moment she turned her gaze from Odile to Felicie.

Felicie kissed each of her children, although Eugene tried to dodge the peck on his cheek.

"I wanna go with you." Eugene's eyes pleaded. "I'm old enough."

"You're old enough to stay here and protect your sisters." Felicie placed a hand on his shoulder, waiting for him to relent. When Eugene finally nodded, she sighed.

At fourteen, he already had some of the military bearing of his father and saw sense in her order. He would protect them.

"Isn't it too dangerous for *you* to be on the streets?" Athalie asked.

"Joan of Arc can take care of herself." Ana lifted her chin, cutting her eyes at Felicie.

"I'm just going to Jean Louis's place. I will be fine." Felicie kissed Athalie on her head, ignoring her mother's sarcastic reference to her favorite heroine from history—the French Saint Joan.

"I will be back soon—promise." Felicie gave Odile a squeeze. "I promise, *ma petite*." Then she plunged outside, into the escalating chaos.

Felicie was weary—and for good reason. She was forty-three years old, seven more than her husband. While André still called her beautiful, she found it more difficult to believe, for she had let the years weigh on her. Although French by heritage, Felicie looked almost Spanish with her long, black, lightly curled hair and brown skin. Her father was a slave, not a white man like Bastien's father, so her skin was not nearly as light as Bastien's.

Felicie slipped past the large oak tree standing sentinel in their front yard, and she pushed open the green gate. She wore a tignon, a colorful headscarf that looked like a turban. Free women of color were once required to wear a tignon when the Spanish ruled Louisiana. That way, one could distinguish those of mixed-race heritage from white women. But tignon or not, no one would have ever mistaken Felicie as white.

Her legs ached as she trudged to the door of Jean Louis's home—a tiny shotgun house next to a small café. She knocked on her son's door, but there was no answer. She eased it open and stared into the inky interior. She called out his name and then sighed when silence responded.

She spun toward the street and stared at the riverfront, where distant smoke billowed near the levee. The Confederates must have set fire to their ships to keep them out of the hands of the Yankees.

Felicie paused, wondering if she should return home, yet she needed to discover Jean Louis's whereabouts. Finally, she drifted in the direction of the riverfront. A steady flow of people rattled past in wagons loaded with their life's belongings in the hope of escaping the city at the last minute.

The morning storms muddied the streets, leaving the sky overcast and gloomy. Felicie mixed in with the crowds as Confederate troops swarmed everywhere, but they looked just as caught up in the chaos as the civilians, even though it was their task to keep order. She spotted many members of the European brigade, made up of French, English, and Spanish battalions, but only a few soldiers from her husband's Native Guard. There was a mad rush of people, talking, shouting, and moving in every direction. She drew a deep breath. Should she return home before wandering too far?

One block down, people of all colors ran with buckets and aprons filled with sugar pilfered from storehouses. It was then that a rumbling roar sounded from behind.

Felicie spun as a mob streamed toward her, hoisting a white man on their shoulders like an animal set to be slaughtered. The man pleaded for his life, lifting his arms to cover his head, hoping to ward off his attackers as they yelled, "Yankee spy!"

"Traitor!" A large man took a swing at him.

"Death to traitors!"

When they reached the street corner, someone looped a rope over the traitor's neck and tightened the noose. Another person tossed the rope's opposite end onto a lamppost before the group hoisted the man into the air like a piece of freight being pulled onto a ship. The man's legs pedaled the air as his body twisted and turned like he was doing some ghastly jig.

Felicie turned and stared at the levee, where the black smoke thickened and darkened, coiling over the city.

∎∎∎

The docks glowed as brilliant flames rose into the air and the fire hissed like rustling wings. Heat seeped into André Cailloux's skin as he rode his horse along the levee where a mountain of cotton, thousands and thousands of bales, was wrapped in an undulating curtain of fire.

Some white folks still believed that dark skin made people resistant to the heat of fires, but André knew from experience that his skin stung just as much as anyone else's. Unlike some free men of color, he was proud of his dark skin and even boasted that he was *the blackest man in New Orleans*—a city with so many shades of white, brown, and black that it defied racial categories.

As André directed his horse along the levee, people ran in all directions, like demons in a white-hot furnace. One white woman stood directly in his path without a bonnet, her tangled hair straggling at her shoulders. She was large, at least six feet tall, with flaming red hair, and she lugged a bucket of stolen sugar in one hand and a pistol in the other. Trailing two feet behind was a man carrying another bucket of sugar with his good hand. On his other side, the man's right arm was severed at the elbow.

André tried to hide his reaction, but he blinked in shock because the man had attached a baseball-sized ball and chain to the stub and fashioned it as a weapon. André had heard of such a person who roamed Gallatin Street, but he didn't think the stories were true.

"Burn the city! Never mind us! Burn the city!" The redhead met his eyes with a look of fury.

Instead of responding, André squeezed his legs and used his reins to steer past wagons filled with more cotton to add to the pyre. It seemed tragic, burning thousands of dollars' worth of cotton, but the citizens would do anything necessary to keep it from Yankee hands.

Confederate ships were also being set ablaze out on the river, and fire swallowed the wooden vessels. In all, they incinerated fifteen cotton ships, sixteen steamboats, and one unfinished ironclad, all pouring out smoke. It seemed the entire river was ablaze. Meanwhile, men broke apart barrels of molasses, which ran down the streets like dark, sticky blood.

"Lieutenant Cailloux!"

André wheeled his horse around and saw another Native Guard officer, Captain Henry Louis Rey, approaching on horseback. They settled side by side to converse, seemingly oblivious to the insanity around them.

Captain Rey leaned over to make himself heard. "We have been ordered to disband!"

Like André, Captain Rey was a free man of color, a mixture of white and black, but he looked more Anglo than African—definitely not the blackest man in New Orleans.

André wondered if he had heard correctly. "What is that you say?"

"General Lovell has ordered us to disband, destroy our uniforms, and hide our weapons!"

André's eyes rounded in disbelief. The Confederacy had organized a unit of free men of color in New Orleans less than a year ago—the only such company in the entire Confederacy, other than one in Mobile, Alabama. Then, the Confederates forced them to purchase uniforms, and now they were being ordered to destroy them!

"What will become of the white troops?" André asked before clamping his lips.

"Lovell plans to remove them to save the city from Federal bombardment!"

André scowled. He had no love for the Confederacy. Like many free men of color, *homme de couleur libre*, he signed up for the Native Guards to save his property and protect his family. The Confederacy threatened both. But still, it was an insult to be told to destroy his uniform and retreat into anonymity as the Yankees descended on the city. He should have known the black troops were just for show. The Confederacy never intended to use them.

9

"What do you mean—to avoid bombardment?"

"If the city is not cleared of soldiers, Farragut has vowed to bombard us, so Lovell is pulling the white militia out of New Orleans."

"Then why is he disbanding the Native Guard rather than pulling us out as well?"

Captain Rey laughed. "You have to ask?"

André never wanted to sign up for the Confederate militia in the first place, but Felicie had convinced him. He resisted for the longest time, but when anonymous threats began to arrive by post, he submitted to Felicie's wishes. He had compromised his convictions for the sake of his wife and family. He had been humiliated, and now the Rebels were disgracing him a second time, casting aside the colored troops at the first whiff of trouble.

Tipping his hat to Captain Rey, André turned for the heart of the city and his home on Baronne Street. The area was clogged with wagons and people, so the going was slow. Smoke from the burning cotton carried in the wind and filled the air like an early morning fog. He passed a couple of fistfights and thought about breaking them up, but there seemed to be a more serious scuffle just one block away, at the corner of Magazine and Common Streets. A frenzied crowd hoisted a man onto a lamppost. A Yankee spy, perhaps? Who could know for sure? Mobs rarely cared.

André spurred his horse forward, pulled out his saber, and roared his fury. Although the musket that the militia supplied was next to useless, André owned his sword—a heavy cavalry saber made in Germany, thirty-five inches long. "Old Wristbreaker," it was called, and it was as sharp as a shark's tooth. Moreover, he was an expert with it.

André held the curved saber over his head, and the mob cleared a path, for they could see that he had no intention of slowing his steed as he made for the man dangling from the rope. The man had already turned blue in the face, but he was still treading air. His neck had not yet broken, so André still had time.

The moment André sliced the rope, dropping the man in front of him on his horse, the mob began to yell every curse in the book. Then the angry crowd surged toward his animal, punching his legs, stinging him like bees. Finally, when someone tried to yank him from his horse, he kicked his attacker's face, sending him flying into the arms of others.

When the half-dead man on his horse began to regain color, he blinked, struggling to determine how he had suddenly wound up on a horse. The last thing he had probably seen was either the gates of heaven opening wide or a dancing devil looking for a fresh soul to devour.

André sheathed his saber and spurred his horse forward to break loose from the crowd. As he did, the man he saved finally regained his senses and stared at André with a look of surprise.

"A colored devil!" The man's mouth gaped. "Am I in hell?"

"You will be if you don't shut up." André frowned, using his knife to cut the rope that bound his hands.

Instead of complying, the man waved an arm at the crowd, shouting, "How did I get on this horse with this devil?"

"I just saved your neck, you fool."

The man grasped his neck, where he wore the remains of the rope-like collar. Surely, he had to know he was safer on the back of a horse with a black man than in the hands of the hundred angry men surrounding them.

"Help! Help me, please!" the man called out to the horde—the very people who just tried to kill him. "This black beast is trying to hang me!"

"André!"

Andre stopped short, searching the crowd when he heard Felicie's voice. He steered his horse toward the crowd and scoured the angry faces as someone hurled a rock, striking him in the shoulder. The half-hanged man continued to bellow for help.

When André spotted Felicie, being jostled and nearly knocked down by the surging crowd, he shoved the lunatic from his horse. The man screamed as he plummeted toward the ground. As soon as he landed, four thugs began kicking him like a dog.

Without thought for anything but his wife, André charged into the cluster. When one man didn't have the sense to dodge out of the way, André's horse knocked him to the ground.

André's eyes locked on Felicie. Leaning from his horse, he reached with his left arm as Felicie's eyes brightened. She sent him a knowing smile, for they had practiced this maneuver many times in an open field for the sheer pleasure of it. As he came by, slowing his horse, she latched onto his arm with both hands and swung from the ground, her long blue dress sweeping the air. Felicie landed behind André, smooth as could be, moments before he turned his horse for an opening, spurring it into a gallop.

"That poor, poor man." Felicie glanced over her shoulder at the mass chaos and the supposed traitor, who would soon be within an inch of his life.

"He thought I was a devil."

"That stupid, stupid man." She returned her attention to her husband, laying her cheek on his back.

They raced back to Baronne Street just as it was beginning to rain when they heard what sounded like thunder. Felicie searched the sky, but André was sure it was the sound of Federal guns hitting the nearby Chalmette fortifications.

2

———

Jean Louis Cailloux gathered his gear, thinking the timing couldn't have been worse. He'd always had doubts whether the Confederate forts could keep the Yankees from New Orleans forever, but did the Union fleet have to choose this morning of all mornings to break past and bear down on the city?

This was the morning that twenty-three-year-old Jean Louis was taking studio photographs of Coralie Bisset, a *Créole noire* beauty, the daughter of a wealthy businessman. While the Bissets were a prominent family among the Creole elite, Jean Louis's father, André Cailloux, was just a modest artisan—a respected cigar-maker, but not what you would call wealthy.

Nevertheless, Jean Louis had his eyes on Coralie, a light-skinned belle of color. She wore a bright blue day dress with large pink bows above the cinched waistline and on each wide sleeve.

"We must be away for home," said Coralie when the city bells began to toll the warning. "That is the signal that the Yankee fleet has made it past the forts."

"*Nous ne pouvons pas.* It may not be safe to leave the building," said Minetta Gerard, Coralie's friend and chaperone for this outing. She peered out of the studio window on Royal Street. "It's madness."

When Jean Louis approached the window, he cocked his head. Minetta was only partly right. There was a growing crowd, but it was several blocks away, near the river. While "madness" was a bit of an exaggeration, he wouldn't be surprised if the city would soon lose control. He caught Minetta's eyes, and she smiled conspiratorially. Was she trying to come up with an excuse to remain in the studio? Was she helping him in his apparent designs on Coralie?

"We should at least finish taking the photographs, *mon amie*," Minetta said.

Like Coralie, Minetta looked to be under twenty years old. But unlike Coralie, Minetta's skin was dark. While Coralie could almost pass as white—*passe-à-blanc*—Jean Louis's skin tone was somewhere between the two of them. Jean Louis didn't know his birth father—a free person of color—but he must have had a fair amount of white blood. His adoptive father was André Cailloux, and it annoyed him to no end whenever his papa boasted that he was "the blackest man in New Orleans."

New Orleans was a colorful tapestry of interwoven bloodlines, for there had been much interracial mixing when Louisiana was under French and Spanish control. Now, under American rule since 1803, Louisiana leaders strived to create the stark black-and-white system that the rest of the country lived under.

"Mademoiselle Gerard is right." Jean Louis nodded at Coralie, who had risen from the chair and nervously fanned her face. "It would be safer to stay inside."

"But my father will be worried."

"Your father will prefer you to remain safe."

"I think it is best if we stay," Minetta agreed.

"Very well." Sighing, Coralie let Jean Louis lead her back to the chair, positioned directly below the skylight in Jules Lion's studio, where ample light poured on the subjects.

Monsieur Lion, a free man of color—French by birth—permitted

Jean Louis to use his equipment and studio to train himself in wet-plate photography.

"Must I remain perfectly still?" Coralie settled back into the seat.

"For now, moving is fine. I will tell you when you need to be still."

"How long do you have to expose the glass plates?" Minetta's warm breath rolled down the back of his neck.

Jean Louis jerked with a sharp intake of air, for he had not noticed Minetta slip up beside him. Suddenly, she was standing so close he could smell her strong perfume as she peered over his shoulder at the upside-down image showing on the glass plate on the back of the camera.

"Today is overcast—so perhaps twelve seconds."

Jean Louis approached Coralie and wheeled out a ghastly-looking device, which resembled an instrument of torture, with its long neck and clamps at the end.

"This will hold your head in place while I take your picture," he explained.

Coralie glanced over her shoulder with wide eyes. "I do not like the looks of that contraption."

"Don't worry. It holds your head still, but it is not painful."

The clamps were fashioned to fit at the back of Coralie's head, hidden from the camera's eye. As he adjusted them, her long, black hair brushed his hands, sending chills up his arm. She had exotic eyes and a long, perfectly sculpted neck. His hand grazed her skin as he finished positioning the head brace.

Minetta scowled when he returned to his position behind the camera. The chaperone did not approve of such intimate contact, yet he ignored her glare and pulled out his stopwatch.

"Tilt your head a little to the left. That's fine. Remain perfectly still now. Here we go." Jean Louis lifted the lens cap and began to time the exposure. "One...two...three...four..."

Just then, a thunderous boom sounded through the air and reverberated among the walls.

"*Mes cieux!*" Coralie jumped as if a firecracker had popped beneath her chair. So much for staying perfectly still.

"Yankee cannons." Minetta peeked out the large window facing the waterfront. "But do not worry. I believe they are still firing down the river, nowhere near New Orleans."

"I knew this was not a wise idea." Coralie rushed for the door, her dress swishing against the wooden floor.

Jean Louis sighed. The moment was forever ruined—as was the photograph. The only way to salvage this morning was to position himself as Coralie's protector.

"Then I will escort you safely home, Mademoiselle." Jean Louis nodded, but before he could offer her his arm, Minetta slipped between them. A very efficient chaperone. He bit back a frown. Too efficient.

"Yes, that would be very kind." Minetta nodded at her friend, who had gone even whiter from fear.

Jean Louis opened the door and bowed. Then all three trooped down the stairs to the street, where a crowd howled in the distance.

"If my father knew I was having a frivolous picture taken on such a terrible day, he would murder me." Coralie lifted a hand to her chest as they hurried along the street.

"I wouldn't fret, *mon amie*," said Minetta. "Your father would be more likely to murder Monsieur Jean Louis."

Jean Louis laughed uncomfortably, although he had a strong sense that Minetta was probably right.

3

—————

André watched his uniform burn. The butternut fabric curled in on itself as the fire consumed it, turning it to ash. He poked at the material until it was an unrecognizable heap at the bottom of the ashcan behind the house. As the flames consumed the fabric, a sense of purging swept over him, as if he were being purified of his compromises. The relief, though, was temporary.

Ten minutes after the uniform disintegrated, an odd mixture of shame and anger burned in his chest. He shouldn't have donned the Rebel uniform in the first place, yet war waged within him, seeing his unit disbanded and disrespected. He trudged back to the house and barely muttered a word to Felicie or the children.

Then the inevitable happened. The Yankee ships arrived in New Orleans at noon.

When André heard the news, he mounted his horse and rode to the levee to investigate in the rain. As he neared the river, he clutched his reins, knowing he would never forget the sight.

A swarm of Yankee ships, standing tall and formidable, was surrounded by the smoking hulks of Confederate vessels. The cotton stacked on the levee still burned, despite the rain, and the piles of flaming bales smoldered like miniature volcanoes.

Between the storms and the arrival of Federal ships, the docks were sparse, leaving only the hardiest of citizens. While André sized up the fleet, the rain suddenly came down in full force, a torrent. He turned his horse, returning the way he'd come. He had seen enough. The Yankees would soon be sending a landing party to negotiate a surrender of New Orleans, and that's when the city's citizens might unleash their fury.

As André headed for home, water cascaded from the brim of his slouch hat, and his clothes hung heavy with moisture. He looked like he had tumbled into the Mississippi River by the time he finally stepped through the door, dripping on the floor.

"Papa!" Odile shouted, running into his arms, then pushing away when she noticed the cold of his wet clothes. She shivered like a dog shaking off water.

"What did you see?" Felicie pulled him aside as Eugene hovered nearby, eager for news.

"The Yankee fleet has anchored." André's grim voice spoke volumes.

"Will they bombard the city?"

"I believe they will attempt to negotiate a peaceful surrender."

"New Orleans will *never* surrender." Eugene raised a fist.

André eyed his youngest son, who shifted from foot to foot as if spoiling for a fight. He had never told his son about his reluctance to join the Louisiana Native Guards, so Eugene probably assumed that he was an eager participant, itching to battle the Yanks. Eugene had no idea that his father would prefer to fight on the side of the blue. His son was too young for such complexity.

Truth be told, he was afraid his son would see him as a coward if he knew he had signed up for the Native Guards for the sole strategic reason of protecting his family and property. Decisions are much more black and white when you are fourteen.

"Have you talked to Jean Louis, *mon mari?*" Felicie pulled him further aside, out of earshot.

"No. Sorry."

"Do you think he is safe? They were hanging that man today."

"They did so because they thought he was a spy. Jean Louis can take care of himself."

Felicie went to the window and stared out. The streets were now a mud bath, and the rain was so heavy that it was almost impossible to see the house across the street.

"Jean Louis will be fine." André patted his wife's arm.

André stared out the window for a moment with a soft shake of his head. Jean Louis had always been a mystery to him. His adopted son hated it whenever he bragged that he was the blackest man in New Orleans. Perhaps that's why André always took pleasure in making the boast in Jean Louis's company. His oldest son needed to learn that you can't outrun your skin color.

For the rest of the afternoon, the entire family, including Felicie's half-brother, Bastien, and Grandmama Ana, remained in the house. Bastien sat in a straight-backed chair in the corner, rocking forward and back, while Ana doted on Odile.

Due to the strained history between Felicie and her mother, André had a distant relationship with his mother-in-law. Felicie was ashamed of her mother's past as a white man's concubine, which was once common in Louisiana. They called it the *plaçage* system because women of color were "placed" as "wives" of white men. It was also called a "left-handed marriage." These women were not wives in the legal sense because interracial marriages were outlawed, but women of color were still expected to be as faithful as a legal spouse. As their reward, white men sometimes gave their concubines money or cottages. This is how Felicie's mother had a place of her own.

André sat in a rocking chair with a book, while his rifle, revolver, and saber were hidden underneath a nearby floorboard. The only weapon he kept on him was a Bowie knife strapped to his side, just in case he didn't have time to retrieve his guns. He rubbed a bruise on his calf, where someone from the mob must have struck him with something hard.

André was thirty-six years old, seven years younger than his wife, and he had maintained a trim, athletic figure, despite Felicie's sumptuous cooking. Although he was also one of the best horsemen and swordsmen in the Native Guards, he was too old for soldiering. André retained a boyish face, he smiled easily, and he had a princely manner about him, especially in uniform.

"Shouldn't you be out looking for Jean Louis?" Felicie asked.

"The boy can take care of himself. I need to stay here with you and the children."

"Are you certain?"

André wasn't, but he didn't say so and was grateful when Felicie asked everyone to kneel for the rosary. When Lent began, Yankee newspapers boasted that the American flag would fly in New Orleans by Easter, which had passed only five days ago. Still, the prophecy was not too far off the mark. André's knees ached on the hard wooden floor as they prayed, but he absorbed the pain as penance for his sins.

···

Jean Louis escorted Coralie and Minetta back to their homes, but he did not linger long at Coralie's house for fear her father would appear. Instead, Jean Louis made his way to the levee, where the crowd had dwindled, and a boat cast off from one of the largest ships, approaching New Orleans with just a single sailor and two Yankee officers.

As the small boat approached, the strangest sight appeared in the background. The great Confederate ironclad ship, the *Mississippi*, a kind of monster *Merrimac*, drifted by, completely wrapped in flames. The *Mississippi* had not yet been completed, and it had been destined to become the most powerful Confederate ship. But it was being reduced to ashes before it ever fired a shot.

Now that the rain stopped and the threat of immediate bombardment was gone, the crowd began to grow. Two Yankee officers stepped onto land, sizing up the Confederate cluster forming around them in a crescent. Jean Louis wasn't sure if the pair of Yankees were brave or just foolish, treading on New Orleans soil without a complete contingent of soldiers. Finally, two respectable New Orleans men met them on the levee and led them toward the heart of the city—heading in the direction of City Hall, where Mayor John T. Monroe awaited.

The mob followed every step of the way, growing in number and becoming more restless. The crowd hurled every obscenity known to man as they pressed close to the Yankees, yet the two officers kept their eyes fixed, ignoring the heat of hostility. Besides, if anyone injured them, the city would pay with cannon fire.

"Long live Jeff Davis!"

"Death to Yankees!"

"Death to the Union!"

"*La mort à Lincoln*! Death to Lincoln!"

Jean Louis nudged a nearby respectable-looking gentleman, noticing he'd not been one of the men hurling curses. He motioned to one of the two Union officers. "Is that Captain Farragut, Monsieur?"

"The fellow's name is Bailey. Second in command."

Bailey and the other officer finally reached City Hall unscathed. The building was a magnificent three-story structure that looked like a Greek temple with fluted Ionic columns. Jean Louis hung back on Lafayette Square, directly across from City Hall, watching until the pair entered. As the crowd became increasingly agitated, Jean Louis wondered if it was too dangerous to stay on the Square.

When he turned to leave, he ran straight into a brick wall of a man. Laurent Bisset stood well over six feet tall—a full five or six inches taller than Jean Louis—and he had shoulders as broad as a barge. While Coralie could *almost* pass as a white woman, her brother, Laurent, definitely looked white. He bore no traces of his African ancestry. Laurent clenched the stub of a cigar in the corner of his mouth, and he carried a gold-tipped cane in his left hand—an ideal weapon with which to bash a person's skull. Laurent shoved Jean Louis's chest, sending him staggering two steps back.

"What were you doing today with my sister?" he demanded.

Jean Louis caught his balance and stood his ground with a glare. He had been so focused on not crossing paths with Monsieur Henri Bisset, Coralie's father, that he had forgotten about her older brother. "I was taking her portrait. It was all very proper. Mademoiselle Gerard was with us."

"I do not care if the Pope was with you. Stay away from my sister."

Instead of answering, Jean Louis took a breath, wondering if he should just ignore him and walk away. Some were challenged to a duel for less cause than this. When Jean Louis turned to go, Laurent yanked him back by the coat collar, still grasping his cane as he twisted the fabric. The man's grip was like a steel trap.

"You are the son of the blackest man in New Orleans, are you not?" Laurent plucked the cigar from his mouth with his free hand and held it inches from Jean Louis's skin.

It seemed as if everyone had heard his father's foolish boast.

"He is not my real father." The moment those words left Jean Louis's mouth, a twinge of Judas guilt knifed him in the heart.

André Cailloux may not be his father in the biological sense, but he had raised him. Denying his stepfather was pure betrayal. Jean Louis tried to squirm free, to get into a position to strike back.

Laurent narrowed the gap between his cigar and Jean Louis's left eye. "I don't care who your so-called father is. He is a piddling cigar-maker who can barely stay in business. What makes you think you can court my sister?"

With the cigar so close to his eyeball, Jean Louis stopped squirming. He couldn't risk any inadvertent contact with its glowing end.

"I was practicing my photography. That's not courting."

"Practice on someone else. If you come too close to my sister, I'll burn you as black as your father."

With the red-glowing tip only inches from his eye, Jean Louis looked around for any sign of a constable—one of the Charleys in the day watch who patrolled Lafayette Square. But today, they had more on their mind than a scuffle between two dandies.

When Laurent shifted the aim of his stogie from Jean Louis's eye to his cheek, the heat prickled his skin. It was less than an inch from his left cheekbone.

"We will have no black blood in my sister's line," he said.

While Jean Louis was tempted to remind Laurent that Coralie already had black blood in her line, he wisely remained quiet.

"Watch your step. Cigar-makers can get burned." Laurent narrowed his eyes.

Jean Louis slowly exhaled when the thug returned his cigar to its proper position, sandwiched between his teeth. Laurent gave him a final shove, spit on the ground, and disappeared into the mob.

Jean Louis's legs shook, and his heart raced as he trudged from Lafayette Square. He wished he had struck Laurent before the threat of burning could immobilize him. Instead, he was humiliated and ached with guilt after denying his adoptive father.

He had never met his real father, and all he knew about him was a name—Antoine Philippe—and the fact that he was a free man of color. Jean Louis asked his mother about him on several occasions, but each time she lashed back and told him to banish that name from his mind—and to stop calling him his "real father." He tried tracking down Antoine Philippe but never succeeded, so all he could do was imagine that he was one of the wealthy men of color who owned large tracts of property.

"Where are you headed, Saint Louis?" came a voice to his right.

Jean Louis spun to find Roussel Pinard, the only friend who referred to him with that nickname. In comparison to a womanizer like Roussel, just about anybody came across as a saint—even Jean Louis.

"I am returning home before the city explodes."

"I do not expect that to happen, *mon ami*," said Roussel. "The city is calming."

It was true. As gray twilight fell, New Orleans had tamed considerably. The sun had nearly set, workers were lighting street lamps, and the noise coming from City Hall had lessened.

"If you are heading home, you must be taking the long route." His friend winked. "It looks to me like you are heading toward Faubourg Tremé."

Right again. Jean Louis had decided to take a longcut through the Faubourg Tremé neighborhood, where many prominent people of color lived—including the family of Coralie Bisset. He knew it was foolish to go anywhere near her house after what happened with her brother, Laurent, but he had to prove to himself that he could not be intimidated. Besides, he figured that the darkness would protect him as he passed beneath her window.

"Are you thinking of sneaking into her bedchamber?" Roussel asked.

Jean Louis frowned. "Only *you* would consider doing such a foolish thing. I simply want to pass by her house."

"I suppose you're planning to quote Shakespeare underneath her balcony. Jean Louis, your romanticism sickens me. Wouldn't you rather join me on Gallatin Street?"

Roussel had to be joking—or making an idle boast. Roussel wouldn't dare risk his neck among the monsters of Gallatin Street—an area lined with dance halls, saloons, and brothels.

Even the prostitutes there were as tough as knuckles. Bricktop Jackson, named for her flaming red hair, had killed several men with her five-inch blade, and she terrified both men and women.

"You couldn't pay me enough to go to Gallatin Street, and I think you have the sense not to go there as well." Jean Louis rolled his eyes. Roussel talked tougher than he really was.

"Suit yourself, Saint Louis. Go on off to church and say a few rosaries for my soul."

"There isn't enough time left in the day to say enough rosaries to do your soul any good," Jean Louis said as Roussel laughed, adding, "*Adieu.*" Roussel headed off in the general direction of Gallatin Street.

Jean Louis still couldn't believe his friend would go there, but he didn't wait around to see. Instead, he made his way into Faubourg Tremé, populated by Creole cottages—compact, single-story houses made of brick and plastered over and painted in pastel colors. Coralie's family house was larger—two stories with beautiful iron balconies, arched Spanish windows, and flowers spilling everywhere. He remained on the opposite side of the street, just staring at the house, ever conscious that if Laurent found him, he would kill him.

Jean Louis wondered if he could convince Coralie to sit for another photograph since the first one failed. He might, but with the Yankees in the city, who knew what would happen next? Sighing, he headed for home, following the trail of streetlights, which saved him from walking in utter darkness. He lived only one block from his parents, and as he turned onto Baronne Street, the stretch ahead led into goblin-like darkness.

He decided to check in with his parents to assure his mother that he was all right. Knowing her, she would be worrying about him when the city was so unstable.

The second he approached the house, his mother threw open the door, her eyes wild. "Where have you been?" She ushered him in after he wiped his wet shoes on the mat.

"Down by the levee." He noticed a look of alarm on her face. "But I'm fine."

"I was afraid for you. They were hanging a man." She gave him a motherly embrace, and Jean Louis noticed his father move out of the shadows of the back room. As they broke apart, his mother took a whiff of his jacket.

"Perfume?" She paused, raising an eyebrow. "Who were you with?"

Jean Louis could tell she was worried that the scent was from one of the women on Gallatin Street. What other kind of woman would wear enough perfume to linger on a man's jacket collar—especially with a scent strong enough to overpower the burning harbor?

"Do not worry, *ma chérie.*" His father approached, putting a hand on Felicie's arm. "He has not been seeing that sort of woman. He has been seeing Coralie Bisset. Am I right, Jean Louis?"

Jean Louis stared at his father but didn't answer.

"I thought I told you to stay far away from the Bisset family. They are not the kind you want to associate with."

"Why? Because they are not the blackest family in New Orleans?" Jean Louis leaned toward his father.

His mother inserted herself between them. "We are not going to have this argument again."

"Is that why you insist on seeing the woman, Jean Louis? Because her skin is like cream?"

"She is a free person of color," Jean Louis said, scowling at his father.

Jean Louis had had it. First, Coralie's brother attacks him for having the audacity to show his dark skin in the presence of his sister. And now his father attacks him because Coralie has skin too light to pass muster for the blackest man in New Orleans.

"I said, is that why you insist on pursuing someone like Coralie Bisset? Because of her skin color?" His father raised his brow.

"No. But I suspect that you have a problem because she is a free person of *very little color.*"

"She is a Bisset. That is what I take issue with."

"Because they are too white for you?"

"No. Because the Bissets are not loyal to their people."

"Their people? Who are their people?" Jean Louis's voice raised an octave.

"*Gens de couleur libres.*"

"You talk about loyalty to your people?" Jean Louis laughed. "You signed up for the Rebel Militia!"

The second he saw the look on his father's face, he knew he had gone too far. His father winced, as if stabbed by his words. Jean Louis also roused his mother, who had been trying to be the peacemaker, standing between them; now she wheeled around on Jean Louis.

"You have no right to say that! Your father joined the militia to keep our family safe."

When all of the soldierly fierceness drained from his father's face, Jean Louis averted his eyes. The last thing he wanted was to hurt his father.

"Papa signed up to fight for our city. Who do you fight for, brother?" Those hot words came from the adjoining room, where Jean Louis spotted his younger brother, Eugene.

"Eugene, go back to bed." *Maman* intercepted her youngest son and steered him in the opposite direction.

Who do you fight for, brother? Jean Louis felt almost sick with guilt at Eugene's words, especially after he betrayed his father with Laurent.

"Good night." Jean Louis spun for the door, but his mama cut him off before he could throw it open and storm into the darkness. She embraced him once again, squeezing him with all her might before pulling back like an alarmed animal.

"What's that smell?" Her nose wrinkled.

"We already went over this. Perfume."

"No. Not perfume." She sniffed the air.

Jean Louis took a deep breath. There was a new smell—the odor of smoke. He had become so accustomed to burning ships and cotton down by the levee that he hadn't noticed the same odor just outside their door. Jean Louis charged outside and saw flames coming from *l'écurie*—the stable where his parents kept their two horses. The blaze sprouted like a fast-growing, fiery vine, crawling up the side of the stable.

"Fire!" Jean Louis looked on in shock. What he saw next would remain fixed in his mind—a man holding a torch, spinning to face him and wearing an animal's head.

In the light of the livid flames, he was sure the intruder wore the head of a bull. The creature's two horns glistened in the glow. Then the monster hurled the torch through the stable door before disappearing into the darkness.

Jean Louis ran toward the building where the torch ignited a pile of hay, leaving the horses frantic, stomping, kicking, and snorting, eyes wild. Suddenly, a blast of violent fire knocked him to the ground. Still, Jean Louis scrambled to his feet and plunged into the smoky structure without a thought.

4

André grabbed two buckets of water near the back door. A New Orleans ordinance required every household to keep two fire buckets at hand, and André had the good sense to make sure they were always filled.

"Alert the watch-house!" André shouted to his son Eugene, who was thrilled by the excitement, judging by the gleam in his eyes. André knew Eugene would do the job and do it fast. But he also hoped the watchtower would spot the fire long before Eugene arrived, and they would alert the firehouses with the city's new telegraph alarm system.

Trying not to slosh water from the bucket, André rushed toward the stable where a red glow flickered through the open door, and smoke poured out as if the stable housed dragons instead of horses. The moment he entered, a wall of heat slammed into him.

His son Jean Louis was trying to smother the crackling fire with a blanket as the flames devoured everything in its path. André glanced at the two buckets, thinking they would not be nearly enough. Still, he tossed the water, and the flames hissed back.

"The horses!" André's heart sank as an entire wall flickered, resembling a pyramid of fire.

Although the stable was beyond saving, he would not let the blaze consume their two horses. He also thought of his and his neighbors' homes. New Orleans was a forest of wooden structures, a city of fuel. He must ensure the fire wouldn't spread.

He jumped into action, heading for his wife's horse first because the flames were already flowing along the roof of the stable directly above the mare's stall. Helen, Felicie's mare, was on her hind legs, pawing the air and coming dangerously close to the fire above, which might ignite her mane.

Taking her by the reins, André tugged her forward when Helen kicked with her hind legs, cracking the wall. Jean Louis, with his back to the mare, nearly took a hoof to the back of the head. André exhaled with a sigh of relief, thankful his son was spared a fatal injury.

When André drew Helen out of the stable, he discovered his neighbors shuffling buckets from hand to hand in a double line that extended from the nearest well to the stable. Fires roused an entire neighborhood, and the law required that every man, slave or free, must help fight a blaze.

André handed Helen's reins to Felicie, who shouted, "Get Jean Louis out of there!"

"He's retrieving my horse!" André started for the stable when he spotted two horse-drawn steam fire engines racing down the street.

The fire company that reached the blaze first would not only get the larger reward but would be in charge of all firefighters. Because of this, fire companies were quick to react and had even been known to sabotage other trucks. He hoped the two teams would spend more time fighting the blaze than each other.

Back inside the stable, André could barely see Jean Louis in the smoke. His son had his horse, Paris, by the reins, and some of the roof was beginning to crumble to the floor, trailing smoke like small meteors.

André studied the area, determining how to best help, when Jean

Louis stumbled to his knees, buckling with a fit of coughing. He vanished from view in the black smoke, but reappeared moments later, and then the panicky horse charged past him, stepping on his shoulder and knocking him flat.

André leaped aside to avoid getting trampled or knocked into a fire-wrapped beam that snapped and almost buckled. While the crackling roof threatened to cave, he said a prayer of thanks when it held as everything else was snapping and hissing around him, warning him that he was running short on time.

Sensing the presence of someone next to him, André turned to discover Thomas, his neighbor who had led the bucket brigade.

Thomas heaved a bucket at the flames and shouted, "Get out of there!"

"My son is still inside!"

His neighbor's eyes went to the wall of smoke, and he cursed before retrieving the next bucket.

By now, André could not see Jean Louis at all—just a cataract of fire giving off billows of smoke—but he had a general notion where his son had fallen. As he dropped to his knees, he heard Felicie's voice from behind.

"André! André!" Felicie stood in the open doorway, a silhouette in smoke. If she came any nearer to the flames, her dress would catch in an instant.

"Stay back!" he shouted.

"André!"

"I'm getting Jean Louis!"

Felicie screamed as a couple of men pulled her from the stable. Clamping a hand over his mouth, André crawled forward, feeling the ground with his right hand. Even if Jean Louis was no longer alive, he was not going to let his son be burnt beyond recognition. He moved forward, ever conscious that the roof was blanketed with a blaze. A falling piece of flaming wood hit him squarely in the back, but he slapped it away before it could ignite his clothing.

When he finally felt the shape of Jean Louis's motionless body,

31

André was completely enveloped in smoke. He held his breath, trying to stay low as he grabbed his son by the armpits and lifted into a crouch position, pulling Jean Louis toward him.

It was said that a man's strength doubled in such situations. While André was a strong man, he felt himself weakening. His head spun from too much smoke. He was choking, and he no longer had any idea where the stable door was. Although his eyes, nose, and throat stung, he couldn't hold his breath any longer and was forced to take a heated, painful gulp of air. A column of fire twisted to his right like a miniature flaming tornado. All he could do was stare, unable to determine where the exit might be.

"André!" His wife's voice cut through the darkness.

He moved toward the sound, still staggering backward as he dragged Jean Louis across the blackened ground with flakes of fire raining down on all sides.

"André! This way!"

He followed her voice but stumbled on a burning piece of wood. For a moment, he lost his grip but quickly adjusted and dragged his son's body as best he could. When Jean Louis's shirt tore in his hands, André tumbled backward.

"André! This way! *Vous devez vous hâter!*" a man's voice called.

That's when the roof collapsed, bringing down an avalanche of fire.

5

New Orleans
Saturday, April 26, 1862

St. Rose de Lima Church was small, but it had been packed since Friday with praying parishioners who must be getting calloused knees by now with all of the reciting of rosaries and lighting of votive candles. Fear had a way of increasing the devotion of even the most hard-hearted man, and the Yankee invasion had certainly stoked those anxieties. So far, their prayers had been answered. The city had survived the first night after the Union fleet's arrival, and there had been no bombardment—yet.

The smell of incense was strong following the early Mass, hanging in the air like the smoke of smoldering cotton drifting over the levee. Once Mass ended, Father Claude Paschal Maistre went outside to the well before he would begin hearing confessions.

The sky was cloudy, but there was no threat of a downpour like they'd experienced yesterday. As Father Maistre took a sip of water from a metal ladle, he looked back at the modest, white-frame structure, which stood on Bayou Road. This Catholic church ministered to the back-of-town folks.

When Father Maistre had the church built in 1857, he made sure it was positioned in the traditional west-to-east orientation, with the entrance on the west. That way, he and the parishioners faced Jerusalem, the Garden of Eden, and the rising sun. Most importantly, they faced the direction from which Jesus would return.

Today, of course, the directions that weighed most heavily on people's minds were not east or west. They were North and South. But all points of the compass had their evil side—even east because it was the direction in which Adam and Eve fled after being cast from Eden. The west symbolized the darkness where the sun sets. The south represented wilderness, and the north told of coming disaster, for many countries had invaded Israel from there.

In the case of New Orleans, Father Maistre welcomed the North's invasion, although he hid his Union sympathies in this Rebel city. He took another long, luxurious gulp of water. Perhaps every direction had its poisonous side, he thought, because the Devil roamed everywhere, like a devouring lion.

Father Maistre, a stocky man with a round face, close-set eyes, and a neatly trimmed beard, tucked his hands in the vast folds of his vestments. When he bowed his head, one could clearly see the full retreat of his hair from his forehead.

When he reentered the church, he eyed the long line outside the confessional at the back of the sanctuary. Like a bucket brigade in reverse, people lined up with their backs to the confessional, so they faced the altar, keeping their eyes on the cross as they examined their consciences. The penitents were all shades—white, free people of color, and even slaves, a gumbo of humanity. The church welcomed everyone, and Father Maistre was determined to keep it that way.

He took his place in the middle booth of the confessional. On each side was a compartment for penitents, entered by way of a curtain. Then the priest took a breath and opened the screen to his right, signaling for the kneeling parishioner to begin. The screen had tiny openings, big enough to let in the person's voice but small enough to conceal the confessor's identity. And so it began...

"Bless me, Father, for I have sinned..."

One by one, people rotated through the two confessional booths, pouring out their life as if they had been holding on to a year's worth of sins and divulged them all at once. With an invasion looming, they wanted to clear their consciences and purify their souls, for who knew if they would live another day. Some were simple recitations, parishioners tallying their sins by numbers only—twelve venial sins, two mortal. But many people were shockingly blunt. They confessed to visits with prostitutes on Gallatin Street. Thievery. Adultery. Drunkenness. Slander. Gossip. Even voodoo. Many smelled of smoke, probably from spending time down by the levee where the ships and the cotton burned.

His day was anything but boring.

The parishioners kept coming until mid-morning when a penitent dropped onto the kneeler with a loud thump in the confessional to his left. Father Maistre couldn't see the person, but the smell of smoke was pungent. After sliding open the screen, he waited for the person to make the sign of the cross and begin. Nothing. Silence. The penitent exhaled but didn't speak.

"You may begin," Father Maistre urged.

The voice finally spoke—in a hissed whisper. "Bless you, Father, for you have sinned."

Father Maistre's heart skipped a beat as the man paused and his statement sunk in. The priest shook his head and said, "Pardon, but I assume you mean, 'Bless *me*, Father, for I have sinned—'"

"No." The voice bit back. "Bless *you*, Father, for *you* have sinned. You have sinned most grievously."

Father Maistre was tempted to ask who he was, but the confidentiality of confession restrained his tongue.

"This is *your* confession, *mon ami*," the priest said. "Not mine."

"But perhaps it *should* be your confession, Père Maistre. God knows you have sinned much."

"Please, if you do not plan on making your confession, leave the confessional and make room for another."

"Have you confessed about what happened in Thuisy?" The husky whisper raised with the slightest hint of a threat.

Father Maistre winced at the mention of the city, closing his eyes.

Thuisy, France. It was the town where he had his first post. "What do you know of Thuisy?"

"Enough."

"What does that mean?"

"It means you would not want me to talk to Bishop Odin."

Father Maistre said nothing.

"Your silence tells me you have not yet confessed the sins you committed while there," the voice said.

The priest was tempted to haul this man from the confessional and throw him out of the church—like Jesus did to the moneychangers. But such an outburst would be enough to get him thrown out of his parish, which is just what Bishop Odin would like.

"What I have confessed is between me and God."

"And *me.*"

Father Maistre wondered if Lucifer himself lurked inside the adjoining confessional.

"Bless you, Father, for you have sinned..." the man repeated.

Before Father Maistre could respond, he heard the creak of the kneeler in the confessional and the curtain swish. The priest wanted so badly to peek and uncover who had just threatened him. But if the other parishioners spotted him looking at the departing confessor, they would think their confidentiality was not protected. He could do nothing but sit and stew, wondering if the threat was real.

How could this man know what had happened in Thuisy, France, when he had run thousands of miles to keep that incident far behind him? A woman cleared her throat in the confessional to his right, breaking him from his thoughts. He slid open the panel and made the sign of the cross in the air.

"Bless me, Father, for I have sinned..." she started.

6

The entire house smelled of smoke, even though the flames had never spread from the stable, thank God. Jean Louis's throat was still raw, and his chest ached if he breathed too deeply, but at least he was alive. When his father dragged him from the stable the night before, Jean Louis had been unconscious and didn't come back to reality until his parents put him on their bed.

His father had saved him—the man he had denied as being his "real father," the man he had accused of not being loyal to his people for putting on a Rebel uniform. The guilt continued to scratch at him, as sore as his throat.

"How are you feeling?" His mother appeared in the bedroom doorway, holding a fresh pitcher of water. Considering the amount used to extinguish the fire, it was surprising there was any left in the well. "You have a visitor. A young woman."

Coralie?

Surely, she would not have taken such a risk by coming here. What would her father think? Not to mention his own father!

"It is Mademoiselle Minetta and her younger brother, Maurice."

Jean Louis's heart dropped. But perhaps Minetta Gerard brought a message from Coralie.

Jean Louis had already bathed and dressed, trying fruitlessly to scrub the smoky smell from his skin. As he stood, his head spun for a moment, but he caught his balance and entered the main room, where Minetta and her brother sat, facing Jean Louis's father and talking together in French.

Maurice was younger than Minetta by several years, but he provided the security that a young lady on the streets would need in such a time. Even with a male escort, Jean Louis was surprised that Minetta's mother allowed her to roam. But with nine children, her mother had trouble reining them all in, especially one as single-minded as Minetta. Her father was too consumed with his work as a cabinetmaker to pay her much heed.

Jean Louis bowed. "*Bonjour*, Mademoiselle Gerard. *Bonjour*, Maurice."

"*Bonjour*, Monsieur." She smiled and looked down at the basket at her feet. "We bring bread and cheese."

"That is very kind of your family," said Jean Louis's mother, taking up the basket. "Send them our deepest appreciation. But I would not have asked you to take such a risk venturing across town for our sake."

"Don't worry, Madame. The streets from Tremé to here were peaceful."

"We are so grateful," added Jean Louis's father, beaming at Minetta. Of course, he was beaming! Minetta's skin tone was much closer to his. Jean Louis tried to banish such thoughts; his father deserved more respect—and gratitude.

His father displayed several fresh scrapes on the side of his face, but it could have been much worse. When the ceiling caved, the stable walls prevented it from landing on them.

While *Maman* carried the food to the detached kitchen, Jean Louis took a seat, and Minetta shared pleasantries, while her brother Maurice looked just plain bored.

Then the conversation suddenly became much more interesting.

"I have heard that the fire was set deliberately," Minetta said.

Jean Louis noticed his father's right eyebrow shoot up in surprise that she would make such a bold statement.

Jean Louis nodded. "I spotted a man with a torch. He was wearing a mask."

"But the city has forbidden them."

That was true. Because of the Yankee threat, Mardi Gras had been suspended for the first time, and masks were banned.

"If our culprit has no qualms about burning someone's stable, it is no surprise that he also has no qualms about breaking a law forbidding masks," said Jean Louis's father with the hint of a grin.

"I see your point." Minetta smiled awkwardly, then turned toward Jean Louis. "So you saw that it was a man?"

Jean Louis scratched his cheek. Actually, he had been so focused on the mask that he hadn't really looked at much else. It all happened so fast that he just assumed it was a man.

"He wore the mask of a bull," Jean Louis said as if that explained why he thought it was a man.

Minetta's eyes went wide. "You mean like Moloch?"

Jean Louis was baffled. "Moloch? You know the man's name?"

For some reason, Minetta covered her mouth as she giggled.

"You will have to excuse Jean Louis," said his father. "He never was a serious student of classical literature."

Jean Louis's face burned hot with embarrassment, but he had no idea what he had said that was so funny.

"Moloch the Destroyer is a horrid devil," explained André. "A god who sacrifices his children in fire, personified by the head of a bull."

"I am sorry, you must think me rude," Minetta said, her eyes still lit by amusement. "I didn't mean to laugh."

"I suppose I simply do not spend much time dwelling on devils," Jean Louis said, sounding more defensive than he intended.

"That is a good thing, as long as you do not dismiss their existence or influence on our lives," André said, putting a hand on his son's shoulder. Jean Louis tried not to flinch at his touch. "But this particular devil—Moloch—made an appearance in the Mardi Gras several years ago."

"I remember the mask. That is why I thought of Moloch when you said it was a bull's mask," Minetta said.

André frowned, scolding Minetta with his eyes. "But you were too young to attend the ball where these devils frolicked a few years ago. You are *still* too young for such things."

"I didn't attend the ball, but I saw the parade. I was not supposed to watch, but I confess. I saw the devils march by our house carrying their torches."

André leaned back in his chair. "That year, many members of the Mystick Crewe were dressed as devils for Mardi Gras. Their theme was *Paradise Lost.*"

"With Mardi Gras suspended this year, a reveler must have dug up an old mask then," Jean Louis said.

"Possibly."

"So, do you think the person who set the fire is a member of the Mystick Crewe of Comus?" Minetta shot a questioning glance at André.

"That is possible." André inhaled. "But that doesn't tell us much since the identity of the members of the Mystick Crewe is a closely guarded secret."

On Mardi Gras, members of the Mystick Crewe of Comus appeared in the afternoon, all wearing masks; then, they participated in the parade and revelries at the Mystick Crewe ball. At the stroke of midnight, they all melted into the night—their identities protected.

"Some claim to know the identities of one or two members," said Minetta.

"It would only be guesswork," said André. "For all you know, Mademoiselle, I could even be a member of the Mystick Crewe."

Jean Louis could not imagine his father, a devout Catholic,

donning the mask of a devil, even for Carnival. His father was as straight-laced as they came.

"But the man might not even be a member of the Mystick Crewe. It is possible the arsonist got his hands on an old mask in storage." Minetta tapped her bottom lip in thought as his father nodded in agreement.

Minetta certainly was a curious sort. Not many women spoke so plainly. His mother did, but that was his mother's way, and he was used to it. He wasn't sure if he liked it in a woman of his own age.

When Felicie returned to the room, they shifted to more mundane matters—the cabinetry work of Minetta's father and the health of her grandmother. Then Minetta said she did not want to put any more strain on Jean Louis's throat with this conversation and excused herself.

"Jean Louis, would you be so kind as to escort Mademoiselle Gerard and her brother home?" His mother sent him an expectant stare.

"But Monsieur should be convalescing. I would not want to put on any added strain." When Minetta lifted a hand in protest, her eyes still had the glimmer of hope.

"My throat is scratchy, but my spirit is strong." Jean Louis rose to his feet. "I would be happy to escort you home."

"Thank you, Monsieur." Minetta was positively shining.

As they exited the house, their eyes instinctively went to the right, where all that remained of the stable was a blanket of black ashes and the stubble of charred wood. The pervasive smoky odor burned Jean Louis's lungs. He swallowed, tasting the soot that still clung in the air, and fought the urge to cough.

Jean Louis and Minetta headed toward Faubourg Tremé, where her family lived—only a few blocks from Coralie's home. Maurice trailed far behind, fixated on the piece of charred wood in his hands, and this gave Jean Louis the opportunity he wanted.

"Has Mademoiselle Coralie asked about me?" He cut his eyes at her, waiting.

Minetta's smile vanished, and she paused before answering. "I have not spoken to her today."

"Then would you speak to her for me?"

Another pause. Then a sigh. Was she upset with his request?

"Yes. Of course, I would be happy to."

She didn't look too happy.

"Would you ask Mademoiselle Coralie if we could meet tomorrow before church?"

"Monsieur, do you think that is wise? What if you are seen by her father or brother?"

"I will be careful."

"I will speak to Mademoiselle Bisset, but I cannot guarantee she will be able to get away from her family to meet with you."

"I will be at St. Augustine's Church tomorrow just before Mass starts. You are a true friend."

Minetta smiled just before her face twisted. A foul stench hit them as they turned onto one of many streets where the garbage was piling up and flies feasted. In recent weeks, pockets of the city had been ignored by sanitation men as the city slipped into chaos. They hurried past a stagnant pond where the carcass of some animal floated and putrefied. Minetta and Jean Louis put handkerchiefs to their faces, and Jean Louis took her by the arm to hurry her along. Even her brother Maurice moved at a quick clip to find fresh air.

Safely past the stench, they noticed the city beginning to stir. Wagons rattled by, and crowds of rowdy men marched along, some carrying clubs and guns, moving en masse in the direction of City Hall and the levee.

"The city is beginning to heat up again." Jean Louis studied the streets with a stern eye. "If Mademoiselle Coralie is too fearful of meeting tomorrow, I will understand."

"Very well, Monsieur."

Minetta touched his hand and stared at him until he had to divert his eyes. She left her hand in contact with his for a few moments before smiling and turning to go.

7

It was mid-morning as André rode to the levee, and the clouds had thickened and darkened to bluish-black, threatening more rain. The crowds had also returned in full force, roused by the sight of the Federal flag flying atop the Mint on Esplanade Street, not far from the river. A contingent of Yankees hauled down the Louisiana flag in the early morning hours and replaced it with the Stars and Stripes, an act that was like poking a hornet's nest with a stick.

André lifted a hand to his face with a sigh. The scratches on his cheek still stung, but it was the squabble with Jean Louis that smarted the most. André had always stressed to his son the importance of being free people of color—ones who owned property and held dignified jobs. Church-going people. He didn't understand why Jean Louis would chase after a nearly white girl from a family that tried to conceal their African blood.

Just as bad, Coralie's father, Henri Bisset, was a large, overbearing man who flaunted his money. It didn't help that the Bissets also ran a cigar-making factory, employing close to two hundred people, while André had only a dozen. In New Orleans, it seemed as if every other man had a cigar in his mouth. But with over one hundred and fifty cigar-makers fighting for business in New Orleans, it was difficult to keep his head above water. Coralie's father was the kind of man who enjoyed seeing his competition financially submerged; in fact, he would gladly shove your head under the water and hold it there.

Surveying the scene in front of the Mint, André leaned over and patted the neck of his horse. He'd had his steed for seven years and was unsure what he would have done had he lost him in the fire. There were still pockets of looting throughout the city as people broke down doors and raided shops for food, but most of the people's wrath was directed at the Mint, a long, three-story, brick building.

In the very center of the structure was a Greek-style entrance with six towering pillars. Perfectly centered on the roof was a large flagpole, from which the Stars and Stripes snapped in the breeze. People threw rocks at the American flag while somebody held up a Confederate flag, waving it in defiance.

Then a roar went up, and André spotted four men on the roof. The crowd cheered them on, laughing and screaming as if they were watching circus performers about to perform a wonder. Taking the cue, one of the men bowed to the crowd while another held up his arms in triumph. When a third man busily pulled down the Stars and Stripes, the mob nearly went berserk. As the United States flag came down, several men threw stones, shattering the Mint's windows, and back up went the flag of Louisiana.

André looked around for any sign of Yankee soldiers. If there were any present, would they dare fire on the four men on the roof?

One of the men above held out the Stars and Stripes like a matador, while another bent over, placing his fingers near his temples and charging like a bull. The crowd ate it up. Soon after, one of the instigators snatched the American flag from the matador and hurled it off the roof. It floated down on the people like a dead autumn leaf, and hundreds of arms reached up, hoping to grab it and take a turn tearing at it.

André's horse skittered and snorted, sensing the sudden boost in tension and anger. He eased his horse from the chaos, observing from a safe distance. But the mob kept growing, as people joined from all sides. Then they contracted inward like a shiver of sharks, converging on their victim. In the center of the tumult was the U.S. flag.

As people screamed, André prayed that no one would be killed in the crush of humanity. But then another cheer went up, and the crowd expanded outward as "Dixie" began to play. It seemed as if everyone was singing or shouting at the top of their lungs; they started singing a new version with lyrics updated to speak to the Rebel spirit of war.

> *"Oh, hear the Northern thunders mutter!*
> *Northern flags and South winds flutter,*
> *To arms! To arms! To arms! In Dixie!*
> *Send them back your fierce defiance!*
> *Stamp upon the cursed alliance!*
> *To arms! To arms! To arms! In Dixie!"*

When the crowd parted, a woman stood, waving the Confederate flag before marching toward the river. Behind her, several men dragged the Stars and Stripes in the mud.

> *"Advance the flag of Dixie!*
> *Hurrah! Hurrah!*
> *For Dixie's land, we take our stand,*
> *To live or die for Dixie!*
> *To arms! To arms!*
> *And conquer peace for Dixie!*
> *To arms! To arms!*
> *And conquer peace for Dixie!"*

André retreated as the mob moved in his direction, heading toward the riverfront. He found safety off the main street, behind a couple of trees, and the crowd flowed past like a mad river at flood stage. Then a man held high a large pair of scissors like a sword, and the singing was drowned out by hooting and caterwauling. The man went to work, snipping off fragments of the flag and tossing them to the crowd like bouquets at a wedding.

It was an ironic image because the tradition of tossing the bouquet arose as a substitute for a wilder French practice—ripping off pieces of the bride's wedding gown, much like they were doing to the flag. It would probably be wise to head back home, away from this insanity, but the antics of the crowd were mesmerizing.

"Monsieur Cailloux, come join the carnival!"

André looked toward his right and spotted his son's friend, Roussel Pinard.

"*Le diable à midi!*" André exclaimed.

Roussel looked soused already—a walking whiskey vat—despite it still being morning, and he had an equally drunk wench hanging on his arm. He was dressed in a gray suit like a dandy, but his collar was inside out, and his top hat was cocked to one side. A scrap of the slashed American flag stuck out of his coat pocket like a multi-colored handkerchief, and his woman also had a piece of the flag sticking out from the bodice of her mud-splattered dress. André scowled in disapproval. Jean Louis's choices in male compatriots were even worse than his choices of women.

"Come join the festival!" Roussel staggered to his right, holding his lady around the waist as they stumbled as one person. The woman, with her long, blonde hair in a tangle, burst out laughing. Then the pair of fools swayed back to the left, bumping into a portly gentleman who shoved them, and they tumbled into a hysterical laughing pile on the ground.

As they fell, André noticed a figure about twenty feet behind them. He sucked in a breath. It was a man in a mask! The mask of Moloch.

André urged his horse forward, but he couldn't go too fast, or he might trample someone—such as Roussel and his wench, who had staggered back to their feet and stood directly in his path, wobbling and laughing.

"Why so serious, Monsieur?" asked the woman.

"Out of my way!" André shouted.

Roussel began to sing. "To arms! To arms! In Dixie!"

The fool. "Out of the way!"

The masked man spotted André and turned to run. When André couldn't maneuver his horse in such a crowd, he leaped from the animal's back and jammed the reins into Roussel's hands.

"Take care of my horse!"

Roussel stared bleary-eyed at the reins that had suddenly appeared in his hands as if by magic. Then André took off on foot at full tilt, his eyes locked on the man with the mask. Moloch barreled into two men, sending them sprawling like bowling pins, and kept running. Curses were thrown as André leaped over one of the fallen men, clearing him cleanly. He gained on the devil, who must be finding it difficult to run with his vision limited by the mask. Then a large man stepped directly into André's path—a man with his gaze fixed straight ahead and utterly oblivious to the foot race.

"Hey!" the man shouted as André tried to avoid a collision, putting his hands on the man's back and pushing off and to the side.

André took his eyes off the Moloch mask during that brief maneuver, but for only a second. When he looked back up, the man was gone. André continued to fight his way through the crowd, spinning as he did, searching the crowd. How hard could it be to spot a man with the head of a bull? Unless he'd taken it off and slipped away.

The singing became louder.

> *"Fear no danger! Shun no labor!*
> *Lift up rifle, pike, and saber!*
> *To arms! To arms! To arms! In Dixie!*
> *Shoulder press and post to shoulder,*
> *Let the odds make each heart bolder!*

To arms! To arms! To arms! In Dixie!"

There! André had just about given up when he saw Moloch slouching down Chartres Street. The masked man was rushing and glancing around, probably thinking he had eluded his pursuer.

Before André could renew his pursuit, a loud boom echoed from the water. A Yankee ship had fired a howitzer on the city, resulting in a dreadful explosion as a shell crashed into the Mint, hurling bricks in all directions. Suddenly, the crowd transformed into a wild stampede. People screamed, and ladies broke down in tears as many scattered, and André was plowed over by two men.

The world went spinning, and André hit the ground, managing to get back up moments before he would've been trampled. He realized that he, too, had better escape before the shells started raining down with devastating power. Had the bombardment finally begun?

André was never going to catch the man in the mask now, so he began searching the crowd for any sign of his horse. He had been a fool to give the reins to a drunk like Roussel. But as he worked his way back to where his pursuit began, he spotted Roussel trying to push his soused companion onto Paris's back. The lady made two attempts to climb onto the horse, but the first time she slid off the animal's backside, and the second time she went completely over the top and headfirst to the ground.

Rushing forward, André helped the drunken wench back to her wobbly feet and gave her a more sober-minded lift onto the horse. She was probably a prostitute, but the Good Lord reached out a hand to fallen women, so the least he could do was the same. In this crowd, it would be safer for her on the back of the horse, where she positioned herself properly, as if in a sidesaddle, even though she wasn't the most proper of ladies. Then André snatched the reins out of Roussel's hands, giving him a scowl.

"Thank you, kind sir, you are most gentlemanly," said the lady, smiling drunkenly and leaning over—almost too far.

André scoffed, putting a hand on her forehead to keep her from toppling out of the saddle.

He took one last look at Roussel, who was still sitting on the ground and scratching his head. Then he cast a glance at the sky, wondering if another shell would suddenly arc from above and blow them in ten directions. He led the lady to safety.

8

Sunday, April 27, 1862
The Next Day

Felicie could not believe what she was hearing.

"What did you say?" she asked Madame Montfort, a matronly woman in a light blue hoop skirt so wide that she could smuggle an entire Rebel unit beneath it.

Madame Montfort, a white Creole, seemed to be taking great pleasure in delivering her shocking news. They stood outside of St. Rose de Lima church, and the woman looked around to make sure they were well out of earshot. She lifted a fan to her mouth and spoke under her breath.

"Yesterday, my husband said that he saw *your* husband leading a young lady on a horse through the city. She was..."

She paused to run her tongue across her lips—savoring her words as if they were a succulent meal of shellfish over rice.

"How shall I put this? Your husband had an adventuress on the back of his horse."

An adventuress. A prostitute, she meant.

Mentioning the word "prostitute" would be taboo anywhere, least of all in front of the church. Even whispering the word "adventuress" had turned Madame Montfort's face beet red as if she had quite literally choked on the word. Her face was squarish, not necessarily plump, and she had such thin lips that her mouth looked like a slash. She never smiled wide enough to show her teeth, but she did offer a sly and subtle grin.

"Are you sure it was my husband he saw?" Felicie asked.

"Yes, I am. I do not mean to raise alarms, but I thought you ought to know, Madame Cailloux."

Madame Montfort scurried away when she spotted André approaching. All smiles and looking grand in his Sunday best coat and top hat, André extended an arm to Felicie, who gave him a long, hard look before latching on. In response, he shot her a puzzled glance as they entered the modest-sized church.

"We have much to be thankful for," he whispered. "The city still stands."

Felicie didn't respond. Although she was grateful that the single cannon shot turned out to be the only one that the Yankees fired at the city, New Orleans was the last thing on her mind. Now that she was privy to the church's gossip, Felicie would have difficulty concentrating on Mass.

St. Rose was a small church, with only about forty pews, but it was thriving and filled to capacity with its mixed congregation of slaves, free people of color, and whites. New Orleans had a rich heritage of mixed flocks, and even the city's gem, St. Louis Cathedral, once included people of all colors worshipping together. For the past thirty years, however, social pressures and new laws had been trying to change all that by re-creating New Orleans in the image of the rest of the South, but St. Rose and Father Maistre resisted.

Felicie and André had built a strong reputation among the free people of color. André was a respected cigar-maker, and both of their sons had been schooled at *L'Institution Catholique des Ophelins dans l'Indigence* in Faubourg Marigny—the best school for free people of color. She gritted her teeth, her neck flushing with emotion when she heard the story connecting her husband with an adventuress. How dare Madame Montfort take such obvious pleasure in the story? Felicie fumed. Could the accusation be true? André struck a dashing figure, and women noticed.

The words of the Mass washed over her.

> *"Judica me Deus, et*
> *discerne causam meam de gente*
> *non sancta: ab homine iniquo*
> *et doloso erue me."*

Felicie knew her Latin, reciting it in her mind. *Judge me, O God, and distinguish my cause from the nation that is not holy; deliver me from the unjust and deceitful man.*

She tried her best not to apply those words to the man standing next to her. She cut her eyes at André. *The unjust and deceitful man.*

She had worked hard for respectability, for legitimacy. Her mother had given birth to three children with three different men, and Felicie had also been headed down that road, with children from two fathers. But Felicie and André were intent on breaking the pattern. They married on June 22, 1847, and André adopted Felicie's first child, Jean Louis, legitimizing him. This was something Felicie never had growing up.

She was the daughter of a concubine, always would be, and you couldn't get any more illegitimate than that. Her very existence was the epitome of original sin.

Felicie sometimes wondered if her half-brother, Bastien, had it easier by not having possession of his faculties. Was he even aware their mother had been a concubine? Probably not. His father, Valentin Encalada, was white, while Felicie's father was a slave who worked alongside her mother on Encalada's plantation.

Bastien may not have the mental capabilities, but he always had the status.

...

"*Maman, it isn't fair!*" *Felicie screamed at her mother. "Freedom doesn't even mean anything to him!"*

Sixteen-year-old Felicie flung her hand in the direction of "him"— her nineteen-year-old brother, Bastien, who just stared at her and grinned.

Her mother reached to embrace her, but Felicie shrugged her away. Her mother and Bastien were being set free. She was not. It was as simple as that. It was as grossly unfair as that.

"I have done everything in my power to convince Monsieur Encalada to free you as well," her mother said, holding back her tears. Felicie hated it when her mother broke down. She was tempted to leave the room.

It was September 21, 1835, and a jury had just approved Encalada's petition to free his concubine and their son, Bastien. "The idiot" was what Encalada called him to his face. With freedom came money —quelques réserves. Bastien and Felicie's mother now had money, and they would probably be buying property next. Meanwhile, Felicie would remain the property of a white man—Bastien's father.

"Monsieur Encalada has put a provision in his will to free you when he passes on," her mother said, trying to soothe her.

"Then I wish him dead!" Felicie grabbed a blue and gray jar from the nearest table and hurled it against the wall, shattering it into a hundred shards.

"Dieu aide-moi! Daughter, control yourself!"

Felicie's mother looked around—a darting, cornered look. The master, Monsieur Encalada, was gone for the afternoon, but other servants could hear, which meant they could snitch.

"I am not your daughter!" Felicie shouted. "What mother allows herself to be freed while her daughter remains enslaved? What kind of mother does that?"

When her mother's lower lip quivered, Felicie bit her lip, praying the woman would keep from tearing up.

Please, no tears, no tears, *Felicie thought.*

She would scream if her mother started weeping. Why couldn't she get angry instead? If her mother had released her rage on Encalada, maybe he would have freed her daughter as well. Felicie always found that anger brought results. Not tears, but red-hot fury.

Felicie had even directed her anger at the master from time to time. She had been beaten for it, but she didn't cry. Or at least she never showed her tears to the servant ordered to strike her. Her mother told her a week ago that if she had been more subservient, perhaps Encalada might have freed her.

Felicie hated her mother for saying that. Especially since she didn't think it was her anger that kept Encalada from freeing her alongside Bastien and her mother. It was her illegitimacy. She was too stained, too broken for that kind of redemption. She was east of Eden, and she had no idea how to get back.

"I will free you," her mother vowed. "I will find a way to save the money."

"You will find a way to please Monsieur Encalada. That's what you always do."

When her mother broke down in tears, Felicie stormed out of the room. Bastien just smiled. He always did.

■■■

Felicie's mother was true to her word. She saved up money, and in 1841 she paid $1,200 to Encalada to purchase Felicie and her first son, Jean Louis, who was two years old at the time. It would take another five years before a police jury would agree to the emancipation of Felicie and Jean Louis. But the 1841 purchase at least took them out of the hands of Valentin Encalada until freedom could be approved.

Felicie's mother could have saved a fortune by waiting for Encalada to die because their emancipation was written into his will. Yet, to her mother's credit, she wouldn't wait another moment to get

Felicie away from him. She paid a sizable amount of money, and contrary to what Felicie had once thought, her mother did not buy property in New Orleans until she first purchased her daughter and grandson Jean Louis.

By the time of her freedom in 1846, Felicie was older and wiser, and she asked her mother to forgive the harsh words of her youth. She wasn't sure if her mother ever did. The guilt of being free while her daughter remained a slave seemed to have done severe damage to Felicie's mother. But Bastien just kept on smiling.

Her mother had worked hard for Felicie's emancipation and Jean Louis's legitimacy. That's why any hint of infidelity on André's part roused Felicie's wrath. Her mother had made many sacrifices to ensure that they had a respectable family name. Let the white men of New Orleans keep mistresses and concubines on the side. That wasn't justified in the eyes of God or Felicie. For André to risk everything with an adventuress…

Felicie looked around the church, wishing she could once more hurl some pottery against the wall, but the only thing she saw were statues of saints. If she found out that what Madame Montfort said was true, one of those statues might just lose a head. So might André.

9

J ean Louis waited just outside of St. Augustine's church, a striking white sanctuary at St. Claude Avenue and Bayou Road. He leaned against a tree, waiting for word about Coralie Bisset.

Coralie's family rented a pew at St. Augustine's. In fact, the Bissets had been part of the mad rush for pews when the church first opened its doors in the early 1840s. He heard stories about how white folks and people of color had competed to see which group could buy up more pews, like a liturgical land rush. The result was that St. Augustine's became a mix of whites, free people of color, and even slaves; many free people of color donated pews to African slaves, and it remained that way today.

The parishioners, all shades of color, had finished filing into the church, and Jean Louis wondered if he had missed his chance to see Coralie. Then Minetta suddenly appeared, slipping out of the sanctuary.

"I must deliver my message in haste," she said, coming up to him out of breath. "Mademoiselle Bisset has agreed to meet with you."

"Splendid!"

"But not here."

"Of course."

Certainly, any meeting would have to take place far from the eyes of the Bisset clan.

"She will meet you at Cemetery Number 1 after church," Minetta said. "At the Bisset family vault. Do you know where it is?"

Jean Louis nodded.

"She goes to the vault regularly to place flowers. Her family will not suspect."

Message delivered, Minetta darted back toward the church, and Jean Louis called out his thanks. Then he turned on his heels and made his way to Cemetery Number 1, a route that took him past Congo Square, which overflowed with newly planted trees. A few blocks away, he found the area—a City of the Dead.

A small city was exactly what it looked like, for the dead were buried above ground in various ways, from oven vaults to sarcophagi topped with parapets and pediments. The stone structures looked like small buildings, and the narrow, twisting pathways made it seem as if you were winding your way through a city built at a child's scale.

Jean Louis knew the burial grounds well and had little trouble finding the Bisset family vault—a long, rectangular structure with a triangular gable, or pediment, on the top. When one family member passed away, the vault was opened, and the remains of the previous family occupant would be placed in an area below, along with the bones of the family's ancestors. Then the fresh lodger would be slid inside and would have the tomb all to himself until the next family member died—but no sooner than one year and a day.

Jean Louis lit a cigar, studying the morbid metropolis. He heard stories of cemetery hauntings, but he didn't believe them. It was easy to disbelieve the stories in the light of a Sunday morning. He had plenty of time before Mass would be over, so he strolled through the City of the Dead. Some of the tombs were huge—finer houses than most of the living in New Orleans would ever see. Not that the occupants of these houses could enjoy the ornate doors, Greek columns, or statues of weeping angels.

The morning stretched on. Jean Louis popped open his pocket watch and groaned. Coralie should have been here by now, even allowing for time to promenade outside of church.

Something must have happened. Perhaps Coralie's family would not allow her a cemetery visit with the city still on edge. No more violence had occurred since the Yankees fired that single shot at the crowd outside the Mint the day before. The Yankees and the mayor had spent Saturday in negotiations for the city's peaceful surrender, and the night had passed quietly in New Orleans, strangely enough.

Today, things seemed relatively normal, so where was Coralie? He paced in front of the Bisset family tomb and pulled out his third cigar. He jammed it into the corner of his mouth and leaned against the tomb.

"Is that how you treat the dead?"

It was a man's voice, not Coralie's.

"Show some respect."

Straightening up and turning, Jean Louis found himself face to face with Laurent Bisset, Coralie's brother.

Jean Louis bowed. "My apologies, Monsieur. No disrespect intended."

Jean Louis's father had suggested he carry a gun, with the city in such a state. But Jean Louis neglected the advice, and now he wished so badly he had a weapon.

"I told you to stay away from my sister," Laurent said, moving in closer.

Jean Louis held his ground. "And who said that I was planning to see your sister?" He tossed his cigar stub to the dirt and ground it with his shoe, shrugging.

"My sister did. She is not any happier about your attention than I am. She sent me here to defend her honor and inform you that she does not wish to see you."

Coralie sent her brother here? That couldn't be. He was lying. According to Minetta, Coralie wanted to meet him.

"What must I do to ensure that you stay away from my sister?"

Jean Louis didn't answer.

Laurent reached behind his back and pulled out a revolver.

Jean Louis nearly lost control of his bodily functions right then and there. He put up his hands. They were slick with sweat.

"Now hold on, Monsieur. There's no call for that."

"Why not? This is the perfect place for an unfortunate incident." Laurent nodded toward one of the nearby platform tombs. "I'm sure there's room for a fresh corpse."

Jean Louis backed up several steps. If he turned and ran, he could lose himself in the twisting pathways among the tall tombs. He glanced behind him.

"I'm a fine shot, Monsieur. You wouldn't get far if you run," said Laurent.

"He doesn't need to run."

Another man's voice. *What in the world was going on?*

Looking over his shoulder, Jean Louis spotted his friend Roussel, who also attended St. Augustine's Church. Roussel was winded from running.

Laurent shifted, aiming at Roussel, but when Roussel slipped behind one of the tombs, Laurent pointed his pistol back at Jean Louis.

"Put down the gun...or I will tell people about your adventures in the North," Roussel said.

The words hung in the air for several beats. Jean Louis had no idea what his friend was threatening to reveal, but it seemed to have an effect. For the first time, he spotted a crack in Laurent's confident bearing.

"If you shoot Monsieur Jean Louis, you know *exactly* what is going to happen," Roussel repeated. "Can you take that chance?"

Laurent shifted his feet, and his gun lowered a few inches, his face contorting with emotion. One could craft a Mardi Gras mask from his expression and scare half of New Orleans.

"Just let my friend go, and nothing more need happen," Roussel said. Jean Louis had never seen his friend in such control. "Let him go, and I will not say a word about your time in the North."

Finally, Laurent lowered his gun and pointed a finger. "This is not over, Cailloux."

Emerging from his hiding place and putting a hand on Jean Louis's shoulder, Roussel steered his friend toward the gate leading out of the City of the Dead. Their backs were to Laurent, providing big targets. But for some reason, Roussel had an unearthly power over Coralie's brother. No shots were fired.

"This is not over, Jean Louis Cailloux!" Laurent shouted. "We shall duel!"

"Act as if you didn't hear that challenge," Roussel whispered.

"I challenge you to a duel, Cailloux! And you are a witness, Pinard! I demand satisfaction."

"I didn't hear that either," Roussel added.

However, Jean Louis had heard the challenge, and there was no denying a duel. He felt light-headed as they slipped through the black wrought-iron gate, back to the living.

10

"The Native Guards have been disbanded?" asked Benoit Montfort, a white Creole who ran a booming tannery in the city.

"Yes." André didn't elaborate. He had grown weary of this conversation, which was to be expected, for he tired quickly of any discussions with Montfort. They stood in front of St. Rose Church, Mass over. It was overcast, with a light wind and comfortable temperatures.

"I do not understand," said Montfort. "We should have at least put up a fight with the Yankees."

Using "we" was stretching it since Montfort had never served a single day as a soldier. Still, he loved the intricacies of war and could talk endlessly about the battles that had so far unfolded in the War Between the States. André had heard him describe every fine detail of the Battle of Manassas, the first major battle of the war. Montfort's beloved Confederacy had won it handily.

Montfort was not an overweight man—just strangely designed. He was thin, except for a band of weight around his middle that looked like he had a bedroll wrapped around his waist. But most distinctive was his enormous mustache, which Montfort meticulously maintained like the keeper of a finely groomed English hedgerow. He was the first person André knew to use the new English invention—the mustache cup. The cup contained an inside ledge to keep one's mustache from getting wet or the wax in his mustache from melting due to the tea's heat.

Montfort also had a habit of running two fingers through his mustache as he pondered great thoughts, which was what he was doing now.

"I'd have imagined that Father Maistre would have spoken out against the Yankee invasion by now." Montfort fixed his eyes on André.

André was one of the few people who knew of Father Maistre's secret sympathies for the North, so he was well aware that the priest was not about to add his voice to the Confederate drumbeat. Montfort was in the clear majority in his support for the Confederacy, especially among white Creoles. He and his wife were among a handful of whites that attended the racially complicated St. Rose de Lima Church, and he clearly assumed that most of the parishioners and virtually all of the priests backed the South. A couple of churches had even donated bells to be melted down and used to make Confederate cannons. But not Father Maistre's bells.

"Father Maistre is quiet about the war." Montfort pursed his lips, straining in thought.

André shrugged. "Perhaps he is more concerned about the salvation of souls than politics."

"But every priest should be on the side of justice. And Bishop Odin says that justice lies with the South. Father Maistre's silence on the matter is very suspicious, don't you think?"

Again, a shrug from André. "Silence is no crime. If it were, Trappist monks should all be put in prison."

It took a few heartbeats for Montfort to realize André was joking, and he emitted an awkward laugh.

André caught sight of Felicie in the corner of his eye. "But I must excuse myself, Monsieur Montfort. I see my wife."

Montfort caught him by the arm before he could escape. "I saw you yesterday, by the way, near the Mint." Then Montfort sent him a sly look.

"Yes, it was a dangerous business, firing that cannon on an unarmed populace," André said.

"You were caught up in dangerous business, all right." Then Montfort smiled and winked.

What was that wink supposed to mean? André hurried away, and soon, he, Felicie, and the children were strolling home from Mass—a long walk, but they had no choice. Their modest buggy had burned in the stable fire. His wife was uncommonly quiet, and he sensed she was angry about something.

He tried to stir up a conversation that would break through her clouded mood. "I am hoping the Yankees will establish a colored regiment. If they do, I will be the first in line to enlist." André gave her a peripheral once over, thinking that his wife might be proud of his determination.

That couldn't have been further from the truth. André blinked when his wife tossed a hand in the air, her eyes ablaze. "Why would you hope for that? Signing up for a Yankee regiment would be just the thing to put our family at an even greater risk."

For André, signing up with a Yankee regiment would be just the thing to regain some of his self-respect and honor. But he should have realized that his wife would put family safety over all else.

Since the children ran ahead, out of earshot, he said, "Black men serving for the cause. It would be a great thing."

Felicie stopped and turned on him. "Do you really think the Yankees would be any different than the Rebel Army? The Rebels had no intention of ever using you on the battlefield, and neither will the Northerners. So why risk your family for a symbolic act?"

"You were the one who convinced me to join the Southern regiment." He meant this as an accusation. The words were laced with blame.

"I did it to protect our family. But signing up for a Federal regiment would do just the opposite in a Confederate city. It would put our family in danger."

"It is my choice." André's jaw twitched. While he let Felicie coax him into signing up for a Rebel regiment, he would *not* let her pressure him out of signing up for a Federal unit. He wouldn't let it happen again.

As they continued in silence, he wondered if he was deluding himself by thinking the Federals would form a regiment. Lincoln was afraid of offending some of the border states that remained loyal to the Union and still kept slaves. Delaware, Missouri, Kentucky, and Maryland. Signing up blacks might push those states into the secessionist camp.

But he could still hope. He and Colonel Rey had talked about approaching the Unionists to discuss black recruitment, but Felicie didn't need to know that.

"Sign up for the Yankees?" Felicie scoffed. "Have you not brought enough scorn on this family?"

"What are you talking about, *mon amour?* Tell me how I ever brought scorn on this family?"

Once again, Felicie came to a halt and wheeled around to face him. She crossed her arms on her chest. "You were seen with a woman yesterday. She was on your horse."

André's face burned with heat. He had done nothing wrong. Acting in the panic of the moment, he simply helped a woman in distress. When he led the prostitute to safety, it dawned on him someone might recognize him and that it might not look good. But he hoped and prayed that with the mob stampeding and Yankee ships firing cannons, the sight of a lady of ill repute on the back of his horse would be the least of people's concerns.

He was obviously wrong.

"*Le diable à midi!* Who told you that?" he demanded.

"Madame Montfort."

That explained Monsieur Montfort's odd winks.

"Madame Montfort is a gossipy old fool."

"So you are saying she speaks falsely?"

"Her *insinuations* are false," he said.

"But the facts are true?"

André didn't make eye contact. He looked around the street to make sure no churchgoers were near.

"Yes, I helped a woman in distress."

André saw Felicie clench her jaw, the way she did when she tried to bottle her anger. He was happy they weren't in their home because she would probably be looking for something to hurl at the wall by now.

"The woman was with Roussel Pinard," André explained.

Felicie rolled her eyes. "Don't tell me you're going to blame Roussel for this."

"Roussel was with the woman, and they were drunk, and he was trying to help her onto my horse, but he was too drunk to be of much use. So I helped her. The Yankees had just fired their howitzer, and the crowd could have trampled her to death."

"Of all of the women in the crowd, you chose an adventuress to rescue? And why was Roussel putting that woman on your horse in the first place?"

"Roussel was watching my horse while I pursued the man in the mask."

He had already told Felicie all about spotting the man in the Moloch mask.

"No other woman has ever ridden your horse," Felicie muttered.

André cringed. The idea of a prostitute riding on the back of his horse had hit his wife's tender spot. He and Felicie had met while riding outside New Orleans, and throughout their courtship, they had always taken early morning rides, coming together over horses.

...

The sun had just risen, and the dew in the grass reflected like a million pieces of glass as André watched Felicie rise above the hill and come into view. They had been courting for less than a month, meeting regularly to ride together. On this day, he'd promised to demonstrate some tricks. He was a fine horseman and welcomed any opportunity to impress her.

She was stunning in her sidesaddle habit—a black skirt, full and flowing. She wore a red vest beneath her black jacket, and a flowered hat tilted on her head. She seemed to be a good horsewoman in her own right. He was always impressed when a woman could maintain such control while riding sidesaddle, legs clamping to the two pommel horns. On this day, she wore a black veil over her face.

He beamed at her as she brought her horse to a stop, side by side with his.

"I am ready for my lesson." She lifted her veil, revealing a mischievous twinkle in her eye.

His smile vanished. He was confused. "Your lesson?"

"Of course. You were going to show me how to vault onto a horse."

André just stared—stunned. He wasn't sure he had heard correctly.

"I was going to show you how I vault onto a moving horse," he finally said, "but you said nothing about a lesson."

"You didn't think I was going to let you have all of the fun, did you?"

André ran his hand along the neck of his horse. "You are not serious, are you?"

"Of course, I am."

"But it's...but...your horse has a sidesaddle. How do you plan to vault onto a sidesaddle?"

Felicie laughed. "I can vault onto your horse, of course. Or at least I can try."

"But...I still don't..." André scratched the side of his face. "If you vault onto my horse, then you'd...you would..."

"Yes, I would be riding the horse astride."

Like a man.

"Don't look so shocked. I am wearing leather breeches beneath my skirt."

André flushed. He had no idea how to respond to that.

"Many ladies wear breeches beneath their riding skirt, even when sidesaddle," she explained.

"No...it's not that...It's..." He wanted to say that most ladies did not discuss such things. He wondered what kind of a woman he had become entangled with.

"Are you planning to show me how to vault? If not, I can turn around and head back into town."

"No, no, don't leave," he said. "Let me show you how it is done, and then we can decide whether it is something you should risk."

He hoped and prayed that once she saw the difficulty involved, she would be content with simply watching. After securing her horse to a tree, André had Felicie hold the long lead line, and she got his horse running in a canter in a counterclockwise circle around her. Then he ran alongside his horse, falling into the same stride and rhythm as the animal. With one swift movement, André latched onto a handful of mane and leaped, raising his right leg high above his head. Once she saw how high he had swung his leg, she would see that it would be futile to try it while wearing a skirt.

After he was securely in the seat, André moved into a standing position on the horse as the animal picked up speed—tricks he had been practicing since he was a boy. Arms outstretched for balance, he looked like he was about to take off flying from the back of the horse.

"I want to try," she said as soon as he dismounted.

"You can't be serious. I have been practicing these tricks since I was a boy. They are much too advanced."

"I realize that. I'm not completely crazy, you know," she said, although André had his doubts about that. "Just show me how to do a simple mount while Gypsy stays put. That's all I ask."

A standing mount. At least she was being realistic. When it seemed clear Felicie would not give up, he insisted she start with the *simplest of mounts. He demonstrated by facing the horse's side and then leaping onto Gypsy, with his belly on the saddle, as he threw his right leg over the other side of the horse and rose into a sitting position.*

"Are you sure you want to do this?"

"Of course. There's no way I could get hurt with something so simple."

That was true. Gypsy stood by patiently as André set Felicie in position, squaring up with the horse's side. Then she jumped, slamming into Gypsy and falling backward onto the ground. Not even close.

André couldn't hold back the laughter as he helped her to her feet.

"Good thing I'm wearing black." She brushed off her dress and laughed. "It will hide the dirt stains."

She tried two more times, with the same result. Gypsy turned her head to peer at this strange person, who kept hurling herself into her side and then bouncing off like an annoying overgrown fly. By this time, Felicie stopped laughing and was getting irritated.

André wanted to help lift her onto the horse, but that would mean grabbing Felicie by the legs as she vaulted atop, which would be much too intimate. Besides, he had a hunch she would resent any help. Instead, he stood by and watched as she hurled herself at the horse twice more before she surprisingly succeeded. She got up on the saddle flat on her belly—but that was as far as she got.

Felicie was stuck. Her skirt was making it quite challenging to swing her right leg over the horse. She kicked her legs uselessly, her feet tangled in the fabric. But she eventually fought her way free, got her right leg over, and sat up straight in the saddle.

"Voila!" She raised her hands, her face shining bright before offering a satisfied sigh and smile at André. "Come on up! Let's ride together."

He stood there, gaping. "Together?"

"Yes, together. If you can ride a horse standing on two feet, I assume you are capable of riding with me aboard."

André didn't even pause to think through this suggestion. He climbed onto the back of the horse, and they spent the next hour riding together.

***

From that day forward, riding horses and learning tricks became their passion, although Felicie decided she actually preferred the sidesaddle after all. Whenever André thought back to that day in the open field, he was always amazed at how willing Felicie was to break conventions in private. But whenever she put forward her public face, it was all about bringing legitimacy and honor to the family name. Nothing unconventional in front of others. So it did not surprise him that Felicie was furious that he had been seen with an adventuress in the most public of settings.

He knew he should apologize, but he reached for an excuse instead. "In the moment, I was thinking of how our Lord showed kindness to fallen women, no matter what people thought."

Felicie scowled. "So you were striving for sainthood by placing an adventuress in your saddle? If that is the requirement for sainthood, I don't understand why men aren't lining up to be saints! I would think it would be a more popular profession than selling produce! Who needs lettuce when you can have a tart?"

André went quiet. There was no talking to Felicie when she got this way. He knew what lay ahead—an afternoon of hearing how he harmed the family name. Felicie stormed off, and André followed a few moments later, keeping a safe distance.

***

Father Maistre discovered it in the offering plate. Most parishioners tossed coins in the offering, but whenever he saw an envelope, his spirits rose because it could mean the contribution of a large amount of cash from one of the church's few wealthy members.

Donations had been sparse the past year, with the city being strangled by the Union blockade.

He eagerly opened the envelope with his sword-shaped letter opener, but his heart sank when it appeared that it did not contain money—just a folded slip of paper. He blew open the envelope, peering inside and hoping to find a sizable donation still lurking in the corner.

Nothing.

When he unfolded the paper and read, his stomach churned. He'd prayed that the man in the confessional, the one claiming knowledge about what happened in Thuisy, France, would disappear into the turmoil of New Orleans and leave him alone. However, this note made it clear that that prayer was going unanswered. He skimmed it with a sense of dread, thinking it worse than he'd ever imagined. Who was this man, and how did he know such details about his past?

Father Maistre read the note three times, with a growing sense of panic. The man wanted hush money to keep quiet about his past, and he asked that U.S. currency (no Confederate dollars) be tucked into the arm of the Saint Rose statue in the corner of the church. In all of her beauty, the sculpture of Saint Rose wore a crown with tiny spikes; this she did in real life, imitating Christ's crown of thorns. Father Maistre had always admired Saint Rose's devotion to poverty, probably because it came so very hard for him. The fear of poverty, after all, was why he found himself in this predicament.

His gaze fell on the coins he'd sorted in front of him. His troubles had been all about money in Thuisy, and it was money that tormented him when he came to America and was chased out of the parish in Chicago. Mammon was the devil on his back, the author of all ill. He drummed his fingers on the table and stared at the coins, thinking it would be so easy to use them to pay his blackmailer. No one would notice.

But people *had* noticed— in Chicago *and* in Thuisy.

He picked a few coins from the top of one pile, like plucking poker chips from a stack. He hesitated for only a moment, and then he dropped the coins into the money pouch hidden beneath his vestments.

As he left the sanctuary, he was reminded, for the millionth time, that Judas had been the one put in charge of the money for Jesus's ministry.

11

Monday, April 28, 1862

The next day, André saw matters continue to unravel with Felicie, but Jean Louis was the point of contention this time.

"Jean Louis has no choice," André said. "He must accept the challenge."

"There are *always* choices." Felicie's eyes flickered with anger, and she lowered her voice, trying to keep a lid on her emotions.

Felicie had just begun simmering down about the incident with the prostitute when Jean Louis arrived at the house this morning, carrying a formal written challenge from Laurent Bisset. Monsieur Laurent had challenged him to a duel for making unwanted advances on his sister.

"People in New Orleans duel over anything," Felicie scoffed. "A wrong glance. A careless word. It is mad!"

"This isn't about a wrong glance." André stared at his son, who was clearly shaken by the note. "This is about our son's honor."

"This is about my son's *life*."

He couldn't miss that she had said "my" son's life. In times like this, Felicie didn't hesitate to remind him that Jean Louis was another man's son.

"If Jean Louis does not accept the challenge, he will be posted."

"I do not care."

"But Jean Louis should care."

Only a few days earlier, André saw a man being posted in the newspaper for turning down a duel. The challenger ran a notice, announcing the man's cowardice.

"No son of mine will turn down a challenge," André said.

Felicie started to snap back, but she refrained, probably because Jean Louis was sitting in the parlor with them, just a few feet away.

"*Maman*, I cannot turn this down," Jean Louis finally said, staring at his mother.

He had come to the house, unsure what to do, but André's words had clearly swayed him. André had been tempted to tell Jean Louis that this duel was what comes from being involved with a woman from the Bisset family, but he held his tongue. The most important thing was to make sure his son did not dishonor his name or the family by evading a challenge.

"I will ask Roussel to be my second," Jean Louis said.

Felicie groaned outwardly as André groaned inwardly with a roll of his eyes. A drunken second was not a wise idea. André thought about offering to back his son, but Wilson's Code of Honor forbade a son, father, or brother from serving in that capacity.

"Roussel has some strange control over Laurent Bisset," Jean Louis said. "He won't tell me what he has on the man, but Laurent is afraid of him. So Roussel would make a good second, no matter what you are thinking, Papa."

"*C'est fou.*" Felicie made a dismissive noise and shifted in her chair, looking around the parlor—her eyes skipping in search of something. She had broken a vase the day before, when they returned from church, so André had removed any other flower vases from the room.

"Choose sabers." André glanced from his son to his wife with a knowing look. "You are more skilled with the saber, and it is safer." The choice of sabers would hopefully be enough to soothe his wife.

"But what if Bisset protests? Dueling pistols have become the norm." Jean Louis shifted his weight, staring out the window with a pained expression.

The French tradition of dueling with swords had indeed given way to the American obsession with guns, but using sabers wasn't unheard of. André even knew of two men who had dueled with sledgehammers and two others who dueled by drinking down two cups—one of which was laced with poison.

"If Roussel has power over Bisset, he should be able to convince him to agree to sabers," André said. "You can fight to first blood." Again, he glanced at his wife for surely this was preferred over fighting to the death. Still, it could result in a deadly wound—and a lot more than just "first" blood.

Felicie rose to her feet and paced the room.

André felt sorry for his son. There was fear in Jean Louis's down-turned eyes, and Felicie wasn't helping matters. Jean Louis would need every ounce of confidence and courage, yet his wife's fear was contagious. When André fought his first duel—with sabers—he had become ill the day before, and his mother volunteered to fight in his place. That was the kind of woman his mother was. Felicie had his mother's determination but not the same loyalty to the Code of Honor.

"*Mon amour*, you spoke yesterday about our family's good name," André said to his wife. "For Jean Louis to turn down this challenge would do much more harm to our name than..." He didn't finish the sentence, but he made it obvious he was referring to the incident with the adventuress.

Felicie pointed toward the door when she caught sight of a tousled head peeking around the wall. "Eugene, I told you to stay outside!"

As she stormed after Eugene, André sighed in relief. With her exit, he and Jean Louis could finish setting the plans in peace. The weapon would be sabers, and the location would be New Orleans' famous Dueling Oaks. But before they could plan further, Felicie returned, still looking like she wanted to break something. If this were her call, she would select china dishes at ten paces as the weapons of choice.

This morning, Jean Louis would compose a letter responding to Laurent Bisset, accepting the challenge.

12

Thursday, May 1, 1862

General Benjamin Butler had entered New Orleans, but all
that Jean Louis could think about was that this could be his
last few days on earth. His father, one of the best swordsmen in the
city, had been training him all week, but Laurent was a larger man—a
savage swordsman. His father said finesse trumped brute strength,
and Jean Louis hoped he was right.

That evening, the arrival of the infamous Yankee general,
Benjamin Butler, had roused the city back to action, and Roussel
dragged Jean Louis to the riverfront, where another mob was
growing.

"How could you even think of missing this?" Roussel said,
tugging him toward the levee, which was packed with people, most of
them shouting curses as hundreds of blue-clad troops landed
onshore.

Jean Louis just shrugged. If he was going to die on Saturday,
perhaps this was as good a way to spend his final two days as
anything. How often do you have the chance to witness an invasion

of your city? Roussel was undoubtedly enjoying it, although much of his pleasure came from the woman latched onto his arm. She was an Irish girl, Colleen McCarthy—blonde hair, a frenzy of freckles, and a full figure. Most likely a lady from Gallatin Street, one of ill repute.

"Your father is a true gentleman," Mademoiselle McCarthy said, leaning uncomfortably close to Jean Louis, the alcohol on her breath overwhelming her perfume. "He rescued me last Saturday when the Yankees fired on the city. Whisked me away on his horse!"

Jean Louis smiled until she got to that last part. Perhaps that's why his parents had been nipping at each other all week long. He assumed it was only because of his duel.

"I think the general is disembarking!" Roussel slapped an arm around Colleen, dragging her forward. Jean Louis trailed behind, his mind still consumed by saber tactics. He should probably be somewhere else, practicing his feints and attacks.

Hundreds of Union soldiers had already disembarked, in perfect formation, and now a drum corps streamed down the gangway. A regimental band onshore played "Yankee Doodle Dandy," trying to drown out the mob's angry shouts.

"Hey, Picayune! Go back East, Picayune!"

"Picayune?" Jean Louis said.

"You haven't heard the stories?" Roussel asked. "The colored barber by the name of Picayune Butler has a son named Benjamin, and someone spread the story that General Benjamin Butler is the barber's mulatto son!"

Roussel and Colleen burst out laughing, the prostitute snorting with hilarity.

The general was flanked on either side by soldiers, and Jean Louis was anxious to catch a glimpse of the infamous man. He fought his way to the front, breaking away from Roussel and his wench. When he caught sight of the general, he saw no sign of black blood in the man, but he had to say that General Butler was one of the strangest, homeliest men he had ever laid eyes upon. The general looked like a misshapen monster, with a huge, bald dome and a dumpy body. But those eyes! They were like the large droopy eyes of a hound dog. General Butler's enormous head was mostly scalp, and it flattened out on the top, while the hair on the back of his head spilled down to his collar.

"Make way for the Beast!" someone shouted.

"La bête!"

The Beast. That was probably the kindest insult being hurled at the general. The crowd was having a grand time tossing commentary about his appearance, but the general showed no emotion.

So this is the man my father admires?

Jean Louis's father said that General Butler was the Yankee officer who first declared that escaped slaves were contraband of war. Before slaves were considered contraband, Yankee officers would send escaped slaves who reached Union lines back to their Southern masters. But once escaped slaves were declared spoils of war, the Federals began allowing them to remain in the North. His father secretly harbored admiration for such a canny political ploy, but most of the city hated General Butler.

"You'll never see home again!"

"Yellow Jack will have you before long!"

"Villain!"

"Diable!"

"Beast!"

The words kept flying at the monstrous-looking man. Having seen enough, Jean Louis decided to head for home, making a detour through Faubourg Tremé, past the Bisset house. He knew it was dangerous to venture close to the property with a duel hanging over his head, but he was desperate to talk to Coralie. He still couldn't believe that she had declared his advances unwelcome. She had never given any such indication before. Perhaps she could convince her brother to withdraw his challenge.

He stood several houses down, lost in shadows, but there was no sign of movement from the Bisset home. He was just getting ready to leave when a side door opened. Stepping out was Coralie's lady's maid, Minetta, carrying a bucket behind the house to the well.

Jean Louis made a beeline for her. Next to the house were two parallel lines of oak trees, with branches intertwining to create a mirror-image of the oaks as they leaned across a narrow lane to form an arch. From behind one of the oaks, he called her name as softly as possible.

"Mademoiselle Gerard. *Mademoiselle Gerard.*"

When Minetta caught him peeking from behind one of the trees, she set down her wooden bucket and hurried over.

"Monsieur, are you mad? If Mademoiselle's brother finds you here, he will insist on a duel this very evening."

"I have to talk to Mademoiselle Bisset."

"Out of the question."

As Minetta moved from the tree's shadow and into full view, Jean Louis couldn't help but notice a greenish-black bruise on her cheekbone, just beneath her right eye.

"What happened?" He motioned toward her face.

"*You* happened."

"I don't understand."

Minetta sighed. "Laurent and his father discovered that I helped arrange the meeting between you and Mademoiselle on Sunday. This was the Bisset way of expressing displeasure. I'm just happy that Coralie convinced her father to keep me on as a maid."

For a moment, Jean Louis felt such rage that he almost welcomed the opportunity to fight Laurent Bisset.

"Did Mademoiselle Bisset really say she did not want to see me last Sunday?"

"No. She was prevented from seeing you by her brother. But he has since convinced her that it is not in her best interests to see you again. Move on, Monsieur."

Jean Louis shook his head. "I will fight for her."

"Even if you win the duel, you have lost Mademoiselle Bisset.

She sees the futility of being courted by you—the son of the blackest man in New Orleans."

Jean Louis detested his father's boast. He lowered his eyes. "Will she be at the duel?"

"Do not expect it. She does not want to see you, Monsieur."

The words sank in, absorbing like poison.

"Believe me when I say that her brother has convinced her that she should not be seen with the son of the blackest man in New Orleans." Minetta smiled.

Was she mocking him?

"Monsieur, there is no shame in your father's boast." She held out her arm and inched up the sleeve of her dress—a provocative move. "I am not ashamed of my skin, and I am slightly darker than you." She laughed. "But not as dark as the blackest man in New Orleans."

If Jean Louis heard that statement again, he would scream.

She took a step closer. "I pray that you are victorious in Saturday's duel. But I also pray that you have the good sense to leave Mademoiselle Bisset alone."

As they spoke, the darkness of the evening continued to slowly settle on them. With his head hung low, Jean Louis did not notice Minetta rise to her tiptoes. She pecked him on the cheek before he knew what had hit him. Then she was gone, hurrying to the back of the house, snatching up her bucket on the way.

13

Saturday, May 3, 1862

Jean Louis was as ready as he was ever going to be. The night before, he had written letters, in case this would be his last day on Earth. There was one for Coralie, which was sure to trigger a spasm of guilt should he fall during the duel. He also wrote a letter to his parents, apologizing for the agony they suffered. In a fit of inspiration, he even closed by saying he was proud to be the son of the blackest man in New Orleans.

He had bathed the night before, a kind of spiritual purification like the knights of old, and he set out his clothes—a dark frock coat and a white silk undergarment with detachable sleeves so there would be no need to roll them up. He selected lightweight boots with wide heels for better maneuverability.

He didn't sleep very much, constantly running saber-fighting tactics through his head. But sheer exhaustion had finally swept over him, and the next thing he knew, he was being roused from bed by his sober-faced father.

It was time.

Jean Louis was his sharpest early in the morning, so an early duel worked to his advantage. He prayed that Laurent was a night person, fuzzy-headed in the early morning. He ate nothing and drank sparingly; the nerves in his stomach were too tight to accept food anyway. It was so strange to realize that he could be no more than a spirit separated from his body within two hours. They were fighting to first blood, but some wounds cannot be mended quickly enough to prevent a duel from going to the *last* drop of blood.

When he was ready to leave, Eugene shook his hand formally and told him he was proud to be his brother. At first, it appeared that his mother was not going to say goodbye. She remained in her room with Odile and Athalie, and he heard only muffled sounds from within. But as his father led him to the door, she came rushing out at the last moment, her face contorted by crying. This was Jean Louis's lowest moment, knowing what he was doing to his mother. He was her firstborn, the oldest boy, and he was tearing out her heart.

"Be safe, be strong," she whispered into his ear as she kissed the side of his face over and over.

Her tears moistened the side of his face, but he did not wipe them away with his handkerchief. Odile and Athalie also emerged from the back room, and they wrapped their arms around him, enveloping him from all sides.

"Do not worry, I will be home soon. Will you have a meal waiting for me?" he asked.

"The finest meal you ever tasted." *Maman* clung to him, tears streaming down her cheeks.

"I am sorry, *mon amour,*" his father whispered, finally prying her loose.

They couldn't be late. If they arrived more than a half-hour late, Laurent had the right to leave and publicly declare his cowardice.

His father had made arrangements to borrow a friend's carriage to travel to the Dueling Oaks. Jean Louis knew that the carriage ride wasn't to conserve his energy. A carriage was needed for one important reason—to carry a body home should the duel go wrong.

They had offered to give his second, Roussel, a ride to the dueling site, but his friend insisted on meeting them there. When they arrived at the Dueling Oaks, there was no sign of anyone except for the doctor, Pierre Allard.

On the outskirts of town, the Dueling Oaks was a wonderland of thick, gnarled oak trees, with Spanish moss hanging like streamers. Jean Louis prayed that Laurent Bisset would not show, allowing him to leave the battle alive with his honor intact. But ten minutes after the hour of eight, Laurent and his second, a man Jean Louis did not know, arrived by carriage—a much more expensive one than what his father had commissioned.

Jean Louis looked in vain for any sign of Coralie, but she had not come with her brother. She would not witness the duel she had started. For the first time, he began to question his sanity in pursuing a woman who did not have the decency to send him a note ahead of a duel. If he survived, perhaps he should follow Minetta's advice and be done with Coralie.

Still no sign of Roussel.

"This is novel," said Laurent. "I have never seen a man's *second* be such a coward that he wouldn't show."

Jean Louis did not respond. Taunting of any kind was a sign of dishonor, and he wouldn't join Laurent's game. Roussel was probably still in bed in a drunken stupor.

They waited ten more minutes. No Roussel.

Jean Louis's father approached Laurent's second and bowed. "I can serve as second in place of Monsieur Pinard."

Jean Louis could not hear the response of Laurent's second, but the man appeared displeased since it was frowned upon to have a family member serve in such a manner. But Jean Louis did not see how having his father as a second could be a disadvantage to his opponent. This duel would be decided among the principals, not the seconds.

Finally, with Roussel still not anywhere to be found, they agreed to the new arrangement. Jean Louis's father consulted further with

Laurent's second; they were expected to try to find some way to reconcile the two combatants peacefully, but this was usually just done for show. Rarely did the seconds come to an agreement, preventing a duel.

"Small feints and light cuts. Remember what I taught you, and you will be fine." His father helped to coil silk bands around his wrist and neck—the typical protection against opening a major artery.

Some duels forbid the more dangerous thrusts, but Laurent did not agree to this stipulation. There would be thrusts, and there would be blood.

The blade fit comfortably in Jean Louis's hand. It was a little less than three feet long, a feather in his hand. The two men were told the limits of their fight—a 65-foot by 20-foot rectangle marked by stones on the ground.

After his papa led him in two *Our Fathers*, it was time. Jean Louis had worried that his father would lecture him about getting entangled with a Bisset woman, but to his credit, he said nothing.

Jean Louis tried to block out such thoughts from his mind, and he focused his field of vision on the small patch of ground and his opponent's hand and saber. The two opponents saluted each other with their swords, and then it began.

Jean Louis feinted a cutover to Laurent's right cheek, but he didn't take the bait. Metal upon metal clanged and carried across the oak grove. The fear had been drained from his body, and adrenaline powered his moves. Jean Louis then tried a simple attack to the right flank, hoping to end the battle quickly and with minimal blood, but Laurent nicely parried.

It was incredible how much energy could be expended in such a short burst of time and in such a compact space. Jean Louis was breathing hard, but he tried not to show any signs of exhaustion. Laurent smiled at him and came at him like a butcher, slicing and hacking. These were easily parried.

His father was right. Laurent lacked finesse, offering only savagery and stupidity. At that moment, Jean Louis's confidence grew as he parried attack after attack. As the frustration began to show on Laurent's face, for the first time he began to think he might just survive this day.

From *en garde* in the 4th, Jean Louis beat Laurent's blade sharply to the left and made a lunge for his right cheek. So close. Laurent parried the cut and showed no blood, but his face dripped with sweat.

Jean Louis bit back a soft smile. It would take only a series of feints and a quick cutover to finish this off. Laurent was beginning to pant.

Jean Louis had been so focused, so single-minded, he hadn't even heard the arrival of another carriage. It wasn't until a woman's voice shrieked through the air that it dawned on him that someone else arrived at the Dueling Oaks. For a moment, he wondered if it could be Coralie attempting to stop the duel, but the voice was Minetta's.

Sure enough, Minetta started to run in between the two combatants, but his father caught her around the waist and held her back.

"Stop this! You must stop! Your friend, Roussel, is dead!" She waved her arms.

The words burned. He must have heard wrong.

"Someone has killed Monsieur Pinard! His body was found this morning at Cemetery Number 1!"

Jean Louis stared at her in disbelief. His mouth parted, but no words came out. His arm had gone limp, and he lowered his guard, his saber pointed at his feet.

Then Minetta shrieked again, only this time she shouted a warning, but it was too late. Laurent had thrust, and at first, Jean Louis didn't even feel the blade enter his side. He stared in disbelief.

The saber had penetrated his body by several inches. As blood started to soak his linen shirt, a wave of nausea sent his head spinning. When the bloodstain expanded out with great speed, leaving his shirt dripping red, his knees went weak, and he dropped to the ground.

14

ndré rushed to Jean Louis's side. His son had collapsed to the ground, but he was trying to sit up while pressing his hands against a soaking red shirt. His breath came in and out rapidly, and he sweated heavily. His eyes showed disorientation, confusion. The doctor crouched, tore open the shirt to get a look at the wound, and began pressing a bandage against the puckering slit in Jean Louis's side.

As the doctor took control, André looked up to see Laurent calmly wiping the blood from the edge of his blade. The furies descended, and he sprang to his feet and bolted toward Laurent, coming at him from behind. He wouldn't hit a man with his back turned, but if Laurent wheeled around, what was stopping him from pulling out the knife strapped to his side and gutting the villain?

Laurent's second saw André coming and muttered a warning. As Laurent spun around, saber ready, André pulled up short and stabbed a finger in his direction.

"*Le diable à midi!* The duel had paused, you whoreson!"

"Back, old man! He should have remained aware."

"You are a coward! You attacked when he was being told of the death of a friend!"

"I cannot help it if he took his eyes away from our combat." Laurent feigned a look of innocence.

"You're a blazing coward!" André pulled out his knife, and Laurent laughed.

"Your blade is pitiful," Laurent said, moving into the *en garde* position.

André felt the fool, holding a small blade in the face of a full-length saber.

"You have no honor!" André shouted.

"Jean Louis lowered his guard, and he should be happy that I didn't disembowel him. I thrust below the naval and to the side. No critical organs were in the path of my blade."

"You cannot be certain." If looks could kill, André would undoubtedly be the victor at this moment.

Infection could kill him just as surely as a thrust through the kidney. André's chest filled with dread as he said a silent prayer for his son.

"He will live," Laurent said.

"You will answer for this. I will announce to the city that you attacked when Jean Louis had turned away upon hearing news of the death of his friend."

"I will deny it. And who will people believe? A Bisset or the blackest man in New Orleans?"

André was tempted to challenge Laurent to a duel, but he could imagine Felicie's furious response. He wouldn't do that to her, not with a wounded son.

"Blasts and fogs upon you!" André spun and returned to his son's side. The doctor was still applying the pressure bandage while Minetta held Jean Louis's hand. Jean Louis stared at André with glazed eyes.

"I think Monsieur Bisset is right," said the doctor. "He appears to have stabbed away from the vitals—but it is always difficult to know."

"The bleeding?"

"It will come under control. You can be assured. No arteries nicked."

André didn't ask any other questions, not with Jean Louis still lucid and listening to whatever they said. He preferred the doctor to concentrate on keeping his son alive. André took his son's other hand while Minetta continued to hold on to Jean Louis. Hearing a commotion from behind, he looked over his shoulder as Laurent Bisset's carriage rattled away.

"Not much of a gentleman, is he?" said the doctor. "Didn't even inquire about his opponent's health."

"You saw him thrust when Jean Louis wasn't looking, didn't you?"

The doctor didn't answer.

"I saw," said Miss Gerard.

"Thank you." André noticed her blackened eye and wondered if she had received it from someone in the Bisset household. "Doctor, you saw what happened, didn't you?"

"I do not know what I saw," he said. "Please, I need to focus on your son."

André grunted and went silent. He pulled out the rosary beads that he always carried with him and began to pray quietly, but he had difficulty concentrating. He had been so focused on Jean Louis and Laurent that he had completely forgotten about Roussel's fate.

"Please, we must talk." He motioned for Minetta to step from Jean Louis's earshot.

Mademoiselle Minetta was clearly reluctant to let go of Jean Louis's hand, but she stepped aside with André, moving beneath one of the large oaks.

"You said that Monsieur Pinard has been killed? How?"

"He was found dead in Cemetery Number 1. Stabbed in the stomach is what I was told."

Stabbed in the stomach. Not much different than Jean Louis's fate.

"Do they have any idea who might have done it?" André

searched her eyes.

"That is all I know. I am sorry."

"*Merci.*" André's eyes drifted back to his son, still prone on the ground and being tended to by the physician. "And thank you for caring for my son."

Miss Gerard's eyes became moist, and she pulled a handkerchief from her sleeve. "If I had not come today...If I had waited..."

That much was true. If she had not interrupted the duel with news of Roussel's death, Jean Louis would not be in this position. But André was determined not to lay the blame on her. He wanted to conserve his wrath for Laurent Bisset.

"You could not have known that Monsieur Bisset would do such a thing."

She dabbed her blackened eye and stared up at him. "That's just it. I should have known."

Had Laurent Bisset given her the black eye?

By the time they returned to Jean Louis's side, the physician had cast a blood-soaked rag to the ground and pressed a fresh one to the wound. Judging by the stain, the flow was being stemmed.

"I think we shall be able to convey your son to the carriage very soon," said the doctor. "I think he will be fine."

"*Merci*, doctor."

"You will want him home where he can convalesce."

Home. When Felicie sees her son's injury, she will want payment in blood. Perhaps from Laurent Bisset. Perhaps from André. Or both. After all, this is *her* son, as she will remind him. Again.

Mademoiselle Minetta took Jean Louis's hand once more and ran her fingers across the back of it, gently massaging. Then she came to attention with a startled, "Oh!" She stared directly at André. "There is one detail about Roussel's death I forgot to mention," she whispered. "Someone saw a man in a mask rushing from the cemetery where his body was found."

"A man in a mask?"

"He was wearing the mask of a bull. He was Moloch."

15

Felicie was on her knees, imploring God to save her son's life. With a prayer book open before her, she immersed herself in the Latin words.

En ego, O bone et dulcissime Iesu,
ante conspectum tuum genibus me provolvo,
ac maximo animi ardore Te oro atque obtestor,
ut meum in cor vividos Fidei, Spei et Caritatis sensus...

Behold, O kind and most sweet Jesus,
I cast myself upon my knees in Thy sight,
and with most fervent desire of my soul, I pray and beseech Thee
that Thou wouldst impress upon my heart lively sentiments of Faith,
Hope and Charity...

When André and the physician carried Jean Louis into the house this morning with a stab wound to his side, she thought with certainty that he was dead. The doctor assured them that the saber had missed vital organs, but how could he be sure? Even if the sword had bypassed anything vital, an infection could be just as pitiless a killer as forged steel.

After a day of tending to Jean Louis's injury and giving the silent treatment to André, she could take no more. With Jean Louis sound asleep and in the care of her mother, Felicie mounted her horse and rode to St. Rose Church. Here, she plucked a prayer book from a pew, threw herself before the altar, and poured out her fears.

Atque veram peccatorum meorum poenitentiam,
eaque emendandi firmissimam voluntatem velis imprimere;
dum magno animi affectu et dolore
Tua quinque vulnera mecum ipse considero ac mente
contemplor,
illud prae oculis habens, quod iam in ore ponebat Tuo David
propheta de Te, o bono Iesu: "Foderunt manus meas et pedes
meos: dinumeraverunt omnia ossa mea."

With true contrition for my sins,
and a firm purpose of amendment while with deep affection
and grief of soul,
I ponder within myself and contemplate
Thy five wounds, having before my eyes the words which
David the prophet put on Thy lips concerning Thee, O good
Jesus: "They have pierced my hands and feet, they have
numbered all my bones."

When Felicie raised her head, her eyes fell on the red-threaded Jerusalem cross woven into the church's altar cloth, flanked by four smaller crosses. These five red symbols represented the five wounds of Christ—the nail to the right and left palms, the piercing to the right and left feet, and the spear to the side, from which water and blood poured.

A wound to the side: Jean Louis's wound.

She asked God why the Devil was trying to steal away her son.

First, he nearly died in a fire, and now his life hung by a thread. Was the Lord trying to teach her something?

She could already count four major wounds in her life. First, her illegitimate birth. Second, her life as a slave, which continued even after her mother and half-brother had been freed. Third, the distance between herself and her mother. All of these were bleeding wounds. But the worst of them all was her fourth wound.

She and André had lost their second child eight years ago. Her name was Hortense, and their little girl did not even reach her first birthday when she was stricken by yellow fever. Yellow Jack. It started with three days of fever, chills, and nausea. But then the Devil went to work, and her child was buckled by strong abdominal cramps. Next came bleeding in the mouth, the eyes, and the stomach. Hortense started vomiting blood. Black vomit.

The yellow fever epidemic was its worst in 1853, killing close to ten thousand people in New Orleans. It was a reign of chaos as the disease spread across the city like a river of oblivion, sweeping people away, sometimes carrying away six people out of a family of nine. Gone.

Felicie was pregnant with Hortense when the epidemic came down on the city, and she would never forget wandering the stricken streets of New Orleans on the night they decided to purify the air. Barrels of tar were placed throughout the city, and at a specified time, they were all fired. It was like walking through Satan's Pandemonium that night, with yellow bonfires burning everywhere and black smoke curling into the sky. The bonfires did nothing to purify the air and stem the deaths. Neither did the firing of four hundred discharges from a handful of six-pound cannons. People continued to die, hundreds upon hundreds each day.

Felicie was grateful that Hortense was not born until January of 1854, when the worst was over. She thought Hortense would be safe, but by summer, she was stricken with yellow fever. It wasn't supposed to happen.

...

"I have come to offer my services," said an old white man as thin as a rail with a stooped-over gait.

He showed up on the second day after Hortense started showing the most obvious signs of Yellow Jack. "I am a nurse at the hospital, and I treated many such cases last year."

By this time, Felicie would welcome any type of help. "What can you do for my daughter?"

"Has she been bled?"

"Yes."

"Good. Good. Lead me to her."

Felicie hesitated. There was something odd in the way he asked to be taken to her. Was that a slight grin on his face? Maybe he was simply attempting to give her a reassuring smile, but it came out all wrong. Still, she would do anything at this stage to help Hortense, so she led this man into the back room, where their child, only five months old, lay in her crib.

The old man shuffled to the window and yanked aside the curtains, letting the light pour in. Then he approached the crib and stared down on Hortense, who was thankfully asleep. A reprieve from her suffering. He reached into the crib and rolled up the sleeve on her right arm. Visible were two round purple spots, each about the size of a dime, the edges a much darker purple than the center.

The old man chuckled.

"What is so funny?"

The old man's smile vanished, and he stared directly at Felicie. "I have it from good authority, Dr. Samuel A. Cartwright, that the suffering of New Orleans was caused by the disturbance of the natural order of things. White people exposed to the sunlight, doing the work of slaves, and black people living the life of free people, cooped up inside. It is not natural, and it caused this disease. You were created to toil outside and white people inside. Restore the natural order, and your child will live."

Before he even reached his final sentence, Felicie had a broom in her hands and was ready to use it as a cudgel. She advanced on him and cracked the broom across his back.

When he let out a roar, Felicie heard footsteps, and Jean Louis barged into the room. Jean Louis, fifteen years old, intercepted the old man before he could attack his mother, heaving him against a dresser and knocking over a statue of St. Francis. It shattered on the floor. Seeing the futility of fighting against a robust youth, the old man rushed from the room, screaming expletives and promising death to their house.

Felicie made Jean Louis promise not to tell of this to his father. If André learned what had happened, he would track down the old man and thrash him within an inch of his life.

■■■

Felicie later learned that this old man actually did work as a nurse at one of the hospitals during the yellow fever epidemic, but he was driven away when doctors found him taking great pleasure in the suffering and death all around him. André never discovered that this angel of death had come to their house.

When Hortense died, Felicie felt her fourth wound—the deepest of her injuries. Was Jean Louis's death going to be the fifth?

Anima Christi, sanctifica me.
Corpus Christi, salva me.
Sanguis Christi, inebria me.
Aqua lateris Christi, lava me.
Passio Christi, conforta me.
O bone Iesu, exaudi me.
Intra Tua vulnera absconde me.
Ne permittas me separari a Te.
Ab hoste maligno defende me.

Soul of Christ, sanctify me.
Body of Christ, save me.
Blood of Christ, inebriate me.
Water from the side of Christ, wash me.
Passion of Christ, strengthen me.
O good Jesus, hear me.
Within Thy wounds, hide me.
Separated from Thee, let me never be.
From the malignant enemy, defend me...

When Felicie finished her prayer, she set aside the prayer book, rose, groaning to her feet, and made her way to the back of the church. Clouds had gathered outside, and the interior of the church dimmed. Felicie dipped her fingers in the font, and just as she made the sign of the cross, a door opened from a room adjoining the altar. It was Father Maistre. Not wanting to talk to anyone at the moment, she slipped into the shadows. If she spoke to the priest, she might break down. She hated showing tears in front of others—as her mother so often did. So she would wait for Father Maistre to leave before she exited the front door.

She watched as the priest genuflected before the altar and then started for the statue of St. Rose—a marble woman wearing a crown of thorns. The priest carried a small sack in his hands and stared at the statue, in earnest, as if in discussion with the saint. Although she could hear him whispering, she couldn't make out the words, but it seemed he was praying. Then she heard a distinct "Amen" before Father Maistre placed the sack in the crook of the saint's right arm, where St. Rose was holding a bouquet of roses. He tucked it in among the marble flowers, deep down so it could not be spotted, and then he genuflected and scurried out the rear door.

Tempted by curiosity, Felicie found herself hurrying across the church, making a beeline for the statue. She reached inside the crook of the statue's arm, her fingers running over some fabric. She pinched a portion of the small sack and jangled it, confirming that it contained money.

She wondered if this was Father Maistre's way of helping some needy soul. But why deliver the money in such a fashion? St. Rose spent her life tending to the poor, so perhaps he thought the gesture would carry symbolic power. Still, it all seemed so odd. But whatever his reason, she made sure the moneybag was safely tucked back in the crook of St. Rose's arm and hurried from the church. As she did, she cast out one last prayer.

Blood of Christ, stream of mercy.
Blood of Christ, help of those in peril.
Blood of Christ, solace in sorrow.
Blood of Christ, pledge of Eternal Life.
Blood of Christ, victor over demons.

16

One Week Later

Gallatin Street.

André wondered why they just didn't call it Sodom or Gomorrah. The street name "Gallatin" sounded so innocuous. At least the older red-light district in New Orleans had a more fitting name—The Swamp. But lurking behind the plain name of Gallatin lay the two most violent streets in all of America.

Pickpockets there wore rings with tiny, embedded knife blades that could cut into a person's pocket. Ruffians carried slingshots— rope with a hunk of lead at the end, perfect for crushing skulls. That is why André and Jean Louis decided to pay a visit during the daylight hours. At night, even the police were hesitant to walk down these two blocks.

Jean Louis had not yet fully healed, but he was well out of danger, bandaged up and doing much better. In fact, he was doing well enough that he insisted on investigating his friend Roussel's murder. The last time that Roussel had been seen alive, he was heading toward Gallatin Street to meet up with Colleen McCarthy, the very same adventuress whom André had helped onto his horse. Since Jean Louis and André decided to track down Mademoiselle McCarthy, that meant visiting Gallatin Street.

The police had done next to nothing in uncovering Roussel's murderer. With stabbings and shootings so common in places like Gallatin Street, it was difficult for the police to keep up with the city's violence—assuming they even cared. Many on the force were paid off not to.

Ah, New Orleans.

But if Jean Louis was going to be foolish enough to step onto Gallatin Street, even in daylight, André insisted that he was going with him—armed with dagger, sword, and pistols. He hoped his reputation as a boxer and swordsman went with him as a form of protection.

André was grateful to God that Jean Louis had survived the stabbing, but he had to admit that he was almost glad for the duel because it may have done the trick to disentangle him from the Bisset family. As far as he could tell, Jean Louis had banished Coralie Bisset from his mind, so the duel was well worth it.

As he and Jean Louis approached Gallatin Street, the smell of fish and manure became stronger with every step.

"Why do you think Roussel became so infatuated with this kind of woman, considering...?" André didn't finish his sentence, but Jean Louis would know his meaning. Roussel's mother had been a prostitute, and his father had been a steamboat worker who had swept into town for a few days. Roussel never met his father.

"He told me he hoped to rehabilitate Mademoiselle McCarthy."

André almost chuckled, but he controlled himself. "Roussel was trying to rehabilitate her?"

"I know what you're thinking," said Jean Louis. "You're wondering why he didn't concentrate on rehabilitating *himself*?"

André looked at his son but did not respond.

"Roussel was not as awful as you might have thought, Papa. He really thought he could rescue Mademoiselle McCarthy."

"That is a noble thing to do."

"I believe he thought that by rescuing her, he was—in his way—rescuing his mother."

André nodded. "Perhaps I underestimated your friend all of these years."

"You weren't the only one. I think Roussel underestimated himself."

"But he must have known the risk he was taking." André inhaled before releasing a cathartic sigh. "Trying to rescue an adventuress could be an adventure in itself. The enforcers on Gallatin Street would not take kindly to seeing one of their women saved."

"I'm not sure he fully understood the dangers."

With those words, André and Jean Louis arrived at the portal to the Gallatin universe. These two blocks near the river were jammed into the space between the French Market and United States Mint—a trio of appetites in one row. Food. Sex. Money.

They stepped into the zone.

Gallatin Street was an incredibly narrow avenue, with tilted buildings on opposite sides so close that you could almost jump from one window to the other and cross the street aerially. It was one long line of bordellos, boarding houses, dance houses, and barrel houses—joints where you could drink all you could for five cents.

Today, under the afternoon sun, the area was mostly empty, the buildings shut for the day. Come nightfall, this place would be packed with shouting, drunken, brawling, puking, scratching, and clawing sailors and women. The women brawled just as much as the men.

They were looking for the Sure Enuf Hotel, a two-story bordello run by a nasty old woman called Mother Colby—an oversized white woman. Many of the buildings along Gallatin Street were rickety old structures, slapped together using the wood from flatboats along the river. They spotted the Sure Enuf Hotel sign from half a block away. It boasted large painted letters, and it appeared as if the customers had been competing to see what kind of damage the piece of wood could endure. The sign was riddled with bullet holes and knife cuts, and one corner was burnt away and charred black. Standing across the street was a large, vacant-looking, young thug, holding a nasty-looking club. Most likely, a member of the notorious Live Oak Boys, hired by businessmen to vandalize and terrorize competitors. A horrid crew.

The bordello called itself a hotel, but that was a misnomer. Never having been to a cathouse, André wasn't sure if you knocked during off-hours or just strolled in. He decided that if the place called itself a hotel, he could walk right in. The door was unlocked, so they entered the main room. A bar of sorts. It was dim—the windows shuttered—and he noticed a couple of broken chairs in the corner. Leftovers from a brawl the night before. The bar counter ran across the back, and behind it was a wall of bottles.

"Hello?" Jean Louis called.

André peeked into an adjoining room, where there stood a roulette wheel and faro table.

"Hello?" Jean Louis said again.

He was answered by a burst of cursing from the room on the opposite side of the bar. A freight-car sized woman barreled into the room, tightening a sash around her robe.

"What y'all think you're doin' here?" she demanded. Her eyes landed on André's sword. "You police?"

"No. We're just looking for a mademoiselle," said Jean Louis. "Colleen McCarthy."

"She's probably asleep, and so would any sensible person at one o'clock in the afternoon," said Mother Colby. "Come back tonight, and y'all can have her by the half-hour."

André felt the heat of embarrassment. "We only want to talk with her."

"It costs the same, talkin' or no talkin'. Come back tonight."

"Isn't our money good enough by day?" André pulled out a handful of coins. This woke up Mother Colby. "What is the going rate?"

"You have it right there," she said, snatching the coins from André's fingers. He had probably just paid double or triple the rate.

"Only one of you can have her unless y'all want to double the money," she said. "Who will it be?"

After André and his son exchanged looks, Jean Louis said, "I will go."

Mother Colby laughed. "Think your papa too old for this?"

"I just want to talk with her," Jean Louis insisted.

"Call it what you want. Follow me."

···

Jean Louis was amazed that Mother Colby could fit up the narrow staircase leading to the second floor. She huffed and puffed with every step. The long hallway was flanked on either side by room after room, none of them bigger than a closet. The rooms had no doors, just flimsy, soiled curtains. Mother Colby stopped at the end of the hallway and said, "Let me rouse her," before ducking through the curtain.

Jean Louis felt conspicuous standing there like a paying customer. If *Maman* knew that he and his father were in this establishment, even for the purposes of an investigation, she would break a vase or two. He wondered if he needed to confess this visit to the priest. Just seeing the row of curtains sparked thoughts that deserved penance.

From inside the room—the crib it was called—he heard the complaining sound of someone being awakened hours too early. Then he heard a slap and a whimper. Another slap. Jean Louis yanked aside the curtain and found Colleen McCarthy sitting up in bed, holding a hand to her red-flared face. Mother Colby took a handful of Mademoiselle McCarthy's blonde hair and gave it a yank.

"When a man pays this kind of money, you wake up when I tell you!" Mother Colby said.

When Mademoiselle McCarthy caught sight of Jean Louis, she

became suddenly alert, and Mother Colby held off on her next slap—hand in mid-motion.

"Monsieur Cailloux?" said Mademoiselle McCarthy, pulling the sheet tightly beneath her neck.

"You got forty-five minutes," Mother Colby grunted on the way out of the room. "That's a bonus fifteen minutes. On the house."

Yes, Jean Louis would definitely need to visit the confessional. Just being in this room was taint enough. He fumbled with his hat.

"Pardon, Mademoiselle, but I am here to talk. To talk about my friend Roussel."

Mademoiselle McCarthy became even more agitated. "I cannot talk about Monsieur Pinard. It is too upsetting."

Jean Louis shifted his weight from one foot to another before asking, "May I take a seat?"

"I said I *cannot* talk to you. Perhaps Mother Colby will return your money."

Jean Louis sat down and leaned forward.

"Just tell me," he whispered. "Did you see Roussel the night before he was killed?"

By this time, Mademoiselle McCarthy was weeping and wiping her eyes with the back of her right hand.

"I am sorry to ask this of you, but we need to know."

"*We?*"

"My father is downstairs."

Mademoiselle covered her face with both hands and said nothing. Jean Louis was conscious that his time was ticking away.

"Please, Mademoiselle. We will leave you in peace if you simply answer a few questions."

She used the corner of the sheet to dab her eyes. "Yes, I saw Monsieur Pinard on that night." She spoke so softly that he could barely hear her words.

Jean Louis matched her soft volume. "You were here with him?"

"We slipped away."

Jean Louis studied her face. He didn't see any bruises, and he would have thought that she might have been beaten for slipping away from her work. But perhaps the bruises were in concealed places. Mother Colby probably knew better than to put bruises on the face. Damaged goods did not attract business.

"Where did you go?"

"We walked along the river. I loved him, Monsieur."

"When did you part with him?"

"It could not have been much later than two in the morning. He said he had to awaken early to serve...to be your second in the duel."

"Did you see anyone else that night? Did anyone threaten him?"

"I drank much. My memory is not good."

Jean Louis leaned over and spoke even softer into her ear. "Would anyone here want to see him dead—for taking you away?"

She stared at him as if shocked he would dare ask such a question in this place. She didn't answer for the longest time.

When she finally shook her head no, Jean Louis asked, "Who would have wanted to do this to him?"

Still no response except a woman in an adjoining room talking in her sleep. She sounded afraid. The walls were paper thin.

"Look at Laurent Bisset," she finally whispered.

"You think Monseiur Bisset murdered Roussel? But why? He hates me, but what did Monsieur Bisset have against Roussel?"

She shrugged and bit her lip, trying to stop her tears from coming. "Roussel was being paid by Monsieur Laurent."

"Laurent Bisset was paying Roussel? For what?"

"To remain quiet."

Blackmail?

"What was Roussel agreeing to remain quiet about?"

"Please, Monsieur, don't ask me to speak anymore."

"This is my last question. I promise."

Mademoiselle McCarthy sighed. "Roussel knew something about Monsieur Bisset."

Jean Louis waited patiently for the rest of the statement.

"Roussel knew that Monsieur Bisset was a bounty jumper."

Jean Louis's mouth opened in silence.

"He did so while traveling in the North," she added.

Jean Louis sat back in awe of the implications. Both the North and the South allowed gentlemen to pay bounties for other men to take their place in the military. A bounty jumper, someone apparently like Bisset, accepted the funds only to renege on the commitment and skedaddle rather than join the military as agreed.

No wonder Bisset would kill to cover his tracks. It was a hanging offense.

■■■

Back outside, André stared in amazement at his son.

"He was a bounty jumper? In the North?"

"That's right. But why do you think Laurent collected bounty payments in the North?" asked Jean Louis. "He could have done the same thing in the South."

"In the North, authorities pay much higher bounties for men willing to take another's place in the military—close to three hundred dollars per bounty. Besides, he would not be known in the North, but people in the South might recognize him or his name."

"I suppose it makes sense. But I thought rich men paid bounties for *poor* men to take their place in the army. Laurent Bisset is rich."

"But he's also a fool," André said. "He probably squandered all of his money and was desperate for quick cash. What I'd like to know is how Roussel found out about Laurent's bounty jumping."

Jean Louis shrugged. "I don't know, but this explains the power Roussel had over him."

They heard the sound of a creaking door and were shocked to see a large woman step into Gallatin Street—one of the tallest ladies they had ever seen. It was the redheaded woman André had seen on the day the Yankee fleet broke past the fort. She was about six feet tall and looked strong enough to whip a wildcat. But she wasn't just large; she had curves. André had done some investigating and learned that her name was Bricktop Jackson, the only prostitute that scared members of the Live Oak Boys. André had heard she carried a two-bladed knife and used it to dispatch several men.

Equally menacing was who followed her out the door: John Miller. He was the man who had an amputation at his right elbow with a steel chain and ball attached. As he stepped into the street, he twirled the ball and chain around and around like a whirligig.

One look at these two nightmares and André clamped his lips tight. He and Jean Louis would finish their conversation at home. As they moved down the block, they had to pass by Bricktop and Miller. André and Jean Louis drifted to the right side of the street and stepped up on the *banquette*—the raised wooden sidewalk. Bricktop and Miller maintained a converging route.

André pulled back his coat to display his weapons—a pistol on his left hip and his sword on his right. He hoped that his reputation with a sword would keep them at bay, but Bricktop and Miller kept approaching. Bricktop made sure they saw her weapon of choice—the knife with a blade on both ends of a handle tucked into a belt around the waist of her earth-colored dress.

Bricktop had been arrested for one of her murders when she stabbed a man a dozen times while her partner in crime, America Williams, helped hold down the fellow. Bricktop's lawyer managed to convince the court that the man with the dozen stab wounds had died of heart disease. Only in New Orleans.

André tipped his hat. "*Bonjour*, Mademoiselle. Monsieur."

Bricktop grinned, revealing that she had lost a couple of teeth, either to disease or fists.

"Bon-jore," she said with a laugh as if the idea of being greeted in French tickled her to no end.

Their paths were about to meet when the front door of a nearby bordello suddenly opened, and a well-dressed man stepped out—only about a dozen feet in front of them. When he started down the *banquette*, meeting André's eyes, the man came to a shocked standstill.

André was equally floored when he saw the man's face. It was Benoit Montfort, a member of André's church! The same Monsieur Montfort who seemed so amused by André's encounter with Colleen McCarthy on the day the Yankee ship fired a shot on the crowd.

André and Monsieur Montfort stared at each other for several seconds. André's thoughts buzzed with reasons why Monsieur Montfort would be stepping out of a Gallatin Street bordello. He was either a customer or, even worse, he could be management.

Similar thoughts were probably going through Montfort's mind about him. If Monsieur Montfort breathed a word of this to his wife, she would be sure to inform Felicie that he and Jean Louis had been seen on Gallatin Street. Things could get very ugly.

"*Bonjour*, Monsieur Montfort," André said, tipping his hat once again.

Monsieur Montfort stammered out a "*Bonjour*" and then hurried across the street. André noticed, strangely, that Bricktop Jackson and John Miller altered their course, heading off in a new direction, the moment they saw Montfort.

André and Jean Louis marched double-time toward the edge of the Gallatin Street district. As they left the area, André cast one last look over his shoulder, and all he saw were Bricktop and Miller standing in the center of the street, legs wide, watching them go, like two hellhounds guarding the gate.

Monsieur Montfort had disappeared.

17

An anti-slavery general. André was impressed.

André rode six miles out of New Orleans to Camp Parapet in Carrollton with the specific intention of meeting this Union General, John W. Phelps, an ardent abolitionist from what he heard. When he entered the main camp—a fortification that stretched from the river north to the Metairie Ridge—he was amazed to see numerous blacks. They were most likely contrabands, escaped slaves who had made their way into the Yankee camp.

"Several planters have sent complaints to General Butler about me," General Phelps said when André was finally given some time to talk with him. They sat across a small table from each other.

The general appeared to be smiling, although it was hard to tell beneath the massive beard that stretched to his chest. "Many slaves have found their way into our camp, but I am not inclined to send them back to their masters."

"For that, we are thankful," said André.

"What brings you out to this camp? I assume you didn't ride this far just to thank me."

André had hoped to work his way slowly to his chief concern.

But generals do not have that kind of time, so he dove right in. "What do you think the chances are that the Federal Army will assemble troops from among the slaves and free people of color?"

This time, General Phelps was definitely smiling. André could see his whiskers rise in merriment at these words.

"I had a notion you might be asking me such a question." He stared at André for a beat or two before continuing. "I do believe that the enlistment of colored troops would weaken the Confederacy."

"Then you would like to do it?"

"It is not a matter of what I would like. I answer to General Butler and President Lincoln. But I do believe that the instrument of military service can prepare slaves for freedom. I think it would be wise to raise up colored regiments to help preserve order."

Now it was André's turn to grin. These were the words he had been hoping to hear. Black regiments would not only preserve order, but they would restore his honor. His former gray uniform would be symbolically superseded by a blue one.

"Will General Butler agree to such a move?" he asked.

"I have my doubts," General Phelps said, puncturing André's hopes. "General Butler does not...he does not believe black men are capable of being trained for military service."

Before Andre could take offense, General Phelps quickly added, "But I do not share his skepticism. I believe that cadets graduating from West Point this coming June could be sent here to drill black troops. It can be done."

But will it be? André was desperate for General Phelps to give him even a glimmer of hope. He wanted so badly to fight for the North and even more so for Jean Louis to fight beside him—father and son. They could put their differences behind them because nothing unifies men more than shared battle. The duel went a small way to bringing them together, but military service would seal their bond.

"In the meantime, I will continue to allow men of color to pass my sentinels without passes." General Phelps waved a hand. "I have not given the same freedom to the white planters, who come looking for their slaves. When the planters are not allowed past my sentinels, they are not very happy."

At these words, General Phelps' smile expanded. It was so broad that André could see his jumble of teeth beneath his whiskers. Then the general gave out a soft laugh, barely audible. But it was enough to give André a morsel of hope.

18

Felicie avoided passing the haunted house of New Orleans on Royal Street whenever she could. It was a stunning three-story property with arched windows, an ornate railing running along the second floor, and a cupola perched on top. But as beautiful as it was on the exterior, she could never forget what happened on the inside.

Bastien walked alongside, and he always insisted on passing the place where the Devil once lived, as he liked to put it. On this day, she gave in to his pleading because it would have been out of her way to avoid Royal Street.

"Madame LaLaurie, Madame LaLaurie," Bastien muttered, with the ever-present grin on his face. "Is this where the Devil lived?"

"Yes, it is, so let us continue on." Felicie took him by the arm, but he was as immovable as a stone gargoyle.

Bastien stood there, gaping at the house, where Delphine LaLaurie once created a torture chamber for her slaves, brutalizing them for years. Who knows if she would have ever been discovered if a fire hadn't broken out in the house in 1834?

The blaze had been started by a cook who decided she would

rather burn alive than spend another day in Madame LaLaurie's living hell. When firefighters and citizens broke in to put out the flames, they discovered seven savagely treated slaves, some with gaping head wounds, all covered in stripes from the lash and weighted down in iron. The slaves were taken away to a city building where several thousand people flocked to see what had been done to them.

"Madame LaLaurie escaped that way," said Bastien, pointing down the street. "She is still alive."

"I doubt that very much. Now let us go," said Felicie.

"Do you think she's still alive?"

"I just said that she is not."

"Did she set fire to our stable?"

"Of course not. That horrid creature is not alive. She is in hell."

It was true that Madame LaLaurie was never caught. On the night that the slaves were rescued—the day of the fire—a mob gathered at her house, itching to bring her to justice. But before the mob could take action, her carriage came racing out the gate, flying toward the riverfront at breakneck speed. Some say she sailed to Mandeville, while others said she hid in New Orleans until she could be safely whisked away. But however it happened, she got away, so the mob took out their anger on her house instead, storming the place and tearing it apart from the inside.

Bastien continued to stare. "So pretty."

Felicie thought he was talking about the house, but he wasn't.

"Madame LaLaurie was pretty. Wasn't she pretty, Felicie?"

"Yes, she was said to be beautiful."

Madame LaLaurie was described as a stately, high-cultured woman, hostess to classical musicians who would fill her house with enchantment and music. According to stories, she would often slip away from an event, go upstairs and beat a slave or two, then return downstairs as the perfect hostess. No one caught on. No one saw blood on her hands.

Felicie finally dislodged Bastien from his spot, and they hurried down Royal Street in the direction of her favorite bakery. As they left, she made the sign of the cross.

"Our Father, who art in heaven..." she mumbled under her breath, exorcising the atmosphere surrounding the LaLaurie house.

Up ahead, she spotted a cluster of finely dressed women heading in her direction, and her heart sank when she saw four Union soldiers crossing the street on a collision course with the ladies. For the past couple of weeks, the women of New Orleans had been at war with the Yankees. Whenever Federal soldiers stepped onto streetcars, ladies would disembark in a huff. Some even spit on the soldiers. Or so she heard.

All four of the men doffed their hats and bowed to the approaching ladies. They stood in the street, politely waiting for the women to pass before they stepped up on the *banquette*. The three ladies, spotting the blue uniforms, came to a sudden stop, each scowling. Felicie noticed that one of them was Madame Montfert.

The ladies made a sharp left turn, for they were not about to pass in front of four Yankee soldiers, and they made a move to cross to the opposite side of Royal Street. They sidestepped the cypress-lined gutters that ran between the *banquette* and the road—gutters often clogged with trash and sewage and cleaned by slaves every day. She hoped that none of these women would feel inclined to spit on a soldier as they passed by each other.

What happened next was worse.

A window opened from the second-floor balcony of a house overlooking the four soldiers. Then a woman emerged and heaved the contents of her tinkle pot over the railing, and a wave of yellow liquid came down in a perfect arch, splattering one of the soldiers on his uncovered head. A direct hit.

The woman leaned over the balcony, feigning shock.

"My apologies, sir! I did not see you down below!" The woman was well dressed—the kind of person who typically had servants emptying the chamber pots.

The captain stared up at the woman, red in the face, wiping his hair with his handkerchief. One of the soldiers unsheathed his sword, even though he could not use it on a lady.

Bastien giggled, and Felicie shushed him. But it was too late. One of the soldiers heard, and when he saw that Bastien was a grown man, the soldier redirected his rage. He charged in Bastien's direction, sword drawn, and Felicie stepped in front with her arms spread.

"Step away, Madame. A true man does not need the protection of petticoats!"

Glancing over her shoulder, Felicie saw that Bastien's near-constant grin had disappeared. He whimpered.

"Please, sir, my brother does not understand the situation. He has a diminished capacity to think."

As the other three soldiers flanked the one with the sword and studied her brother, Bastien came close to tears. It was evident that although her brother appeared to be a full-grown man, he was a young boy on the inside.

"I apologize for my fellow New Orleans ladies," she said, locking eyes with Madame Montfort, who stood just beyond the soldiers, taking pleasure in the Yankees' predicament.

The men were at a loss. They could neither attack Bastien nor vent their wrath on women. The lady who had started it all continued to gaze from the balcony, smiling at the havoc she had caused.

"My good gentlemen, take this as my souvenir!" She hurled her chamber pot from the balcony.

One of the soldiers ducked before it could strike him in the head.

"Show it to General Butler! He will be pleased to know that his ugly countenance is all the rage!" The woman sent them a look of disdain from the balcony.

As the pot bounced to the ground, Felicie inhaled, her lips curled inward, and her eyes widened with shock. An image was pasted on the inside— the face of General Butler, which was a distinctive head if there ever was one.

"All of the ladies are adorning their chamber pots with his lovely face!" The lady sent them a sly smile with a toss of her head before slamming her window shut.

When one of the soldiers hurled the chamber pot into the street with a look of rage, Madame Montfort's gaggle of women burst out laughing. The soldiers glanced from the women to Felicie, realized they were in a no-win situation, and marched away double-quick.

"You did not have to apologize for us," said Madame Montfort to Felicie when the soldiers had gone. "We have nothing to be sorry for. These monsters have invaded our city and deserve far more than having a chamber pot emptied on their heads."

Felicie ignored her, turning to comfort Bastien, who was still shaken by the soldier who had threatened him with a sword.

"It is true about the chamber pots," Madame Montfort said, moving closer to Felicie. "Many fallen women have taken to pasting General Butler's picture in the bottom of their chamber pots. But perhaps your husband already knew that, seeing as he is in the habit of consorting with adventuresses."

"I would not be talking about husbands so openly in the street." Felicie put a hand on her hip. "Not when your husband was once a patron of the ballroom in the Orleans Theater."

Madame Montfort's gleeful mask dropped and was instantly replaced by a look of horror. Felicie had never used this knowledge before; out of respect, she had never said a word to Madame Montfort about her husband's past. But the lady had pushed her too far. Knowledge was power, and this particular piece of knowledge gave her the ability to shut Madame Montfort's mouth.

The lady turned back to her friends and beat a quick retreat. It would probably be a long time before Madame Montfort dared to bring up the story of André and the adventuress ever again. Felicie had first-hand knowledge of Monsieur Montfort's past, for Felicie had been there, in the Orleans Theater ballroom, so many years before.

She had been at a quadroon ball.

...

All seventeen years of age, Felicie was given the job of pulling on a rope that dangled from the ceiling. By pulling on it like a bell ringer, she powered the punkah—a giant-sized fan that moved up and down like the wing of some enormous bird, pushing a cool breeze down upon the women seated on a platform carpeted in crimson.

The women were known as quadroons, a term that technically meant they had one-fourth of African blood. But in truth, some of the women were probably octoroons (one-eighth African blood) or even griffes (three-quarters African). Whatever the percentage, they were objects of desire for many white men in New Orleans, and a quadroon ball was where the men could meet such women with the gloss of respectability.

No men of color were allowed into a quadroon ball, nor were any white women. This was purely a place where a white man could add a black concubine to his possessions and perhaps recreate what it must have been like to have a harem in ancient days.

This was the first time Felicie had been asked to work at such a ball, and she hoped it was the last. Not only was the incessant pulling on the rope burning her arms, but her mind kindled with fury. She watched as a white gentleman in his twenties approached a woman with European features and soft-brown skin—probably an octoroon. On the surface, this ball did not appear any different than a white folks' ball.

Many of the men had paired off with women of color and were dancing or strolling around the ballroom, probably checking out the women's conversational skills. If a woman passed muster, the man would cut a deal with the lady's mother, and she would become a placée; she would be "placed" in a formal relationship—a cross between a mistress and a wife. As the New Orleans custom dictated, the woman would probably be placed in a Creole Cottage on rue de Ramparts, while the white man became known as her Protector. This was the plaçage *system in action.*

Whenever Felicie complained about the plaçage system, her mother would chide her, saying it was better than being forced into prostitution. But the plaçage system sounded like nothing more than a formalized form of forced prostitution to Felicie. Besides, what did her mother know? She, too, was once a concubine.

Most of these discussions ended in an argument with tears—mostly her mother's.

"What price is your mother asking for you?" came a voice from behind.

Still pulling on the rope, Felicie cast a glance over her shoulder and spotted a portly young man, probably six or seven years older than her, moving in her direction. He had a pasty complexion speckled with a few angry red dots and an enormous mustache that looked large enough to strain his neck. He bowed. She was surprised he had the strength to raise his head back up with that weighty mustache.

"I'm sorry, sir, but I am not a participant of this ball," Felicie told him.

Surely, it was apparent she was a slave. She wondered if he was making fun of her, but she had to answer politely regardless.

He smiled and moved closer, sniffing her neck.

"Y'all smell as nice as any of the ladies here. Are you sure your mother wouldn't make a bargain for you?"

"I'm not my mother's for her to bargain with, sir."

Felicie belonged to Master Valentin Encalada.

The man moved around to the front, sizing up Felicie as he might a prize horse. "You are more beautiful than any of the women I have observed this night."

Felicie pulled harder on the rope as she gritted her teeth. If this man wasn't careful, she might just string him up by the neck.

"Are you certain you couldn't take a spin on the dance floor? We don't need that punkah operating continuously. A little heat never bothered anyone."

Felicie felt a drop of sweat slide along her arm on the inside of her long-sleeved muslin dress.

"I'm sorry, sir, but I could get in trouble if I were to do something like that."

The man took a step closer. She could smell the drink on his breath. If he grabbed her, surely somebody would come to her assistance. These were genteel events, not saloon dances. Of course, if this were a Bal de Cordon Bleu—an even more formal dance for quadroons and white men—this gentleman would already have been escorted from the premises. Bals de Cordon Bleu required formal invitations, but all that was needed to attend an ordinary quadroon ball was a one-dollar entrance fee—and the proper racial mix. White man. Mixed-race woman.

"Please, Mademoiselle. Rules are made to be broken. I think you—"

"Monsieur Montfort, I'm afraid you are mistaken," came a woman's voice, cutting through the sound of music in the ballroom.

Madame Arnaud, one of the ladies supervising the ball, had come to the rescue. Although, from the look on her face, she probably thought she was rescuing the gentleman from Felicie, not the other way around. She scowled as if Felicie were the cause of trouble.

"Monsieur Montfort, this is nothing but a slave," Madame Arnaud said, her eyes locked on Felicie. "There are many proper ladies from which to choose."

She took Monsieur Montfort by the arm and steered him away from the temptation. That was surely how Madame saw Felicie—as a tempter, every bit as delicious as the apple in the Garden. She was the fruit that could not be tasted.

Monsieur Montfort looked over his shoulder and gave Felicie a farewell wink. Felicie pulled so hard on the rope that she ran the risk of yanking down the entire punkah, like Samson bringing down the pillars. Her arms continued to burn.

■■■

That night at the quadroon ball was the first time Felicie had met

Benoit Montfort. He never made an advance on her again, for he paired off with a quadroon woman that very night, and he made the woman his mistress, placing her in a house on Rampart. When he married his white wife four years later, he disposed of his quadroon mistress, as some (but not all) men do. Madame Montfort was not one to tolerate a harem of any size.

"Madame LaLaurie was pretty." Her brother, Bastien, snapped Felicie back to reality, tugging on her sleeve. "She was pretty, wasn't she, Felicie? Was she pretty? Madame LaLaurie was pretty, I think."

Felicie said nothing. She pulled Bastien along, this time dislodging him from his spot. They made their way to the bakery, and she hoped it would be open for business. These days you never knew.

19

May 18, 1862

Coralie sat before the ornate, gold-framed mirror while Minetta stood behind her and gently draped the white veil over her head. Coralie wore the kind that covered her face in gauzy lace, so her features were barely visible, a ghostly image. She wore a yellow dress trimmed with three white flounces, and her hair was styled like a Greek goddess. In preparation for church, she pulled on a pair of cream-colored, long gloves and leaned in closer to the mirror.

"Will this veil catch a young man's fancy?" Coralie smiled at her reflection.

"That's not the purpose of a veil," said Minetta, who had long ago made it clear that she would speak her mind bluntly with Coralie. Terrified of confrontation, Coralie grew to accept forthrightness from her lady's maid.

"The veil is a sign of your modesty and humility before God," Minetta added.

Coralie laughed. "That's what you say. But I think it's most useful as a way to tantalize men. When you hide something from them, they want nothing more than to see what is hidden. Works every time."

"But veils conceal what is special before God. A veil covered the Ark of the Covenant, and a veil covers the holy sacrament during Mass."

Coralie studied her face in the mirror from several angles. "That is precisely my point. I am special enough for men to duel over."

As Minetta reached for a veil for herself, draping it over her head, she sometimes wondered why she tried to teach matters of the spirit to Coralie. She donned the mantilla, a chapel veil that fell down the sides and back of her head like a waterfall in white.

"How is Monsieur Jean Louis recovering?" Coralie asked.

The strange thing was that Coralie's interest in Jean Louis had heightened since the duel. When Minetta delivered the news of the violence that had unfolded, Coralie seemed strangely thrilled by the idea that Jean Louis could possibly die in a duel over her.

"He is doing much better."

Coralie spun around on her stool. "Monsieur Jean Louis has not been disfigured in any permanent way, has he?"

"I do not believe so."

"No wound is visible?"

"None. Remember, he was struck in the side."

Coralie smiled. "I am very relieved."

Minetta suspected that Coralie would be more upset if Jean Louis had been disfigured than killed. But the subject of the duel gave Minetta the opening she was looking for. She wondered how much Coralie knew about her brother's whereabouts on the night of Roussel's murder.

As Minetta pulled back the veil and helped Coralie with her pearls, she approached the subject delicately.

"That was very sad about Monsieur Roussel Pinard, would you not say?" Minetta clasped the necklace shut at the nape of Coralie's neck.

Coralie scowled. "I have changed my mind, Minetta. The cross would be better against the yellow of my dress."

Minetta began to remove the pearls. "I was asking about Monsieur Roussel. That was very tragic, don't you think?"

"Oh yes, of course. But why speak of such things on a Sunday morning? This is a day to celebrate life—and love."

"Very true, Coralie. I was only wondering if you or your brother knew Monsieur Roussel."

Coralie turned toward Minetta and furrowed her brow. "Why would I know Monsieur Roussel? He was not the sort of man with whom I kept company."

"Of course not. But what about your brother? Did he know Monsieur Roussel?"

"I don't believe so. In fact, I believe that Laurent had the greatest disdain for the man."

"He spoke of him?"

"Only in the most critical of terms. He thought Monsieur Roussel was a reprobate. I saw them arguing once or twice, but those were the only times I ever saw them together."

Minetta draped a silver crucifix around Coralie's neck. The cross stood out sharply against her olive skin, flashing in the sunlight pouring through the open window.

"What do you think they were arguing about?"

"I am not sure about this crucifix." Coralie cocked her head, staring at her reflection. "It makes me appear too pious. Perhaps the pearls were better after all."

"Pearls before swine," Minetta muttered under her breath.

"What was that, Minetta?"

"I said that is fine. Pearls are very fine, but so is the cross."

Coralie studied the crucifix in the mirror; then, she stood back, tapping her right toe. "Yes, let's return to the pearls."

The next question had to be worded very carefully.

"I am so pleased your brother was not harmed in the duel,"

Minetta said. "He must have trained very hard. Did he train the night before the duel?"

Minetta unclasped the crucifix and nested it gently among Coralie's many necklaces. She reached for the pearls.

"Actually, this one is even better." Coralie pointed at a short, gold chain with a floral design.

Minetta shifted from the pearls to retrieve the chain. "I was asking if your brother trained the night before the duel."

"Laurent train? I do not think so. He was gone most of the evening."

"Celebrating with friends?"

"I have no idea. He seemed quite confident about the duel, so I think he went out drinking with friends. I was so excited that night that I had difficulty sleeping, and I remember my brother returning very late. He and father argued, but that is nothing new."

That was true. Coralie's father waged running battles with his children, so arguments were commonplace in the house. Laurent's father was especially disappointed in the trajectory of his only son, and Minetta wondered if the duel was Laurent's attempt to gain his approval. But why would either of the Bisset men kill Roussel, who was supposed to act as Jean Louis's second in the combat?

"Yes, I think that is very fine." Coralie leaned back in her seat and took a final assessment of her appearance. "Thank you, Minetta. Would you please water the plants until we are ready to leave for church?"

"Yes, Coralie."

This was no simple chore, for the Bisset house overflowed with flowers, spilling from window boxes and sprouting from a battalion of flowerpots, adding a frenzy of color to every room. She retrieved water from the well in the courtyard, which was good enough for plants but not drinkable. For drinking water, they purchased water by the barrel and stored it in large Ali Baba jars.

Minetta hadn't progressed very far in her duties when she heard a burst of shouting from the parlor. Men's voices. Laurent and his father were going at it again.

"Put away the revolver! Are you a fool?" Monsieur Bisset's voice boomed through the house.

A revolver? Arguments in the house never went that far.

"These infernal Yankees need to be taught a lesson in manners!" Laurent bellowed.

Water pitcher in hand, Minetta tended to a batch of flowers just outside the parlor door. It was a good place from which to eavesdrop, although she wondered if it was a bad idea to get too close if guns were being drawn.

Coralie's voice was soon added to the mix. "What is happening, Papa? I do not understand the anger—or the gun."

"The beast, General Butler, has issued a new order," said Monsieur Laurent. "It strikes at the heart and the honor of every Southern lady in New Orleans."

Laurent let loose with a string of expletives that made Minetta's ears burn. Then Monsieur Bisset explained the situation in calmer tones.

"The new order says that any lady who insults or shows contempt to a soldier or officer of the United States will be looked upon and treated the same as a prostitute."

Minetta could hear Coralie gasp. She pictured her feigning a fainting spell and being lowered onto the fainting couch.

"It's an outrage against our ladies' honor!" Laurent bellowed.

"I said put the gun away," ordered Monsieur Henri Bisset. "I have told you time and time again that your temper will be the death of you! Use your wits for once!"

"The last time I used my wits, you said you would disown me!"

"That wasn't using your wits! It was foolish beyond words!"

Minetta had no idea what they were talking about.

"But we must do something about the Yank invaders," Laurent said. "We cannot stand idly by and watch our women abused in such a Philistine fashion. This is perhaps the greatest crime ever committed by an occupying army."

"There are other ways to subvert the Yankee menace than displaying your gun and waving your sword. That will only get you killed."

"Papa, if a lady is accused of insulting an officer, would she really be placed in jail—like a lady of the night?" Coralie asked.

"I would put nothing past these Yanks."

Minetta heard the rustling of fabric and scooted to the far side of the room, where she nonchalantly began watering plants. Coralie swept into the room and went straight for her.

"Minetta, I have something more important for you to do than watering."

"Yes, Mademoiselle?"

Coralie brought her voice to a near whisper. "I would like you to paint over the inside of my chamber pot. *Immediately*."

"Understood, Mademoiselle."

"Please. Before we leave for church."

Minetta smiled to herself as she left the room and made her way upstairs to Coralie's bedchamber. Coralie was taking no risks. She was not about to be arrested for owning a chamber pot with the picture of General Butler painted on the inside.

20

When Father Maistre opened the back door to the church, a refreshing breeze rushed over him, carrying with it the scents of flowers. He peered into the dark, but he could hear nothing but the hum of insects and the clattering of tree branches brushing against each other in the wind.

He ducked back inside, wringing his hands and distracting himself by running through his rosary beads for the second time. His mind continued to buzz, and he sprinted through his prayers as if the loop of beads were a racetrack. Until today, he had kept his Union sympathies hidden, except to a few people. But what he was doing on this night might just pull his mask off completely.

Well past midnight, he heard a gentle rap on a side door that led into the small sanctuary near the statue of St. Rose. When he eased open the door, the faces of two black men greeted him, and behind them was a cluster of moving shadows.

"Father Maistre?"

The priest opened the door wide to give the two prominent leaders passage—followed by six slaves: an old woman, three young men in their twenties, and two young women. Of the final two, one was in her thirties, and the other probably not even twenty.

The first leader shot out his hand. "Abraham Galloway."

"John Scobell," said the other.

"Father Claude Maistre. Come in."

"Bless you, Father."

Galloway was in his twenties, a well-dressed man of mixed-race descent. He had thick, black hair with gentle curls and bangs that draped over one eye. Scobell was darker skinned, also in his twenties —tall, trim, and clean-shaven, with close-cropped hair and broad shoulders.

Father Maistre, candle in hand, led the group across the sanctuary. One of the slaves paused to dip his hand in the baptismal font, scoop out a mouthful of water, and gulp down the holy water. He obviously had never been in a Catholic church before. Another slave's eyes didn't leave the altar as they crossed the sanctuary.

"I hope there ain't no bones beneath that altar," one fugitive whispered.

"Do not worry. It is only the bone of a saint's finger," Father Maistre said. "Nothing to be afraid of."

"Just as long as that finger don't wander the church at night and start pokin' me when I sleep," said another slave.

While the priest genuflected before the altar, most of the fugitive slaves gaped at him. The old woman, figuring it was the fitting thing to do, got down on one knee, but she had to be helped back to her feet once her knee hit the floor.

Father Maistre led them into the sacristy, a small room at the back of the church. The priest enjoyed art, and one wall of the room displayed several paintings. Another area was lined with vestments hanging on a pole.

In the flicker of candlelight, one of the escaped slaves peered at the painting of the Sacred Heart and scratched his head. It was a typical image of Jesus pulling his vestment aside to reveal a red heart encircled by thorns and bleeding from a lance wound. Flames sprouted from the top of the heart, which was crowned by a cross.

"Saint Margaret Mary said that Jesus's heart is an ocean of infinite mercy," the priest said.

The slave turned toward Father Maistre, his eyes glowing with reflected light. He offered a crooked smile but said nothing.

"This is where you can stay for the time being—until we can get you out of the city safely." The priest shifted his gaze to the elderly woman. "Madame, you and the other ladies may take my room in the rectory next door. The men will have to settle for sleeping on the floor."

"Where y'all gonna sleep?" Scobell eyed the area.

"One of the pews in the sanctuary will suffice. I'd invite you, men, to sleep on one of the pews as well, but if anybody walked into the sanctuary unannounced..."

"That's fine to me. This place is heaven compared to my old quarters." One of the young men studied the large crucifix on the wall, his profile revealing scars from a lashing. He also had a shackle still clamped around his right ankle. While the chain had been lopped off, the iron band remained like a piece of cruel jewelry.

Father Maistre nodded. "Someone should stay awake, so I thought I would be the first. I'll be in the sanctuary praying."

Scobell smiled. "Like the Garden of Gethsemane?"

Father Maistre chuckled. "I promise to do a better job staying awake than the apostles."

While the fugitive slaves settled in for the night, Father Maistre headed for the sanctuary, where he knelt and prayed for the next half hour. The room was dark except for the light of Christ that always remained lit on the altar—a red glow like the Sacred Heart itself, never quenched.

The priest leaned against the pew and felt a wave of drowsiness come over him, and for a moment, wondered if he would succumb to sleep. His drowsy state was forgotten the moment the door behind him scraped open, sending his heart rate skyrocketing. Sweat trickled down the back of his neck as footsteps crossed the sanctuary floor and shadows flickered across a wall. He spun, expecting the worse, only to exhale with relief when he saw Galloway and Scobell.

They sat in a nearby pew and faced Father Maistre.

"Thank you again, Father." Galloway draped his arm on the back of the pew.

"Thank you for helping out a good Baptist man like myself," added Scobell.

Father Maistre smiled, wondering for the hundredth time why he risked his church by sheltering fugitive slaves. Still, he downplayed the threat he brought upon himself and his congregation.

"You are the ones to be thanked. I am not dealing with the kind of dangers you must have faced leading these people through our swamps. The terrain couldn't be easy, especially since you two are obviously not from around these parts."

"You're right there," Scobell said. "I'm from Richmond, although I can speak with many accents as if I was from different parts."

To Father Maistre's amazement, he spoke the last sentence with a Scottish accent.

Galloway smiled. "I'm from Bern, North Carolina, and we both came this way attached to General Butler's army."

"In what capacity?" Galloway and Scobell obviously could not be soldiers since blacks were not allowed in the Federal Army.

"I do whatever I can," said Scobell.

Most likely a spy. Father Maistre had heard of groups of slaves and free blacks operating in the South. The Lincoln League, they were called. But all of this was better left unsaid.

"Do you suppose General Butler will change his mind on the contraband situation?" Father Maistre asked.

When General Butler oversaw Fort Monroe out East, he had initiated the contraband policy, in which escaped slaves were accepted into Yankee lines and considered spoils of war. But in New Orleans, no such thing was happening.

Ever since the Yankee occupation began, slaves had been fleeing the plantations in droves, but they were being turned away at Union lines. That's why they needed shelter in places like St. Rose de Lima Church.

"It's President Lincoln's orders that the general is following," Scobell said. "Things are a lot more sensitive in a place like New Orleans, and they're trying to avoid upsetting the planters by turning back fugitive slaves at Union lines."

Scobell straightened with a look of disappointment. "The planters are already riled as can be, so I don't see how accepting contrabands could make them any angrier—especially after General Butler passed the Woman's Order."

"True."

"It burns me that Federals are hurling contrabands back to the wolves," Galloway growled.

As the man continued relating some of the horrors slaves had experienced out on the Louisiana plantations, Father Maistre worried that Galloway's voice might carry into the night. Still, he didn't want to squelch the man's passion.

"I'm sorry if I go on so much." Galloway sighed, before letting out a full-bodied yawn, arms stretching to the sides.

"Nothing to be sorry for."

"Would you like me to keep watch so you can catch some sleep, Father?"

"You're the ones who need the rest. I will continue to remain awake."

After Galloway and Scobell excused themselves, Father Maistre was alone with his thoughts and prayers, trying another round of the rosary. His mind, however, drifted to the threats that had been made by the unknown man in his confessional. The money that he left by the statue had disappeared within a day, and he had heard no more threats about his past scandal.

Once again, drowsiness came over him like a slow-growing fog inside his mind, and he moved into the head-bobbing stage.

Then he heard a bark.

His head shot up.

Another bark.

Father Maistre had obtained a dog the week after the Yankees took control of the city. It was a German Shepherd—a dog that was easy to train and a good protector. He named the dog Martin after the French saint Martin of Tours, famous for giving his Roman soldier's cloak to a beggar. His German Shepherd was his own cloak of protection.

Martin didn't bark unless he had a good reason.

Father Maistre rose from the pew and moved through the church to the side door, just past the statue of Saint Rose. He stepped out into the utter darkness of night. The wind had picked up, and he heard two competing tones of insects, an orchestra of crickets and cicadas. Then a crunch. Feet on stones? He turned to his right. Nothing but blackness.

He wandered over to Martin's doghouse, where the German Shepherd was staked to a long chain. Crouching, he ran his fingers behind Martin's ears while the dog licked his other hand.

"You hear something, boy? Or did you just see a rabbit?"

Father Maistre's eyes, well-adjusted in the dark, wandered to a shed behind the church, noticing the door was ajar. He was usually good about keeping it closed. Father Maistre picked up a heavy stick, wishing he'd brought along something more substantial, like a candlestick. He paused outside the shed to listen. Was someone breathing behind the door, or was it his runaway imagination? He waited. If someone was inside, they couldn't remain silent forever. But the crickets were so loud that they drowned out any faint sounds of movement. As he gently pushed open the door, it gave a soft creak. When he peered through the gaping doorway, there was nothing but another level of darkness, a deeper pitch of black.

One step into the shed. He turned left, but all he could see were various garden tools. He pivoted right, and his skin nearly leaped from his bones. An animal's head emerged from the darkness, moving toward him at high speed.

The head of a bull lunged for his face, and it let out a roar. He stumbled back a step, knocking over a rake, as the attacker swung a club, aiming for his head. Instinctively, Father Maistre held up his hands and intercepted the arcing arm, grabbing the attacker by the wrist. But the bull-faced creature slammed a fist against his throat, leaving him unable to breathe, as if someone had jammed a lump of hot coal down his throat, burning and blocking his airway. He buckled over, gagging and coughing and trying to scream, but all that came out was a garbled moan.

Instead of attacking him a second time, the bull threw open the shed door so hard that it banged like a gunshot, knocking a couple of cans from a shelf attached to the wall. Then, the malign spirit sprinted into the darkness.

The priest fought for air, chest heaving, throat in agony, and he stumbled into the night, falling to the ground. It seemed like an eternity before he could suck in a single breath, the lump in his throat squeezing off the air passage, leaving only the thinnest capillary through which to wheeze.

When Galloway and Scobell eventually found him, the priest was sitting on the moist ground, holding his neck and gasping. He remembered Galloway trying to speak to him, but he couldn't talk or even think straight. As he began to calm, it slowly dawned on him that he was holding the attacker's club in his hands. Somehow, in the struggle, he had ripped it out of the bull's hand.

When he realized the end of the club was still warm to the touch, it dawned on him that he was holding a torch. The attacker must have put out the flame when Father Maistre came to investigate. Had this demon come to set fire to the church?

Breathe. Father Maistre had little time to think of much beyond staying alive.

21

A ndré noticed a raw redness around Father Maistre's neck, like a rash, but mixed with the bluish-purple bruise. The priest said the attacker had hit him squarely in the voicebox.

"And he wore a mask?" André asked, draping an arm over the edge of a pew in St. Rose's. Two days had passed since the priest had been attacked.

"The man wore the same kind of mask as your firesetter—a bull. I fear he was coming to set fire to the church..." Father Maistre closed his eyes and dropped his chin in thought. "He probably knew I was hiding contrabands."

"But how could he have known you were hiding slaves?"

"No idea," said Father Maistre from the next pew. "You and Felicie would not have told anyone."

"Not a living soul. Any idea who might have been beneath the mask?"

Father Maistre's fingers continued to trace the bruised mark on his neck; then, he took a sip of water before answering. "I only know he was young, and he was taller than me. But that could be almost anyone."

Father Maistre was barely five feet, five inches.

"If you need assistance in watching the church, you can count on Jean Louis and me."

"Thank you, André. But enough of this unpleasantness. Tell me. What's happening with the Native Guards that the Yankees might be assembling?"

André smiled. He had not told anyone about the recent moves to raise up a black unit on the Union side, but news always had a way of trickling out.

"Captains Rey and Davis are hoping to meet with General Butler to propose that he raise up a unit of free men of color."

"Do you really think General Butler will listen to their ideas, given what happened with General Phelps?"

"You know about Phelps?"

Father Maistre nodded. Brigadier General Phelps had approached General Butler to arm fugitive slaves and raise up three regiments of African soldiers to help protect Camp Parapet. But General Butler said Africans were only suitable for carrying spears, and he told him to use them to cut down all the trees between Camp Parapet and Lake Pontchartrain. Phelps resigned in protest.

"Are you willing to face the consequences when your Confederate neighbors learn that you are trying to rally support for black Union troops?" the priest asked. "You're playing with fire."

"I will have my honor back."

The priest rubbed his throat and stared at André. "No one blames you for wearing the Confederate uniform."

"I blame myself."

"You had little choice."

"Little or not, I had a choice. I chose wrong."

"If you fight for the North, you might have more than one man in a mask trying to burn down your house."

"Sounds like you're trying to talk me out of fighting for the Yanks."

"I just want you to be well aware of the cost."

"You are taking the same risks in hiding contrabands, Father."

"But I do not have a wife and children."

Strangely enough, André wasn't as much concerned about the opinion of his neighbors as he was the opinion of his younger son, Eugene. He feared that Eugene would not understand why he switched his loyalties from the Louisiana Native Guards who defended New Orleans to the Yankees who occupied the city.

"I have considered the risks." André exhaled, picturing the image of Eugene's face once he learned of his decision.

"What does Felicie think?"

"I have not spoken to her about this yet." That conversation would be even more complex than the one with Eugene.

To change the subject, André asked about the kinds of conversations Father Maistre would face if his Unionist loyalties became known to people like Bishop Odin. But they hadn't gone too far down this conversational byway before they heard an impatient pounding on the sanctuary door.

"Shall I open it?" asked André, and the priest nodded.

The man at the door was Benoit Montfort, and he did not look happy.

"Where are they?" Monsieur Montfort demanded, bumping shoulders with André as he barreled past.

Father Maistre gave him a blank stare. "Where are who?"

"Don't play fast and loose, Father. Where are the fugitive slaves?" Montfort glanced around the sanctuary, even scanning the ceiling as if he thought he might find a couple of slaves gripping the lights like flies.

"Where did you get the notion that there are fugitive slaves in the church?"

"Don't play games with me," Montfort said, eyeing the door leading to the sacristy. "Bishop Odin would not be pleased."

"The bishop would also not be pleased about a parishioner walking in like he owned the place," André said. He flexed a hand, making a fist at his side, and took a step closer to Montfort.

"Would you mind if I had a look around?" Montfort asked, eyeing the door to the priest's quarters.

"I do mind." Father Maistre lowered his chin and stared down Montfort from under his brow.

"Your salary is paid for by church members like me," Montfort said. "And if I find out that you have been harboring contrabands, you will lose the financial contributions of people like me."

Father Maistre visibly flinched at Montfort's statement, as if the parishioner had flicked him in the nose. The priest had a reputation for enjoying fine art, fine food, and fine wine, and André knew he had an attraction to money that didn't exactly square up with the Sermon on the Mount. But to his credit, the priest stood his ground.

"Your money does not entitle you to invade my church."

Montfort's eyes lingered on the doorknob of the sacristy. If Montfort was trying to uncover the priest's secrets, he needed to be reminded that he had secrets of his own.

"It was nice seeing you the other week," André said, cocking his head, staring at Montfort, and waiting. While it took a second for the meaning to sink in, André raised a brow at the precise moment Montfort realized he was talking about spotting him on Gallatin Street. "I see that your money goes to other causes than the church."

Montfort's face flushed red. "The same could be said for you, Cailloux. With your son, were you? It's so nice to see fathers and sons pursuing similar interests together."

André maintained a stiff smile. "I am just saying you should keep such things in mind as you make threats."

Father Maistre followed this exchange, his head bobbing between them, clearly mystified by their veiled references.

"I don't have to justify myself to you, Cailloux." Montfort looked ready to burst like a steamboat boiler pushed to its limit.

Montfort stared at the sacristry door for a few heartbeats before charging toward it. André leaped to his feet, wondering if he should strong-arm the man away from the door. If the contrabands were uncovered, it would be the end for Father Maistre in New Orleans.

André hesitated just long enough for Montfort to throw open the door and storm inside. André was right behind. He gripped the edges of the door and leaned inside the sacristy.

When Montfort found nothing in the small room, he rifled through the vestments along one wall, hoping to uncover anyone crouching behind them. He shuffled up and down the vestment wall, the clothing swishing as he pushed through them. A couple of the vestments hit the floor as Montfort spun and gave André a final glare before marching through the sanctuary in a sevenfold rage. André and Father Maistre said nothing until Montfort exited, slamming the front door behind him.

André stared at the entryway and let out a deep breath, turning to the priest. "You could have told me that the contrabands were no longer there. I about had a heart attack."

Father Maistre smiled and flung up a hand. "I was going to. They were moved just this morning."

Putting both hands on his hips, André looked back at the sanctuary door. "He can still cause trouble. He's a big donor to the church."

"I'm not bending to his will. I don't care how much money he has."

André nodded. He wished it were true that Father Maistre didn't care what the man donated, but he knew the priest better than that.

22

August 1862

André was free on the back of a horse.

He was in charge, he was the master, and the horse beneath him did his bidding. With a simple signal, he could make this nine-hundred-pound beast turn right or left. On the back of the animal, he had the authority of a ship captain, who could pivot a monstrous vessel with just a word, a single command.

Although he was technically a free man of color, *gens de couleur libres*, he didn't feel this freedom in the city confines; he was surrounded by potential masters on every street corner. Over the past few decades, the city's white fathers had piled law upon law to constrain free people of color.

Just six years ago, the state forbade people of color from incorporating new religious, charitable, scientific, or literary societies. Each law was like a shovel-load of soil added to the mountain that he was forced to climb day after day. Ever since the Americans took over Louisiana, they had been piling on laws and restrictions, making it seem he was trudging uphill.

But out here on the edge of the city, accompanied by his wife, they were free from all of it, and everything was speed, everything was whipping wind as his horse carried him at high velocities. Gone was the uphill trudge.

The land was mostly flat, and he rode on the back of Paris, his stallion, while Felicie rode beside him on Helen. This happy plain was their Eden, a perfect, unbroken landscape, making it seem like he was the first father of all creation and Felicie the first mother.

In his mind, the real Eve was not a white woman, as he had seen in so many stained glass windows and paintings. In the beginning, Eve was a free woman of color, like Felicie, with traces of every human running wild through her bloodstream. And Adam? He was the blackest man in the Tigris and Euphrates river valley.

They brought their horses to a canter and eventually found a shady spot beneath their favorite tree—a leafy oak on the edge of the field. The air carried the summer scents of thriving grass. To their left was a patch of big-leaf hydrangea, pink with clusters as large as mop heads. André stretched out on the soft, black ground and laid his head in Felicie's lap. She plucked long stems of grass and ran them across his cheek. It was mid-morning, and the sun had put the idyllic day on a low simmer—just enough to keep them warm without boiling. Their two horses, Paris and Helen, nibbled on grass, emitting loud, moist sounds.

"You have decided to join the African Brigade?"

"Let's not talk about that." André turned with a distant look in his eyes, staring at their surroundings. The day was perfect. Why let anything intrude on perfection?

"We *have* to talk about it. I hear that General Butler has changed his mind and now wants to raise a black unit."

André, his head still in Felicie's lap, stared straight up at her. "How did you learn that?"

"I hear things."

The Confederates had recently staged a successful sneak attack on Union troops in nearby Baton Rouge. Although the Yankees had beaten back the Rebels, André knew there was fear that the Confederates might attempt to take back New Orleans under General Breckinridge. General Butler needed more men with which to defend the city. Some believed he would reverse his earlier decision and raise up a unit of black troops after all.

André didn't say anything more. He closed his eyes as the breeze danced across his face, hoping Felicie would drop the subject.

Of course, she didn't.

"I'm asking you. If the Yankees decide to raise an African Brigade, will you join?"

Letting out a groan, André pushed himself up to face his wife. "I am thinking on it."

"Remember the children."

"Jean Louis can take care of himself."

Felicie gave him her patented look of displeasure. "You know I am talking about the young ones."

"I have to do what is right."

"No matter the threat to our children?"

André didn't have to answer her. As head of the household, this was his decision. She was the one who had pressured him into joining the Native Guards that served the Confederate side.

"You convinced me to wear the wrong uniform," he said.

"Only to protect our house and family."

"It was a humiliation, a compromise."

"Sometimes, we must make compromises." She tossed up a hand, her eyes pleading with him.

He sat up and stared at her long and hard, unsure whether to go any further with this subject. "Like the compromises your mother made?"

Felicie's face twisted, her eyes flashing with anger. "That is different. She gave away her virtue. That was too costly a compromise."

"And I gave away my honor. Don't take away my chance to regain it."

"So you hate me for convincing you to do what's best for our family?"

"I could never hate you, but I am going to do what is right this time."

"*This time?* Do you think I led you into sin the last time? Was it so difficult to wear a Confederate uniform?"

André nodded slowly. He didn't want to argue. Not here, not now.

"I want to know," she insisted. "Did I lead you into sin?"

"Call it what you want. You convinced me to ignore my conscience."

"Your conscience might have lost us our property—and our freedom."

"I am signing up for the Yankees' Native Guards." He stood with conviction.

She leaped to her feet in turn. "I thought you said you were only considering it."

"I said I do not want to talk about this."

"But you're putting *our* family at risk."

"Every family, black or white, who sends a man or son to war is taking a risk." André spun for his horse, running a hand down its flank. "We're not any different than other soldiers' families."

"Of course, we're different!" Felicie's arms flailed. "A family of color carries so much more risk! We live in a Confederate city that already hates us for who we are. Why give them another reason to harm us?"

"Someone set fire to our property—and that happened while I was still technically a part of the Confederate unit. It cannot get any worse than that."

Felicie brushed the slivers of grass from her dress and stepped next to her horse, which nibbled grass side by side with André's—beneath the shade tree.

"Of course, it could get worse. It could get much worse for us."

He resented Felicie for bringing up this subject before they got back to the city. Why spoil their ride?

"This is my decision, not yours," he said sharply.

"You convinced Jean Louis to duel, all because of your sense of honor, and it almost got him killed. Now you want to put *all of us* at risk."

André was tempted to leap onto his horse and ride off.

"You have long sought legitimacy for yourself and for our children," he said. "Has it occurred to you that I seek legitimacy too? Has it ever occurred to you that serving in that Confederate unit felt like the same as being a whore—a concubine?"

"Like my mother?"

"Yes. Like your mother."

"But my desire for legitimate children did not put our family at risk," she said. "Your search for legitimacy does just that. My desire is not selfish."

"And mine is?"

Felicie didn't answer, thank God. If she spoke her mind, his resentment might transform into hints of hatred.

"I do not think that putting my life on the line for the Union is selfish."

Again, Felicie did not respond. She stared at him, and he glared back. So much for Paradise. Then she let out a grunt and threw herself up and onto the saddle—a move he had taught her long ago. She rode off without another word.

■■■

Jean Louis found Coralie even more enticing behind her veil.

Coralie wore a maroon dress, and her entire head was covered in a white gossamer veil sprinkled with a flower pattern that obscured much of her face, except for her dark eyes. She'd adorned her coiffure with some pink flowers above her left ear. The veil also covered much of the exposed skin of her neck and shoulders, making it difficult to discern her light brown skin. She could almost be mistaken for a white woman behind her veil.

Almost.

Jean Louis had to catch himself to keep from staring.

"I am so glad we could complete our unfinished business, Monsieur Cailloux," said Coralie.

Jean Louis tried to read her thoughts by observing the look in her eyes, for he could see little else of her expression. She had smiling eyes. *A good sign.*

"Is the camera prepared?" asked Minetta, who had come along as a chaperone—as usual. "We do not want to tempt fate by taking too long with this activity."

"This activity" was another photography session after the last one had been interrupted by Yankee cannon fire. Surprisingly, the whole thing had been Coralie's idea, with Minetta acting as a go-between. Jean Louis was sure that whatever relationship he had with Coralie had gone up in flames, so he was stunned when Minetta came to him, asking if he would like to complete the photography session with Coralie.

Minetta wondered if it was wise for him to attempt another session, considering the bad blood with Coralie's family. She was obviously trying to discourage him, but Jean Louis was no longer afraid of what Laurent might do. He had bested the man in the duel, even though he was the one who had come away with the wound. Next time, Laurent would bleed.

Today, as he set up for the portrait, he tried to banish Laurent and Coralie's father from his mind. Instead, he marveled that his near-death in the duel had revived Coralie's interest in him. Perhaps a little spilled blood was worth it.

"How would you like Mademoiselle to pose?" Minetta stepped forward, seeming to be in an unusual hurry to see this thing over.

But Jean Louis was in no hurry. He would like nothing more than to stretch out this session as long as possible.

"Do you think you could make my photograph into a CdV?" Coralie took her seat and positioned the folds of her dress.

Just the rustle of the fabric drove Jean Louis mad with excitement. He hoped he didn't come across as giddy as a schoolboy.

"I could sell a thousand copies if I made your image into a CdV." When Jean Louis noticed the sudden alarm in Coralie's eyes, he added, "Not that I would dare. I only meant that people would flock to buy images of the mysterious and beautiful woman in the veil."

This seemed to please Coralie...judging by her eyes.

A CdV, or *carte de visite*, was all the rage ever since Napoleon III had his photos published in the new form. The photographs were small, about two by three and a half inches, and they were printed on albumen paper, which gave the image a brownish tint, and then mounted on thicker stock. Everyone these days seemed to be carrying photos of loved ones on cards or mailing them to relatives. Cardomania was what they called it.

Jean Louis wheeled out the neck brace to hold Coralie's head in place, and his hands brushed against the wispy-thin veil. If Minetta hadn't been there, he didn't know if he could have resisted kissing the back of her neck.

"I hear there is talk that General Butler might raise a regiment of African soldiers." Coralie gave him a sideways glance

"I have heard the same." Jean Louis inserted the glass plates into the camera.

"Does your father intend to join if a unit is formed?"

Jean Louis did not wish to spend his limited time with Coralie discussing his father, so he gave her a quick answer. "I would not be surprised if he joined."

"That is too bad." Coralie cast her eyes down and fluffed her skirt. "I surely hope you would not do anything to betray our city and our Confederacy by joining with the Yankees."

"Of course, I would never join a Yankee unit." Jean Louis, eager to please, gave her a look of confidence.

Coralie's eyes lit up. "I am glad to hear that."

In truth, Jean Louis had considered signing up. The pay was supposed to be good, and he imagined he would look fine in uniform. But what good is a dashing uniform if Coralie disapproved of its blue color?

He changed the subject. "I am so happy you decided to permit me to take your photograph a second time. I hope this will not create any problems with your family."

"They do not know of our meeting, and they will never know."

"I understand completely."

Jean Louis made some final adjustments to the camera, trying to think of something charming to say but came up empty.

"Now, please tilt your head slightly to the right." He motioned with his hand, using his forefinger and thumb to shape an L. "There. That is perfect. Hold that pose."

He removed the cover, exposing the glass plate to the onrush of light and image. Then he counted down the exposure—like someone counting down the firing of an explosive.

23

It was official. On August 22, 1862, General Butler called on Africa.

He announced General Order 63, which declared that the United States Army was enlisting free men of color to form three new regiments in the Louisiana militia, pending approval by President Lincoln.

Within forty-eight hours, free people of color had closed over a hundred businesses for the day so men could swarm the enlistment offices. André was one of them. Jean Louis was not.

In the days to come, André became a common sight on the streets, riding along on his horse, stopping to encourage black men to enlist. He commanded respect from high atop his stallion—and wore a captain's uniform.

Today, he stood in his bedroom and stared at the blue uniform before putting it on. On each shoulder was an epaulette—bright gold with quarter-inch diameter bullion fringe befitting a captain. He slipped on the single-breasted frock coat and began to button it one by one. Gold buttons, each showing the American Eagle. He next donned a sword belt and crimson sash. Last were the white dress gloves and a blue, soft, wide-brimmed hat encircled by an officer's cord and showing the U.S. wreath boldly in front. The ultimate flourish was the ostrich feather on the left side of the hat.

He was ready to meet the day.

André spent the morning on the streets recruiting. The sight of a black man in uniform would inspire many men to sign up. As he rode slowly through the city, he took note of the envy in their eyes.

He also noticed something in the eyes of the whites—shock. The sight of a black man in a dress uniform had many of them scowling, some shouting names. But if he could brave a battle, he could brave ineffectual insults, which passed through him like ghost bullets.

He stopped by Jean Louis's tiny house, but his son was gone, and a neighbor said she thought he was down at the family cigar factory, a small operation on Union Street, just a couple of blocks from the waterfront in the Third District. Although Jean Louis was a carpenter by trade, he spent some time at the family factory when his business was slow.

Sure enough, André found Jean Louis alone in the small workroom, sorting through tobacco leaves and selecting filler leaves that would form the core of the next cigar. The Cailloux family could afford to hire only a dozen—a stark contrast to the large factories where long lines of workers sat at tables in warehouses, rolling cigars. They faced enormous competition from the big factories run by other free men of color, such as Lucien Mansion and Georges Alcès.

"I will take over your work while you head down to the enlistment office," André said to his son.

When Jean Louis looked up and fixed his eyes on the uniform, André hoped it would work its magic and inspire his son to finally do his duty. He saw how his son lusted after such a uniform, but Jean Louis just shrugged and returned to the tobacco leaves.

"I said I can take over for you here," André repeated.

"I would rather stay and work alone if you please, sir."

André's jaw fell slack, and he blinked with disbelief.

With the filler leaves rolled, Jean Louis picked out a binder leaf that would hold the core together. The leaves—brown sheets of dried vegetation—looked like old parchment. His son was a fast roller and could craft more than a hundred cigars in a day, but he also knew his son was bored by the work. Jean Louis much preferred carpentry and photography to the tedium of cigar-making.

If André's uniform wasn't going to be enough to get Jean Louis to the enlistment office, maybe he needed to be reminded of other benefits.

"The Yankees are promising land and good pay—thirty-eight dollars upfront to those who enlist. More later."

Jean Louis shrugged again and kept working without even as much as a glance. He was probably afraid that if he looked at the uniform again, he might not be able to resist.

"You are planning to enlist, are you not?" André stepped closer, angling his head, hoping to catch his son's eye.

Jean Louis still didn't answer. He had wrapped the filler leaf with a binder leaf and placed the bunch into a mold, which would compact and bond them together before the final step—enveloping them in the wrapper, the outer jacket of the cigar made from the finest quality leaf. The cigar's uniform.

"I am speaking to you, son. I have been named a captain, and I am raising a company for the 1st Regiment."

As Jean Louis shuffled through a stack of dark-brown tobacco like an oversized deck of cards, ignoring him further, André could take it no longer.

"Look at me when I speak to you!" André swept the pile from the table.

Jean Louis stared at the tobacco on the floor. "That is good filler you just dumped on the ground."

"I said look at me when I am talking." André had always prided himself on shaping his son by applying the same, steady pressure as the mold that pressed the cigars into a perfect cylinder. He demanded respect. He expected it.

Finally, Jean Louis turned his eyes on him. André had never

experienced such a yawning gap between him and his son. He was done with asking. He would order him to enlist. He was a captain in the 1st Regiment and expected his commands to be obeyed.

"You *will* enlist." André's eyes burned hotter with each word.

Jean Louis rolled another leaf, grinding his teeth, pushing back with equal fervor, letting each word drip with defiance. "I will *not*."

André had the strength to drag his son to the enlistment office if he desired to, but a captain shouldn't resort to physical force. A word was all it took to make a man move. But not today. His words sailed off into oblivion.

"If you are my son, you will enlist."

He saw fear creep into his son's eyes. He had him. *If you are my son...*

Then a slow smirk crept across Jean Louis's face. "Then I guess I must not be your son."

André's arm cocked back as if it had a mind of its own, but he held back his hand when his son flinched. It was enough to see Jean Louis cringe under the threat of violence.

"I am sorry, Papa." Jean Louis exhaled when André lowered his arm.

"*Le diable à midi!* Is this about the Bisset woman? Has she steered you away from the good cause?"

"This is my decision." A flash of determination danced in Jean Louis's eyes before he picked up the scattered tobacco leaves from the floor and brushed away the dirt. "I will not betray our city."

André could not believe his ears. He thought it would be tough explaining to Eugene why he joined the Yankees, but he hadn't expected this from Jean Louis.

"But you *are* willing to betray your own people," André said. "You are willing to betray *every person of color* in your city."

Jean Louis stared at the palms of his hands, then glanced over at André's darker skin. He held up his palms.

"But we are not the same color."

This time André could not control the sweep of his hand. Like a striking snake, his hand flashed from his side and smacked Jean Louis's cheek with a whip-crack. André had lost all control—of his son, and it seemed, of himself.

Jean Louis's skin was light enough to show the redness of the slap. He held his cheek, his eyes glimmering, but he didn't utter one word or strike back. He simply stood and exited the cigar factory.

PART II

PARADISE REGAINED

"If I find in myself a desire, which no experience in this world can satisfy, the most probable explanation is that I was made for another world."

— C.S. Lewis

"Long is the way
And hard, that out of hell leads up to light."

— Paradise Lost, Book ii, Line 432

24

September 1862

Jean Louis wondered if he should have walked rather than wait for a New Orleans streetcar. He could have been home long ago if he had simply trudged back. For slaves and free people of color, the wait could be eternal because they could only ride in cars marked with a large black star. Yet Star Cars seemed to come as infrequently as Halley's Comet.

"You been in New Orleans long?" Jean Louis asked a young man of color—a soldier waiting alongside him.

"Came here with my mama in '50," the young soldier said.

Jean Louis still couldn't get used to seeing men of color, *libres*, dressed in Union blue—although the word "man" was generous for this young soldier. He looked fifteen years old, if that, and yet he wore the uniform of a second lieutenant. Either he lied about how old he was, or he looked astonishingly young for his age.

"You born free?" Jean Louis asked.

"Yes, sir. So is my mama."

With his constant references to his mother, he also appeared to be a bit of a mama's boy. Jean Louis introduced himself and found out that the young second lieutenant's name was John Crowder, and he was in the same regiment as his father, André. If Crowder was shocked that Jean Louis wasn't in uniform, he didn't say so.

Crowder was a curious one, for although he had a baby face, he also had a serious, studious air of maturity. His curled hair was short and perfectly parted down the middle; his nose was broad and his eyebrows thick, giving him an intense look. He was thin and of average height, but he had a habit of rising on his tiptoes as if to give himself a few inches more.

"Where'd you get your education?" Jean Louis asked.

"John Mifflin Brown taught me, sir," Crowder said. He was polite, too.

John Mifflin Brown? He was a well-known black clergyman in New Orleans—highly educated, a pillar of the city. Jean Louis was impressed but didn't say so.

Jean Louis nodded as another streetcar came and went—an all-white car, of course. As they watched it pass, a couple of other soldiers joined the growing cluster of people of color. Now that he was hemmed in by blacks in uniform—the very uniform that his father tried to force on him—he tugged at his collar as a bead of sweat rolled down his back.

Over the past few days, it became increasingly more uncomfortable to be seen wearing civilian clothes. Was he doing the right thing by giving in to Coralie's wishes and *not* fight against the Confederacy?

Jean Louis cut a quick glance at Crowder, thankful that the soldier had been kind about his civilian status. When two other black officers arrived, they didn't give Jean Louis a second look; they were more intent on harassing the boy for his youthful appearance.

"I think folks is starin' at you, Chowder, because they're not sure whether to salute you or change your diapers." One of the officers—a captain—laughed, elbowing the other in the ribs.

"Judging by the smell comin' off his person, I put more stock in them thinkin' he needs a diaper change," said the second officer, a lieutenant.

Jean Louis watched from the corner of his eye, noticing Crowder's reaction. Although he was clenching his jaw, the young man ignored the two soldiers. Jean Louis frowned, for these two soldiers had to be the most pusillanimous, dirty, low-life men. Within seconds, it began to drizzle. When a passing horse dropped a sloppy load of manure that nearly splashed on Crowder's shoes, the other soldiers burst out laughing.

"Don't worry 'bout the smell, folks!" The captain sent the other blacks waiting for the trolley a look, barely containing his laughter. "The boy here just filled his pants."

Several in the crowd tittered. Then the rain became a steady drizzle, and Jean Louis was as miserable as a wet possum. He tried to distract himself from the rain by reigniting his conversation with Crowder, asking him about his life in New Orleans. The young man was beginning to explain that he started out working as a cabin boy on steamboats on the Mississippi at age eight when Jean Louis noticed Laurent Bisset approach the streetcar stop. Jean Louis tensed, and he no longer heard whatever Crowder was saying.

Laurent had a cigar clenched in his teeth, as usual, and he grinned malevolently in Jean Louis's direction. Then, to Jean Louis's shock, Laurent decided to stand among the small group of white folks, set apart from the blacks. Laurent was a free person of color, not white, but his African features were subtle unless one looked closely.

"You know that white man?" asked Crowder under his breath.

"What's that?"

"I asked—do you know that white man?"

Jean Louis pulled out a cigar and lit it, shielding it from the drizzle. "His name is Laurent Bisset, and he isn't white."

Crowder turned and stared at Laurent, who blew smoke in their direction. The cloud didn't reach them, given the space between them, but it still delivered Laurent's message of disdain.

"He ain't white?" The young lieutenant's jaw dropped.

Jean Louis shook his head and was tempted to announce it for everyone to hear, but he wondered whether anyone would believe him. Besides, he was not about to snitch, not even on Laurent Bisset.

A few moments later, another streetcar pulled by two horses, one black and one white, approached. Jean Louis and all the surrounding soldiers leaned in to get a good look at whether it carried the star. When it was obviously another half-full, whites-only streetcar, they pulled back in synchronized disappointment.

Laurent, meanwhile, flicked one last devious grin in their direction with a wink and stepped up to enter the whites-only car. He disappeared inside, seconds before Crowder, the young man at Jean Louis's side, suddenly bolted forward.

Jean Louis gasped. The young man intended to board the streetcar!

...

Crowder was fed up. He was a soldier. No matter how young or dark his skin, his uniform deserved respect. If the city could integrate the horses pulling the coach, they could do the same for the passengers. Heck, a racial imposter was already on the inside, so why not him?

He would rather face a mob of angry white passengers than stand another minute with the two officers harassing him. When the car pulled up and the man called Laurent Bisset climbed aboard, Crowder followed him.

As Crowder stood on the first step of the streetcar, he turned to the two soldiers who'd been heckling him, Moss and Lewis, and grinned. "Ain't you two boardin'? Or you too afraid?"

Lewis cussed back at him, but neither soldier moved. Moss was wide-eyed, clearly terrified at the idea of forcing his way onto a whites-only streetcar. The man that Crowder had been talking to—

Jean Louis Cailloux—met his eyes, obviously concerned that he was about to risk his life to ride a streetcar.

Crowder saluted to the waiting crowd and then entered. Every eye in the car was on him as the conductor made his way to the back, his scowl displayed like a battle flag, but Crowder stood his ground.

"Off this car, boy!" The conductor's lips twisted with a snarl.

"I am an officer of the Army of the United States of America."

"You're a trained ape of the United States of America is what you are, so get your monkey butt off of this streetcar, or I'll toss you off."

Crowder put his hand to his holster as a warning, but he didn't dare draw his gun. Outside, he could hear a few black folks applauding, including Jean Louis. He doubted that Moss and Lewis were, though.

The middle-aged conductor was soft around the waist and faltered in his steps as he eyed Crowder's gun. The man was afraid to put a hand on an armed soldier. Laurent Bisset narrowed his eyes, saying and doing nothing. He just sat there, waiting. However, a white man, younger and more robust than the conductor, rose to his feet and came to the conductor's aid.

"I am an officer of the Army of the United States of America." Crowder looked at the man and sat down. While there were plenty of empty seats near the other passengers, he chose one that was three rows apart from anyone.

"Boy, get your sassy ass out of that seat," said the young white man.

Crowder stared straight ahead. "I am an officer of the Army of the United States of America."

In his peripheral vision, Crowder noticed the conductor step aside, allowing the large white man to squeeze past and move in close. He inhaled, bracing for whatever came next, deciding it would be futile to throw a punch—and highly dangerous. Instead, he remained fixed in his seat, his shoulders tensed, his body rooted.

"I am an officer of the United States Army, and if you lay a hand on me, you will be reported to General Butler." He glanced out the window at the other people of color, who now watched in awe. "Remember what happened to Mumford for desecrating the flag."

William Mumford was a Confederate who had been hanged back in June for tearing down the American flag from atop the U.S. Mint.

The white man immediately leaned away from Crowder. The threat had worked, and the man took a step back. But that's when Bisset shot from his seat. At first, Crowder thought that Bisset, a man of color, would come to his aid. But within seconds, Bisset's murderous face made it evident he would perfect his act by playing the role of an outraged white man. He lunged forward and grabbed Crowder beneath the armpit, trying to raise him to his feet.

"Boy, I'll desecrate you as much as I please!" Bisset scooted behind him so he could get both hands beneath his armpits, ripping Crowder from his seat.

Crowder wanted so much to fight back, until he thought of his mother and how she would feel if she received a letter telling of him being beaten to death on a streetcar.

Within seconds, the white man regained his courage and joined Bisset. Suddenly four thick arms were tugging and pushing him down the aisle. Crowder struggled and squirmed like a fish on the end of a line. Careful not to throw any punches, he finally broke free.

"This is worse than wrestling a hog in mud," the white man panted, aiming for a better grasp.

As a woman screamed, Bisset's fist came down on the back of Crowder's neck like a cudgel. Crowder spun and came face to face with Bisset, who spit in his face. Crowder wiped it off with a glare, wanting so badly to announce to everyone in the streetcar that Bisset was an imposter. But he couldn't betray the secret of a free man of color, even one as despicable as Bisset. Crowder's jaw clenched. He was on the verge of forgetting any common sense and responding in kind. Everything in his body told him to break this man's nose. That would wipe the smirk from Bisset's face.

"I am an officer of the Army of the United States of America." He ground his teeth and closed his fist.

"Who cares?" Bisset scoffed, looking at the other passengers before turning his hard eyes on Crowder. "This here is the Confederate States of America!"

Crowder broke loose once again and tried to slide back into his seat, but Bisset latched onto his shoulders and yanked him back with tremendous force. A woman leaped from her seat, jabbing her umbrella in his stomach just before Bisset punched him in the gut. Crowder buckled, wheezing, making it easier for Bisset to drag him to the back of the streetcar and hurl him forward. Bisset gave him a kick to the rear end, sending him sprawling.

Crowder stumbled, trying to keep from falling, but he slipped in the mud and fell to his knees. One of his hands landed in a mixture of mud and manure. As he swirled his hand in a puddle, doing his best to clean it off, he glanced up to see Moss and Lewis grinning.

When Moss chuckled, an elderly woman snapped at him, asking, "What're you fools laughing at?" She rushed to Crowder's side, pointing at him. "At least this soldier boy dared to do something!"

Crowder glanced from the elderly woman to Moss and Lewis in time to see their smiles vanish.

"Amen, ma'am." Jean Louis, joined by an elderly man in the crowd, bent to help Crowder back to his feet. "Those men are fools."

Once Crowder stood, the old woman pulled out a handkerchief and handed it to him so he could wipe off his hands.

"That was a brave thing you done, young man. 'Bout time someone showed some gumption 'round here." She cast a scornful eye at Moss and Lewis. "If you two fools can't fight on a streetcar, how you suppose you gonna fight Rebels on a battlefield?"

Moss dropped his eyes, unable to respond, while Lewis glared hatred. Crowder sighed. He may have won this battle with the two men, but he had a sense that his war with them was just beginning.

25

W hat a sight!
　　　　Over one thousand free men of color streamed along
Canal Street, a river of blue uniforms, a Mississippi of music and
marching men. There were three new regiments, the first of this war
to be comprised of black men fighting for the Union. André had
never been so proud.

He was captain of E Company in the 1st Regiment—Halleck's
Guard they called themselves, in honor of President Lincoln's
general-in-chief, Henry W. Halleck. In theory, General Butler said
the regiments were comprised of only free men of color, but André
knew better. In his company, which consisted of close to one hundred
men, he was well aware that a handful of them were slaves. The
company encompassed all colors, from black to bright, yellow, and
brown—all descriptors of the shades in between.

The men sang strongly as they streamed along Canal Street.
Colonel Stafford, the 1st Regiment's white commander, had even
equipped some men with band instruments—drums and plenty of
brass, from a cornet in B flat to a bass in E flat, all with bells that
rested on the soldiers' shoulders like rifles. Music powered their steps.

"En avant, grénadiers!
ça qui mouri, n'a pas ration.
En avant, grénadiers!
ça qui mouri, tant pis pou yé!"

"Forward, Grenadiers!
Those who die, no ration.
Forward, Grenadiers!
Those who die, all the worst for them!"

André maintained the appropriate emotional distance from his men—a cool detachment—but he had taken a liking to several officers below him. A young man by the name of John Crowder, a second lieutenant, had particularly impressed him.

Lieutenant Crowder had recently earned notoriety for trying to force his way onto a whites-only streetcar. He was thrown off, but his attempt triggered a string of similar protests, and the incidents quickly took a dangerous turn. In one case, some black soldiers even punched the streetcar driver, and in another instance, a soldier pulled a gun.

A compromise eventually stipulated that black *officers* could ride on white streetcars, but enlisted men could not. A small step in the right direction.

Whites and blacks lined the *banquette* along Canal Street as the troops marched past in precise formation. André had become hardened to the hostile gazes. He had a knack for blocking out the taunts and jeers, and pockets of black folks did a good job drowning out the insults with raucous cheering. Hats were waved. Young boys climbed trees for a good view. Several small black boys ran up and down the long parade line, stopping to imitate the marching men.

One man's voice managed to bellow above the clapping and cheering. "March on back to Africa! When the first bullet flies, y'all will be runnin' for cover, so y'all run on back to Africa as fast as you can scoot!"

André had heard the accusation time and time again. Even some of their own white officers were convinced that they would scatter and run at the first sign of live bullets. André intended to prove them wrong, but how could he be sure? These men had never seen action before, nor had he.

But he left that worry for another day. Today, they were marching and singing with pride.

"Yankee Doodle went to town
A-riding on a pony,
Stuck a feather in his cap
And called it macaroni.

"Yankee Doodle, keep it up,
Yankee Doodle dandy,
Mind the music and the step,
And with the girls be handy.

"I see another snarl of men
A-digging graves they told me,
So 'tarnal long, so 'tarnal deep,
They 'tended they should hold me.

"Yankee Doodle, keep it up,
Yankee Doodle dandy,
Mind the music and the step,
And with the girls be handy."

■■■

Father Maistre stood on the dusty road that ran in front of St. Rose Church on the edge of town, watching the black soldiers march through the area. These troops regularly came through his parish on their way to and from Camp Strong, located at the Louisiana Racetrack, where horses and gambling once thrived before the war. The camp's location at one of the city's "temples of chance" was only fitting, for the Union Army was taking a big gamble on these untested soldiers. *Libre* civilians flocked to the camp, eager to watch the troops.

The priest buried his hands in the wide sleeves of his black cassock, his fingers clenched around the latest note he'd received from his blackmailer. It was the first demand in several months, and just when he had begun to wonder if his ordeal was over, another note appeared in the offering two days ago.

Father Maistre wasn't sure how much more money he was willing to pay for silence. He had already made a couple of payments, and the church's funds were running dangerously low with the departure of several white families. Rumors of his sympathy to contrabands had driven away Monsieur Montfort and his wife, along with most other whites. And now this—another demand for payment.

Perhaps he needed to remove the guilt hanging over him by making a public confession and freely admitting to his past sins. Maybe it was time for his penance to begin.

As Father Maistre returned to the church, he glanced over his shoulder, noticing two women in veils leaving the camp behind him. Dingy clouds of dust that hung over the road flicked around their skirts; the veils came in handy to keep the dust away from their faces. Since the pair had been watching the black soldiers, he assumed they were women of color. It was hard to tell, though, through their face coverings. He smiled and stopped to wait when it became obvious that they were heading toward him. As they neared, one of the women lifted her thick veil, revealing herself to be Felicie Cailloux.

"Good morning, Father," she said.

He wasn't supposed to notice as a priest, but she was striking in her blue day dress—a solid-color blouse and patterned skirt. The woman at her side raised her veil, revealing her darker skin and tired eyes. He smiled in greeting this unfamiliar woman, thinking her dress and face looked much more weathered than Felicie's.

"How can I help you ladies today?"

"This is Madame Boreé, wife of one of the soldiers in my husband's regiment," said Felicie, and Father Maistre bowed in her direction. "We have an important favor to ask of you, Father." Felicie's eyes drifted toward the church with a raised brow before she tilted her head toward it.

"Please. Come inside." He gave her a knowing look.

Something told the priest that small talk would not be appreciated as they headed for St. Rose de Lima, so they walked in silence. Once inside the small church, Father Maistre drew up two chairs for the ladies, retrieving a third for himself.

"What may I do for you, Madame Cailloux and Madame Boreé?"

Madame Cailloux turned to her friend. "Would you prefer if I explained?" When the woman nodded, she continued, "Madame Boreé recently approached the *Société des Fleurs de Marie*." Madame Cailloux paused, letting the reference to the benevolent society in New Orleans sink in. "She asked if the Society would arrange for a Mass to be sung in honor of our Native Guards."

Madame Boreé jumped in, her words heated. "The Society agreed to approach my parish priest, but he..." She took a breath with a look of horror. "My priest told them he would gladly sing a Mass for the soldiers of color, but only if it was their *funeral Mass*."

Father Maistre's eyes widened. "You heard him correctly? He would not say Mass for their protection?"

"He spoke loud and clear," Madame Cailloux said. "He was only willing to say Mass if it celebrated the deaths of these men!"

He knew that Confederate sympathies ran deep among Southern priests, but to speak such thoughts...

"Would you like me to talk to this priest?"

"No." Madame Cailloux gave a tilt of her chin, her eyes firm. "We are asking if *you* would say a Mass in honor of the Union's Louisiana Native Guards instead."

Father Maistre sat back with a long pause.

"I told her you were a man of strong convictions," she added, piling on the pressure.

Father Maistre scratched his temple. Up to this point, his Union sympathies were a subject of speculation but still hidden. To say this Mass would be taking it to a new level. His Yankee thoughts and sympathies for black soldiers in blue uniforms would be exposed, which meant the few white families remaining in St. Rose's parish would whittle down to nothing if he took such a stand.

As the families departed, so would their money.

Strange. Father Maistre had just been thinking he needed to make a public confession as a penance for his sins. Was this his chance—to say this Mass? He hadn't expected God to take him so seriously so soon. Doing something that depleted his pocketbook and the church's coffers was about as tough as it got, and he could see that the two ladies were perplexed by his slow response.

Father Maistre finally exhaled with a nod. "I would be honored to say a Mass for your husbands and the other soldiers."

For the first time since they met, Madame Boreé smiled.

Father Maistre grinned as well, but alarm bells were going off in his head. What in the world had he done?

He had lifted his inner veil and revealed his secrets. That's what he had done.

26

The church was packed.

With the slow trickle of white families leaving St. Rose in recent weeks, the sanctuary had been looking sparse and pitiful like a dying vine. But on this day, every seat was taken, and *les libres* lined the back and side aisles of the sanctuary. Many men of color had shown up in uniform, overflowing the building with blue.

Father Maistre stepped forward to give his homily, outstretching his hands and repeating a portion of the Mass, first in Latin, then English.

"Brethren, pray that my sacrifice and yours may be well-pleasing to God the Father Almighty," he said. "May the Lord receive this sacrifice at thy hands, to the praise and glory of His name, to our own benefit, and to that of all His Holy Church."

Father Maistre paused and scanned the silent congregation. His gaze landed on André and Felicie Cailloux, who were seated in the front row with their children.

"Know this." He locked eyes with André. "I am here to say that your sacrifice is acceptable to God, even if the service to your country is not acceptable in the eyes of this city. Your sacrifice is acceptable to

God, even if it is not acceptable in the eyes of the enemy. It is acceptable to God, even if it is not acceptable to men who wear the same uniform as you. Know this: It is *acceptable!*"

As Father Maistre spoke, he shifted his gaze to other soldiers and families, and his eyes picked out the face of Benoit Montfort, who had slipped in and stood at the back, watching him like a hawk. Once again, the priest extended his arms and recited a portion of the Mass, first in Latin, then English.

"This is the Lamb of God who takes away the sins of the world. Happy are those who are called to his supper. Lord, I am not worthy to receive you, but only say the word, and I shall be healed."

After another pause, his eyes settled on Monsieur Montfort.

"Only say the word, Lord, and I shall be healed. When God says a word, all must obey—storms, disease...even demons! So I say, when the demon of fear torments you, look to your Holy Commander. Look to the one riding on high, look to the one wielding the sword of the Spirit, look to your Everlasting Commander, look to your Omnipotent General, look to the Soldier of His Spirit marching within you! Only say the word, Lord, and we shall be healed!"

"Amens" rang out from all corners of the church.

By the time that Communion came, Father Maistre noticed that Benoit Montfort had slipped away.

■■■

Jean Louis wondered if he was a fool to be taking such risks.

In the past week alone, he had secretly met with Coralie twice. On this full-moon evening, he waited behind the Bisset home, hidden behind Coralie's favorite tree. The tree seemed to spread as much horizontally as vertically. Two massive lower branches shot off to each side, only about four feet from the ground. Jean Louis would lift Coralie onto one of the branches, and they would talk freely and without a chaperone. If either of the Bisset men—father or son—found him here, they would shoot him on sight.

Tonight, Jean Louis carried with him a gift—a CdV of Coralie. The photo had turned out better than he could have hoped. The picture showed her in all of her mystery, veil draped over her face, revealing a tantalizing profile just below the thin material.

Upon approach, Jean Louis heard men's voices coming from the house, and he moved back a couple of steps, positioning himself behind a vertical shaft of the tree that concealed him completely. As he listened, the back door of the Bisset house opened and slammed against the home, revealing Monsieur Henri Bisset and his son, Laurent. As both men emerged from the house, the light of the full moon cast their shadows along the ground, and Jean Louis pulled back behind the tree.

Had they learned of his visit? Were they coming to put a single shot in his forehead?

Henri Bisset hurled a choice curse word at Laurent and smacked the back of his son's head. "I have had it with your incompetence!"

"I am sorry, Papa."

When it seemed they had not come in search of him, Jean Louis slowly exhaled, thankful they had other things on their mind.

"I asked you to do a few simple tasks, and have you carried them out successfully?"

"No, Papa."

Jean Louis could not make out Laurent's expression from this distance, but the tone of his voice was pitiful. He was like a big dog broken down by abuse. Jean Louis's heart almost went out to him. Almost.

The two men, puffing on thick cigars, stopped about six feet from the back door. Jean Louis squinted, noticing something in Monsieur Henri Bisset's right hand—a bundle of rods, bound together to form a powerful cylinder. This *fasces* was a symbol of power, but Jean Louis was well aware of its various uses. One of them was to inflict punishment.

"Are you still certain that no one else knows about your bounty jumping in the North?"

"Roussel Pinard was the only one who knew."

Jean Louis's heart sped up. Were they about to confirm his greatest suspicion—that Laurent had murdered Roussel to keep him quiet?

"What about the prostitute?" the father asked, cigar smoke puffing out as he spoke.

"Roussel did not tell her anything."

"How can you be certain?"

Jean Louis held his breath, wondering if Henri Bisset would order the death of Colleen McCarthy, the Gallatin Street adventuress.

"I said she knows nothing." Laurent's voice continued to wilt.

"That is not a good enough answer."

"I am sorry, Papa."

"You need to be certain she knows nothing."

Jean Louis looked around for any other hiding places.

A scattering of trees stood behind the house, but most of the trunks were too narrow to provide much cover. Behind him and to his right was a stable where the Bissets kept four horses. The door was ajar, and he wondered if he could make a run for it without being spotted. He was too exposed behind this tree.

When the home's back door squeaked on its hinges and both men turned toward the sound, Jean Louis held his breath.

"Coralie, what in the world...?" her father asked.

Coralie had exited the house, expecting to find Jean Louis waiting for her. Instead, she found her father and brother.

"What are you doing out of the house at this hour?" Her father's voice raised.

The second the two men turned toward Coralie, putting their backs to Jean Louis, he hurried across the yard. It was his only chance to reach a place of greater safety. Thankfully, the grass was thick and muffled his steps. He managed to squeeze through the stable's open door, careful not to nudge it, making it squeak. He wondered if Coralie had seen him spirit through the dark.

"I asked you!" Henri pointed with a snarl. "What are you doing coming out the back door at this time of night?"

"I am sorry, Papa. I needed some fresh air."

"You did not ask my permission to leave the house."

"I am sorry."

"That's not enough. You know that punishment must follow."

Her father said it matter-of-factly, as if he had said it many times before. Jean Louis remembered the *fasces* in the man's hand and wondered if he would dare strike his daughter with such a weapon. He vowed that he would not remain stationary in this stable if her father clubbed Coralie. If he had to, he might just kill him.

"Please, Papa, I did not mean to disobey. I came out here looking for you to ask your permission to leave the house for a short spell."

She spoke this falsehood with conviction.

"That is no excuse. Your brother must be punished for your misbehavior, Coralie."

Her brother must be punished? Peering out from the slightly ajar stable door, Jean Louis watched as Laurent and his father made their way to the tree where he had been hiding only moments before. When Coralie stepped into the yard, visible in the moonlight, she looked panic-stricken.

"I'm sorry, Papa, please don't!"

"You should have thought of that before you disobeyed."

"Please, Papa, don't hurt him."

Monsieur Bisset, teeth clenched around the stub of his cigar, pointed the *fasces* at his daughter. "Get back in the house this instant. If you do not, your brother's punishment will be greater."

Coralie backpedaled, retreating into the shadows. Jean Louis could hear her sob as she reentered the house, and the back door clicked shut.

"By the tree," Monsieur Bisset snapped at his son.

Jean Louis watched in horror as Laurent removed his shirt and leaned over the lowest branch of the tree—one of those that snaked about four feet above the ground. With the first strike, the bundled rods cracked against Laurent's broad back as he grunted.

Jean Louis was grateful that Coralie was not the one being struck, but his world had suddenly turned upside down. He saw Laurent in a different light as the bundled rods struck a second time, and the young man grunted and exhaled the pain, taking his sister's punishment. Then Monsieur Bisset plucked the cigar from between his teeth and jammed it against Laurent's back, and Coralie's brother let out an unearthly bellow.

Unable to watch any more of this, Jean Louis pulled back from the door and stood motionless in the center of the stable. He sucked in a breath as three more cracks sounded through the air. Tonight, the Devil was getting in his licks. Jean Louis hated the sound of suffering, so he shrank even deeper into the stable. He was afraid he might startle one of the horses, but he had to get away from the thump of wood on flesh.

When silence finally settled around him, he hung his head, thankful there would be no more violence tonight. Then he raised it back up, staring into the dark stable, suddenly afraid that Laurent or his father might decide to enter. He retreated deeper into the building, where he found a large pile of hay, and he waded into it, preparing to bury himself in the cuttings should one of the men enter. As he lowered into it, he touched something that felt like vermin and jerked back. Still, Jean Louis took a steadying breath and carefully probed the hay to discover what was buried beneath.

As he parted the hay, he clamped his lips tight to keep from shouting when he saw a hollow eye staring back at him. At first, he thought it was the head of a horse buried inside. Had Monsieur Bisset beheaded one of his animals for pleasure? But as he dug deeper, he realized it was not a horse.

It was the head of a bull, and it wasn't real.

It was a mask, the mask of Moloch. It was the very same one he had seen on the man who set fire to their stable.

27

Jean Louis took his morning coffee at the French Market, the culinary heart of New Orleans along the river. It was the only place where meat could be sold in the French sector, and the butchers' stalls featured an assortment of bloody temptations—slabs of meat hanging from hooks. In the fish market, baskets overflowed with a variety of fish, crabs, and shrimp. It smelled of heaven.

Since the Civil War came to New Orleans, much of the spirit had been sucked from the market, but as the city entered the fall of '62, it slowly came back to life. People began to fill the area, searching for vegetables, fruits, and flowers, but Jean Louis's draw this morning was the coffee.

He relaxed at a brand-new coffee stand that had just opened in the French Market—Café du Monde. A fresh brew was the lifeblood of New Orleans, but the war had choked off shipments, forcing cafes to experiment with foodstuffs to mix in with the beans, stretching their supplies. Some tried adding acorns or beets to the beans, but the Café du Monde had come up with an ingenious supplement —chicory.

He took a sip of the steaming hot coffee and savored the hint of nutty flavoring that chicory gave the drink. He looked around the square and noticed that a local dentist was set up across the way, flanked by a four-piece brass band. The dentist carried a nasty-looking pair of pliers, for he was there to pull teeth, and the band was there to drown out any wails of pain. His assistant was already working the crowd, searching for anyone who looked like they needed a rotting tooth yanked. The assistant, a young man who did not even look twenty, struck up conversations with passersby, staring into their mouths as they chatted.

"*Bonjour*, Monsieur Cailloux."

The greeting caught Jean Louis with his coffee mug just touching his lips. The drink nearly spilled as he lowered it and turned to see Minetta approaching. She carried a beignet, a warm, powdered pastry—crispy on the outside, soft on the inside. The fresh smell made Jean Louis's stomach rumble.

He stood and bowed. "*Bonjour*, Mademoiselle. Would you care to join me?"

He hoped no one would see this as an illicit rendezvous, but gallantry called for the invite. She smiled and took a seat.

"Do you come here often?" Minetta asked.

"Before the Yankee occupation, I came to the Market regularly, but this is my first time at Café du Monde."

"I could afford only one item, and my sweet tooth won out." She bit into her beignet with a smile, her eyes glazing with pleasure.

Jean Louis leaned in closer, lifted his mug, and whispered, "A toast to Mister Lincoln."

Minetta touched her beignet against the mug. "A toast."

They exchanged their approval of President Lincoln's recent actions with a knowing look. They could not speak of his proclamation aloud—not in a crowded coffee shop with so many Confederate ears. Lincoln had recently announced that come January 1, 1863, all slaves in states that are in rebellion will be "thenceforward, and forever free."

Forever free.

The words rang like a bell of jubilation in some parts, but in others, they resounded like a fire alarm. New Orleans was one of those places. The announcement was just another outrage in a Confederate city controlled by Yanks.

Since Lincoln's proclamation was off-limits, Jean Louis wondered if he should divulge what he recently learned about Laurent and his father, but that would mean revealing he'd been surreptitiously meeting Coralie by the tree.

"I hear that your late-night visit to Mademoiselle Coralie did not go as planned," she said.

Jean Louis hid a smile beneath another sip. Minetta and Coralie must not keep many secrets.

"I was there that night." He set down his mug.

Since she already knew of their rendezvous, he figured he might as well tell her everything he uncovered that night. "While I was waiting for Mademoiselle Coralie, I overheard Laurent and his father talking about Roussel Pinard. Roussel knew that Laurent was a bounty jumper."

"Laurent a bounty jumper? Are you sure?"

Jean Louis nodded. "I also heard it from another source—the adventuress, Mademoiselle McCarthy."

Minetta took another dainty bite of the beignet, careful not to let the powder snow on her dress. "Coralie told me that Laurent and his father argued the night of Roussel's death. She said her father was furious about something Laurent had done, so it could be they were fighting about the bounty jumping. Do you think they discovered that Mademoiselle McCarthy also knew about it?"

"Laurent said no one besides Roussel knew what he had done. But I don't think his father believed it."

"And you think they silenced Monsieur Roussel? Did they actually say they had done the deed?"

"Not in so many words. But if Roussel knew Laurent had been a bounty jumper..."

"If they killed your friend, what can you do about it? The city has

174

more on its mind than the murder of a *libre* rascal like Roussel." She dabbed her mouth with her handkerchief and dropped her eyes. "I'm sorry. He was your friend, and I should not speak ill of the dead."

"Do not apologize. I knew very well that he could be a cad. But he was also a friend."

Minetta shot him a conciliatory smile. "I will be happy to keep my eyes open for any evidence of their complicity in your friend's murder."

"*Merci.*"

As Jean Louis stared into his mug, the four-piece brass band struck up a tune. That could mean only one thing—the dentist was hard at work. He and Minetta looked over at the poor man seated in the chair with his mouth open and his eyes wide with fright. The dentist had his arm around the man's neck from behind, like a strangler, while he reached into the mouth with his pliers. The assistant stood in front, pinning their victim into the chair. A crowd began to gather, and people cheered as the dentist gave a great twist on his pliers, and his "patient" was nearly lifted from his seat. Because the band was playing, Jean Louis could not hear any screams, but he could imagine them.

"You seem strangely fascinated by the dentist, Mademoiselle."

Minetta turned back to face him. "It's sometimes hard to look away from pain."

"Even if it is being inflicted by Monsieur Bisset on his children?"

Minetta looked down at her hands. "No. Not that. I always look away from that."

Jean Louis told her all about how he had witnessed Laurent take a beating for Coralie's misbehavior.

"Does this happen often?"

"All the time," Minetta said. "Taking his sister's punishment was Laurent's idea when he was a boy. His father was about to strike Coralie when Laurent intervened and asked if he could be struck in her place. Their father happily obliged, and he discovered something strange and, in his mind, wonderful. He learned Coralie would be much more compliant if she knew her older brother would take the beating in her place. So the tradition continues to this day."

"I am surprised you've never told me."

"Mademoiselle Coralie asked me not to say a word to anyone. She is terribly ashamed."

"I must say that this puts Monsieur Laurent in a different light. I did not think of him before as heroic."

"He is very protective of his sister. His behavior among men may not always be the best, as you know, but he would never strike a lady. He would kill any man who struck his sister."

Jean Louis took another sip of coffee as a strange and sudden sense of camaraderie with Coralie's brother came over him.

"But what about—?" He looked into Minetta's eyes, afraid to mention it. He put a finger to his eye.

"What about my black eye earlier this year?" Minetta raised a brow with a sigh. "That came compliments of their father."

"I assumed it was Laurent who gave it to you."

"Monsieur Laurent would never do such a thing. In fact, he openly argued with his father about such treatment of women. I only wish he showed the same honor to men such as yourself. But I think he sees his father in them and is only happy to bully them."

"So... which one of them would be capable of killing my friend Roussel? The father or Laurent?"

"Either one, I would say." Minetta finished her last nibble and looked back over her shoulder. The band played again, and another man was nearly being lifted out of his chair by his tooth. Jean Louis cringed and looked away. An empathetic pain passed through his chest as he dropped his gaze. When he finally dragged his eyes up to meet Minetta's, he sent her a slight smile.

"If Mademoiselle Coralie should ever be discovered meeting me behind the house, would her brother be punished for it?" Jean Louis asked.

Minetta nodded. "The consequences would be especially severe."

One day ago, Jean Louis would not have cared a whit what Monsieur Bisset did to Laurent. But now...

"Are you certain you should go on seeing Mademoiselle Coralie?" Minetta crossed her arms.

Jean Louis sighed and said nothing.

"Her father is a dangerous man." She leaned forward, pointing. "You could be putting your life at risk by meeting her. You could be putting *Coralie's* life at risk."

"What does Mademoiselle Coralie say? Do you think she wants to continue seeing me?"

"I do not know. But I suspect she will go on, no matter what the risk. You may need to make the decision yourself."

"And end it?"

"Yes, end it."

"But I am not afraid of Monsieur Bisset."

"I am not saying you are. But think of the danger. If their father discovers that you are seeing his daughter behind his back, he might give both of his children the beating of their lives."

Suddenly, the nearby crowd erupted in laughter and applause. Jean Louis and Minetta looked over and saw the dentist standing on his stool, holding his pliers high in the air like an upraised sword. He could not see what was caught between the man's pliers from this distance, but he imagined that it must be a bloody tooth.

■■■

"We're finally shipping out," said Lieutenant Crowder to his friend, Leviticus Exodus Amos, whose mother couldn't get enough of the books of the Old Testament. Everyone just knew him as Levi, a tall, skinny lieutenant with the most prominent Adam's apple Crowder had ever seen. His neck looked like a snake that had swallowed a hog whole.

Crowder and Levi strode across Camp Strong, heading in the direction of the junior officers' quarters.

"We've been assigned to fatigue duty." Crowder said, sending Levi a bland look with a sigh.

The 1st Regiment of the Louisiana Native Guards was heading to the Bayou Lafourche to open the Opelousas Railroad. The Yankees had no intention of releasing them into battle, but that didn't stop Levi from being uncommonly optimistic.

"That don't bother me none 'cause we might stumble on some treasure while diggin' in the ground," Levi said.

"I wouldn't count on it."

"It can happen, especially if the people who done the buryin' put a rooster head in with the treasure." Levi put a hand to his ear and tilted it to the ground. "If you listen real close, the rooster head will start in a crowin' under that soil and lead you right to the treasure."

Crowder rolled his eyes. Levi was a font of useless information. Once his friend got going on a topic, it was like trying to stop a fast-moving train. When he started telling Crowder about how it's also a good idea to follow sleepwalkers because they can lead you straight to treasure, Crowder looked for any opportunity to change the subject.

"Maybe we'll see some action while we're doing the work on the railroad," he said. "Stumbling across Rebs is far more likely than stumbling on treasure."

"I'm all right with that. I can't wait to give those Rebs a good thrashin'."

Like most soldiers, Levi was itching for a fight. However, if Crowder was honest, he would admit that he was a little afraid of seeing action. He had joined the military because his mother needed money, but he didn't relish the idea of being shot at. Crowder prayed he could learn to hide his fears, especially in the presence of men like Lewis and Moss. Any sign of fear, and those men would strike.

Crowder and Levi entered the junior officers' quarters—a cramped room with a line of bunk beds down each wall. Crowder had the bottom bunk in the middle of the room, and Levi filled the bunk directly above him. Through the dim room, dust hung in the sunrays streaming through grubby windows. There was enough light to see someone sitting on the edge of his bed, shuffling through papers.

"Well, I'll be jinx swing!" Levi exploded. "What do you think y'all doin' on Crowder's bunk there?"

"And those are my letters!" Crowder said, moving in quickly.

When the man looked up, Crowder's heart clenched, seeing Captain Lewis's curious grin. He looked like he'd stumbled upon a treasure of his own.

"Hello, Chowder." Lewis stood, two sheets of paper still in his clutches.

Crowder motioned toward them. "Those are my *personal* letters."

Lewis grinned. "Letters from your mama. A mama's boy. Why am I not surprised?"

Lewis held up one of the letters, easily keeping it from their reach. His confidence and swagger never failing, he laughed while keeping them at bay.

"In this one, Mama asks if you have warm socks. That's so sweet. Maybe you could have her come to camp and tuck you in for the night." With a grin, he glanced at the paper he still held above their heads.

Crowder tried to snatch it out of Lewis's hand, but the captain was too quick, leaving him grasping at thin air. Crowder stood back, shoulders slumped, staring at him, knowing there was nothing he could do. The embarrassment burned through him.

"Ain't nothing wrong with warm socks." Levi patted Crowder on the shoulder, glaring at Lewis. "Warm feet keep away the Devil. Dead spirits like folks with cold toes."

Lewis blinked, unsure how to respond, and turned his attention back to Crowder. "How old are you really, Chowder?"

"Eighteen and none of your business." Crowder stood a bit taller.

Lewis cursed and laughed. "*Eighteen!* That's a lie."

It was a lie, but he would never admit it. What would Abraham Lincoln say if he knew that a black lad of sixteen was an officer in a company of men, some as old as forty-five?

"Put that letter back into my haversack."

"Gladly, boy. I have already finished reading your precious mother's letters, and I am sure my men will enjoy hearing about your mama's boy relationship. By the way, who is this Liser wench living with your mama? Is she your missus?"

"She is not."

"You two sound very cozy to me. This Liser person also sounds like she is contraband. Slave material. Is that the only kind of whore you could find—a real dark one?"

"You ain't so fair-skinned yourself," Levi said, leaning toward Lewis. "You're darker than me, and I'm as dark as the inside of a cat's belly."

Lewis's grin vanished. He looked Levi up and down. "You sayin' that I'm as dark as slave contraband?"

"You got a problem with dark skin?" Levi sent him a challenging look with crossed arms. "If y'all do, maybe you should tell that to Captain Cailloux."

Lewis's jaw clenched. It was no secret how proud Cailloux was of his dark skin, wearing it like a badge. And most knew that the captain, even at thirty-six years of age, could whip anyone in the regiment. Lewis would not dare to insult dark skin while Captain Cailloux was within range.

"Do not forget to write Mama tonight." Lewis shoved the letters into Crowder's hands, crumpling them in the process. "Maybe you could ask her to give you a bath while you're at it."

When Crowder didn't reply, Levi broke into a smile, adding, "Baths are good. Maybe y'all oughta try one some time." Levi's eyes danced with humor. "My grandmamma always had us sit in a tub of river water and face the setting sun. Then she dipped her hands in the water, making the sign of the cross. Do this, and y'all don't get stomach pain, as long as you keep your toes above the waterline."

"Shut up, Levi," Lewis said before exiting the junior officers' quarters.

After he was gone, Crowder smoothed out the papers on his bed and returned them to his trunk. It wasn't until he sorted through them that he noticed one was missing.

■■■

With André shipping out in two days, Felicie wondered if this would be their last ride across the open plain on the edge of New Orleans. Her heart clenched at the sight of him riding next to her. Could she bear being separated?

Felicie straddled her horse like a man, so she could ride with greater speed and abandon. She lightened her body in the saddle and squeezed with her legs, and her horse, Helen, increased speed. It was easy to communicate her wishes to Helen; just a gentle squeeze of her calves, and her horse picked up the pace. No need for anything like a stick to keep her moving at high speed. André kept his horse in perfect pace with hers, and as they raced across the open field, she savored her steady rise and fall in the saddle, in perfect sync with her horse's stride. Leaning forward and lifting slightly out of her saddle, she shortened up the reins.

Felicie and André exchanged glances as their animals remained side by side, their horses' heads bobbing with every footfall. Under the harsh sun, the shadows of their horses ran alongside, silhouetted against the grass.

André once told Felicie that he would take riding horses over gliding across a ballroom any day. This was his preferred form of dancing, moving in unison, stride for stride, following the beat of the hooves, communicating non-verbally. André said nothing was more magnificent than a man in a uniform riding a horse, but she disagreed. There was nothing better than a *husband and wife* riding together.

When they stopped to rest their horses, Felicie slid from her saddle and handed André her reins with a sad smile. "Will you be in any danger?"

André had to be back to camp within an hour, and Felicie sensed that it might be a long time before they would be together again, just the two of them. After she and André sat with their backs against their favorite tree, their shoulders touching and their horses grazing a short distance away, André took her hand in his.

"Unfortunately, it does not look like General Weitzel has any intention of using black soldiers in battle," André said.

Unfortunately? Felicie would never understand men.

General Godfrey Weitzel was not fond of black regiments, and he had made it clear that he had no faith in their fighting ability. Weitzel even tried to resign rather than command black soldiers, but General Butler would not accept his resignation. While Felicie thought Weitzel was a fool to underestimate men like André, his prejudice might keep her husband out of harm's way.

She leaned her head on André's shoulder and tried to banish any thought of war. She placed a hand across his chest, where his heartbeat thrummed under her fingers. She leaned into him, putting her ear on his chest, trying to memorize every drum of his pulse. They embraced one another for a long time before he peeled her arm away and stood.

"Time to return to camp." He helped her up, putting a hand on her hip and staring into her eyes.

Felicie brushed the hair from her wet lashes, embracing André as they kissed. Afterward, she rested her cheek on his shoulder as a gentle breeze drifted around them. She squeezed her eyes shut, trying to commit to memory how it felt to be embraced by her husband.

"You will come back to me, won't you?" Her voice was just over a whisper.

André hesitated before answering, "I will come back."

"I will pray a rosary for you twice a day." She pulled back, studying his every feature.

"Your prayers and Saint Michael will protect me."

"And Gabriel? Will he protect you too?"

"And Gabriel."

"And Raphael and Uriel?"

"And every angle you can think of...We are on the side of the angles."

Felicie held on to him for dear life and began to sob. "I cannot live without you."

"Je t'aime, ma chère." He brushed her tears dry before taking her by the hand and leading her to her horse.

"Je t'aime, mon cher," Felicie whispered with a final kiss to his cheek before he helped her into her saddle.

They galloped side by side one last time before slowing to a canter and heading back to Camp Strong and what lay beyond. But Felicie couldn't help but sense they were being banished from Eden forever, with their way back barred by a hundred thousand muskets carried by men in both blue and gray.

28

When the 1st Regiment of the Louisiana Native Guards marched out of New Orleans on October 25, black soldiers belted songs about bringing back the four limbs of Jefferson Davis. They talked about shooting Rebels as easily as picking off possums from five feet away. But now, three days later, the thrill had been replaced by grumbling.

André walked alongside the rail line, making sure no one was slacking off. It made him feel like a plantation overseer, so he made sure he also toiled alongside the men—work that was terrible and demeaning. They had to get down on their hands and knees to rip out weeds.

The Native Guards had been ordered to clear miles of railroad track, which meant yanking out the grass by hand. Without scythes, they battled massive plants that completely obscured large stretches of the tracks, growing so thick that trains could not pass. Retreating Rebels had also damaged as much track as possible and scattered logs on the rails—anything to impede the transport of Northern supplies. The job of the Native Guards was to clear and repair it. They rebuilt culverts and replaced rails that the Confederates had torn out, but it was the monotony of yanking weeds that was most discouraging. This seemed never-ending.

The only consolation was that it wasn't just black troops doing this horrible work. The Louisiana Guards worked alongside the 8th Vermont, inching their way along the New Orleans, Opelousas, and Great Western Railroad like some vast insect with a thousand legs and arms, chewing up grass. About the only one who seemed oblivious to the tedium of the work was a man in André's company named Levi, who kept a steady stream of commentary as they toiled.

"If y'all got a high fever, get yourself a pigeon that ain't never flown out of a cage, cut him wide open, and plop him on the person's head," Lieutenant Levi explained cheerily to another soldier. "The pigeon blood will draw down the fever. Works ev'ry time."

Since Levi's chatter never seemed to slow down his work, André let him be. He had a solution for everything. Indigestion? Make a tea from the inside skin of a chicken gizzard. A rash? Rub it with hair taken from a black cat's back. Stomach cramps? Keep a tub of water with stale bread under your bed.

After three miserable days of hard work under the sun, they finally reached a bend in the tracks that led to Des Allemands station. It was also when they received momentous intelligence. Confederates were suspected of holding the station, which meant they might be approaching their first spot of action. Captain Cailloux saw an instantaneous change in the demeanor of his men. Smiles returned, and backs straightened. They would no longer scrabble on the ground on all fours. They would fight like men.

André also understood the significance of this moment. No other black unit had fought in this war, so they were about to make history. A surge of energy swept through his body as his troops formed a line of battle, with enlisted men standing shoulder-to-shoulder in two ranks. The rear-rank men stood a forearm's length from the front-rank men and would shoot over their right shoulders when the time came. The two ranks would simultaneously send a single swarm of lead, hitting the enemy in a deadly cluster.

The 8th Vermont formed their line of battle on the track's right side, the north, while the Louisiana Native Guards positioned on the left. Black and white, separated by the definitive line of tracks. Just in front of the troops was a flatbed that carried two pieces of artillery. The sky was clear, except for a few shreds of cloud against the blue. There was a light breeze, with temperatures cool and comfortable. It was a perfect day to fight. In the distance, André spotted a wide-winged bird, its wings forming a V as it slowly circled. Probably a turkey vulture.

"You are about to meet the enemy for the first time!" declared Colonel Thomas from atop his horse. "Not a man must falter!" He paused to let that sentence sink in. "*Not a man must falter!* If any one of you hesitates, I will shoot him on the spot!"

Colonel Thomas moved his gaze up the ranks.

"We are fighting for the glory of God and the salvation of our country!" he continued, fixing his eyes on the black troops. "This is your opportunity to get your revenge for the blood that has flowed from the lacerated backs of your mothers...the lacerated backs of your wives...and the lacerated backs of your sweethearts! Woe to any man who flinches!"

The train moved forward, pushing the flatcar toward the bend in the tracks. Around that turn would be a pack of Confederates, aiming several hundred rifles in their direction. The drums began to beat, and the lines surged forward, with the file closers in the rear to keep everyone in order and prevent anyone from fleeing in the face of fire. A file closer had the authority to execute anyone who dared run.

André gritted his teeth, well aware of what the white commanders thought of them, but his men would not run.

The flatcar, artillery on board, squeaked forward as the infantry followed. The bend in the tracks approached a simple turn that might just become the most significant turning point in everyone's lives. The train station and the Confederates were around that corner; the war was right around that bend. André tried to banish all thoughts of death, including his. But he realized that today might be the day when he peeked behind the veil and saw what lay on the other side of physical existence. He tried to convince himself that peering behind the thin barrier into the afterlife would be as glorious as the first time he lifted a veil to see Felicie's face.

André asked St. Michael the Archangel for protection. He spoke aloud in French—a language most of the Louisiana men spoke.

> *"Saint Michel Archange, défendez-nous au combat. Soyez notre protection contre la méchanceté et les pièges du diable. Que Dieu le réprimande, nous prions humblement. O Prince de l'armée céleste, jette en enfer Satan et tous les mauvais esprits qui rôdent dans le monde à la recherche de la ruine des âmes. Amen."*

> *"Saint Michael the Archangel defend us in battle. Be our protection against the wickedness and snares of the Devil. May God rebuke him, we humbly pray. O Prince of the heavenly host, thrust into hell Satan and all the evil spirits who prowl about the world seeking the ruin of souls. Amen."*

Several of the men, one of them being Lieutenant John Crowder, joined the "Amen."

But as they wheeled around the bend, André could sense deflation and disappointment sweep over the soldiers like a wave. Despair was palpable, for just ahead of them sat the Des Allemands train station—deserted and smoking. The Confederates had fled the station—nowhere to be seen.

There would be no battle today, which meant they would return to picking weeds on all fours like beasts of burden.

André had rarely been so disappointed.

29

The Buffalo House was his father's favorite haunt, but Laurent never liked stepping foot into this saloon at Franklin and Dyads Streets. Like all taverns in this area, things could get quickly out of control. That's why the proprietor, Bison Williams, carried around a cudgel as he waited on tables. He could deliver your food if you behaved, and if not, he would deliver a blow to the side of your head.

Laurent's father attended fights at the Buffalo House regularly, and on this day, they picked out a table in the dark corner. From there, the two men had a good view of the violent pairing between Looney Powell and Oyster Johnny. It made Laurent's forehead ache just watching the men as they circled each other, making periodic headbutts—their skulls bonking together like colliding coconuts. They crashed again and again, like demented rams, for about forty-five minutes before Looney finally wound up on the floor, knocked out cold. Oyster Johnny staggered from the stage, his forehead glaring red as he accepted a drink from Bison Williams, spilling much of it down his bare chest.

Laurent's father leaped to his feet and applauded wildly when the match ended. The man loved his violence, and he had spent his life trying to train his son to absorb it on every part of his body. Laurent's back still stung from the most recent strikes of his father's bundle of rods, the *fasces*.

Laurent never knew his mother, but he had hazy memories of his father "training" his mother how to absorb violence as well. If she were here today and Laurent ever saw his father lift a hand to hurt her, he would not hesitate to kill him. But his mother ran away from home when Laurent was only four and his sister was two—at least that's what his father told him. Laurent sometimes wondered if there might be a body buried behind their house.

Even today, Laurent had fantasies of taking up a club and beating his father senseless. Perhaps he could borrow Bison Williams' cudgel.

"Wish I could knock some sense into that priest," said Laurent's father after he had taken a seat and calmed down a bit.

"Pére Maistre?" asked Laurent.

"What other priest do you think I'm talking about? Who else is stirring up trouble?"

Nodding, Laurent took a sip of his lager when two unsavory characters strolled into the Buffalo House. It was John Miller, the man with the ball and chain for an arm, and his lover, the prostitute Bricktop Jackson. Laurent would never strike a lady, so he wasn't sure what he would do if Bricktop Jackson ever came after him with a knife. She'd sliced up several men over the years and struck an imposing figure at six feet tall. But he still didn't think he could wallop a woman, even an Amazonian monster like her.

"Evening, Monsieur Miller, Mademoiselle Jackson," said Laurent's father, saluting with an upraised mug. "What brings you here this evening?"

"Moloch brings us." Miller grinned, revealing a mouth with half of its teeth missing.

"Moloch the Destroyer," said Monsieur Bisset. "I should have known."

Laurent noticed a couple more undesirables walk into the joint, and his body instantly tensed. In strolled Red Bill Wilson, the fellow who organized the Live Oak Boys a few years back. He had a massive, bushy red beard in which he kept a knife concealed. Two more Live Oak Boys stood behind Wilson—Charley Lockerbee, better known as Charley Lagerbeer, and his son Albert. Albert was considered the most ferocious fighter of the bunch, a wild wolf of a man.

Miller and Bricktop turned to look at the new arrivals. They did not consider Live Oak Boys allies, but they didn't count them as enemies either. Although the gang was paid by businesses to wreak havoc on competitors, they didn't work for anyone but themselves. They were chaos-slinging freelancers.

Miller nodded at them silently, then turned back to Monsieur Bisset. Laurent wondered if he should slip out of the saloon before things exploded. Whenever the Live Oak Boys arrived at an establishment, trouble was sure to follow.

"About that Moloch mask," said Miller. "You still got it, ain't you?"

"Of course," said Monsieur Bisset. "Does your friend need to borrow it?"

"Yes, *our friend* would like it." Bricktop leaned a bit too close for comfort.

"What's the mask gonna be used for?" Laurent swallowed, shoving his fear deep inside.

"Ain't none of your business." Bricktop jabbed him in the shoulder.

"It is our business because it's our mask." Laurent sat up a little taller, feigning the confidence he lacked.

Miller blinked, clearly startled that Laurent would speak up the way he did, and he stared back as if waiting for him to crumble. Laurent returned the glare. From the corner of his eyes, he noticed the proprietor, Bison Williams, emerge from a back room, still brandishing his cudgel. Bison had spotted the three Live Oak Boys, and he naturally assumed the trio had been sent to his establishment to tear things apart. One of the cooks appeared just behind Bison, brandishing a cleaver.

Laurent had a hard time keeping his attention on Miller and Bricktop, for the saloon was getting close to the edge of insanity.

"We want the mask," said Miller. "No questions asked."

Monsieur Bisset smiled, placating them. "Of course, you can have it."

"We want it *now*." Miller curled a fist at his side.

Laurent raised his eyebrows. The mask was hidden in their stable, which meant taking Bricktop and Miller to their property. It wasn't ideal, but with the number of people filing out of the kitchen wielding weapons, it would get him out of the saloon.

"I can take you." Laurent, suddenly on his feet, started for the door.

"Why the sudden change of heart?" Miller grinned at the line of cooks holding knives and bracing for the worst. "You afraid a little action's 'bout to start in this here place?"

"Do you want the Moloch mask or not?" Laurent growled. Then he shot a look at his dad, who sent him a judgmental stare.

Laurent swallowed, narrowing his eyes in return. He no longer cared if his father or the others could see his fear. He wanted out of this place, and he quickened his pace toward the front door. Miller, Bricktop, and his father followed several steps behind.

"Wish we could've stayed to see what happened," said Miller after they exited. Seconds later, shouts, screams, and the smashing of furniture sounded from the saloon. The Live Oak Boys were at it again.

30

It began with what started as a normal baptismal service. The family collected outside the church to symbolize that the child had not yet officially entered the flock. About twenty people gathered around as Father Maistre breathed on the infant boy three times, making a sign of the cross with his breath. He noticed that among the group were Felicie Cailloux, her two sons, and two daughters. André was off to war.

It was January of 1863, only a couple of weeks after Abraham Lincoln's Emancipation Proclamation took effect with the New Year. All slaves within rebellious states were considered "forever free." Many expected the Proclamation to ignite slave uprisings throughout the South, but they hadn't yet materialized. The only modest insurgence in New Orleans was this simple baptismal service led by Father Claude Maistre.

"Go forth from him, unclean spirit, and give place to the Holy Spirit, the Paraclete," the priest prayed.

The infant, Nicodème, was the child of slaves. Father Maistre used his thumb to make the sign of the cross on the baby's forehead and chest. "Receive the sign of the cross upon your head and upon your heart. Take to you the faith of the heavenly precepts; and so order your life as to be, from henceforth, the temple of God."

Next, the priest applied a dab of salt to the baby's mouth. Just as salt preserves food from corruption, this salt, this symbol of wisdom, would protect the baby from the corruption of sin and Satan. Then came the exorcism, a rebuking of the Devil's influence on the child's future. He made the sign of the cross three times over the baby, who was still licking his lips to get at the salt.

Father Maistre applied spittle behind the infant's ear, honoring the miracle that Jesus performed when he healed the deaf man. With this, the priest declared that the child's ears shall be opened to the Living Word of God.

All of this was by the book.

Then, after anointing the child with oil and renouncing Satan, the small group filed deeper into the sanctuary and approached the baptismal font. There, Father Maistre removed his violet stole and put on a white one. The baby was a calm spirit until the priest poured water upon his head three times, all while saying, "I baptize you in the name of the Father, and of the Son, and of the Holy Ghost."

Nothing unusual whatsoever.

It was not until the baptism had been completed that things changed dramatically.

"From this day forward," Father Maistre proclaimed to the small gathering, "baptisms and marriages for all persons of color will be inscribed in the principal register without discrimination, *together with the whites.*"

His words left the people momentarily stunned. Then came smiles and applause. Applause in a sanctuary! Father Maistre brought out a massive baptism register and showed them a new record containing only one name on its blank pages.

"Today is a fresh start for our nation and for St. Rose de Lima Church," he said. "Today, all baptized children will be freed by God. The first name in this new book, the one you see here, is that of a white child. Today, I will add a new name, the name of this black child."

With his hand shaking slightly, he dipped his pen in ink and began to write. The nib scratched against the paper. When done, he lifted the book and displayed it for all to see. The name was as big and bold as if he were John Hancock, writing on the Declaration of Independence.

Nicodème Gossett.

He had no idea that a single name on a sheet of paper could lead to so much trouble.

...

They agreed to meet at a pirate's grave.

Jean Louis did not want to meet Coralie at Cemetery Number 1 because he associated it with his friend Roussel, who had died there. So they chose to meet at Bienville Street Cemetery, another city of the dead with monuments rising above the ground. He and Coralie were to meet at the tomb of Dominique You, half-brother of the notorious pirate Pierre Lafitte. The grave that held the remains almost looked like a large dollhouse—a white square base topped with a slanted cap that resembled a dwelling roof.

As Jean Louis waited for Coralie to show up, he read the inscription. "*Intrepide guerrier, sur la terre et sur l'onde, Il sut, dans cent combats, signaler sa valeur Et ce nouveau Bayard, sans reproche et sans peur Aurait pu sans trembler, voir s'crouler le monde.*"

In English, the inscription said, "Intrepid warrior on land and sea. In a hundred combats showed his valor. This new Bayard without reproach or fear could have witnessed the world crumble without trembling."

Intrepid warrior. For what seemed like the thousandth time, Jean Louis was stabbed by guilt for not signing up for the Native Guards.

Although the man in this grave had been a pirate, he had gone on to win redemption by fighting in the Battle of New Orleans, and

General Andrew Jackson said he displayed uncommon gallantry. Jean Louis thought about his father, whose troops continued to toil west of New Orleans, and he wondered if he should be laboring beside him. On the other hand, he wasn't the only free man of color who did not sign up for the Native Guards, and his mother needed someone to protect her because families of Yankee soldiers faced trouble on all sides. That was how he justified his action—or inaction. But still, here lay a pirate, a *pirate* who fought for what he thought was right.

"He could have witnessed the world crumble without trembling," Jean Louis whispered, tracing the man's name on the monument.

Even the priest, Father Maistre, had shown uncommon gallantry this week by daring to inscribe the names of black baptized children alongside the names of white children. If a priest can be fearless, then what about him?

"*Bonjour,* Jean Louis."

He spun as Coralie approached, making her way through the city of death—with Minetta at her side. Mademoiselle Coralie wore a walking dress of patterned blue organdy, covered by a darker blue mantle to keep her warm on this chilly, January day. As they neared, Coralie raised her white veil, revealing a coy smile.

Minetta stayed back to give them privacy, and they strolled together, moving a short distance from the pirate's tomb.

They talked about frivolities, to begin with, but then Coralie surprised him. She switched to something substantial by mentioning the latest controversy surrounding St. Rose de Lima Church.

"Is it true about Père Maistre?" Coralie asked.

"Is what true?"

"That he has begun inscribing slaves' names alongside the names of white people?"

They stopped to face each other. Since the pair had advanced in their relationship, Jean Louis took her right hand. Coralie's white gloves acted as the final barrier preventing skin-on-skin contact.

"It is not just slave children. He is also inscribing the names of free people of color in the baptism and wedding registries, alongside white people. Does that not please you?"

"I can understand free people of color. But the names of *slaves*. They have no place in the same registry book."

Jean Louis shot a look at Minetta, who remained at a distance, staring at the inscriptions of various tombs. When Minetta looked up, their eyes met. Minetta was a free person of color, but her parents had once been slaves before being manumitted. He studied her face but couldn't tell if she was offended by Coralie's words.

"I thought..." Jean Louis swallowed and looked away.

If he spoke his mind, would he offend Coralie? He wanted to say that he admired Father Maistre for taking such a bold stand. Yet, in the end, he forced a smile.

"We do not need to speak of such things." He kissed her hand.

"Oh, but we must." This wasn't like Coralie—to be so forceful with her opinions. "I am concerned that you and your family remain members of that church."

"Are you concerned, or is your father concerned?"

Coralie let go of his hand. "Are you saying that I have no thoughts of my own?"

He took her hand back in his. "That is not what I am saying. I just did not think that you held such opinions."

"I am a free person of color and proud of it." She raised her chin a notch. "I could pass for a white lady of standing if I so wish, but I am proud to be a free person of color. And I do not believe that slaves should be listed alongside the names of people with my pedigree."

"What about my pedigree?" Jean Louis studied the back of his hand before searching her eyes. "My skin is darker than yours. Does that bother you?"

Coralie's eyes dropped. "It does not bother me—as it does my father. You are a free man of color, but the priest is inscribing the names of *slaves*. That is much different."

"You mean because their skin is as dark as my father's skin?"

"I did not say that. Besides, he is not your real father."

Jean Louis let go of her hand. "That is not true. He is my real father."

"You know what I mean."

"My father is the blackest man in New Orleans."

"I thought you did not like that boast."

"I am the son of Captain André Cailloux, and I am proud of it."

"I am sure you are," she said, taking his hand. She ran her fingers across the back of his knuckles. "But that is not my point. I have always admired you because you desire to advance from your past."

Jean Louis stared at her in shock. She had reflected his own words back at him, leaving him speechless.

She took his other hand. "Your desire to advance from the past— that is why I thought you would happily do as I ask."

"What is it that you ask?"

"That you leave St. Rose de Lima Church."

Leave St. Rose's? She had asked him not to enlist in the Louisiana Guards, not to fight alongside his father. And now she was asking him to leave his family's church?

Jean Louis glanced at the inscription on Dominique You's grave once more—the line that said he "could have witnessed the ending of the world without trembling." Jean Louis was facing a lady not quite twenty years old, and yet he was trembling. While he did not want to lose her, she was asking him to renounce his family church! Deciding not to enlist in the Native Guards was one thing. He could justify it because his mother sympathized with his decision and did not want to lose a son to war, along with a husband. But this request—to leave his church—would devastate her.

At the same time, he could not say no to this woman.

"I will have to think about it," he said.

"What is there to think about? I thought you and I saw the world through the same eyes."

"I have to think about it." He dropped her hands—probably a bit too forcefully. To make up for it, he raised one hand up to kiss the back of her glove. "I am sorry, Coralie, but I cannot make this decision lightly."

Carefully, she placed the veil back over her face. "I am sorry as well, Monsieur."

Then she turned away and walked back to Minetta, whose gaze kept shifting from his face to hers. As Jean Louis watched the two women disappear among the graves, he kicked a stone and sent it ricocheting off a tomb. Minetta shot a quick glance over her shoulder, sending him a soft smile, just before they disappeared around a corner.

31

André sat across from John Crowder, the young second lieutenant. The sun was just dropping over the bayou, lighting up the sky with yellows and oranges. The clouds were thin, wispy, and grey like they had been drawn hurriedly with charcoal. Several oversized birds perched in the tupelo trees while a mass of exposed roots writhed at the base, gripping the bank like a tangle of serpents.

"You did the right thing, son." André puffed on a cigar.

"I know, sir."

Crowder was a confident boy—emphasis on "boy." André wondered if he could even be eighteen. With such a youthful look, it was not surprising Crowder had stirred up trouble with some of the older soldiers in the 1st Louisiana Native Guards—most notably Captain Lewis and Lieutenant Moss. Despite his age, Crowder had more respect for military discipline and the chain of command than almost anyone he knew.

André tapped off some ashes. "That man needed to be disciplined, and Captain Lewis knows that."

Crowder used his right thumb to rub the palm of his left hand as if erasing something. "Yes, sir."

A soldier had exposed himself to a woman who came to camp to assist with nursing. According to André's understanding, Captain Lewis had done nothing to reprimand the man for his actions. Some even said Lewis found the incident funny. But not Lieutenant Crowder. He disciplined the private for his disrespectful behavior, making Lewis look like a fool.

André exhaled, blowing smoke into the breeze. "The lady who was accosted...She helped you recover from an illness, didn't she?"

"Yes, she did, sir. But that is not why I defended her honor and disciplined the private, sir. I would do it for any lady." Crowder seemed a bit angry. Defensive.

"Do not worry, son. I am on your side. What you did took courage."

"Just doing what's right, sir."

"And that isn't always easy."

Silence descended between them, but the marsh buzzed with insect life and resounded with bird calls in the dusk. André also discerned several frogs croaking. It almost sounded like someone turning the crank on a mechanical device.

"Has Captain Lewis given you any problems since then?"

Crowder paused for a few beats before answering. "No, sir."

André studied the young man, and while he didn't believe him, he also didn't expect Crowder would complain. In fact, he hoped the young officer wouldn't file a grievance because the boy needed to handle Lewis on his own. Something about this young soldier had André's fatherly instincts kicking in, and each encounter with him was just another reminder that Crowder was out here doing what he wished Jean Louis would—wear the uniform and fight for the North.

André took one more puff and frowned, trying not to think about the Bisset girl getting her hooks into Jean Louis.

After dismissing Crowder, André stretched his joints and moved through the darkened camp. He passed by a white soldier from the 8th Vermont, a sentinel. And as he strode by, the sentinel did not bat an eye at him; he gave no recognition of his authority. Not a whit.

André wheeled around. "Soldier, did you see me pass by?"

The sentinel, a private, turned to face him. "No, I did not."

"Do you see me now?"

The white soldier looked at him, from head to foot. "I reckon I do."

"Then I suggest you come to attention and shoulder arms."

The soldier hesitated, staring at André as if he were nothing but an empty uniform. "I only come to attention for my superiors."

"I am a captain. I *am* your superior, private."

"You're a colored, and a captain's title don't change that."

If such insubordination had been shown to a white officer, the man might be shot.

André moved within a few inches of the soldier. "What is the first line of your general orders?"

"To salute all officers, according to their rank." The private spoke like a resentful schoolchild forced to recite.

"I could have you court-martialed for your refusal to recognize my rank."

The soldier exhaled a heavy sigh. "Your uniform cannot conceal the color of your skin. Your skin is your true uniform."

The soldier had not once used the word "sir."

"Stand at attention, or I will have you disciplined, soldier!"

The private smiled. "That will not happen, and you know it."

André's stomach clenched, knowing he had no true recourse. This was not the first case of white soldiers unwilling to salute black officers, and he had heard of none being disciplined for insubordination.

The private spit on the ground and shrugged. "Even if you had *two rows* of buttons, I wouldn't salute you."

"I will see to it that you are in custody by nightfall."

"I look forward to it."

As André marched off, he knew his threat was nothing more than the wind.

32

It was late morning, and Felicie was just getting ready to head out to the detached kitchen to begin cooking when she heard a rap on the front door. It was Minetta, and she had a troubled look, a nervousness that ran counter to her usual confident manner.

"Is Monsieur Jean Louis here?" Minetta asked.

"No, he is not." Felicie was about to suggest she check Jean Louis's residence down the street, but she thought better of it. Why would she send an unmarried woman to her son's place?

As if she could read her thoughts, Minetta said, "I already checked his home, and he was not there. I hoped he would be with you."

"I'm sorry, but I don't know where he is."

The distraught look on Minetta's face and her strong desire to see Jean Louis did not bode well. She wondered if her son had begun courting this young maid. Why else would she dare to go to his lodging place unescorted?

"Please, come in, Mademoiselle. Is there anything I could do to help?"

After a moment of hesitation, Minetta stepped across the thresh-old. "Thank you, Madame Cailloux."

"Please, take a seat. What is this about?"

Minetta hesitated, and her eyes caught sight of something behind Felicie's back. Felicie spun to discover Odile peeking around the corner from the children's bedroom. As Felicie rushed over, Odile retreated to her room. A few moments later, all three children emerged, and Eugene took his two sisters out back to play.

"I'm sorry," Felicie said, motioning for her to sit once more.

Minetta lowered into a wooden chair and smoothed out her dress. She wore a deep-blue visiting dress, the color of a lapis lazuli precious stone. She adjusted the light-blue cape around her shoulder before fiddling with the buttons that ran up her sleeve. "Perhaps you can help. It has to do with Father Maistre and the church."

Felicie took a seat. "I may be able to help. I am friends with Père Maistre."

"Yes...Yes...That is what I understand."

Minetta looked over her shoulder as if searching for Jean Louis at the door, hoping he would enter. When nothing of the sort happened, she sighed and returned her worried gaze to Felicie.

"If it concerns the church, then I am just the person with whom you can confide." Felicie reached across the table to pat her hand.

Minetta nodded. "I have overheard things...about Father Maistre's decision to register the names of black children alongside the whites."

Criticism of Père Maistre was not news to Felicie. "Many are not happy with him."

"But there is more. I believe that Père Maistre might come to some harm."

Felicie leaned forward, her body posture urging Minetta to confide. "What is it you heard, Mademoiselle?"

"There might be an attempt to set fire to the church this evening."

Felicie straightened in her chair. "May I ask how you obtained this information?"

"I really do not want to say. But believe me when I tell you that I overheard a conversation about setting flame to the church this very night."

Minetta was a maid in the Bisset home. Where else would she have heard such statements except from Monsieur Henri Bisset or his son, Laurent?

"I do not know Father Maistre personally, so I thought..." Minetta's voice trailed.

Felicie took Minetta's right hand. "I will take you to the church, and we can tell Père Maistre to be on guard."

"But if these men find out that I overheard them and warned the priest..."

"There is no reason they would. They did not observe you eavesdropping, did they?"

"I do not believe so," Minetta said.

"Then you are safe, Mademoiselle. I can carry the news to Father Maistre myself, and you needn't be involved beyond this."

But Felicie knew her assurances could only go so far. Ever since the Louisiana Native Guards left to fight for the Yankees, she constantly worried about André's safety in the field and her family's safety in a city of Confederates. Now she also had a priest and a young maid to worry about.

■■■

Jean Louis kept watch from inside the tool shed, a stone's throw from the back of the church, while Father Maistre kept guard at the front of the building. Night had fallen, and Jean Louis crouched near the shed door with a revolver in his right hand, loaded and ready. He was a fine shot. His father had taught him well.

When Jean Louis stopped by his mother's house earlier in the afternoon, she told him what Minetta had overheard, most likely from Henri and Laurent Bisset. That threat had brought him to the church, where he was keeping guard through the night.

Adjusting his position, he leaned his head out of the door and into the night air. Insect life pulsed all around him, and frogs called out to each other from the nearby pond. The hairs on the back of his neck raised when their steady rhythm was punctuated by the scream of a female fox, a vixen. It almost sounded human, like a woman crying through the dark.

He waited.

Soon, an owl joined the chorus, its call hovering in the air. Jean Louis was amazed at how noisy the night could be. He hoped to distinguish human movement amidst all of nature's instruments.

Another half-hour dragged by, and he wondered if he should check in with Father Maistre, but then the insect life suddenly quieted, as if a conductor had motioned for the entire orchestra to stop playing.

Jean Louis's senses went on high alert, and then—*there it was.* The sound of rocks crunching underfoot. A twig breaking. Then silence. Human sounds? Could be. But it could also be just one of the long-tailed weasels he had seen hunting in this area, looking for stray cats to attack.

Then he heard what sounded like the striking of a match.

From inside the shed, he could see nothing directly. But he noticed a faint glow of light seeping through a crack in the shed wall.

Someone, just on the other side of the door, had lit a torch. If the intruder was Laurent, it was not going to be easy confronting the man. But Jean Louis actually feared the man's father even more.

Rushing forward, Jean Louis barged out of the shed and raced toward the light. He aimed his pistol at the torchlight—a ball of fire that almost seemed to be floating in mid-air about twelve feet away.

"Stay where you are!"

He made out the silhouette of an enormous head—the devil's head. The head of the bull, Moloch the Destroyer. The mask swiveled in his direction, and the arsonist immediately hurled his torch at the church wall and ran.

Should he stop to douse the flame or chase the devil?

Jean Louis chased the devil.

He didn't think he could hit the moving target in the dark, so instead of firing his pistol, he took off running. But he didn't have to pursue very far. The oaf tried to run with the mask still over his head —a difficult thing to do in the pitch black. The arsonist let out a strangled screech as he tripped over a branch and tumbled face forward. Jean Louis holstered his gun and pounced as the man struggled to get back to his feet, tackling him and knocking him flat.

Straddling the arsonist, Jean Louis put his hands on the man's shoulders to keep him pinned to the ground. However, this man wasn't nearly as strong or as fierce as anticipated. He expected much more fight. The man also wasn't very tall, and for a moment, Jean Louis wondered if he had just apprehended a child. Looking over his shoulder, he saw that the torch had not spread flames to the door of the church. It had bounced off the door and sputtered safely on the ground.

Capturing this devil was all so surprisingly simple.

Father Maistre came running up, out of breath, his eyes lit with excitement. "Is this the man?"

Then the arsonist began to sob, and it suddenly dawned on Jean Louis that this was *not* the man. It was a woman.

He reached down and yanked at the bull's head, which seemed almost half the size of the person he had brought down. As he removed it, the person let out a yelp, reminding him of the vixen's call in the night.

The person beneath him had a full head of hair. It definitely was a woman.

"*Mon Dieu!*" Father Maistre sucked in a breath.

Exactly. The arsonist was Colleen McCarthy. The adventuress. Roussel's friend.

■■■

Mademoiselle McCarthy sat in a straight-backed chair in the church sanctuary, facing the two men, looking scared out of her wits. She stared into the coffee mug that Father Maistre slid toward her as Jean Louis took inventory of her appearance. It was strange seeing her in men's trousers, her hair tangled, her blouse dirtied. He glanced to the corner where the bull's mask lay like some beheaded animal.

The adventuress had been hysterical when they brought her into the church, but Father Maistre managed to calm her down. Even though Jean Louis wanted to start pelting her with questions, the priest motioned for him to hold off. They stared at Mademoiselle McCarthy as she slowly brought the cup to her lips and tested the heat, drinking her coffee.

Finally, Jean Louis could hold back no longer.

"Why did you try to burn the church? Were you the one who burned our stable?"

Mademoiselle McCarthy's head jerked up like it was connected to puppet strings. "Burn your stable? Heavens no, Monsieur! Why would I do such a thing?"

"The same could be asked for what you did tonight." Jean Louis paused, taking in her look of shame, adding, "The person who set flame to our stable was wearing the same head of a bull."

"It's not my mask." She averted her eyes, staring back into her coffee.

Jean Louis was about to press her with another question, but Father Maistre stopped him with a wave of his hand, pausing before lowering his voice and offering a kind smile. "It is obvious to us, Mademoiselle, that you were forced to do this thing. I do not think you would start a fire of your own accord."

Slowly, she nodded her head. "I would not, Père Maistre."

"I did not think so. What did they threaten you with to get you to do this?"

When his question triggered more tears, the priest handed her a fresh handkerchief and waited.

Mademoiselle McCarthy took it and blew her nose. "They threatened my child. My baby boy. He is not even two months old."

Two months old? Colleen McCarthy had not been visibly pregnant when Jean Louis and his father had paid her a visit on Gallatin Street. But she had been seeing Roussel regularly just before his death.

"Is your boy Monsieur Roussel's child?" Jean Louis asked, following the priest's lead by talking in a soothing tone.

She nodded, then shrugged and said, "I hope he is."

Father Maistre put his right hand on hers. "Who threatened your child?"

Again, a shrug with more tears.

"Was it Monsieur Bisset?" Jean Louis asked.

She stared at Jean Louis, her eyes red from crying, and wiped her nose. "Why would Monsieur Bisset ask me to do this?"

Jean Louis pointed at the bull's mask in the corner. "I believe that belongs to Henri Bisset."

"I don't know who the mask belongs to. I only know that..." She winced. "I only know it was given to me, and I was told to wear it and set fire to the church. I'm sorry, Père Maistre. I had no choice." She sighed and fumbled with the handkerchief in her hands. "Once the fire started, I would have made sure you were awakened, Father. I would have made sure you...you weren't hurt."

Father Maistre nodded and patted her hand. He and Jean Louis remained quiet, hoping she might volunteer the name of the person who made her do this.

When she didn't, the priest gave her a pointed look. "Who asked you to start the fire?"

"I can't give you that name. My child is at risk, and speaking would put him in danger."

"Was it Monsieur Montfort?" Father Maistre guessed.

She looked up in shock. Father Maistre had hit the mark. Mademoiselle McCarthy sighed and sobbed a little more before giving them an almost imperceptible nod.

"But why would he force you to set fire to the church?" asked Jean Louis. "Is it because Father Maistre has begun mixing black and white children in the baptismal registry?"

"I don't know!" she cried. "I just know that if he finds out that I failed...if he finds out that I talked with you." More tears ran down her cheeks as she shook her head. "I don't want anything to happen to my baby boy!"

When Father Maistre stood, his chair scraped the floor. He disappeared into the back room only to reappear with a screwdriver. "Do not worry. You are about to succeed in setting the fire, Mademoiselle. Jean Louis, please. I could use your help."

To Jean Louis's amazement, the priest proceeded to remove the church's back door, and then they dragged it a safe distance from the building. Along the way, Father Maistre explained that they were going to burn the door while it was safely detached—but not until they had a few buckets of water handy to douse the flames once the door was scorched. After it was sufficiently scarred by fire, they put out the flames and reattached it to the church.

"Mademoiselle, you may now tell Monsieur Montfort that you succeeded in setting fire to the church." Father Maistre's words were visible as a fog curled from his lips due to the chill in the night air. "I will tell people that I awoke to the smoke and managed to put out the flames before it could spread beyond the door. Your clothes smell strongly of smoke, so he will be convinced that you did your job. He will not suspect that we talked. Go before he wonders why you are gone so long."

In a daze, Colleen McCarthy made a move to leave.

"Wait!" Jean Louis lifted a hand. "You almost forgot something." He dashed back into the church and reemerged, carrying the head of the bull. "You don't want to leave this."

"*Merci.*"

As they watched her depart, with the head of Moloch beneath her arm, Jean Louis asked, "Do you think she would testify in court against Montfort?"

"Would *you* if your child's life at stake?" Father Maistre asked.

"I suppose not."

"Then we will need to get to Montfort another way."

Suddenly overwhelmed by weariness, Jean Louis nodded and then headed in the direction of home and bed.

33

John Crowder strode through camp in a state of fury, a letter from his mother clutched in his hands.

He read the latest communication from his mother three times—each time in greater disbelief. Someone had written to her, saying he was in trouble with the military authorities for smoking, drunkenness, and carrying on with women, disobeying commanders. Now his mother feared that he no longer loved her because what son would do such things, bringing shame to the family?

This had to be the work of Lewis and Moss. After catching Lewis rifling through his letters, he believed the spiteful captain had lifted his mother's address and written to her, filling her head with all sorts of trash.

When Crowder tracked down Lewis and Moss, he found the pair around a campfire with five other soldiers, devouring desiccated vegetables—an unholy mixture of cornhusks, tomato skins, and other vegetables and foodstuffs too difficult to identify.

Crowder hesitated. He'd prefer not to create a scene in front of the others, for that was just what Lewis would want. The man craved an audience. As Lewis sent him a taunting grin, Crowder noticed he was missing a front tooth. Perhaps someone had done Crowder a favor by punching him. The lieutenant stood still as his emotions almost got the better of him. It was as if a hundred pins were pricking his brain, but he took a calming breath, dampening any ill thoughts.

"We need to talk, captain." Crowder sent Lewis a challenging stare.

"I'm listenin'." Lewis crossed his arms, the sardonic smile still displayed, pulling at his lips.

"Not here."

"You afraid to talk before the men?"

"This ain't for their ears."

Captain Lewis slowly rose to his feet. Moss started to rise, but Lewis snapped a command. "Stay put! I got this."

Crowder moved from the campfire's glare into the dark as Lewis followed close behind, stopping only to clear his nose on the ground.

"That's far enough, wonder boy. You got somethin' to say to me, then say it."

Crowder spun, squinting at Lewis's silhouette, backlit by the campfire. "I know you been sendin' letters to my mama."

Although Crowder couldn't see Lewis's expression in the dark, he could sense the smirk. "Now why would I be writin' to your mama, boy? You think I wanna court and spark your old lady, that what's buggin' you, Chowder? Rest assured. I don't want to bed down with your mama."

Crowder knew that Lewis wanted him to get angry, throw punches. Lewis would like nothing better than to file charges and get him thrown out of the military.

"I'm just warnin' you, Lewis. Stop writin' letters to my mama."

"Or what?"

"Or you will have to answer to me."

Lewis belly-laughed so hard that he leaned over, gasping for breath. While he was down, Crowder was tempted to kick him in the face. It would be so easy. He was younger and stronger, but Crowder would not strike a fellow officer, no matter how provoked.

"You have been warned," Crowder said, striding past Lewis and knocking him in the shoulder.

"I have been warned?" Lewis spun, arms wide, looking at the other soldiers. Some chuckled, but others dropped their gaze, not wanting any part of it. "I have been warned! That is rich!"

Crowder strode past the group, his insides churning. He looked around, needing to vent his anger. As he marched through the long line of dog tents, men stared, and whispering sprang up on both sides.

■■■

André could not believe his ears. "I am sorry, sir, but did I hear you correctly?"

Colonel Stafford leaned back in his chair inside his spacious canvas wall tent. He looked to be in his late thirties or early forties, a trim-waisted white man with a long nose and beard of medium length, squared off at the bottom as if his barber used a ruler to cut it in a straight line. His eyes were deep-set but friendly, and his shoulders were slightly sloping.

"It is true," Colonel Stafford said. "General Banks would like to remove all black officers from the regiments."

General Nathaniel Banks. André was beginning to despise the man who had replaced General Butler in New Orleans at the end of '62. It may have made the city's residents happy, but it did not please the free soldiers of color. General Banks brought with him a history of disdain for the very idea of black troops.

"General Banks claims that colored officers are detrimental to the service," said Colonel Stafford. "He says it annoys, embarrasses, and demoralizes both white and black troops."

André could not imagine giving up his captain's stripes, his uniform, or his authority.

"But I do not plan on giving up without a fight," said Colonel Stafford. "I will not see any of my officers removed. Not a one."

André believed him because Stafford had turned out to be the most vigorous defender of colored troops. Stafford regularly complained to his superiors about the tattered clothing, lack of supplies, and failure to pay the colored soldiers. In fact, Stafford was nearly thrown out of the service over a conflict with the white soldiers who made up 1st Louisiana Cavalry. When Colonel Stafford tangled with the calvary's Captain Richard Barrett, he actually rode the man down and nearly got court-martialed for it.

If anyone was going to stand for the free soldiers of color, it would be Colonel Stafford.

"Thank you, sir."

"But if I am going to be able to make a case for you and your fellow black officers, I need to see greater discipline in your ranks."

André was tempted to point out that discipline deteriorated because of the men's frustration with the lack of supplies and the backbreaking, demeaning labor. But there were no excuses in the military, so Colonel Stafford was correct. Discipline was falling to pieces.

"I heard that seventy men reported ill for duty on a single day," said the colonel.

"Yes, sir, it is true, sir. I have disciplined those who were clearly not ill. It will not happen again."

André spoke with conviction, although he did not know how he could guarantee such a thing.

"And if you see any hints of pillaging—*any hints*—act swiftly and decisively to end it."

"Yes, sir."

Colonel Stafford had already stood up for the 1st Regiment when they were accused of pulling up cane from the fields of the James Zumpt's plantation—even though he probably suspected that there actually had been some pillaging of the countryside. André had the same suspicions.

"You know, captain, I once had similar opinions of black troops," Colonel Stafford continued. "I did not think them fit for battle."

"I did not know, sir."

"But I have men like you to thank for changing my perspective."

"That is kind of you to say, sir."

"I am confident that you can keep your men in line. No more mass illnesses."

"Yes, sir. But what do you think the chances might be that white officers will replace our black officers?"

"I prefer to leave prophecies to prophets, captain."

"Yes, sir."

As André exited the tent, his right hand went instinctively to the double bars on his shoulder boards. If anyone tried to rip these from his captain's uniform, he would fight them to the bloody end.

34

March 1863

S pending the day with the horses just wasn't the same without André. Felicie had decided to go riding with Jean Louis on this overcast Saturday morning, anything to alleviate her fears about her husband's safety. They had stopped to rest the horses, and she watched as Paris and Helen continued to share their affections.

Letting out a soft vibrating sound, a horse's form of greeting, Paris wandered over to Helen and began nibbling at her back, his way of scratching the mare. Then Helen returned the favor, using her teeth to scratch Paris before resting her head and neck over his.

She had hoped her horses would bring her out of her gloom, but the concerns of the day had infiltrated her mood no matter her love of riding. She did manage about a quarter of an hour when she solely concentrated on her horse's movement and the breeze on her face. But the moment she and Jean Louis left the open field and returned to the bustling hub of New Orleans, the anxiety came rushing back, as if it had been lurking on the edge of town, just waiting to pounce.

Before André had left New Orleans with his regiment, he

assured her that the government rations and money he sent back would do more than just sustain the family; it would actually make their life easier. But the deliveries from the Union government had been only sporadic at best. Even worse, the government's promise of a $100 bonus and a $13 per month salary had proven hollow. André and the other free soldiers of color had yet to be paid a dime.

If she didn't have Jean Louis, who helped keep the cigar factory afloat and made some extra money with his carpentry, she didn't know how the family would eat. She was even more thankful that Jean Louis hadn't gone off to war with her husband, although she could see that the decision ate away at her son. His face looked troubled on this cloudy morning.

André's 1st Regiment was being shifted to Baton Rouge, about eighty miles away, and she worried the move might bring him closer to the line of fire. The soldiers, André included, probably relished being closer to the action, but not Felicie and the other wives. She also heard that there had been recent trouble concerning black officers in the Louisiana Native Guards. All of the officers of color in the 2nd Regiment had been forced to resign, replaced by white officers. If that happened in André's 1st Regiment, her husband would be devastated.

Adding to this mountain of worry, there was the recent attack on the church, which could have been so much worse if Minetta had not warned them of the threat. All in all, the food on their supper table each night might be sparse, but the worries were plentiful. If she could convert her fears to food, she and her family could dine for years.

■■■

Jean Louis had hoped that a morning ride would raise his spirits, but it did little to chase away the darkness. As he and his mother rode slowly back into town, he fought the urge to trot past the Bisset house. Over the past month, he had strolled or ridden past the house every week—sometimes multiple times in a single week. He hadn't seen Coralie since the day she asked him to leave St. Rose de Lima Church.

Jean Louis hadn't left the family church—not yet anyway.

Every time he went past the Bisset house, he hoped for a chance glimpse of her on the balcony. He saw Laurent a couple of times from a distance, but Coralie's brother never spotted him, thank God. Jean Louis still believed that Laurent and his father were involved in the attempted arson at the church. It couldn't be a coincidence that Minetta overheard them talking about setting a fire, and then Colleen McCarthy shows up that very night with a torch in her hand. Mademoiselle McCarthy said Monsieur Montfort had given the orders to torch the church, not the Bissets, but there had to be a link. The Montforts lived only a few houses down from the Bissets.

"You are awfully quiet this morning," said his mother, interrupting his stream of obsessive thoughts.

"Just distractions." He smiled slightly.

She returned the smile. "I know. We are all worried. About your father, about everything."

When it came to his father, it was more than just worries. Jean Louis's guilt had also been growing. He let Coralie sway him from the Native Guards and from his father. Now, his father, *his true father*, was in Baton Rouge with the 1st Regiment, and he didn't know when he would see him again. He wanted so badly to talk with him. Even one half-hour would be all it would take to set things right.

As they moved along rue de Chartres, he and his mother passed by the Old Convent of the Ursuline nuns, which was now the residence for the archbishop. It was a stately white stucco structure with two long rows of windows on the first and second floors. On the third floor, several dormer windows looked out from the roofline like alligator eyes. Dismounting and tying up their horses, Jean Louis and his mother greeted a small parade of Ursuline nuns as they scurried past. It was a busy afternoon because Saint Joseph's Feast Day was only three days away. Before the war, Saint Joseph's Feast Day had been a festive time for masquerade balls in New Orleans—not as wild as Mardi Gras, but a crucial day, nevertheless. This year there would be no balls, but people still observed the feast of the patron saint of the dying.

"Let's go see the altar." His mother motioned her head toward the Chapel of the Archbishops, which flanked the large convent.

Jean Louis shrugged, and so they went into the chapel, where the traditional Saint Joseph Altar had been set up just to the left of the main one. Being the father of Jesus, Saint Joseph represented fatherhood, and that was a difficult reminder for Jean Louis. Once again, it nudged his thoughts back to his own father.

In silence, they approached the side altar—three-tiered to symbolize the Trinity. At the center was Joseph, carrying his son Jesus, and gathered all around him was a bounty of fruits and vegetables and cakes, spilling toward the floor like a waterfall of food. It was a feast for the eyes and the nose, an exuberance of color and scents. There were lilies, palms, and carnations sitting near bread baked into the shape of a cross. Legend has it that if you tossed a piece of Saint Joseph's bread into the heart of a storm, your house would be protected.

There were also carpenter's tools on the altar—a special significance to Jean Louis since he worked with wood. But most important were the fava beans, which some considered lucky. When famine hit Sicily, legend had it that the fava bean plant was the only thing that continued to thrive, saving people from starvation. The fava bean took on a special meaning in a city as hungry as New Orleans.

Jean Louis asked Saint Joseph to pray for them, to intercede on their behalf for the safety of his earthly father. Then they genuflected and exited the chapel. The gloom hanging over him remained, for he was walking the streets in civilian clothes when he should have been wearing a uniform. The shame he experienced couldn't have been greater than if he were walking down the street without a stitch of clothing.

When they turned a corner for their horses, his day got even worse when he saw the Bissets on the same stretch of the *banquette*. Approaching along rue de Chartres was the father, Henri, along with Laurent, Coralie, and another man he didn't recognize.

Most upsetting of all, the unknown man and Coralie walked arm in arm, and their attitudes seemed amorous, not cousinly. The man was so light-skinned that for a moment, Jean Louis thought he might actually be white. But Jean Louis's eyes had been trained to pick out small African clues, and he decided he must be a free person of color —a very light-skinned man of color.

The Bissets walked four abreast, taking up the entire *banquette*, and Minetta followed right behind them like a good servant.

Coralie's veil was drawn back, and Jean Louis saw the shock in her eyes when she spotted him coming directly toward them. She averted her gaze and smiled at the man who was latched onto her arm. Was this a new lover, his replacement? Did this light-skinned man receive the stamp of approval from her father that he had never been given?

Jean Louis linked his left arm with his mother's as she quickened her pace, pulling him forward. There was no way they could all fit on the *banquette*, for the Bissets already took up the entire width of the sidewalk.

They were on a collision course, like two advancing armies.

Who would give way? Who would step down from the *banquette* into the muddy street? He could tell that his mother had no intention of stepping aside. In fact, her pace quickened even more.

Gentlemen should be the ones to step aside, of course, and Jean Louis noticed the light-skinned man release Coralie's arm so he could politely step from the *banquette*. Not to be outdone, Jean Louis did the same, leaving the walkway to let everyone pass.

But Laurent, his father, and Coralie kept on coming, and so did Jean Louis's mother. There still was very little space for all to pass, especially with his mother and Monsieur Bisset on the inside track. A flicker of confusion crossed the face of Coralie's new beau, who probably wondered why Laurent and his father did not step aside as gentlemen should.

Jean Louis's mother and Monsieur Bisset closed the distance as if preparing for hand-to-hand combat. If his mother were carrying a rifle, she would be lowering her bayonet at this point. She ran Monsieur Bisset through with her intense gaze, and he glared back at her.

At the very last moment, before the two armies crashed together, Minetta rushed ahead to save the day. She took Coralie by the arm and drew her back behind Laurent and Monsieur Bisset. Shocked, Coralie hissed at Minetta, but the maid was stronger, and she pulled Coralie aside.

At first, Jean Louis thought his stubborn mother would maintain the inner track and run head-on into Monsieur Bisset. But seeing Minetta's generous concession, his mother rewarded the maid by moving to the outer lane, vacated by Coralie, and passed by, nearly brushing shoulders with Laurent.

"A blessed Saint Joseph's Feast." Felicie made eye contact with Coralie's new beau, who stood in the street as he tipped his hat and returned the greeting. Jean Louis tipped his hat to Coralie and also said, "A blessed Saint Joseph's Feast," but Coralie had pulled down her veil to hide her face.

Jean Louis's eyes shifted to Minetta, who cast a devious smile. He tried to smile back, but the stress prevented him from doing so. Would Minetta pay for what she had just done, drawing Coralie out of their path? Would Monsieur Bisset use his bundled sticks, his *fasces*, to strike her?

If Jean Louis ever learned that Henri Bisset struck Minetta again, he wasn't sure he could keep from murder.

35

May 7, 1863

On Good Friday of all days, Bishop Odin returned to New Orleans from a trip to Rome, and he brought along a small army of French priests. Father Maistre wondered how long it would take him to uncover what he had been doing at St. Rose de Lima Church during his absence.

Evidently, not long at all.

Father Maistre found himself seated at a long, narrow table in the archiepiscopal residence on rue de Chartres. Many priests had gathered for their monthly meeting, and at the head of the table sat Bishop Jean-Marie Odin, a moon-faced, clean-shaven man with a slightly receding hairline. He was a pious man, and Father Maistre admired the great sacrifices and risks the bishop had taken for his flock when he lived in Texas. But as sacrificial as the bishop might be, he had a blind spot for the Confederacy.

Father Maistre looked around the room, and his eyes fell on the tapestries along one wall. He was always drawn to the one violent scene amid more peaceful Biblical images. This tapestry depicted

John the Baptist's head being served up to Herod on a platter. Instinctively, Father Maistre ran his fingers along his neck as he swallowed.

Less than a week after the bishop returned to New Orleans, Father Maistre had offered thanksgiving for the Emancipation Proclamation at a Thursday High Mass. The church that day had been so packed that some people couldn't even squeeze through the door. People of color from all parishes had been flocking to St. Rose's.

"God watches, and His justice finally prevails!" Father Maistre had declared from the pulpit. "Men might perish in the work, but a principle—a faith set loose—spreads and bears fruit!"

Men might perish in the work. He wondered if he might be one of those men. Already, he had been given frosty stares from the many Confederate-leaning priests in the room. He could deal with a few cold shoulders, but what happened next was much more difficult.

A young priest, Father Alexandré Lemoine, asked permission to make a statement. He stood, his arms rigid at his side. He had delicate features to go with his delicate wire-rim spectacles. He had a placid air about him. While he was not a fire-breather, he had a strangely strong voice to go with his frail appearance.

"I am sorry, bishop, but I cannot sit in a gathering that includes a man convicted of a crime."

Father Maistre grabbed his armrests, his stomach dropping, as if the floor opened beneath him.

Murmuring sprang up on both sides of the long, narrow table, like apostles wondering who the betrayer was in their midst. Father Maistre had expected a rebuke from the bishop about his pro-Yankee statements, but not revelations about his criminal past in France.

After Bishop Odin called for attention, he turned to Father Lemoine and said, "Please explain." It all seemed so staged.

"My conscience and my God have bid me to reveal that one in our midst has violated both civil and canon law because of greed." The young priest ignored Father Maistre, keeping his eyes locked on the bishop.

"This is a serious charge, Father Lemoine. Are you certain of your information?"

"I am certain. This priest fled from Thuisy, France, because if he had remained, he would have been imprisoned."

That was true. Father Maistre fled France for England and then Belgium in June of 1849. Whoever had been blackmailing him had probably given Father Lemoine that information once Father Maistre stopped making payments. It's also possible that Father Lemoine could have been the one blackmailing him, but he doubted it. The young man was just a bit player in this drama, orchestrated by Bishop Odin.

"And this person is in this very room?" asked the bishop.

Father Maistre grunted. "Enough of the theatrics!" He slapped a hand on the table. "Just say the name."

When every head swiveled in his direction, Father Maistre wondered if Father Lemoine was going to stab a finger in his direction and declare, "That is the man!" like some actor in a melodrama. Instead, he looked at him almost apologetically, as if he did not want to reveal his name.

"I do not deny that I left France under...clouded circumstances," Father Maistre said.

He could see that some of the most outspoken Confederate priests were taking great pleasure that the criminal in their midst was him.

"And what were these clouded circumstances?" The bishop leaned his elbows on the table and steepled his fingers.

Father Maistre smiled. "Perhaps you would like to tell the gathering."

"But how can I do that? I am not aware of what happened," the bishop insisted.

Father Maistre fought the urge to roll his eyes. The bishop knew the circumstances very well.

"You were accused of embezzling money from the church coffers in Thuisy, France," said Father Lemoine. Again, he spoke gently, without theatrics, and his information was impeccable.

But Father Maistre was not going to let him off easily. "Is there a reason why you brought this up in this meeting and did not meet with the bishop or myself in private first?"

Father Lemoine stood there, gaping, flushing red.

The bishop cleared his throat. "Father Lemoine is not on trial here."

"And I am? If I am already on trial, then the wheels of justice move awfully fast. By supper time, I can be hanged."

Bishop Odin scoffed. "No one is talking about hanging anyone."

"Just a figure of speech, Your Excellency." Father Maistre bowed his head.

"Am I to gather that you don't deny committing a crime in France?" the bishop asked.

"I do not."

Bishop Odin stared at him as if contemplating what should be done with his misbehaving priest. "How do you think you can maintain your current ministry with this public scandal hanging over your head?"

"It needn't be a *public* scandal." Father Maistre frowned with a shake of his head, looking at each person one by one. "I trust the confidentiality of this room."

That was a lie. He didn't trust the Confederate sympathizers on each side of the table, who were probably already chomping at the bit to spread the tale of his crime.

"Perhaps it would be best if you retired quietly to a monastery where you could do penance for your crime."

Ah. There it was. Bishop Odin already had a plan to remove him from New Orleans.

"Perhaps you could go to Gethsemane Monastery in Kentucky for a time."

Father Maistre snapped to attention. Bishop Odin must know that after his problems in Chicago and Fort Wayne, Indiana, he was supposed to spend some time at Gethsemane Monastery contem-plating his actions. But he never showed up in Kentucky and wound up in New Orleans instead.

Mammon, that devil, had gotten his revenge. Father Maistre studied the palm of his hand, and he thought about the baptisms he had been performing lately. Since the beginning of the year, he had performed close to two hundred, many of them of black children. For the first time in his priestly life, he felt a true calling.

So, without a single word more, Father Maistre stood, turned, and headed for the door. Perhaps many of the priests in the room thought he was obedient, leaving for Gethsemane Monastery that very moment. Perhaps even Bishop Odin thought he was going to Kentucky, although Father Maistre doubted it.

Whatever they might be thinking, they would discover the truth soon enough. Father Maistre was returning to his church.

He wasn't going anywhere.

36

Felicie arrived at St. Rose Church for confession, even though the bishop strictly forbade it. In fact, the church was mobbed that Saturday morning, primarily by free people of color looking to support the renegade priest.

Felicie was thrilled to see the turnout, for her hackles had been raised by the heavy-handed bishop. Just three days earlier, Bishop Odin had announced that Father Maistre was under interdict, which meant he was forbidden to say Mass or perform any of the sacraments, including confession. So come Saturday morning, what did Father Maistre do? He heard confessions, and Felicie and Jean Louis were among the first to arrive.

Felicie would like nothing better than to march to the bishop's residence and give him a piece of her mind, but Father Maistre had calmly convinced her to hold her fire. Still, she was spitting mad.

Not only was Father Maistre forbidden to hear sacraments, but parishioners were not allowed to attend any Mass said by the priest, and they could not receive the sacraments from his hands. But the people came anyway.

"Will you say Mass tomorrow?" Felicie asked Father Maistre

later in the morning when the church had cleared. She and Jean Louis stayed behind to find out if there was any way they could help his cause with the bishop.

"Black parishioners in this city have nowhere else to go," the priest said.

Felicie nodded. She thought about saying something uncharitable about Bishop Odin, but she bit her tongue.

"Besides, I am only following orders." A slight grin tugged at Father Maistre's lips. "Captain C.W. Killborn has ordered me to continue to minister to my flock."

Captain C.W. Killborn was from the Provost Marshal General's Office, in charge of military law enforcement.

"Why would he become involved?" asked Jean Louis.

"To ensure that priests are not being pushed out of their parish for pro-Union views. He supports me."

Felicie drew a hand along her black veil, which she had pulled back from her face, and she ran the edges between her fingers. She had to approach this next question tactfully. "But won't the bishop say he has other reasons than your political views for ousting you?"

The "other reason" was something the entire city had learned over the past two weeks. Felicie was shocked when she found out that Father Maistre had fled France after pilfering money from his church. When the sin came to light, the priest confronted the issue head-on by addressing his congregation—yet another packed service.

"My battle with the bishop pales in comparison to what your husband and his men are facing." Father Maistre stood and started for a bank of candles along the wall. "Let us light some candles for their courage and safety."

Felicie tried not to think about the dangers André was facing as she lit several votive candles. They had received word that the Louisiana Native Guards left Baton Rouge on May 20 and were heading to Port Hudson, a Confederate fortress on the Mississippi that was holding firm, along with nearby Vicksburg. Attacking a fortified position was as dangerous as it gets.

She and Jean Louis joined the priest in lighting candles and saying the rosary, and the prayers rose like smoke from a burning battlefield. Felicie still had a hard time bottling her anger toward the bishop. Prayer helped, but she was distracted by so many competing thoughts. She had noticed a sullen spirit in Jean Louis ever since he had encountered Coralie with another man. Jean Louis knelt beside her, but his hands did not move up the beads of his rosary. Father Maistre also remained in the sanctuary, praying on the opposite side of the church.

When Felicie sensed someone entering the sanctuary, she turned and was jolted to see Benoit Montfort standing about twenty feet away, arms folded across his chest. So much for calming her spirit.

"Good afternoon, Père Maistre...Madame and Monsieur," said Monsieur Montfort.

Father Maistre looked up and scowled. "Good afternoon, Monsieur Montfort. Confession has just ended, but I could make an exception for you."

Monsieur Montfort sighed and rolled his eyes. "Making light of the sacrament is unbecoming of a priest."

"I am serious. If you have something on your conscience to place before God, I am willing to hear your confession."

"And you know perfectly well that you are under interdict and not allowed to hear confession. No Catholics are allowed to worship in St. Rose."

"God can be worshipped anywhere," snapped Felicie, answering scorn with scorn.

Montfort shrugged. "I am here to collect the keys of the church."

"On whose authority do you ask for the keys?" Father Maistre stood with narrowed eyes.

"On the authority of Bishop Odin, of course."

"I don't believe it," the priest said bluntly. "Why would he send you? He might send someone from the Provost General Marshal's Office, but not you."

Felicie wondered the same thing. Montfort would probably like nothing more than to see Father Maistre lose complete control of his church, so most likely he had taken it upon himself to obtain the keys.

"I am trying to settle this peacefully. If you do not hand over the keys, military force can be used."

Father Maistre laughed. "Military force? The provost marshal general supports me. You will find no help from the military."

"Remember, I tried to do this peacefully," said Montfort.

"With threats? Do you call that peaceful?" Father Maistre's voice raised.

"I am not threatening you. I am simply giving you information to help you make your decision to step down willingly. You will not maintain control of this church for much longer. It is a matter of *when* you hand over the keys."

Father Maistre returned to the bank of red votive candles and calmly lit another. "I light this one for the salvation of your soul, Monsieur Montfort."

But Montfort did not hear. He had already left the church.

After Felicie watched him exit, wishing him dead, she looked down at her hands and noticed that in her anger, she had snapped her rosary beads, breaking them apart. They scattered on the floor like shattered glass.

37

John Crowder was proud of his uniform, but sometimes he wished he could tear it off in this heat and humidity. While it was still early, his uniform weighed a ton, keeping the heat and steaming moisture against his skin. To their left was a swamp, where bald cypress rose from the water, thick at the base and tapering up out of the murky surface. All around the trees, cypress knees protruded—pointed projections that erupted from beneath.

"Glad I don't live too close to those." Levi pointed as the group made their way through murky land. "If y'all live within one hundred feet of a swamp, y'all will grow webbed toes. It happened to an uncle of mine who sprouted them and even started growing duck feathers. And that's the honest truth, 'cause if I'm lyin', then I'm dyin'."

"Keep talking, and you *will* be dyin'. I'll throttle you myself," said Lieutenant Moss through gritted teeth.

It was hard to know when Levi was joking and when he really believed what he said. Just twenty minutes ago, he talked about how people sometimes used monster-sized alligators to tow steamboats.

"Just hook a team of gators to the steamboat with cables, and they'll pull it like a team of horses."

Levi kept up a steady stream of conversation as they passed a dilapidated home. An old white lady sat in a rocker on the porch of the shack, which didn't seem much larger than the chicken coop out back.

"You'll never take Port Hudson!" The old lady shook a fist.

"If y'all don't shut your mouth, we'll set your house on fire and burn you up!" one of the soldiers shouted, glaring at her.

The old lady just cackled, until she watched some of the men make off with all of her chickens. Then, she squawked more than the birds, springing out of her chair with surprising speed, pounding on the back of one of the soldiers with weak fists. The young man caught her by the hand and spun her around, laughing and pushing her from him.

As they moved on, the soldiers of the Native Guard kept their eyes peeled for blackberries, wild cherries, and muscadine grapes, free for the picking. All around them were giant magnolias, their heavy branches leaning over like the limbs of giants, their flowers blooming white and pink. Spanish moss clung, hanging off the oaks and cypress trees much like the veteran officers' silver beards.

"Well, I'll be jinx swing!" Levi's jaw dropped when they came upon a field where a cow lay sprawled out, close to death.

Crowder stared in amazement—and disgust—as Levi set aside his rifle, crouched by the cow, and began squirting milk into his mouth. The animal's enormous ribs showed through its skin as it breathed in and out like bellows.

"There has to be something wrong with doin' that." Crowder winced and looked away.

"I'm thirsty!" Levi grinned. "Why let good milk go to waste?"

Crowder had to admit that the milk was tempting, and he would give anything to gulp some down. Levi leaned over the stricken animal, taking in several more squirts before pulling back to wipe his mouth.

"If you drink the milk of a dyin' cow, it gives you strength against the Grim Reaper." He gulped another mouthful, milk spilling down his cheek as his large Adam's apple bobbed up and down.

After licking his lips with a chuckle, a few other soldiers gathered around him for their turn, but Crowder was not one of them. Although it was blazing hot and he was trying to conserve the minimal water in his canteen, he wasn't *that* thirsty.

Federal soldiers, thousands of them, were converging on Port Hudson, north of New Orleans, and Crowder prayed that the fortress might fall before they reached it. He had to admit he was afraid of battle, even though he should be proud and excited for the chance to fight like free men.

The other Native Guards seemed awfully excited, but he was not ready to die. Although dying in battle would be much more glorious than in a cot from the fever, it might be more painful. It all depended on how he went. If a cannonball took off his head, his body wouldn't know what hit it, and he'd be gone in a flash. Crowder had become quite the praying man over the past two weeks because you never knew when you'd be taking your last breath and paying a visit to the Lord. The veil between this existence and the next was fragile. He tried to imagine what it might be like to stop breathing, to become all spirit and no body, but the thought had him spooked.

The cow soon took its last breath, kicked off its mortal coil, and the men moved on.

■■■

The morning of May 27 broke open with a beautiful blue sky, and the soldiers took that as a good omen, for the heavens matched the color of their coats. But General William Dwight was already drinking heavily and would be soused before any firing started.

André gave a slight shake of his head as he watched the general down another shot. He averted his gaze and turned to Colonel Chauncey Bassett, who had taken over the 1st Regiment when

Colonel Stafford was removed for cursing out a white officer tormenting black soldiers. While André was devastated when Stafford—their staunchest ally in the white world—was relieved of his duties, at least Colonel Bassett was an abolitionist and seemed to be a friend.

"What is the terrain ahead like?" André asked Colonel Bassett.

"General Dwight says the ground is smooth going all the way to the fortress." Colonel Bassett stroked his thick black beard as his deep-set, penetrating eyes stared off into the distance.

"Is there a problem, sir?" André studied his profile.

"No one has reconnoitered the ground." Colonel Basset's monotone voice dropped.

If no one has gone before us for any type of reconnaissance, then how does Dwight know it's smooth going? A rock settled in the pit of André's stomach.

Colonel Bassett snapped out of whatever he was thinking about and lifted a finger, his eyes unusually bright. "But General Dwight said our men will have support from white troops. And your company will carry the colors, Captain."

"Thank you, sir." Carrying the colors was a great honor, for the flag is the rallying point, but it was also a primary target.

The battle had officially begun at 5 a.m. with an hour-long bombardment of the fortress by Union ships. And now the two black regiments—the 1st and the 3rd—were taking roll call.

"Pontius Pilate!"

"Julius Caesar!"

"General Butler Jones!"

The 3rd Regiment was comprised of many former slaves, who had taken on new names of their choosing—quite colorful ones at that. Meanwhile, the 1st Regiment soldiers, most of them free men of color, primarily had French names like André Cailloux and Anselmo Planciancois.

All of the men whooped and cheered when Sergeant Planciancois was handed the flags to carry and was commanded to "protect, defend, die for, but do not surrender these flags."

Sergeant Planciancois saluted. "Colonel, I will bring these colors to you in honor or report to God the reason why."

Another cheer sounded. The men were bristling for a fight, smiles all around, many vowing that they would take no prisoners. André had an enormous responsibility because white soldiers were still convinced that the black troops would break and run as soon as they encountered fire. It was André's job to prevent that—whatever he had to do. General Dwight said the fate of the Negro race lay on the conduct of the Native Guards in this battle.

"I regard it as an experiment." Dwight stared at the ranks with steel in his eyes. "You may look for hard fighting or a complete run away."

A complete run away? André would never let it happen.

The Native Guards, about one thousand men strong, made their way across the pontoon bridge set across Foster's Creek. As soldiers filed onto the floating bridge, engineers barked the command, "Route step!" They couldn't march in unison because it could damage the wooden bridge, which had been built across floating India rubber pontoons—inflated rubber bags.

On the other side of the bridge, they worked their way through the willow trees, finally reaching the edge of the forest. When André studied the land before him, it was worse than he imagined. General Dwight did not know what in the world he was talking about, for the terrain was anything but smooth. On their right was a swamp with an army of cottonwoods in perfect formation rising out of the murky black water. It was probably crawling with alligators and snakes. On their left was a tangled mess.

The Rebs had felled trees and created an abatis—a wall lying on the ground with branches sticking toward them like wooden spears. The area was rutted by gullies and overrun by thick underbrush.

But most ominous of all was what lay just in front of them.

They faced high bluffs, where the Confederates had fortified themselves. The Rebels had the high ground. A ridge ran along their left where the Southern men could fire on them from rifle pits before reaching the bluffs.

This is smooth ground? André exhaled, rubbing the back of his neck. *Is General Dwight out of his mind?* The second his men emerged from the willow woods, they would be exposed, much like a shooting gallery.

"It's a death trap," one of his troops muttered from the back.

"Silence!" André sent a sharp stare over his shoulder.

But the soldier was correct. No sane person would lead a regiment into this open space.

Lieutenant John Crowder stepped in next to André. "What do you think?"

André shook his head. It was suicide, but he had his orders, and he had to follow them. Even worse, as men of color, if they didn't charge into this death trap, the news that his troops backed down—that black troops wilted under fire—would spread across the country.

For the first time, André wished he wasn't the blackest man in New Orleans. He didn't want to represent an entire race of people. It wasn't fair that he was forced to carry that weight.

When General Dwight did something, the entire white race wasn't judged by his behavior. But the people of color in New Orleans would be judged by what André and his men did here today.

Still, these soldiers were real people, not symbols. They had brothers, sisters, wives, fathers, and mothers. Could he sacrifice them?

André's stomach churned, leaving him to wonder what came next. He stared at the bluff and spotted soldiers moving within their rifle pits. They, too, waited for his decision.

38

Colleen McCarthy placed her twenty-five cents next to the other coins on the front stoop at the Sure Enuf Hotel, where she and the others put their weekly bribes. A pair of policemen would soon come by to collect them. On this day of the week, many policemen's pockets jangled as they walked their beats.

Colleen stared at her money with a sigh. Paying twenty-five cents was tough, but at least she didn't have to shell out a dollar per week like the ladies in the elegant parlor houses. Once a year, the police made arrests just for show, and Colleen prayed she wouldn't be made an example. She could never afford the ten-dollar fine.

Ever since Roussel had been killed, Colleen spent most mornings in tears, losing hope of ever escaping this viper's pit. Baby Roussel kept some hope alive, but the added mouth to feed made it more challenging to give up even twenty-five cents of her earnings. Some of the girls advised her to leave the baby on a church's doorstep.

As she trudged back up the stairs, Colleen's eyes fell on the hem of her dress, which was becoming more tattered and dirtier by the day. She had once prided herself with lovely dresses (two of them), but the stink and grime of this place stuck to her like a second layer of skin. She envied the snakes that could shed theirs.

Entering the hallway leading to her crib, she came up short and gasped. Standing at the far end of the hall, holding her child, was Bricktop Jackson. Next to her, cooing at her baby, was Miller.

"What are you doing with my child?" Colleen rushed forward, ready to attack, not caring if they killed her on the spot.

She had left her baby with Claudette, the girl in the adjoining crib, while she took care of her twenty-five cents.

"I'm sorry," said Claudette, peeping her head from behind the curtains of her small room. "They insisted they see the child."

"Give me back my baby!"

Colleen was ready to throw herself on Bricktop, but she realized that would be as effective as throwing herself at a brick wall.

"Easy, little filly, easy." Miller stepped into the hallway and caught her by the waist.

"Careful now, you're going to upset the baby." Bricktop shielded the child—as if she had a maternal instinct.

"Give him back!"

When Miller slung his left arm around Colleen's shoulders, the chain attached to it thumped against her spine. "Calm down. You'll get your baby...in due time."

Colleen's skin crawled with the weight of Miller's arm around her as he drew her inside her room. She dropped onto her bed, the corn husks in the mattress crackling beneath her.

"What do you want with me now?" She flicked her eyes at him, sucking in a breath, praying that whatever came next wouldn't be harmful to her or her child. Her mind whirled with possible scenarios, but one look at Miller's size reminded her she had no power or options.

"Easy." Miller grinned, sitting next to her. His stink was so foul that Colleen had to breathe through her mouth. She closed her eyes as he added, "We're just payin' y'all a polite call."

Bricktop, with the baby still cradled in her arms, stepped inside the room and yanked the curtain shut with a swish, concealing them from the rest of the house.

"We just wanna talk a bit, honey. We hear stories 'bout you and that priest."

Colleen averted her eyes, staring at the floor.

"We hear you been talkin' to him." Bricktop swayed the baby in her arms, watching Colleen with an unwavering stare.

"Don't know what you're goin' on about," Colleen muttered at the floorboard. "I burned the priest's place. Why would I talk with him?"

"That's just the thing," said Bricktop, speaking all sweet and like. "We looked at that burned door. Seems strange the fire didn't spread any farther than that."

"The priest woke up, threw water on it. What did you expect me to do? Stick the torch in his eye?"

Miller laughed. "That would've been just the thing! I like the way you think, lassie. Maybe there's hope for y'all after all."

Bricktop leaned over and made a cooing sound to Baby Roussel. She was such a tall woman that when she straightened back up, her head came close to bumping the short ceiling. She looked like a giantess, cradling a baby.

"We're just here to give you a friendly warning," Bricktop said. "If we find out you been talkin' to the priest..."

"I ain't been talkin' to no priest."

"That's good, lassie," Miller said.

When she looked at Bricktop, the lady was waving her double-sided knife, enticing the child as if it were a toy. Roussel reached for it, his tiny fingers coming so close to the sharp blade.

"Get that thing away from my child!" Colleen attempted to lunge for her child, but Miller clamped her down.

Bricktop sent her a glare, keeping the blade inches from the baby's outstretched hand.

"This here will get a lot closer to your baby's soft skin if I find out you been talkin' to anybody about the fire and who sent you to do it."

239

Tears streamed down Colleen's cheeks as she shook her head, her voice cracking. "I ain't been talkin' to no one."

"That's good, that's good." Miller squeezed her leg. "That's what we like to hear."

"But if we find out that y'all has already done so..." Bricktop raised a brow, letting her silence fill in the blanks.

Then, the giantess placed the knife in Roussel's clutches, letting him grip the handle.

"No!" Colleen stood as her baby shook the blade like a rattle.

Miller grunted and grasped the blade moments before it came close to the child's forehead. Bricktop grabbed the baby's wrist in tandem and slipped the knife from the child's hand before any damage could happen.

"Babies shouldn't play with knives." Bricktop waved the weapon at Colleen. "Let that be my motherly lesson for the day."

Then, to Colleen's overwhelming relief, Bricktop stuck the blade in a holster before placing Baby Roussel into her arms. Colleen held him so tight she nearly smothered him, and within seconds, the child began to cry.

■■■

Jean Louis and his mother attended Mass at St. Rose's every possible day—weekdays included. Before Father Maistre was suspended, the weekday Masses usually drew only a scattering of people—mostly elderly. But when Jean Louis entered the church on Wednesday, May 27, he found the place packed. He noticed that even Minetta had begun attending. If the Bissets knew she was going to Father Maistre's church, they couldn't be too happy about it.

"How is Coralie?" Jean Louis asked Minetta after Mass had let out.

The air was already muggy for May—clear, hot, the air dripping like a soaked towel. Minetta wiped the side of her neck with a handkerchief as she stared back at him—as if dumbfounded by his simple question. Was she shocked that he was still holding on to Coralie in his mind?

"You haven't heard?" she asked.

"What haven't I heard?"

"I suppose you wouldn't know since it has not been officially announced in the papers."

Jean Louis felt a sinking sensation. "What's happened?"

Minetta stared at the ground for a few moments before finally looking up at Jean Louis. "Mademoiselle Bisset is betrothed."

"Betrothed?"

Minetta touched him on his shoulder. "I'm sorry."

He had seen her with another man, but he didn't think...How could this happen so quickly?

"Does she really want to marry of her own free will?" he asked, holding out hope that she had been forced into the union by her father.

"I believe so. I'm sorry."

Jean Louis studied the area in front of the church where people were still gathered. His mother, who was talking with Father Maistre, kept shooting looks at Minetta and him.

"Do you think you could arrange a meeting between me and Mademoiselle Coralie?"

Minetta stared at him in disbelief. "That would not be wise."

Jean Louis dug his toe in the ground. When he looked up, he spotted Colleen McCarthy of all people heading in their direction. She was dressed like a Gallatin Street woman—wearing a gown so short that it revealed her ankles, certainly not the kind of dress women wore to Mass. She carried a baby in her arms.

When other churchgoers noticed her approaching, Jean Louis's skin began to burn, and he knew he must be getting flushed. With his light skin, his blush of embarrassment would be easy to spot. Being seen outside of the church with an adventuress like Colleen McCarthy will surely set tongues wagging. He was especially terrified that people might think the child in her arms was his.

While Mademoiselle McCarthy looked distraught and he felt for her, his mother's steely gaze was more pressing. But he didn't have time to contemplate how to handle his mother's reaction because Colleen strode right up to him. Minetta, obviously enjoying his discomfort, hid a smile.

"You have to help me," said Colleen, skipping any social niceties.

"Mademoiselle, this is not the place." Jean Louis glanced around, muttering under his breath.

"I don't have time to choose a suitable place. They will kill me and my child."

Minetta's sly smile vanished. "Kill you? Who?"

Jean Louis held his breath as what seemed like a hundred sets of eyes were on him. He motioned her to the side. "Please. Let's step under the tree, and you can tell us what happened."

He sent Minetta an urgent look, nodding for her to join them. The last thing his family needed was for him to be seen talking alone with a woman like Colleen McCarthy. The three of them moved beneath the cover of a nearby magnolia.

"I decided to run away." Colleen looked over her shoulder, scanning the area.

"From...from the...hotel?" Jean Louis wasn't about to use the word "bordello" within spitting distance of the church.

"I could not stay there another day. I had to leave with Roussel."

"With Roussel?" said Minetta.

"My child."

Minetta looked at the infant as if contemplating the meaning of the name. "I see."

"You must hide me, Monsieur Cailloux. Madame Montfort will try to have me killed by that Bricktop lady when she finds out I have fled."

Jean Louis's jaw dropped. "*Madame* Montfort?"

"Yes." Colleen nodded with authority.

"You mean *Monsieur* Montfort."

"No. *Madame* Montfort."

"But I thought it was Monsieur Montfort who...who forced you to set the fire."

"I lied when I said that because I am more afraid of Madame Montfort than I am of her husband. In truth, it was Madame Montfort who forced me into setting fire to the church. And she will send Bricktop and that man with the chain of an arm when she finds I have fled. She doesn't tolerate people running away from her bordello."

Her bordello. Jean Louis ran a hand along his jaw, swallowing. *Madame Montfort also runs the bordello?*

"Wait a moment." Minetta turned her wide eyes on Colleen. "You tried to set fire to the church? And you were forced to do so by Madame Montfort?"

Colleen looked at Minetta as if noticing her for the first time. "And who are you?"

"A friend of Monsieur Cailloux. We can help you," said Minetta.

Jean Louis gaped, blinking at Minetta, thinking she'd gone crazy. There was no "we" anything.

"Thank you, Mademoiselle." Colleen squeezed Minetta's hand.

Jean Louis shook his head, trying to catch up. "I thought Mother Colby is the one who ran the Sure Enuf Hotel."

"She runs the day-to-day operations, but Madame Montfort is actually the one in charge. You have to hide me from her. You have to hide me in the church. I must seek sanctuary."

Jean Louis and Minetta exchanged glances. "I think Father Maistre has enough to handle without adding you and your child to his causes," Jean Louis told Colleen.

"But Monsieur..."

Jean Louis was afraid she was going to melt into sobs. They had already drawn a lot of attention.

"You can't send me back. If they know I came here today..." Her eyes welled with more tears. "They've already threatened my baby with a knife."

"Monsieur Cailloux can shelter you in his apartment." Minetta waved a hand at Jean Louis, who stared at her, stunned.

When Minetta noticed Jean Louis's look of disapproval, she touched his arm with a gentle smile. "Don't worry. I will stay with Mademoiselle McCarthy at your place."

Jean Louis put a hand to his forehead. *Two* unattached women in his apartment? That was even worse!

"You can stay at your family home down the street," Minetta quickly added.

Jean Louis shook his head. "No."

Before Minetta could protest, he continued. "You may stay in my apartment, but I will stand guard outside. I can sleep by daylight, and you and Mademoiselle McCarthy can have my room through the night."

"Thank you, Monsieur." Colleen offered a hint of a smile, her lips shaking.

For a moment, Jean Louis was afraid the woman was going to kiss him on the cheek, and he instinctively backpedaled. Thankfully, she stayed put.

Minetta took Colleen by the hand. "Quickly. Let's go there straight away, and you can explain everything."

Jean Louis obeyed orders like a good soldier. As they turned for his home, the back of his neck prickled. He could tell that not only his mother but at least a dozen other churchgoers stared at them as they left. He also noticed a man across the street disappear around the corner of the house.

He wasn't sure, but he had a sneaking fear that the man was missing one arm, and in its place was a chain with an iron ball dangling from the end.

39

Port Hudson
Wednesday, May 27, 1863

About one thousand men strong, the 1st and 3rd Louisiana Guards remained within the protective canopy of the willow forest. Just beyond them stretched open ground—terrain as rough as anything John Crowder had ever seen.

Once they moved into the open, hot lead would begin raining down on them from the bluffs like a hailstorm in hell. General Dwight was a fool to think they could reach the Confederate lines before being decimated. They were walking into a horrifying enfilade, in which the enemy would scorch them all along their flank.

Crowder cut his eyes at Levi, who pulled a lava-hot pepper from his pocket and popped it in his mouth. Levi recently gathered them at one of the houses they passed and now ate them like candy.

"They boil the blood—just what y'all need before a battle." Levi chewed and swallowed without breaking a sweat, reaching for another and pushing it toward him. "Want one?"

"No, thank you." Crowder waved him off with a grimace.

"Suit yourself." He popped it in his mouth.

As the bugle sounded, six companies of the 1st Regiment surged out of hiding, followed by nine companies of the 3rd Regiment. They marched out of the woods at quick time.

This is it. Crowder eyed the bluffs, which were about six hundred yards away, thinking they might have well been six thousand.

At first, nothing happened, as Crowder eyed the eerily quiet landscape. It seemed they were being lured into the open as the hidden Rebel troops waited for the right moment. Within seconds, a crack of multiple guns echoed through the air, and the Confederates fired on them—the dismal hiss of bullets flying by.

When a man behind him collapsed with a groan, Crowder kept his eyes fixed straight ahead. *No turning back, no turning back.* Every particle in his being screamed at him to turn and flee into the woods. Why commit suicide on the insane orders of a drunken general?

The regiment increased their pace to double quick and was now four hundred yards from the bluff. As the men hustled through the chaos, a splatter of red erupted from someone's temple a couple of steps in front of him. The lines began to fall into disarray and confusion, but Captain Cailloux called above the noise, encouraging the men to hold firm.

"Stay together. Press forward! With me!"

Two hundred yards away, they fired a volley—and then all hell broke loose. The Confederates opened up with their artillery, and the skies cracked apart. The Rebels fired canister—thin-walled metal cylinders packed with musket balls, jagged pieces of metal, and even nails. Now he knew exactly what people meant when they said soldiers were "mowed down." Lines of men collapsed as if an invisible scythe swept across the battlefield, lopping people down in groups like chopped grass.

Everywhere Crowder looked...it was screaming bloody chaos. The very air was tormented with flying debris, bullets, and cannon shots. When Crowder tripped and tumbled onto a fallen soldier, he tried not to look at the man's face—at least what was left of it. What was he doing here? He wasn't even seventeen years old!

He scrambled to his feet and saw bits of metal flying through the air like a twister had hit a hardware store and was flinging deadly bits of metal every which way. He heard Levi scream, and at first, he thought his friend had been hit. Instead, the man ran forward with a wild, warrior's cry.

Crowder did a double take, thinking Levi had gone crazy, when something pricked his side. John winced but kept moving, charging until a fist of pain battered his gut and twisted his inside with a fire blazing so hot, he thought he'd incinerate. He sprawled forward, arms out and his rifle flying. When he inspected his side, he noticed a blackened hole in his gut, dribbling blood.

He also noticed that he had landed on a dead man.

■■■

André watched in horror as their flag was shredded by Minié balls and flying metal. Sergeant Planciancois continued to wave the flag until a shell ripped right through it and thundered into the side of his head. The sergeant fell onto the banner, dead in an instant, half of his head gone, when two other soldiers converged on the flag, fighting over who would pick up the colors. Louis Leveiller and Athanase Ulgere, both corporals, had their hands on the flagstaff and were screaming at each other to let go.

A Minié ball settled their argument, ripping through Leveiller's neck, spouting red in all directions. Leveiller collapsed on top of Planciancois's corpse, leaving Ulgere grasping the pole in shock.

Soldiers ran for cover in a nearby willow swamp, but a round of artillery hit the trees, splintering them and the men hiding behind them. André saw a three-foot piece of willow go flying under his nose like a spear point. The smoke thickened the air with a devilish glut of sulfur and whistling metal.

Sword raised, André moved along the line of soldiers, shouting in both English and French. "Follow me! Follow! *En avant, mes amis!*"

When he looked down, he noticed that his left arm was a dangling mess. He supposed some bones were shattered, but due to the frenzy and terror, there was no pain. He hadn't even noticed the bullet tear through his arm. It was like he was dreaming.

But they had to keep moving, keep pressing forward. Black men do not retreat; black men do not run under fire. The Confederate lines—the bluff—were only one hundred yards away. But it seemed as if they still had a million miles to go.

40

"Tell me. What is going on?" Felicie demanded.

She'd spotted her oldest son in hot conversation with Mademoiselle Minetta and *that woman*. From the looks of her, she was a Gallatin Street lady. A fallen woman. An adventuress—like the one her husband had helped onto a horse so long ago, it seemed.

Felicie stood on the stoop of her son's place. He rented a small Creole shotgun house—so long and narrow that you could fire a shotgun and send a bullet straight through from the front to the back door.

"Where is the woman?" It wasn't a question. It was a demand.

"What woman?" Jean Louis shrugged.

It couldn't be good if Jean Louis denied the existence of a woman she had seen just an hour earlier in front of the church. And what about that child? She had a terrible feeling it belonged to Jean Louis. Why else would the lady bring it to him, looking so desperate?

What had Jean Louis done now? She wished so badly that André could be here to deal with this.

Felicie stepped across the threshold into the front parlor and eyed the back room. The house was only the width of a single room, and the parlor spilled into a bedroom, then a kitchen, then a bath, then into the postage-stamp backyard.

"What woman? You know perfectly well that I mean the woman carrying the child in her arms."

She made a move for the bedroom, but Jean Louis cut her off.

"I do not know that woman." He blocked her path.

"Then why did she walk right up to you? Why did she pick you out among the people outside of church? Is that your child?"

Jean Louis looked genuinely shocked. Then, to her surprise, Mademoiselle Minetta stepped from the back room, holding the child in her arms.

"You should tell your mother." Minetta gently rocked the child as it slept.

"I don't want to put my mother into any danger."

"She won't be in any more danger than she already is," Minetta whispered, trying not to wake the baby.

"Yes." Felicie wasn't concerned about lowering her voice. She turned to her son, using her most forceful tone. "Tell me what is going on."

Jean Louis sat down in a straight-backed chair while she and Minetta also took seats.

"I'm waiting," said Felicie.

Jean Louis sighed and proceeded to reveal some astounding things. How this child was probably Roussel Pinard's, how the adventuress, Colleen McCarthy, had been forced into her current life and threatened if she didn't attempt to set fire to the church, and how her oppressors were Monsieur and Madame Montfort.

The last piece of news was the most staggering of all. From all appearances, Madame Montfort was the epitome of propriety. She was the one who seemed so shocked when her husband spotted André helping an adventuress onto his horse. How could they have kept that side of their lives so well hidden?

"I do not care much for Monsieur and Madame Montfort,"

Felicie said, "but I find it hard to believe they would be running a house of ill repute on Gallatin Street!"

"It's true."

This statement came from the bedroom doorway, where the adventuress leaned against the doorjamb. She looked haggard, bleary-eyed.

"You woke up." Minetta stood with a tender look. "But you need to rest."

"I had to flee from the Montforts." Colleen trained her eyes on Felicie, ignoring Minetta's comment. "And now I need to hide, or Madame Montfort will kill me."

When Felicie stared at Colleen, she saw her mother in her face. Felicie's mother had been forced into the life of a concubine. The *plaçage* system may have been a more socially acceptable arrangement than the station Colleen was forced into, but it was still basically the same. Felicie had been running from her mother's past ever since, so she understood what it meant to be on the run. She knew exactly what this woman was fleeing from.

Felicie changed her mind in a heartbeat.

"Jean Louis, we must help this woman," she said. "And if you need additional weapons, I know where your father has stashed some extra guns."

■■■

Minetta slipped out the back of the Bisset house carrying a small bag with several days' worth of clothing.

While Jean Louis kept an eye on Colleen McCarthy and her child, she had returned to the Bisset house because Monsieur Bisset would get suspicious if she didn't show up for work. She told Monsieur Bisset that she had to spend a couple of days at a sick relative's home, and he grudgingly agreed.

With a bag of clothes slung over her shoulder, she knew she should go directly back to Jean Louis's residence, but she had been shaken by everything that Colleen McCarthy said about the Mont-forts. Monsieur and Madame Montfort lived only three houses down from the Bissets, so she passed them almost every day of the year. They seemed like such ordinary, genteel folk—pompous, but nothing stood out as uncommon. It still seemed hard to believe what Colleen was saying about them. They owned a Gallatin Street cathouse, and they were threatening to murder Colleen and her child?

Her doubts and curiosity drove her to stroll past the Montfort residence, even though it was in the opposite direction from Jean Louis's home. She stood behind a tree and stared at the house—a large home with stacked porches, or galleries. The house was pure white with galleries that spanned the entire width of the house on both levels. Beautiful French doors gave access to the second-floor rooms at several spots along the upper gallery.

Minetta could not resist. The house looked quiet, so she dashed across the front lawn and slipped along the side, peering through some bay windows but saw no signs of life. Even bolder, she set aside her bag and crept up the short flight of steps on the side of the house, screened from the street by thick vegetation, and entered.

Minetta had been inside the first floor several times, so she knew its layout. She paused to listen for any sounds of movement. Nothing. No shuffling of feet upstairs. She passed through a breakfast nook, down a hallway to a curving staircase just off the foyer at the front of the house.

She had never been on the second floor before, but she was heading there now, moving silently up the polished wooden stairs.

The room at the top of the staircase was locked, which immedi-ately raised her interest. She hurried along the upstairs hallway to the master bedroom and out a set of French doors to a second-floor gallery—an expansive balcony. She hurried along the exterior to two additional sets of French doors and tried each. One was locked, but the second pair opened, so she entered the locked bedroom from the outside.

As she closed the French doors behind her with a soft click, she turned and let out a mild, startled gasp. Lined up and mounted on two different walls were Mardi Gras masks. Devil masks.

They hung on the walls like animal-head trophies. There were several red-horned masks, two that had more of an Egyptian god appearance, one that looked like a goat, another a bull, another a fish, another a fly. These looked awfully similar to the devil masks from the Mardi Gras float for *Paradise Lost*. Minetta was glad she had entered by daylight.

The room was tidy and clean, with a large roll-top desk jammed against one wall. The wood squeaked as she raised the desktop. Positioned squarely in the center of the desk was a neat stack of papers. She lifted the top sheet and read the names: Moloch and Dagon. Beneath each devil name was a list of people, including a few familiar ones, such as the infamous Bricktop Jackson and John Miller. They were listed beneath the word "Dagon." She stared at the masks and thought that Dagon might be the fish god.

She flipped through more pages. More names of devils, each seemingly corresponding to masks on the wall. And more names of people in New Orleans. She was so engrossed in this discovery that she almost didn't hear the sound of footsteps coming up the stairs.

Minetta pushed the stack of papers back in order, her hands shaking. She closed the roll-top, wincing as the wood scraped and made a slight squeak. She looked around, but there was only one place to go. She rushed through the French doors and onto the second-floor gallery.

She crouched behind an oversized potted plant with tropical foliage, peering through the glass in the French door. Minetta watched as Monsieur and Madame Montfort entered the room and approached the roll-top desk. She couldn't hear what they were saying—just a barely audible murmur. When Madame Montfort saw the state of the pages on the desk, she glanced around as if she knew somebody had been rifling through them. Minetta hid further behind the vegetation, closing her eyes, sure she had been seen.

She waited for the hammer to fall, but the Montforts did not storm onto the balcony, demanding to know what she was doing.

When her nerves stopped crackling, Minetta peered back into the room. Madame Montfort retrieved a mask and pulled a file folder from inside of it. She and her husband examined the folder for a spell before sliding it back inside the disguise.

Did the masks serve as their file storage?

The people listed beneath the names of the masks were beginning to make some sense. The Montforts maintained files on all those people, and the files were stored in corresponding masks.

"Mademoiselle!"

Minetta was jolted back to reality and turned to look at the street with a gasp. Laurent Bisset and his father stood on the front lawn, staring up at her.

"Mademoiselle Minetta?" said Laurent. "What are you doing up there?"

Minetta made a run for it. She had only one way to go—through the French doors leading into the master bedroom. Even in her dress, she knew she could outrun Monsieur Montfort. It was Laurent and his father she was terrified of.

Rushing through the master bedroom, she pounded down the staircase, hearing startled sounds coming from the Montforts just behind her. She had three exits out of the house from which to choose—the front, back, or side doors. Three exits, two men out front. She chose quickly, selecting the back door. She threw it open with a bang, flew down the short flight of stairs, and saw nothing to her right but open grass and trees ahead. As she darted across the lawn, a figure shot from her right and nearly threw her off her feet.

It was Laurent's father, quick and strong for his age. As soon as he put his hands on her, she could only think about the bundle of sticks that he used to beat his son—the *fasces*. Would he dare to use them on her?

■■■

Jean Louis felt a stab of déjà vu as he sat outside his house, armed to the teeth with a sword at his side and a pistol and hunting knife on either hip. It reminded him of the evening he kept guard on the church. That night, he had apprehended Colleen McCarthy in the act of arson, but on this day, he was serving as her protector. Life had some strange twists.

It was early afternoon, and Mademoiselle McCarthy was inside, feeding her child. Minetta had told Jean Louis she needed to head back to the Bisset house to gather her things, but that was hours ago.

He was happy to protect Mademoiselle Colleen and her child, especially if the baby really was that of his late friend, Roussel. It gave him a sense of purpose since he had given up the chance to fight alongside his father.

Jean Louis perked when he noticed a man coming down the street, his head down and arms swinging by his sides. He didn't see an oak club in the man's hands, so he didn't think it was one of the Live Oak Boys from Gallatin Street. Besides, they usually traveled in packs, and this man was alone. But as he neared, Jean Louis's alarm bells went off, for it appeared that it was Laurent Bisset.

Jean Louis drew his pistol.

"Put away the gun, Cailloux. I'm not armed." Laurent raised his hands.

Jean Louis didn't put away the gun. Why would he take the word of a Bisset?

Laurent shrugged and forged forward as Jean Louis stood.

"I bring news." Laurent came to a stop, folding his arms over his chest. "Your girl has been taken."

His girl? Coralie?

"What are you talking about?" Jean Louis's throat went dry.

"Your girl. Minetta. She has been taken by the Montforts."

Was this a trick to get him away from Mademoiselle McCarthy?

"Why would they take Minetta?"

"Because they found her rummaging through their house, and they're convinced Minetta knows where you're hiding Colleen

McCarthy. They won't hesitate to hurt her to uncover the information."

"Where have they taken her?" Jean Louis's breath seemed to catch in his throat. If they touched a hair on her head…

"They've got her at Bill Swan's Fireproof Coffee-House on Levee Street."

Jean Louis exhaled, his stomach clenching. How could he have put Minetta in such danger? He should be the one taking on the risk.

"Why are you telling me this?" He sent Laurent a side eye, wondering if he was tricking him into walking into a trap.

"Because I don't treat women the way my father does—or the way the Montforts do."

That was consistent with how Minetta described Laurent, but it could still be a ruse.

"Have the Montforts hurt Minetta?"

"They struck her, but when I last saw her, she was not hurt badly —yet. However, I cannot guarantee that she will make it through what happens next. She's just lucky that this is the day of the grand-national rat-killing match."

Laurent must have seen the confusion in Jean Louis's face because he smiled and explained.

"This is the biggest rat-killing match of the year, and the Mont-forts have a lot of money riding on it, so they can't deal with Minetta immediately. But as soon as the match ends, who knows what they'll do to Minetta—and you. In the meantime, I told the Montforts and my father that I would look for Colleen McCarthy. I can stall as long as possible, but I will eventually have to report back to them that I could not locate her. You need to get Minetta out of Swan's place this afternoon."

Jean Louis didn't know what to say; he didn't know whether to even believe this story. Did Laurent oppose violence to women with such intensity that he would go against the Montforts, much less his father? Minetta certainly gave that impression.

Jean Louis shot out his hand. "I am extremely grateful."

256

"I am not doing this for you, Cailloux." Laurent crossed his arms, ignoring Jean Louis's olive branch. "I do not believe in treating women this way, either Minetta or Colleen McCarthy. If you were the one being held prisoner, I would not lift a finger to help you."

With those words, Laurent spun on his heels and strode off. Jean Louis drew back his outstretched hand and scratched his head. Should he dare show up at Bill Swann's Fireproof Coffee-House? It was true that they held rat-killing contests there, but how could he trust Laurent Bisset?

Jean Louis decided he had no choice but to take the risk. However, first he had to whisk Mademoiselle McCarthy to his parents' house for sanctuary. Then he had a saloon to storm and some rats to kill.

41

Lieutenant Crowder held his hand to his gut as he crawled off the corpse. He had no idea what soldier lay beneath him because there was not enough of a face remaining to make an identification. Bullets continued to hail down, pattering the ground. The corpse twitched as another bullet struck the body.

Crowder tried to stand, but as he rose into a half-crouch, the pain wrapped around his entire midsection and triggered a spasm in his lower back that took his breath away and knocked him off his feet. He laid against the pebble-covered ground and gasped, fighting to breathe normally again.

Trying to distract himself from the pain, he watched a beetle maneuver across the terrain inches in front of his face. He pulled his hand away from his stomach wound, hoping that the bleeding had stopped, but his hand was covered in fresh blood.

Still gripping his gut, he rose into a crouch and scooted sideways on the ground, crab-like, moving toward a tattered piece of blue fabric torn from a soldier's body in a blast. It would make a tolerable bandage.

When the pain became too great, he dropped to his side, trying to

The Dixie Devil

catch his breath. The piece of cloth was only a few feet away, but it seemed as if it was going to take all his strength to get there. Groaning, he heaved himself forward like a sea lion and took hold of the clothing fragment. He moaned as he shoved it into his body, his gaping wound burning from the effort to plug the hole in his side.

"Crowder!" Someone called his name from amidst the scattered bodies.

Most of the living soldiers had moved toward the bluffs. The only men he could see were dispersed across the dirt like fallen scarecrows. Many were dead, but somebody had clearly called his name.

"Crowder! Over here!"

He surveyed the mangled men, thinking it sounded like Lieutenant Moss. When he finally saw an arm lifting from the ground as if waving, it seemed odd and nightmarish, like a corpse waving farewell.

"Crowder!"

The voice came from about fifteen feet ahead. The man's mouth was moving, and his eyes still had the light of life. It appeared to be Moss, but the man's face was dark with blood smears, so it was hard to tell.

"Crowder, help me!" Moss's terrified eyes beckoned.

A large chunk of wood had speared Moss in the back. Crowder rose to his right elbow, and he paused to take a breath, bracing and praying for the energy to rise a foot off the ground. Then he forced himself into a crouch, the pain intensifying in his belly and back, managing to stumble across a dozen feet before collapsing with a yell.

"Crowder, I'm dyin'. Save me!"

Crowder tried to assess Moss's situation. While the wood shaft sticking from Moss's back didn't seem to penetrate too deep, he couldn't be sure. With a bullet in his belly, Crowder figured he might be in more serious shape, but Moss seemed much worse off mentally.

"Say a prayer. Would y'all say a prayer for me, Crowder?"

Crowder nodded and then began. He lay on his side, staring intently at Moss. "Our Father which art in heaven, hallowed be thy

259

name. Thy kingdom come, thy will be done in earth, as it is in heaven. Give us this day our daily bread. And forgive us our debts, as we forgive our debtors. And lead us not into temptation, but deliver us from evil..."

It took as much energy to stumble through those few words as it took to stagger across five feet of battleground. He paused to catch his breath.

"Don't stop, John. Keep praying."

Crowder blinked a couple of times. He believed this was the first time Moss addressed him by his first name.

He prayed on, turning to his favorite Psalm: "Thou shalt not be afraid for the terror by night; nor for the arrow that flieth by day; nor for the pestilence that walketh in darkness; nor for the destruction that wasteth at noonday. A thousand shall fall at thy side, and ten thousand at thy right hand; but it shall not come nigh thee."

■■■

"Leave the field, Captain! Your arm!" In the chaos around him, someone was telling André to pull back.

André's injury—his right arm shattered just above the elbow—was clearly garnering attention, yet he didn't feel any pain. That would come later. The appendage no longer seemed like it was there. It was just a dangling shred of bone and flesh.

But there was no way he would leave the field. If he left, so would his men, and he couldn't allow that to happen. Black men don't retreat. He stared at a man sitting on a log. Most of the soldier's right leg was missing, but he was still firing his rifle. If this man was fighting on, so would André.

"Follow me!" he continued to scream over the sounds of war, encouraging his dwindling ranks as hell unfolded.

A few men retreated, but most pushed forward into the mouth of the battle like planks of wood sliding into the path of a rotary saw blade and then shredding to pieces. As if the shells and Minié balls were not enough, André and his men reached a flooded ditch, and he had to shout and scream to keep them moving into the water. With chaos blustering on all sides, the men held their rifles and cartridge boxes high above their heads to protect them from getting waterlogged.

He noticed the ranks begin to dwindle as men either died or stopped to find cover behind boulders and tree stumps. Some ran into the swamp, taking their chances with the gators and poisonous snakes. Still, most of his men were with him. Although promised, there had been no artillery support, but they pressed forward.

"Suivez-moi! Ne soyezpas découragés!"

The water was cold and deeper than he thought as he stepped into the ditch. This was a baptism by both water and fire. The water swallowed him from below, and the fire fell from above while a wave of smoke came over them, moving fast like a fleeing ghost. When it flowed over and through them, the way ahead looked clear. Only about fifty yards to reach the Confederates.

Then a black blur came racing toward him. He caught a glimpse of it from the side, and for a moment, he thought it was a black bird swooping toward him. Suddenly, it was as if the sky caved, and he was being buried alive in the rubble of the collapsing atmosphere.

For a moment, he was back in their burning stable, which was flaming and collapsing on all sides. Only this time it was as if the entire world was burning and falling in on him, burying him beneath an everlasting mountain of debris. Just as everything went black, he was thrown into the air, rising in his ascension as if the swooping bird had taken him in its talons and lifted him into the broken sky.

42

F elicie handed a cup of coffee to Colleen McCarthy, careful not to spill. Jean Louis had brought the woman to their house for safekeeping while he went to find Minetta. Although her son acted calm on the surface, Felicie could sense his anxiety. And while she tried, she couldn't squeeze any information out of him before he left on horseback.

"Do you know where my son went?" She wondered if Mademoiselle McCarthy had any clue about what was happening.

Colleen shook her head, then sipped her coffee. She kept glancing back at her child, asleep in a pile of bedding on the floor.

"Why did he have to leave to find Minetta?" Felicie asked. "I thought Mademoiselle Gerard was going to stay with you and help with the baby."

Colleen set down the cup and stared into the coffee for a few moments before answering. "I saw your son speaking with Laurent Bisset, and then he brought me to your home. That's all I know."

"Laurent Bisset? Do you have any idea what he and Jean Louis discussed?"

"No, Madame." She gave her a look of sympathy before studying her child.

Felicie exhaled and stared out the front window for a moment. While she believed Mademoiselle McCarthy, she had a sense something was wrong. She said a silent prayer for her son before following Colleen's gaze to the child on the floor.

"You loved Roussel Pinard, did you not?"

"Oh yes, Madame."

She waited for a beat before being as blunt as possible. "Do you know why the Montforts wanted to kill him?"

Mademoiselle McCarthy put a hand to her mouth. "How do you know? They're going to think I told you!"

The woman began to shake, looking as if she were getting ready to bolt, but Felicie took her hand. "Do not worry, Mademoiselle, it wasn't anything you said. When I learned that the Montforts ran the house where you worked, I thought they might be behind Monsieur Pinard's death."

Mademoiselle McCarthy dabbed her eyes with her sleeve, her hands still shaking. Felicie handed her a white lace handkerchief.

"Was Roussel planning to take you away from their...business operation on Gallatin Street? Is that why they had him killed?"

Colleen just stared into space. Felicie didn't think she was ever going to answer, but eventually, she gave a slight nod.

"When we saw each other that night, Roussel said he planned to take me away and head north to Chicago. The Montforts would not allow that. I feel it's all my fault."

Colleen scratched at the palm of her hand as if punishing herself. She had a skin disorder, but she seemed unusually savage in her scratching.

Felicie cupped her hands over hers. "You can't blame yourself for what the Montforts have done."

"The Montforts pretend to be upstanding citizens," Colleen said, "but they collect information on all sorts of people and use it against them. They had damaging information on Laurent, which they used to force him to set fires."

"Like the fire at our stable?"

Colleen nodded.

"But why us?"

"Because the Montforts hate you. That's all they need to justify any action."

"What information did they have on Laurent to force him to do such a thing?"

"He was a bounty jumper. They also used this information to pressure him into blackmailing Father Maistre because they knew about the priest's money scandals in his past."

Felicie leaned back, amazed at the scope of the Montforts' dealings. "They had something on almost everybody, it seems."

"That's how they operate. Then they forced me to set fire to Father Maistre's church when he stopped paying blackmail money. I fled from them because I had a feeling that if I stayed in that place much longer, I woulda showed up dead in Cemetery Number 1."

"Like Roussel?"

"Like Roussel. The Montforts didn't kill him themselves. They never get their own hands dirty. They hired two monsters—Bricktop Jackson and John Miller."

All of these stories of murder and blackmail, one after another, suddenly overwhelmed Felicie. For the first time, she realized the depth of the danger facing Colleen McCarthy—and now Minetta and her son.

■■■

Jean Louis paid his fifty cents to enter hell and stepped through the swinging doors into Bill Swan's Fireproof Coffee-House. It was packed from wall to wall, the noise and steam accosting Jean Louis from all sides. Bill Swan, the proprietor, was a former member of the

Live Oak Boys, offering free drinks to gang members in exchange for protection.

The place teetered on the edge of chaos. Jean Louis watched one man lose control and shatter a glass against a wall, but one of the Live Oak Boys slammed an oak club against the back of his legs, at knee level, and the man crumpled. They dragged him out by the legs and probably rifled through his pockets before kicking him into oblivion.

Jean Louis was happy there was no sign of the Montforts or Laurent's father because they would probably be the only ones here who could recognize him and realize why he had come. He kept his slouch hat tipped over his eyes just in case.

Swan may have called the place a coffee shop, but the drink of choice was beer, and it flowed like floodwater. The main barroom was dark, even on a bright afternoon like this, and it was stifling hot. He noticed a wide staircase leading up to the second level, guarded by a Live Oak Boy. Most likely, Minetta was being held upstairs. Jean Louis carried his pistol and a hunting knife, fully prepared for a fight.

People began spilling out the back door because it was almost time for the national rat-killing match. He hoped that the Live Oak guard at the staircase would also head out the back door, but no such luck.

Jean Louis followed the crush of people flowing outside, hoping there might be an external entrance to the second floor. He found himself in a small outdoor arena, surrounded by several rows of bleachers.

Most people chose to stand, packing themselves around a small pit, about twelve feet long and ten feet wide. A wooden wall, about three feet high, enclosed the square pit. It had a twelve-inch overhang to keep dogs from leaping out of the arena and tearing into the spectators.

Scanning the crowd, Jean Louis still found no sign of the Montforts, but that was not surprising. They put on a respectable front and would probably not dare to be seen at such an event; they were perhaps holed away in a room somewhere, monitoring the proceedings in secret. However, he did catch sight of Bricktop Jackson and John Miller. It was hard to miss the giant woman with flaming red hair and the man with a chain and ball for an arm. Jean Louis retreated into the crowd.

"The first dog belongs to Thomas Jennings of New York!" announced Swan, who acted as referee and stood in the center of the dirt-floor pit. "His dog, Modoc, is twenty-three pounds and is known to have killed twelve full-grown rats per minute for five straight minutes. In case y'all can't do your own matriculatin', that's sixty dead rats in five minutes!"

Modoc trotted into the arena to the sound of whoops and clapping. He was a bull terrier, a muscular mutt with the typical egg-shaped, white head and strange, triangular-shaped eyes. He looked to have jaws as strong as steel machinery.

The dog's large, pink tongue dangled as Mr. Jennings of New York strode over to a row of large burlap sacks, which were lined up on the first row of the bleachers. He heaved one of them over his shoulder like some demented Saint Nicholas, the fabric moving and rippling.

When Swan gave the signal, Jennings untied the top and turned the sack upside down, spilling out dozens of fat rats. As the rodents tumbled, they scattered like a panicked mob, darting for an escape route but running into the walls that surrounded the pit.

Modoc herded the rats into a squirming heap of brown fur, pouncing whenever one of them made a break for it. It took only a single bite to kill each rodent. Modoc became a killing machine, as one rat would take a chance and leave the pack, only to have its body broken in a split second. Jean Louis could hear the rats' bodies snap from where he stood. The crowd was stirred into a bloodlust frenzy, turning the place into a miniature Roman circus.

Once every last rat was sprawled out on the slaughtering ground, the rat master took any potential survivors to a table with a circle on top. About a half dozen rats were placed inside the ring, and Swan poked each rat three times with a stick. Four rats were indeed dead, but Jean Louis watched as two mangled creatures struggled to crawl away. One of them stopped moving early on while the other bloody bugger inched its way across the surface, smearing a trail of red behind. When this rat managed to crawl out of the circle, the crowd applauded; the referee declared the valiant vermin officially alive, keeping it from being credited to Modoc's kill count.

As the crowd waited for the next dog, a stocky man bounded into the pit. He wore a purple cravat and a jacket that looked like it had been mauled by a terrier. It was time for a bit of entertainment, so this clown opened one of the sacks and reached in his bare hand, which drew a screech from a lady in the crowd. He plucked out a rat and swung it around his head by its tail, like a lasso, and acted like he was going to let it fly into the audience, which caused an entire row to duck. The man then buttoned up his coat and started stuffing it with rats, and he began squirming and dancing around the pit, looking like a man with a terrible itch. The crowd roared and hooted until the clown finally undid his coat buttons and out popped six rats.

As Jean Louis watched the crazed behavior of the crowd, an idea came to him with complete clarity. He glanced around the arena, noticing how mesmerized the people were by this human rat catcher and the canine versions.

Once the crowd was utterly captivated by the next rat massacre, he clamped his hunting knife between his jaws and crawled beneath the bleachers. When he neared the sacks, he sliced the back of one of them, much like a doctor making an incision, and he turned it around, so the gaping hole faced outward, toward the arena. Rats poured out like maggots squirming from an open wound.

It took only two seconds before the screaming began.

The sack contained at least one hundred rats, which poured into the stands. Women screeched, and men bellowed as vermin scurried in all directions. People leaped to their feet and ran, making it sound like a herd of elephants was passing overhead. The bleachers seemed on the verge of collapse. Grabbing another sack of rats and tucking it under his arm, Jean Louis ran for his life.

When he came out from beneath the bleachers, he saw that the arena had become a frenzied swarm of people. Some men enjoyed the sport and took to chasing down rats or bashing them with their canes.

Jean Louis had only ten feet to cross from the bleachers to the door leading back into the coffee house. Once inside, he untied the sack, pouring out more rodents.

"Rats!" Jean Louis darted into the main room of the coffee house. Like some mad Pied Piper, the rats streamed behind him into the main room, scattering toward all corners. A couple of drunks danced around the room, trying to stomp on the racing rodents, while the Live Oak Boy who guarded the staircase to the second floor began chasing them with the oak club in his hands, bashing the vermin and laughing hysterically. With the guard occupied, Jean Louis bounded up the staircase.

Upstairs, women were running down the hall as if the place were on fire. Jean Louis opened door after door after door, screaming about the rats at the top of his lungs, and moved down the long, second-floor hallway. He almost reached the end when he opened a door and finally found who he came for—Minetta. She had been tied to a chair and gagged.

Before ducking into the room, he saw John Miller's looming figure at the end of the hallway. When Jean Louis realized he had been spotted, his throat went dry. John Miller rushed toward him, but the hallway was clogged with screaming women. It was like trying to run against a torrent of floodwater.

Jean Louis had time, but not much. He slipped inside Minetta's room, pushed a dresser in front of the door, and went to work on her gag and bindings. Thankfully, the knots were poor, and he had her free in no time.

But "no time" was also what they had left. John Miller had begun trying to wedge the door open.

"Can we get out the window?" Jean Louis glanced from the door to her worried eyes.

"The bedding." Minetta nodded, rushing to twist a sheet into a narrow rope as Jean Louis pushed the bed closer to the window.

Jean Louis tied one end of the fabric to the bed's metal frame while Minetta tossed the other end outside. Meanwhile, Miller had started bashing the door with his chain and ball. If he got inside, Jean Louis's skull would be next to take a beating. The vision of the rat being clubbed flashed before him as he shook off the sense that it could be him next.

"Go, go, go!" Jean Louis helped Minetta onto the bedsheet rope, and she slid down with impressive speed, like a fireman down a pole.

By this time, Miller hammered a hole through the door and reached through, fumbling for the lock. Jean Louis snatched up a fireplace poker and whacked his hand, probably breaking several bones. There was no way now that this guy was going to let him live.

As the door splintered, Jean Louis raced to the window. He grabbed hold of the bedsheet, but before he could climb through the window, he looked up and saw Miller only a few feet away, swinging his chain and ball. He ducked as the missile whistled inches above his head, smashing the window instead of his skull.

Miller prepared to strike again, and Jean Louis had no choice but to drop the bedsheet and take evasive action. He leaped to the side but wasn't quite quick enough, and the ball crashed against his upper arm. It was a glancing blow, or his arm might have snapped. Still, it stung like the dickens.

Jean Louis eyed the open door, but Miller cut off that path, backing him into a corner. Miller swung the ball and chain over his head and closed in on him. A split second before Miller struck, Jean Louis snatched a lamp from a nearby end table and held it out. As the ball and chain spun around its base, Miller found himself weighed down by the lamp, which was wrapped in the tangled chain.

Miller roared his frustration and began unwinding the chain from the base, giving Jean Louis enough time to escape. The last thing he saw before lowering himself down the makeshift rope was the bruiser rushing the window, swinging his chain. Miller hadn't had the time to completely unwind the chain from the lamp, so he attempted to hurl the entire light at Jean Louis. It smashed through the window, showering glass on the brim of his hat, as Jean Louis slid toward the ground. He looked up just as Miller stuck his head out the window, hurling down curses.

"My horse is out front!" Jean Louis motioned Minetta forward.

Hand in hand, they sprinted toward the front of the coffee house. Jean Louis glanced over his shoulder as Miller ducked back inside, probably on his way to cut them off. Jean Louis's hands were shaking so badly when he reached his horse that he had a tough time untying the reins from the hitching post.

"Hurry, hurry, hurry, hurry!" Minetta moved from foot to foot, wringing her hands.

"If you stop screaming in my ears, I will!"

"He's coming!"

Reins finally freed, he heaved Minetta on top of the horse. The thug exited the front of the coffee house and spotted him. Even worse, Jean Louis noticed that Bricktop Jackson also emerged, wielding her double-sided knife. Seeing a rat scurry by his feet, Jean Louis plucked it from the ground and heaved it at Miller. The rodent missile caught him squarely in the face, buying Jean Louis just enough time to mount his horse.

The man with the wicked arm flung his ball and chain at the back of Jean Louis's steed, hoping to stun the animal. But the weapon whistled through empty air, and the horse took off down Levee Street.

Jean Louis looked over his shoulder with a sigh of relief, but they weren't in the clear, not by a long shot. Their two pursuers were already leaping onto horses and taking off in pursuit.

43

The 1st and 3rd Regiments pulled back. They had thrown a thousand bodies at the fortified bluffs, resulting in hundreds of casualties. At least that's what it looked like to John Crowder as he surveyed the universe of death around him. There seemed to be as many bodies on the ground as there were retreating.

"You think I'm gonna die, John?"

Lieutenant Moss had been talking of death for several minutes straight, and John gave him the same reassurance each time.

"You ain't dyin' on me. Trust me on this. You ain't dyin'."

Lieutenant Moss was still stretched out on the ground because he was afraid the Confederates would start taking target practice at him if he sat up. Crowder continued to press the blue cloth to the bleeding hole in his belly. The bullet must not have hit any major arteries, or he would already be dead. He hoped and prayed he'd stemmed the bleeding.

As the black troops retreated across the killing ground, Crowder took off his hat and waved it, calling out for help like a marooned sailor waving to a passing ship. He caught the eyes of a pair of black soldiers.

"Take him first." Crowder motioned toward Moss.

"Is he even alive?" one of the soldiers asked. They hadn't even noticed Moss lying there like a corpse.

"I'm still kickin'," said Moss, opening his eyes.

The two soldiers helped Moss to his feet, each of them wrapping an arm around him. In addition to the piece of wood in his back, Moss's left leg may have broken because he hopped away, flanked by his two human crutches, screaming in pain.

After they left and Crowder was alone, he waved his hat again, trying to draw more help. When a bullet plucked the ground, kicking up a puff of dirt only a couple of feet away, it dawned on him that waving his hat also looked like an invitation to be shot at by Rebel sharpshooters.

"You need a ride, John?" A voice came from behind him.

Crowder twisted to get a look, never happier to see Levi. In awe, Crowder laughed. Levi looked completely unscathed.

"You get it in the gut?" Levi nodded toward Crowder's makeshift bandage, asking the obvious. "Here, let me carry y'all."

Crowder braced. Any amount of jostling would spasm his back like someone was taking a handful of his muscles and twisting them like taffy.

While Levi was a wiry man, he was stronger than Crowder supposed. Levi nodded to prepare Crowder before crouching and putting both arms under him. When he stood, doing a deadweight lift, Crowder let out a strained moan.

"When I get y'all back to camp, I'll get ya a handful of gum moss and corn shucks, a thimbleful of anise seed, all mixed up with rainwater." Levi held him and strolled off of the battlefield, as calmly as taking a stroll down Canal Street. "That'll clear any bad blood you might have."

That was the last thing John Crowder remembered before fainting from the pain.

▪▪▪

Willis Terrill found General Dwight sloshed and seated on the ground, leaning against a tree. General Dwight was a stocky man with a round head and a hairline in as much retreat as his troops. The black soldiers were pulling back from the battlefield, but it was Terrill's opinion that the units should not have been sent to the slaughterhouse in the first place. The Rebel fortification was impossible to breach, especially without artillery support.

But Dwight wouldn't know any of that. He was bleary-eyed and drunk and positioned nowhere near the battlefield.

Colonel Nelson, who oversaw the 3rd Louisiana Guards, had sent Terrill, his aide, to report the horror—and the futility—of this approach.

"Colonel Nelson requests permission to withdraw," Terrill told the general.

General Dwight stuck a hand inside his blue jacket, Napoleon style—although he wasn't doing it to strike a glorious pose. He was scratching his belly. The general stared at Terrill as his drunken mind worked overtime to analyze the information.

"Tell them to charge again." General Dwight waved a hand.

Terrill blinked in astonishment. "But, sir, both regiments have been cut up badly and have lost half of their men."

"I said, tell them to charge again!" General Dwight squirmed on the ground, threatening to stand, but evidently decided it took too much energy. He waved his hand once again, like a drunken orchestra conductor. "Let the impetuosity of the charge counterbalance the paucity of numbers."

"But it is impossible for them to take the fortifications, sir."

"Do not tell me what is impossible!"

Once again, General Dwight moved to stand, but instead, he reached for the bottle at his side. Terrill couldn't believe this was the man who had fought so gallantly at the Battle of Williamsburg one year earlier. Dwight, a colonel then, lost half of his command in the battle and was left for dead. He only lived because he was discovered by Confederates and taken prisoner until released in an exchange.

Surely, a man with that experience understood what he was telling these regiments to do. Why would he give such a command?

"Tell them to charge!" Dwight waved a finger in the air. "Tell Colonel Nelson, I shall consider that he has accomplished nothing unless he takes those guns!"

"Yes, sir," said Terrill before retreating in the face of the general's fury.

Terrill had no choice but to relay the orders, so he re-crossed the creek to give Colonel Nelson the dire news.

"Are you sure you heard correctly?" Nelson asked.

"Absolutely. I told him the troops had been cut in half, but he insisted on another charge."

The colonel sighed. The day was about to get even bloodier.

44

Jean Louis raced his horse down Levee Street, which ran along the river, just where the Mississippi made a mighty big bend. Minetta had a tight hold on him from behind, and he kicked in his heels, driving his horse forward. People in their path scattered to all sides.

Just behind were their two indefatigable pursuers—John Miller and Bricktop Jackson, riding on separate steeds.

Jean Louis made a sharp left, his horse kicking up dust as it galloped into the French Market; he hoped to lose Miller and Bricktop in the chaos and clutter of the busy area. But as they shot into the market square, a clothes pole man stepped right into their path, just as he was shouting, "Cloooooothes pooooles!"

Balanced on his left shoulder were a bundle of wooden saplings, each about ten feet long and trimmed cleanly of branches. When the man caught sight of the charging horse, his eyes got very wide, and his "Cloooooothes pooooles" transitioned into a drawn out, "Oooooooooooh noooo!"

"Watch out!" Minetta screamed into Jean Louis's ear as if he needed to be told.

The man froze, which was a good thing. If he had moved, he might have stepped into their path. Jean Louis veered his horse right, and his left leg clipped the very end of the clothes pole bundle, spinning the man from his feet.

The close call and quick riding maneuver cost them precious time. Shooting a glance over his shoulder, Jean Louis could see Miller closing in and preparing to whip his chain and ball to split their skulls.

Miller gained ground until he was almost beside them, and the black, baseball-sized missile whistled toward Jean Louis's head, missing him by no more than five inches. In desperation, Jean Louis rode straight into the market, a long, narrow structure that contained over a hundred stalls where merchants sold food, flowers, and baskets.

People scattered, tables overturned, and one man dove headfirst onto a table loaded with clams to avoid being trampled. Miller and Bricktop were still right behind him, one on each side. Once again, Miller began to twirl the ball and chain above his head like a deadly, steel lasso.

Jean Louis leaned over his horse's neck to avoid the ball that orbited above Miller's head like a black moon, with Minetta leaning as flat as she could on his back. He shifted his horse and sideswiped Miller's steed, sending it to the right—and into a stall where slabs of raw meat hung from hooks. Miller's chain, still spinning, wrapped around one of the hooks, yanking him from his horse and hurling him into a side of bloody beef.

With Minetta still holding tight, Jean Louis shot out of the other end of the market-house, making a sharp right when he reached St. Louis Street.

"She's still on us!" Minetta shouted over her shoulder.

Jean Louis glanced back and saw that Bricktop had lost ground but was still in sight, her red hair flying wildly like flames sprouting out of her head. With Jean Louis's horse tiring, he had to lose

Bricktop by deception, not speed. Up ahead, on the left, loomed Cemetery Number 1, the perfect maze.

When Bricktop fired her gun, Minetta glanced back to see the woman trying to aim from a galloping horse. It was a clumsy attempt and a waste of bullets.

Jean Louis directed his horse left down Basin Street and raced along a tall wall that enclosed the entire cemetery. They finally approached the entrance and thundered through the gate.

A jumble of aboveground tombs—tall structures, typically five to eight feet high—stood on all sides of the center alley, giving them the perfect cover as Jean Louis steered down a narrow path to the right. Once they were clear of the main alleyway, he leaped from the horse before it even came to a complete stop.

After Minetta jumped from his steed into his arms, they left the animal, losing themselves in the maze on foot. They stood a better chance on their own rather than dragging along a noisy, seven-hundred-pound horse.

Together, they weaved their way through the jumble of tombs, turning left, then right, then left again—a ghastly maze. They didn't even pause to see if Bricktop was behind them until they reached a tightly packed group of tombs, each of them at least seven feet high. This was a good spot to pause, stay out of view, and catch their breath.

"You have any idea where we are?" Minetta panted when they finally stopped running.

"No, but hopefully, that means Bricktop doesn't either," he whispered.

They went quiet and listened for the sounds of pursuit. They heard the stomp of horse hooves, but was it Bricktop's or theirs? Was she on foot or horseback?

Jean Louis pulled out his gun, and carefully they pressed on. If they could find one of the cemetery exits, they could lose her for good. They passed by a large tomb, where Mary, the mother of Jesus, peered down on them. When they reached a stretch of shorter crypts, they crouched and listened, but there were no sounds except for the distant shouts of street vendors and some squawking birds.

"If we keep going straight," Jean Louis whispered, "I think we'll come back to the Center Alley."

"From there, we could work our way to the exit on Conti Street."

"Good idea. The exit onto Tremé is probably too far away."

They continued moving stealthily among the tombs. When they reached the Conti alley, they crouched further to stay hidden behind the profile of a lower platform. Jean Louis peeked around the corner with a sigh of relief. There was no sign of the red-headed killer.

They snuck into the alley running along the wall facing Conti Street. Just off to the right, not too far away, stood a massive tomb for the Portuguese Benevolent Society. This new tomb had 24 vaults wrapped around it on all sides, like a chest of drawers in stone. When they reached it, the Conti exit would be just to the left.

As they rushed forward, someone stepped from behind a sarcophagus. There stood Bricktop in the center of the alley, legs shoulder-width apart, aiming her gun with two steady hands. Jean Louis and Minetta changed course as the gun went off, blasting the edge of a tomb just to their left.

"Back to the Basin Street exit." Jean Louis tugged Minetta, dashing toward the Center Alley. All the while, Bricktop ran on a parallel path through the forest of tombs.

"Hold on," Jean Louis panted, pulling Minetta back as they neared the edge of the alley.

They huddled behind a tall tomb with a triangular top, which reminded Jean Louis of a miniature church. That's when he saw a flash of red hair down the alley. He aimed and fired, his bullet bouncing off a stone a few feet from where she disappeared.

Not even close. Jean Louis pressed against the vault and steadied his breathing. He only had a couple of bullets left. He had to be sure he could hit Bricktop, which meant getting close.

"Stay here," he whispered, turning to Minetta, but she was gone. Jean Louis's heart dropped.

"Minetta," he hissed, moving along the narrow path, squeezing between tombs.

When there was no sign of her, he hoped she was heading back to the Conti Street exit, leaving him to fight it out with Bricktop near the Center Alley. Splitting up was a smart move, although it also took her away from the protective cover of his revolver.

Jean Louis couldn't leave the cemetery without knowing that Minetta was safely away. But where was she? He looked at the different paths in front of him, torn about which way to go. He peeked around the corner into the Center Alley, looking to his left— and suddenly heard a sound coming from his right.

As Jean Louis ducked behind the tomb, he was relieved to see a funeral procession entering Center Alley from his right—near the Basin Street exit. Jean Louis thought about using the group for cover, but Bricktop would have no qualms about firing into the mourners to get at him.

An elderly black man in military dress led the procession with his sword raised. Behind him were three boys dressed in surplices, two carrying candlesticks, and the third held a large silver cross. Then followed the priest and the coffin, carried by four strong men. Six-foot-long white streamers came off both sides of the coffin and were held aloft by girls in white dresses. Last of all were men and women, the mourners, all carrying lighted candles and singing.

"I walk in the graveyard, I walk through the graveyard
To lay this body down;
I go to the judgment in the heat of the day
When I lay this body down;
And my soul and your soul will meet in the day
When I lay this body down."

Jean Louis left the narrow path, crouching as he darted among the vaults. Beads of sweat raced down his forehead, one cutting a course over the bridge of his nose. He couldn't stop worrying about where Minetta had gone.

He moved parallel to the funeral procession, which was off to his left, but their singing made it difficult to pinpoint Bricktop's location. That's when the singing stopped, and the screaming began.

He scooted as close to the Center Alley as possible, remaining hidden behind a seven-foot-tall vault. He could see flashes of clothing as mourners and singers scattered and screamed. Had Bricktop attacked the procession, like a wolf among sheep?

"Cailloux! Cailloux, show yourself!"

Then he heard the whimpering of a young girl.

He peered around the vault, horrified to discover a young black girl, who couldn't be more than ten years old, shivering in her white dress. Bricktop held a gun to her temple.

Jean Louis dropped his head, knowing he had no choice. He stood and stepped from behind the vault. "Let her go, Bricktop. She's just a child."

"I don't want to hurt her. I want to hurt *you*—and your betrothed, Mademoiselle Gerard."

Betrothed?

"I don't know where Mademoiselle Gerard has gone."

"And I don't believe you!"

Several of the men from the mourning procession tried to encircle Bricktop.

"Stay back!" She yanked the girl around like a doll, holding on to her collar with one hand—still pressing the gun to the child's temple with the other.

The men lifted their hands and retreated.

The minister, a stocky man with a deep voice, said, "Let the girl go."

"Shut up!" Bricktop waved the gun at him before jamming it

back to the girl's head. "Give yourself up, Cailloux, and the girl will be fine."

"All right, all right." Jean Louis placed his revolver on the top of a short, squat vault.

When one of the men made a move to pick up the gun, Bricktop aimed at him. "Leave it there!"

The man hopped backward, arms up.

As Jean Louis took two slow steps toward Bricktop, various scenarios played out in his mind. If she shot him, would she really keep her word and free the girl? And if she let the child go, how was she planning to escape this angry mob after she killed him? Would the crowd be so thankful their girl was safe they'd let Bricktop flee? Or would they converge on Bricktop once the girl was out of harm's way?

Jean Louis watched Bricktop's eyes as they danced, her mind whirling.

She motioned to the crowd. "All of you move by that fence where I can see you."

The funeral mourners gathered by a low, black wrought-iron fence that encircled a parapet vault. Jean Louis figured Bricktop planned to shoot him, ditch the girl, and make a dash for her horse, which she had tied up near the cemetery entrance off Basin Street.

"Okay, Cailloux, move closer."

Jean Louis continued to move toward her one slow step at a time, unsure how to avoid a public execution. If he didn't sacrifice himself, the little girl would die. He knew Bricktop's reputation. She would have no qualms about shooting a girl.

"Where is Mademoiselle Gerard?" Bricktop raised her chin, sending him an evil eye. "I want both of you."

"I have no idea," Jean Louis insisted.

"You lie!"

"It's the truth!"

"Tell her, man! Tell her where to find the woman," said one of the men from the procession.

Jean Louis looked at him helplessly. "I really don't know where she is. She ran off."

"Come close." Bricktop edged back several feet, closer to her horse and the exit, never taking her eyes off Jean Louis. "Close enough that I can't miss."

Jean Louis glanced at Bricktop's famed knife, tucked into the belt cinched around her ample waist. The knife had a five-inch blade on either end with a German silver grip in the middle.

"Maybe you'd prefer to stab me," Jean Louis said. "I hear you're pretty good with the knife. How many men have you killed with it?"

Keep her talking.

"Move it!" Bricktop's face flushed almost as red as her hair.

Jean Louis quickened his pace. He was only about fifteen feet away now.

"Is this close enough? You can hit me from here, can't you?"

"Closer!"

He obeyed. He moved within twelve feet.

"How about this? Can you shoot me now?"

"Closer!"

She was really taking no chances.

As Jean Louis took one step closer, he saw the ghostly flash of a figure moving from behind one of the parapet tombs. The rustle of fabric and the gleam of a sword had Bricktop spinning to face the commotion. In a split-second decision, Jean Louis rushed forward and yanked the little girl away. At the same moment, Minetta—who had leaped from behind a tomb—drove a sword into Bricktop's side.

Bricktop roared and tried to shoot Minetta in the face, but Jean Louis shoved her massive frame, knocking her to the ground. As Bricktop stumbled, the gun fired, the bullet ricocheting off a marble tomb.

Minetta swung the sword at Bricktop, slicing off some fingers from her gun hand, leaving Jean Louis to scoop up the weapon. And while he should have put a bullet in her head right then and there, he paused, unsure whether he could execute an unarmed woman.

His indecision gave Bricktop the seconds needed to make a break for her horse near the Basin Street exit. Jean Louis aimed at the fleeing redhead, but he couldn't bring himself to shoot a woman in the back.

As Bricktop hobbled toward her horse, bleeding from her side and hand, Minetta shouted out at her. "Jackson! If you think you're safe from the Montforts, then check out the room in the house where they keep the devil masks!"

Jean Louis had no idea what Minetta was talking about, but it certainly caught Bricktop's attention. She turned and gaped, her face turning white.

"The Montforts keep files inside the devil heads! Look inside the Dagon mask, and you'll find a file on yourself—and Miller!"

Bricktop closed her mouth and narrowed her eyes but said nothing.

"Don't believe me? Look inside the Dagon mask!"

Bricktop hurled a curse at Minetta and mounted her horse, galloping for the exit.

Minetta growled in frustration, probably wondering if her words had penetrated Bricktop's thick skull. Jean Louis's eyes went to the sword in Minetta's hand, still red with blood.

"Where in the world did you get that blade from?"

The elderly man in the military uniform stepped up to Minetta and bowed. "Thank you, Mademoiselle. I couldn't have done better myself."

"And thank you, Monsieur, for the loan of your sword." Minetta offered it back with a nod.

He pushed it toward her. "It is my gift to you. You saved our girl."

Minetta nodded wearily and tried to smile but was soon shaking uncontrollably. Thinking she was in shock, Jean Louis put an arm around her and drew her away from the mourners. Soon, he spotted his horse wandering through the graves and led her in that direction, leaving the mourners to go back to their burial.

Strangely enough, after everything they'd experienced, one thing continued to echo in his head. It was a word spoken by Bricktop to describe Minetta.

Betrothed.

45

Trees shattered overhead, but the Native Guards remained relatively unscathed, crouched in the willow forest and firing futile shots at distant Confederates. Rebel shells ripped through the canopy, splintering wood and showering branches upon them. But it certainly beat rushing into the wide open, where their human limbs would do the splintering rather than tree limbs.

"Why we even botherin' to shoot?" a private by the name of Hawkins asked Levi. "Our bullets ain't got a chance of hitting anything but dead air."

"It's all for show. It's all for show." Levi tore into a cartridge and began pouring powder. He paused to laugh hysterically. It was true. Their shooting was all a ruse.

Levi had witnessed the day's confrontation between Colonel Nelson and Lieutenant Colonel Henry Finnegass, a white man from the 3rd Regiment of the Native Guards. Finnegass told the colonel "he would be damned" if he would lead his men to slaughter yet again. Nelson pointed out that General Dwight, their drunken leader, had given a direct order to attack again, but Finnegass wouldn't budge.

"General Dwight needs to hear our guns goin' off to be convinced we done followed orders, so we're given' him a show, free of charge," Levi said. He turned, with a big grin, and began firing from the forest, knowing full well that the Confederates were too far away.

About the only thing they might hit from this distance was a passing bird, but General Dwight wouldn't know that. He was too far away to see what they were doing but close enough to hear their guns going off.

Hawkins lowered his voice to a whisper. "Ain't that a court-martialing offense, not attackin' on order?"

"Ain't no skin off our noses." Levi shrugged. "It's Nelson who might get court-martialed...or Finnegass...or both. Besides, we *are* attackin'—just not out in the open."

A cannonball ripped into the willow tree above them, and a branch, heavy enough to knock out a man cold, came crashing down with a thunderous roar. Levi barely dodged it, but one of the smaller branches put a four-inch scratch across Hawkins' cheek.

"When we get back to camp, make yourself a tea outta crushed cockroaches," Levi said, pointing at the red slash. The cut wasn't too deep, but it would soon start stinging. "A tablespoon of roach tea every hour—that'll take care of any infection, boy."

Hawkins touched the cut and winced. "Ain't we shot enough to convince Dwight we been attackin'?"

"Gotta give 'em a good show. Gotta give that old drunk his money's worth." Levi slapped Hawkins on the shoulder and proceeded to reload.

■■■

Lieutenant Moss had become hardened to the sight of arms and legs piled up outside the medical tent. The doctors had been chopping off limbs and piling them like firewood. The stench was pungent, and the flies were thick.

Moss studied his bandaged leg, thankful he had both limbs. The doctor had considered taking his leg to be on the safe side. Amputation was the operation of choice.

Leaning on a single crutch, Moss hobbled into a large tent, a dismal house of pain where several ailing men were sprawled out on bloodstained cots. The stench of day-old blood was powerful. He spotted Lieutenant Crowder on the far side of the tent and tottered over to him. There were no chairs for visitors, so Moss eased himself onto the ground. His wound burned, sending hot trails of pain down his back as he sat. Crowder was asleep, and for a moment, Moss was afraid he was no longer alive. Leaning over, he placed his hand near Crowder's mouth and could feel a soft puff of air between his slightly parted lips.

Moss decided he would pray for John Crowder. He felt guilty for the way he had treated him over the past few months. He never felt comfortable tormenting this young officer—the youngest of officers—but he did it to impress Captain Lewis.

Captain Lewis was among the missing, and Moss wondered if he had become food for buzzards. No one knew for sure who was still on the battlefield because no crews had yet been sent to retrieve the bodies of the black soldiers. As a result, many were unaccounted for, including Captain André Cailloux.

Moss began to pray in whispered tones, turning to fragments of Psalms taught to him as a child. "Though a host should encamp against us, our hearts shall not fear: though war should rise against us, we'll be confident. You shall set us upon a rock, for my soul trusteth in thee. In the shadow of thy wings, give us refuge until these calamities be overpast."

He believed that the Lord had delivered him from destruction, and John Crowder had been the angel that God used. If John had not called out for help to both God and their fellow soldiers, he might still be out on the field, melting in the sun. He was ashamed of his cowardice on the battlefield. He had never been so terrified of simply rising to his feet. He remembered thinking that if he moved so much as a muscle, the Confederates would spot him and shoot him dead.

Only Crowder's prayers had calmed him.

Moss had finished reciting all of the bits of Psalms he knew by heart when he noticed John Crowder staring at him, eyes wide open.

"Thank you, Lieutenant," John spoke. Barely audible. "Keep praying."

So Lieutenant Moss started back in with the Psalms, only this time he prayed much louder. When his prayer ended, John's eyes were partially closed. The young soldier began to say something, but it was very faint.

"What did you say, John?" Moss leaned in closer.

"Liser. Tell Liser I had hoped to marry her."

It took a moment for the name to sink in. *Liser*. It was the name of the slave girl that John Crowder had fallen in love with. Moss knew this because he and Lewis read the letters that Crowder had written to Liser and his mother. They had had a good laugh over them. Now, the memory of their mockery burned him as badly as the pain in his leg.

"I will write to Liser and tell her that you *will* marry her."

A slight smile appeared on Crowder's face. "Not sure she wants to marry a corpse."

"You ain't dyin' on me. Trust me on this. You ain't dyin'." Moss used the exact words that John had spoken to him on the battlefield.

Crowder must have recognized them because his eyes widened just a bit, in earnest. He glanced down as if he were trying to get a glimpse of Moss's leg.

"Yes, I still got my leg attached," Moss said. "Thanks to you."

Crowder smiled again. "Wish they could amputate my belly. But removing my midsection would make me two feet shorter."

Moss found himself at a loss for words. He stared into space.

"The battle..." Crowder started but began mumbling something else.

"What did you say?" Moss leaned in once more.

"The battle...Did we take Port Hudson?"

Moss paused. "Yes, we did. The Rebel fortifications came down."

Crowder stared at him with glistening intensity, mumbling, "You don't have to lie."

Was it that obvious? Moss thought that telling him the fort had fallen would prove that he hadn't been injured in vain.

"Please don't lie," Crowder repeated.

Moss sighed. "Port Hudson did not fall. Not yet at least, but it will."

"Did we attack again?" Crowder asked. "Did more friends die?"

This time, Moss did not have to lie to give him a shred of good news. He moved within a few inches of John's ears and whispered, "No one else had to die. General Dwight ordered another attack, but..." Moss looked around to make sure no one was eavesdropping. "No attack was made. Colonel Nelson told us not to."

Moss didn't spell out all the details—how Nelson had told the troops to fire from the protection of the willows, even though he knew they couldn't hit Confederates from so far away. As planned, General Dwight heard their guns going off and assumed his orders were being obeyed. No further charge was made by the black units. No more suicides.

An awkward silence fell again between Moss and Crowder. Moss sighed. How do you console a man you tormented for so many months?

Finally, he put a hand on Crowder's shoulder. "I'm sorry, John, for what we...for the things I said and did."

At first, Crowder didn't answer, and Moss was afraid he either didn't hear him or didn't want to absolve him of his sins.

But eventually, Crowder spoke. "Thank you. Tell the preacher. Tell him."

"Yes, I will tell the preacher my sins."

"No...Tell the preacher I want to talk to him."

The gravity of the situation suddenly dawned on him. Crowder *needed* a preacher.

Moss stood with a firm nod. "I will find him."

Moss couldn't move very fast with his injury, but he pushed his leg to its limit as he hurried from the tent. There was only one preacher and one priest attached to the two black regiments, but surely they were somewhere amidst the hospital tents. Moss popped his head into multiple tents and found repeated scenes of misery, but he didn't see the preacher until he checked the row of men laid out under a sycamore tree.

"Reverend, Lieutenant John Crowder needs you," he panted, doing his best to catch his breath.

The preacher, who was holding a soldier's hand, glanced up at Moss. "I will be there shortly." He looked back down at the soldier—a bearded man with one arm.

"No. He needs you now, Reverend."

The preacher looked at Moss once more, taken aback by the force of his words.

"I said I'll be there soon."

"Soon may not be soon enough. *Now!*"

"I am tending to several hundred soldiers, lieutenant—"

"*Reverend, now!*"

Moss was determined not to let down Crowder. If Crowder died before the preacher could hear his final words, he would never forgive this man. He would never forgive himself.

Moss thought about going for his weapon and threatening the preacher if he didn't come immediately. But the fellow must have sensed that he was determined—or insane. He finally rose to his feet and snarled, "Take me to him."

Moss rushed back through camp, his leg stabbing with every footfall, and he prayed that Crowder would still be alive. The preacher seemed to soften when he entered the tent and saw the young officer so close to death.

He crouched beside Crowder, took his hand, and said, "Let his portion be with Abraham, Isaac, and Jacob, with Job and David, with the prophets and apostles, with martyrs and all thy holy saints, in the arms of Christ, in the bosom of felicity, in the Kingdom of God to eternal ages."

When the preacher knelt down close to Crowder to hear his confession, Lieutenant Moss quietly exited the tent to give them privacy.

When he reentered the tent, about fifteen minutes later, John Crowder, the youngest officer on the field, was dead.

46

Madame and Monsieur Montfort made a bundle of money at the rat-killing competition, but not nearly as much as planned. Having an entire sack of rats released into the stands has a way of discouraging patrons from hanging around and betting. An entire round of rat-killing had to be canceled because they had lost too many rodents in the frenzy. While the spectators had a jolly time, smashing rats with canes and clubs, it cost Madame and Monsieur Montfort money. To make matters worse, Minetta Gerard had escaped in the chaos.

"Bricktop and Miller better catch Cailloux and that Gerard wench, or I will see them flogged," said Madame Montfort as she and her husband entered their home. She was counting on Bricktop and Miller to inflict the severest of penalties. They moved through the foyer toward the main staircase.

"I am not confident that Bricktop and Miller will get the job done properly." Monsieur Montfort frowned, shrugging off his coat. "They haven't been as reliable of late. They are also becoming too dangerous and difficult to manage."

"You might be right. Perhaps we should have Bricktop and Miller killed once they take care of Cailloux and Minetta." Madame Mont-fort nodded with a stiff upper lip, pulling off her gloves.

"Put them down?" Monsieur Montfort inhaled, doing a double take. "But how? And who would dare do it?"

Monsieur and Madame Montfort certainly wouldn't be the ones. They never did their own dirty work, and they rarely made appear-ances on Gallatin Street—although her dense husband sometimes ventured down there during daylight hours to visit the women. That's how he happened to be spotted by the Caillouxs almost a year ago.

Stupid, stupid man.

She sometimes wondered if she should have her husband put down.

Madame Montfort carried her reticule, a purple handbag that matched her dress and had a golden drawstring. Inside was a consid-erable sum of money. They moved wheezing up the stairs to hide their latest earnings, for they stashed much of their cash-at-hand in one of the masks hanging on the wall—the Beelzebub mask. Her husband had suggested storing it in the disguise that represented Mammon, but that was much too obvious.

Madame Montfort clucked her tongue with a shake of her head. The praying mantises had it right. Once your husband has served his function, chew off his head.

Monsieur Montfort paused on the staircase to catch his breath. "Perhaps Bridget Fury could carry out the extermination of Bricktop and Miller. She is good with poisons."

"Bridget Fury has softened since her latest stint in prison." Madame Montfort pursed her lips in thought. "But she has also become much more manageable, so let me give it some thought."

As Madame Montfort unlocked the door, she noticed a few drops of what appeared to be blood on the threshold.

"What in the world...?" She stooped for a closer look, nudging the door open a little farther.

When she straightened back up and stared into the room, she

froze. Bricktop Jackson and John Miller stood by the roll-top desk, where a file was opened and spread across it.

Bricktop had cut into the mask of Dagon with her knife. Her dress was soaked red with blood, but she seemed oblivious to the wound that had saturated an eight-inch diameter patch of fabric. All of her attention was on the Montforts.

Bricktop and Miller glared. *They knew.*

"Now hold on one second," Monsieur Montfort said as if he could talk his way out of this.

The Montforts turned to run, but the two attackers were on them in seconds with their ball and chain and knife. Two more rats were exterminated.

■■■

Felicie saw the newspaper in Jean Louis's hands, and her heart nearly stopped. He came to the house with an undertaker's look on his face.

"Have they posted the lists?" she asked.

"No lists. The government's keeping out most news about Port Hudson until the siege is over."

Felicie nodded. The paper published lists of the dead and injured in the aftermath of major battles. But although there hadn't been any solid news, there was no shortage of rumors about the fighting at Port Hudson. She didn't sleep more than a few minutes in the night, her mind running away with every imaginable worry.

"Is there something more in the paper about Monsieur and Madame Montfort?"

"Yes, another article," he said.

This brightened Felicie's mind. She knew it was a sin to glory in gore, but she was immensely relieved when she learned that the Montforts had been found murdered in their home. Bludgeoned and stabbed, over and over and over. It didn't have to be so horrific to satisfy her sense of justice. A simple, painless poison would have been enough to ease her mind that the Montforts were no longer a threat.

"But there is something else." Jean Louis took her by the arm and led her from the front room to the dining room. "I want to be the first to show you." He ushered her to a chair, adding, "Sit."

Suddenly, her heart was galloping again. Her son looked so deadly serious.

"I will not sit. You're scaring me, Jean Louis."

"Please sit."

"I will not." She stood firm.

"Please." His eyes pleaded.

Now her heart was flying out of control, and she unconsciously placed her right hand on her son's shoulder to steady herself. Why was he scaring her so badly if the paper hadn't published lists of the dead or any other news about Port Hudson?

"They did have one item," he said.

Feeling the shiver of a sudden chill, she lowered herself into a chair, and Jean Louis spread out the newspaper on the table in front of her. It was a copy of *L'Union*, which was published by pro-emancipation activists. The name "Cailloux" leaped from the page. The headline said that Captain Cailloux was a hero.

Too terrified to read, she looked up at her son, who had tears building in his eyes.

No, no, no! Felicie didn't want a hero for a husband. She let her eyes fall on the paper for only a moment, taking in one sentence.

"In Captain Cailloux, the cause of the Union and freedom has lost a valuable friend."

That's it. That's all she could read.

Her hands began shaking uncontrollably. As Jean Louis crouched to put his arms around her, Felicie covered her mouth, thinking she would be sick. Her body revolted on all fronts. First, came the shakes, then sickness, and now, the sense of heaviness, like a black cannonball roosting in her core and pulling her through the floor.

"He died a hero, they say," Jean Louis whispered, still rocking her in his arms.

"I can read!" She pushed at his chest.

"I'm sorry."

"Don't! Don't say a word! And if you tell me he's a hero again, I'll scream!"

Jean Louis didn't say anything more. Instead, he tightened his arms, comforting her the best he could.

"This cannot be right," she said. "They make mistakes. Papers make mistakes."

It was true. When the papers published lists, it was not unusual to list an injured soldier as being dead or a dead soldier as being wounded. Her eyes drifted to the article. But this was much more than a name on a list. This was an entire story.

"They got it wrong." She shook her head. "This is somebody else. Not André."

She pulled away from Jean Louis, raging as she jumped to her feet and walloped a vase of flowers, sending it crashing against the nearest wall. Anger was always her first response. Not tears. Anything but tears. Tears reminded her too much of her mother, her weak mother. But she couldn't fight back the complete despair that threatened to swallow her whole.

Felicie sat back down and began to rock back and forth in the chair, hugging herself, trying to keep her emotions contained, trying to fold into herself and disappear. It seemed that she was choking as her sentiments continued to manifest themselves in physical ways.

Jean Louis stood by, helpless to do anything but tear up when her broken voice finally floated through the room.

"Who will I go riding with?" She looked up at him, her eyes filling with pain. "Who will I ride with?"

"I will ride with you, *Maman*." He dropped to his knees, clasping her hands.

"Why didn't they let him ride in the cavalry?" she asked. "They should have let André ride in the cavalry, and he'd be alive. He can ride circles around those men. Why didn't they let him?"

"Free men of color don't ride in the cavalry," Jean Louis said. "They march."

"I gotta go to him," she said, jumping to her feet. "I gotta ride to Port Hudson. I gotta see if it's true."

Jean Louis rose and stepped in front of her, wrapping her in a bear hug. "Not now, *Maman*. Please, not now. You have three other children to think about."

"They are with my mother today, and they can stay with her. I have to leave!"

Although Jean Louis didn't argue, he maintained his hold on her. She fought him, pounding him on the shoulders as if her body had been taken over by another force. And then, as if someone had punctured an inflated bag, she collapsed inward, her knees gave out, and she crumbled. Jean Louis held her up and carefully lowered her into a kneeling position on the floor.

She squeezed out words between sobs. "They could be wrong, couldn't they, Jean Louis?"

"You're right, *Maman*. They could be wrong. His body hasn't been found yet, so they could be wrong."

Felicie straightened her back, alert to these new words, this new hope. She had two thoughts—one hopeful, the other horrific. If they hadn't found his body, there was still a chance he might be alive. But there was also a chance he was lying out there in the field, injured and in pain.

"Please, Jean Louis, I have to ride. I have to find him. Why haven't they found him? He might be alive! Why haven't they found him?"

"*Maman*, that is the problem..."

■■■

Levi was beyond furious. He was in another realm of fury entirely. He grabbed his gun and marched for Telegraph Road.

"I'm bringin' back Cailloux!" he shouted over his shoulder.

"Don't do nothing foolish." Lieutenant Moss limped, trying to keep up. "There ain't no flag of truce. Y'all will be picked off by Rebel sharpshooters!"

"I'll Shadrach those devils. I'll walk through the fire and not be touched!"

He meant every furious word. The day after the assault on Port Hudson, flags of truce had gone up, and Union soldiers had been sent out to collect bodies—*the bodies of the white soldiers*. They collected the dead from the white units that had attacked the fortifications on the same day as the black troops.

But the bodies of the black soldiers still lay out in the sun, a feast for the birds and flies in this disastrous heat.

Right on cue, two flies buzzed Levi's face. When he swatted them, he looked like a crazy man, punching at the air. Then he strode forward, determined to find André Cailloux's body before the sun melted it to an unrecognizable heap.

He stood at the edge of the willow forest and stared across the ragged moonscape in front of him. He remembered Captain Cailloux holding out his sword and rallying the troops at the very front of the lines, somewhere near the flooded ditch. He gazed up at the bluff to his left and thought he saw the movement of Rebel sharpshooters. He would be a fast-moving target, and they would probably make a game out of it—shoot the black man sprinting alone across a no-man's land. If Levi stopped to examine a body to find Captain Cailloux, he would be an easy target. He was counting on God's intervention to keep from being riddled with bullets.

He made the sign of the cross and kissed the crucifix around his neck.

Then he took off running across the battlefield.

■■■

There was no stopping his mother. She would have jumped on a horse and started riding for Port Hudson the moment Jean Louis delivered the news, but he calmed her down enough so that they could take the time to pack supplies and obtain a travel pass from the provost marshal. They had no problem getting one, for the name Cailloux had become famous almost overnight as the story of the attack on Port Hudson spread through the city.

Jean Louis thought his mother was going to go insane when he informed her, as gently as possible, that her husband hadn't been found because none of the African bodies had yet to be removed from the battlefield. At least that was the story making the rounds. He prayed it was one of a million false rumors.

After all, not all stories could be true because some of them flatly contradicted each other, especially the sketchy details of the battle. Pro-secessionists claimed that the Louisiana Native Guards had fled at the first sign of fire, but most other reports said the black troops had fought bravely. The words *gallantry, coolness,* and *courage* were tossed around in abundance.

Some newspaper reports even said his father led the charge as the black troops scaled the abatis, poured into the fort, and overwhelmed the Confederates in hand-to-hand combat. He liked to think that was the truth.

Once they were saddled up and ready to head out of New Orleans, Minetta insisted that she be allowed to join them. After everything they had gone through together, he wasn't about to stop her. Both Minetta and his mother dressed all in black, including the veils over their eyes, while Jean Louis wore all black except a white shirt with a black armband.

"You should be very proud of your father," came a voice to his right.

Jean Louis spotted three women heading in their direction—all women of color, wearing tignons on their heads.

"I am, ma'am," he said, tipping his hat.

He wished they had already left town because he knew his

mother hated these conversations. So did he. It seemed every free person of color looked at him with an unspoken question, asking why he wasn't in Port Hudson fighting alongside his father. He could see it in their eyes when they stared at him, wondering why he wasn't wearing a uniform.

A couple of people had asked him that question directly, but he didn't give them an answer. He wasn't about to offer excuses. He also didn't tell them that he had recently checked into the possibility of enlisting; that too would smack of an excuse. He hadn't even told his mother he was thinking of joining. She wouldn't take the news well.

"We are sorry for your loss, Madame Cailloux, but I am sure your husband is leading the charge through heaven's gate," said one of the ladies.

"Thank you, ladies, you are too kind," Minetta interjected before Felicie could reply. Smart move. She spoke for his mother because Felicie wouldn't be nearly as polite.

"Do you think you will be enlisting, Monsieur?" asked another one of the ladies.

There it was. The blunt-force question.

He wished he could confirm, but this was not the time or place to drop that bombshell on his mother. Instead, he absorbed the punishment in their eyes, tipped his hat, and said, "Good day, ladies, but we must be on our way. We are riding to Port Hudson."

"Godspeed," said another lady, waving her handkerchief at Felicie.

Jean Louis helped his mother and Minetta with their horses before mounting on his father's stallion, urging it forward with a trot. Before they even reached the edge of the city, his mother nudged her horse's sides, moving at a near gallop as he and Minetta struggled to keep pace.

If anyone else stepped into their path to offer condolences, they'd be taking their lives into their hands because Felicie was not stopping for anyone.

...

In less than a minute, Levi had become target practice. He heard whoops from the bluff, followed by cracks, then puffs of dirt kicking around him. He ran in a zigzag pattern, and his zigs and zags became quite extreme as he dodged boulders and broken tree limbs that had been shattered by cannonball fire during the battle.

Levi had put a dab of peppermint beneath his nose, but even that was no match for the odors rising from the ground like a foul fog. In some areas, he danced around to avoid stepping on bodies. He had never seen anything like it. The corpses had already become bloated and greenish in color, and flies had descended in Old Testament swarms. He now knew why Satan was called Beelzebub, the Lord of the Flies. Levi was running through hell.

He had already survived one mad dash across this stretch of Pandemonium, back on the day of the battle, so he was pushing the odds by doing it again. He had a strange calmness as he leaped over a deep gash in the land. A bullet ricocheted off a boulder immediately to his right—the closest shot yet.

Up ahead loomed the main bluff. Stretched out before it was the flooded ditch—the farthest point that the troops had reached. He looked for any sign of captain's bars on the corpses' uniforms, but that meant taking a careful look at the horrors around him. Most of the bodies were already a liquid feast for maggots.

Levi could stomach just about anything, but this was too much. He stopped, bending to retch, which ended up saving his life. When a bullet whistled by his ear, he was hunched close to the ground, still emptying his stomach of the last of his rations, thankful to be alive. He sucked in a few hurried breaths, looking around. If he had remained standing, he would have been one more casualty on the field.

Finally, he stood, wiping his mouth, and crisscrossed the area in front of the flooded ditch. When he discovered several bodies drifting in the water like pontoon floats, another wave of nausea plagued him.

He had a stomach of steel, but this was too much for one person to handle. He laid a hand to his gut, unable to stand another moment on this field.

As he prepared to race back in full retreat, he caught sight of some captain's bars on the uniform of an unrecognizable body. It certainly looked like Cailloux's uniform. He scooped up the sword closest to the body and turned and ran.

This time, on his return trip, the Rebels only fired a few parting shots at him. He thought he heard several of them applauding his performance.

47

Port Hudson
June 1863

Colonel William B. Shelby read the note two times. He couldn't believe his eyes. The words were from the Yankee general, Nathaniel Banks, and Shelby read them yet again.

General Banks had just informed Shelby, the Confederate colonel of the 39th Mississippi, that he didn't have any dead left out on the battlefield.

The Rebel colonel had sent a message to General Banks requesting a truce so the Federals could collect the dead black soldiers still lying out in the field along Telegraph Road. He even offered his own men to help with the nasty business. And the general's response?

In his exact words, he "had not any dead there."

Colonel Shelby stared down from the bluff overlooking the ragged land running alongside Telegraph Road. General Banks most certainly "had dead there." He could see them from his vantage point. Most importantly, he could *smell* them.

Colonel Shelby turned to his aide, who wore a bandana over his nose to filter out the odor of decay.

"I have heard of sieges where they try to starve you out," Colonel Shelby said. "But I do believe this is the first siege in which they are trying to drive us out with stench."

"Do you really think they'd leave their dead out there just to torment us?" asked the aide.

"Smells that way."

Colonel Shelby put a scented handkerchief to his nose as they continued to stare down on the field of bones.

"It's like Gehenna, sir," said the aide.

Colonel Shelby blinked in bafflement. "That's Biblical, ain't it?"

"It is, sir. It's a valley outside of Jerusalem where the Romans dumped the bodies of criminals and animals. An accursed place."

"And it's called Gehenna?"

The aide nodded. "A place where souls and bodies are destroyed."

"Make sure the newspaper reporters hanging around camp know about this. And use that word: Gehenna. They'll eat it up."

"Yes, sir."

As the aide departed, Colonel Shelby put the scented handkerchief back to his nose and stared down on the battlefield once again, noticing movement here and there. Probably rats or other animals. It certainly was not human.

■■■

"I been here over a week, and they ain't lettin' anyone near the field," said the young girl, Liser.

Felicie and Minetta sat outside Liser's tent as the young black girl cooked up a batch of soap over an open fire. It took an entire day to cook up the animal fat and lye to create the soap to clean the soldiers' uniforms. Then it took three to four days just to wash a load.

Felicie, Minetta, and Jean Louis had arrived in camp the day before, but they stumbled across Liser just this morning. She was a kind girl, all skin, bones, and smiles. But when Felicie started asking her about the black soldiers still lying out on the field, Liser's easy smile vanished. It was obvious she didn't want to talk about such a subject with the wife of one of the men still out there. She changed the subject as quickly as she could.

"Y'all could get yourself a Certificate of Good Character, you bein' wife to a hero," said Liser, stirring the soap with a long stick. "I'm sure y'all could too, ma'am," she added, looking at Minetta. Women needed a certificate before they could become a laundress working on Suds Row.

Liser was right. Felicie could easily get a certificate, and being a laundress was actually a good idea, for many wives did it to stay close to their husbands. This girl, who couldn't be more than sixteen, had a good head on her shoulders. If Felicie and Minetta were going to remain near Port Hudson, they could become laundresses, one of the most respected and highest-paid jobs among camp followers.

"Are you the daughter of one of the soldiers?" Minetta asked Liser.

"No, ma'am. I was the girl of one of the soldiers. Lieutenant John Crowder's his name, ma'ams."

"I see. Were you betrothed?" Felicie asked.

"Not yet, but he was fixin' to get on his knees and ask me." A pause. "He was fixin' to before all this happened. He gone."

Felicie dropped her eyes as Minetta asked, "A casualty of the battle?"

Liser stared into the cauldron, stirring the soap. Tears formed in her eyes.

"They got him back in camp alive and all, but he didn't make it more than a day or two. At least that's what they tell me."

"I'm sorry." Felicie sent her a look of kindness before staring into the distance. At least this girl knew the fate of her beau.

Minetta glanced from Felicie's grief-torn eyes to Liser. "I hope he got a good burial."

"He did. His friend, Lieutenant Moss, showed me his grave."

Liser looked at Felicie guiltily. "I'm sorry, ma'am, to be talkin' 'bout his burial when your husband..."

Felicie touched her hand. "That's all right. I am happy John Crowder is at rest."

"It ain't fair them leavin' the soldiers out on the field when they've given their lives," Liser said. "The officers claim the Rebels start shootin' whenever they try to get the bodies, but I ain't believin' it. They got them a truce flag and collected all the white soldiers without bein' shot at."

Liser stared into space—and then abruptly changed the subject once again. "Bein' a laundress pays good, ma'am. Y'all should do it. They like married ladies doin' the cleanin'."

"Thank you, Liser."

Felicie watched her stir for a few minutes before catching movement down the trail. She looked up to see Jean Louis coming down Suds Rows, passing by multiple clotheslines, all loaded with laundry. A tall, thin, dark-skinned man ambled along by his side, and in his hands was a sword. He carried it with the blade resting on his palms like he was presenting it to royalty.

"This here is Levi," said Jean Louis, introducing the man. "He fought alongside Papa."

"Pleased to meet you, Monsieur Levi," said Minetta. "And this here is Madame Cailloux."

Levi made a deep bow. "I'm honored to be meetin' the wife of so great a man, Madame."

"Thank you."

"And this here is Liser," added Minetta.

Liser cast her eyes downward.

"Liser!" Levi exclaimed. "Well, I'll be! Y'all John Crowder's gal, ain't you?"

Liser stopped stirring. "You knew him?"

"Knew him good. We marched side by side. A fine man."

Felicie's eyes shifted to the sword, and she let out a gasp.

"Where'd you get that sword, Monsieur?"

"The battlefield, ma'am. I believe it belonged to your brave husband. Do y'all recognize it?"

She nodded. It was a heavy cavalry saber, almost three feet long. Curved and very sharp. *Old Wristbreaker.* Felicie clamped her lips, holding back the tears that threatened.

"Then it's an honor to present it to y'all, ma'am."

He placed the sword gently in her hands, and she stared at the blade, turning it over to examine it thoroughly. She took the sword and pressed the edge along her forefinger, blood dripping from the tip.

"*Maman*, what are you doing?" Jean Louis moved in quickly, disarming her before she could do severe damage.

It had just been a whim, drawing that blood. A momentary madness. Felicie wasn't sure why, but the urge to bleed came over her. She would draw a drop or two, maybe more. A coldness came over her, and Jean Louis put his arm around her. She shivered.

"Did you see my husband?" she asked Levi. "Did you see him out on the field?"

"I believe I did, ma'am."

"And you're sure it was him?"

"I recognized his uniform, and this sword seems to confirm it."

"His uniform?"

"Yes, ma'am."

He recognized his uniform? Why didn't this man say he recognized André's face?

She tried not to think about what that meant.

48

————————

Jean Louis was knee-deep in rancid swamp water. Every step was a chore, as his shoes sank into the mud, and a slurping suction gripped his feet. Over the past week, he had tried several times to access the battlefield through the proper channels, but he was always blocked by sentries.

Cutting through the backwater was his only option.

"This is a fool's mission," said Levi, who had agreed to lead him to his father's body.

"You've seen battle, and you dodged bullets to locate my papa," said Jean Louis. "And now you're telling me you're afraid of a little swamp water?"

"It ain't the swamp water that spooks me. It's what I can't see lurking below it."

True. The pair had already spotted two alligators and a water moccasin winding its way along the surface of the murk. Who knew what lay beneath each footfall? But Jean Louis was determined to pass through this stretch of willow swamp. Levi had pilfered a stretcher and was holding it well above his head to keep it dry. Jean

Louis led the way, using a long stick to probe the water, checking the depth. So far, the swamp was only up to their thighs.

"You even sure we're still goin' in the right direction?" asked Levi.

"I'm sure."

He wasn't.

If the stories Jean Louis heard were true, Levi was fearless on land, but the man was clearly terrified of water. Although the soldier couldn't swim, Jean Louis promised him that the water would never get over his head.

"Hold on, hold on," said Levi. "Gator—ten feet to your right."

Jean Louis saw two knobby projections sticking out of the water, coated with a scummy green skin of festering vegetation. He examined the knobs for a good five seconds before poking it with his stick. Just as he suspected. A log.

They kept going, pushing through as mosquitoes feasted on their necks and foreheads. Jean Louis slapped at a couple that landed on his neck, his fingers smearing with dabs of blood and mosquito parts.

"You sure you remember where my father's body lies on the battlefield?" Jean Louis asked.

"I'm sure, but I ain't sure you want to be seein' it, sir."

Jean Louis tried to chase the thought from his mind. He was doing this for the honor of his father and mother—although she would probably kill him if she knew the risk he was taking.

Then the inevitable happened. He took a step, and his foot wouldn't come back up. Slowly, he began to sink. The muddy bottom of the swamp steadily pulled him in.

"Stay back, Levi, stay back."

Levi came to a sudden standstill and stared as Jean Louis felt himself slowly descending. His feet continued to sink in the mud until the water level soon reached above his waist. Fortunately, he stopped sinking before the water reached his chest or, even worse, covered his mouth and nose. Levi, still holding on to the stretcher with one hand, managed to use his free hand to take hold of the coil of rope slung over his shoulder. He tossed one end to Jean Louis, but it fell about five feet short.

"You're gonna have to move a few feet closer," Jean Louis said.

"If we both get stuck, we're goners, sir."

"We don't have a choice."

Levi paused before he took a deep breath and inched his way closer, one small step at a time, and then he stopped.

"My feets is sinkin', sir. Can't go no farther."

"Try it from there."

He threw the rope three more times, and three times it came up short. Only two feet away.

"Just one step closer should do it."

"One step closer might kill me, sir."

"Then tie the rope to the stretcher and toss me the stretcher."

"Good idea."

Backing up a step, Levi tied the rope around one of the stretcher handles, and then, with the other end of the rope looped around his left hand, he heaved the stretcher at Jean Louis.

Jean Louis caught the stretcher—in the forehead.

His vision went spinning for a moment, but he now had his hands on the stretcher with the lifeline attached. He tightened his grip.

"Ready, sir?" asked Levi.

"Ready."

Levi began to yank, like pulling wagon wheels out of a muddy ditch, and Jean Louis suddenly fell forward into the water. With his feet still stuck in the mud, he started flailing with one hand, trying to raise himself up. But without his feet planted on firm ground, he couldn't do it. It was like his feet were caught in concrete while his upper body was bent forward, submerged in the murk.

Pull, he thought. *Pull, Levi!*

He felt the tug of the stretcher in his hands and prayed that Levi tied the rope securely. If it came loose from the stretcher, he was done for. With his face still underwater, his lungs burned, and the need to breathe overwhelmed every other thought. His body had used up every bit of air he had stored in his cheeks, and his lungs screamed for more. He felt Levi tugging, but his feet remained anchored. His head was on the verge of exploding, but he didn't dare open his mouth because he would be breathing in his own death.

Finally, a foot popped free from the suction grip with a slurping sound, and he took one enormous step toward Levi. When his right foot landed on something firm, he rose, gasping for air and pulling his second foot free. Levi stumbled and fell backward into the swamp water, scrambling to stand. Once on his feet, he stared at Jean Louis with crazy eyes.

"Hate to say it, sir, but ya'll are covered in leeches." Levi pointed at him with a wince.

Jean Louis put a hand to his cheek where a thick, brown, slimy leech suctioned to his face. He used his fingernail to pry the leech loose and then flung it aside.

When Levi discovered that he, too, had four leeches suckered to his neck, he had enough. He beat a retreat the way they came, stripping off leeches and shouting his disgust with every step he took.

Jean Louis followed, sloshing through the water, conceding defeat.

■■■

On June 14, over two weeks since the first attempt to take Port Hudson, the Federals tried again.

Another disaster.

The Rebels mowed them down, the same as before, killing another four hundred and injuring more than a thousand. This time, the black soldiers were held in reserve and were not sent into the grinder.

Meanwhile, the bodies of André Cailloux and his men remained scattered along Telegraph Road. Jean Louis knew that his mother still hoped to search for bodies if she were allowed. In fact, she sometimes threatened to take a gun and force her way onto the battlefield. But at this stage, there was no way he would allow her near the field, even if she were permitted. The condition of the bodies would be something out of a devil's dream.

"We should all head back to New Orleans," he told Minetta one evening as they went for a ride together. The area was riddled with swamps and choked by dense woods, but they found an open path to run the horses—taking them away from the smells and sounds of battle. "This siege could go on forever."

"I don't think your mama is going to agree to leave," Minetta said as they dismounted and tied up their horses.

They walked arm in arm across the prairie, thick with flowering blazing star. A field of purple spread like a painting—the long, narrow flowers pointed skyward like purple caterpillars crawling up a stalk of grass.

"She has no choice but to leave." Jean Louis sighed. "I need to report back for the 7th Louisiana Regiment."

The 7th Regiment was a colored unit being formed for the protection of New Orleans. Confederate General Richard Taylor had moved his troops dangerously close to the city, and measures had to be taken.

"And I'm not leaving here without *Maman*," he added.

"But she won't leave until she gets your father's body. She'll think she's deserting him."

Jean Louis dropped her arm and spun to face her. "Do you think I'm deserting my father by going back to New Orleans?"

"Of course not. I'm just saying you should know your mother by now. She won't leave his body."

Jean Louis leaned down and plucked a reed, then twirled it between two fingers. In the distance, he noticed a groundhog standing and peeking above the tall grass, eyeing them.

"I deserted my papa by not enlisting when I should have, by not fighting alongside him. I should've been there that day. He shouldn't be out there alone right now."

Minetta enveloped him. "You didn't desert him. You needed to be home to protect your mother, your brother, your sisters."

"He wanted a son who could be proud of being the son of the blackest man in New Orleans."

"But you *are* proud of him."

"I wasn't always."

"No son is."

She moved around until she stood in front of him. She took his right hand with her left and then placed her other hand directly over his. Her skin was darker than his, and her eyes were dark brown too, with spangles of reflected light. Minetta tiptoed to kiss him on the forehead, moving to his cheek before claiming his lips.

■■■

Felicie threw a tin drinking cup at her son, and only quick reflexes prevented it from putting a mark on his forehead. It clanged against a tree and bounced to the ground.

"Don't you dare!" Her voice rattled with emotions that broke her heart a second time.

For the past couple of days, she was bound by a slogging weariness. Her bones ached almost as much as her heart, but she worked alongside Liser doing laundry, fighting the filth of the camp, which seemed more fruitless than laying siege to Port Hudson. Lice ran rampant, and rain turned everything to mud. Between the sludge and her grief, she was barely moving through her existence, mired and immobilized.

But when Minetta told her what Jean Louis was thinking of doing, she came to life.

"Don't you dare!" Felicie's eyes lit up.

"But my father dared." Jean Louis tried to talk some reason into her.

"And look where it got him!"

Only one day after the second disastrous attempt to take Port

Hudson, General Banks was at it again, calling for one thousand volunteers to storm the fort. Although it was a third suicide charge, it motivated Jean Louis. Instead of going back to New Orleans to join the 7th Louisiana Regiment, as planned, Jean Louis stayed in Port Hudson with plans to join the next wave of attacks. He wanted to fight on the same killing ground as his father.

"You are not even enlisted," Felicie said when she had calmed down just a bit.

"But I can enlist."

"I think you should do what you originally planned," Minetta said, almost pleading. "Head back to New Orleans and join the new regiment being formed to protect the city."

"But that's the safe choice," Jean Louis said.

"What's wrong with that?" Felicie screamed, slapping his face.

Felicie looked from her hands to the mark on her son's face with astonishment before sitting on a stool, sighing, and dropping her head. "Go to New Orleans with my blessing and join the 7th. Anything is better than attacking this fortification."

"I need to do this for Papa." Jean Louis lowered his voice, still holding his cheek.

"Return to New Orleans and enlist there," Minetta urged. "Do this for your mother."

"Please," Felicie begged, her body beginning to shake once again.

Felicie was desperate. She thought her mind would crumble like dry earth if her son tried to attack the same deadly bluffs. They called such attacks "forlorn hopes" for a reason.

"Please, Jean Louis, stick with your original plan," said Minetta.

"Why? And take the coward's way out?"

"No. Because a forlorn hope is a fool's mission."

"But who will be with Mama if I leave for New Orleans? I don't want to leave her alone."

"I will stay here with *Maman*."

Felicie took note that Minetta had just called her "mother."

"And how will the two of you get back to New Orleans safely if I am gone?" Jean Louis asked.

"I am not returning until I can get my husband's body," Felicie said. "They will provide a military escort for his body. It will happen."

"Please, Jean Louis," Minetta said. "New Orleans needs protecting more than this fort needs more dead. Don't worry about us. We're safe here surrounded by thousands of blue uniforms."

When Minetta put her arms around Jean Louis, Felicie raised her eyebrows, taking note.

"I want to see you enlist, but join a regiment that serves a purpose," Minetta said.

Felicie was amazed to see her son melt under this young woman's touch. What Felicie's fury couldn't do, Mademoiselle Minetta's soothing tone could. Jean Louis stared at his feet.

"You may be right," he said, looking up at Minetta.

"I know I am."

And then she kissed him, right in front of Felicie and the Lord Almighty—and right on the lips.

49

When Jean Louis returned to New Orleans, leaving his mother in the hands of Minetta, he was stunned to see the reception that the Cailloux name received. He enlisted in the 7th Louisiana Colored Regiment and was greeted at the recruiting office as a kind of hero, even though it was his father who had earned the praise.

He approached St. Rose de Lima Church wearing a blue uniform for the first time. His father had always struck an imposing figure in his uniform, and he hoped he captured some of that magic, but he doubted it.

"My, you're looking much like your father," said Father Maistre upon greeting him. Jean Louis smiled, and the priest motioned him into the sanctuary. After genuflecting, they sat in one of the back pews.

"I hear that the 7th Louisiana was formed for a sixty-day task of keeping the Rebels at bay," said Father Maistre. "Do you think the Confederates will dare attack the city?"

"I have my doubts."

"And your mother? She and Mademoiselle Minetta have remained near Port Hudson?"

"My mother has no intention of leaving until she has my father's body."

"I can believe that. He was a hero."

Father Maistre did not exaggerate. Jean Louis had read many of the accounts from all points in the country. The men of color who fought at Port Hudson had gained the country's attention, especially his father. While many Southern sources tried to downplay or deny the heroism of the black soldiers, some northern papers exaggerated in the other extreme. He read one account that said a Negro soldier lost his gun, so he bear-hugged a Confederate soldier and ripped the skin from his face with his teeth.

Jean Louis knew from sources such as Levi that the Union soldiers didn't even get any closer than fifty yards of the Confederate line, making it rather difficult to bite somebody's face off. But he was still gratified at the generous exaggerations.

"Thank you for all you did for us here—for Mademoiselle McCarthy and her child," Father Maistre said. "And for me."

"How is Mademoiselle McCarthy?"

"I have found her a position as a cleaning lady, and she attends St. Rose's faithfully."

"What has happened with Bishop Odin?"

"Ah, Bishop Odin. I am still under interdict. But I also still have these." Father Maistre reached into the folds of his vestments and pulled out a set of keys to the church. He jangled them like sleigh bells. "I recently advertised for a special Mass that I'm saying on July Fourth, and I invited all true friends of liberty, without distinction of race or color."

"In other words, you're still causing trouble." Jean Louis chuckled and shifted in the pew, his arm resting on the back of the seat. "That brings me to the reason for my visit. I bring a request from my mother."

"Anything for your mother."

"When she returns to New Orleans with my father's remains, she would like you to say the funeral Mass."

Father Maistre made a sign of the cross and then kissed the crucifix that dangled from his neck. "*Précieux Jésus*, I would be honored. Is she sure?"

"She is sure."

"She realizes that I am still under interdict from Bishop Odin."

"She hasn't forgotten."

Father Maistre beamed.

...

For the third time, Levi crossed the killing ground along Telegraph Road. Only this time, there were no Confederate sharpshooters taking target practice at him or cannons firing shells into the willow swamp. He walked unscathed across the shattered land.

The Confederates had surrendered Port Hudson on July 8.

The forlorn hope that Levi had volunteered for—another suicide mission—had never materialized. In fact, the Rebels had surrendered just as General Banks was making final preparations to blow up the tunnels they dug beneath the Citadel and Priest Cap strongholds. Levi and the rest of the forlorn hope were going to rush into the breach, where they most likely would have been wiped out—just like the other two charges—so it was a good thing it never came off.

News had reached the Confederates that nearby Vicksburg had fallen to General Grant on July 4th. The Rebels at Port Hudson finally realized that their position was hopeless, especially with their food depleted and disease spreading. They handed over the Port Hudson garrison, munitions, armaments, and materials of war to the Union's General Banks.

The Federals had lost many more lives than the Southerners, but the Confederates had lost Vicksburg and now Port Hudson. The Mississippi River was firmly in the control of the Yankees.

Levi was amazed that when the Confederates finally gave up,

they came down from the parapets and swapped stories with Yankee soldiers, shaking hands like long-lost relatives. Only a few hours before, they had been shooting at each other.

With the siege ended, at last, the dead black soldiers that had melted into the ground could be retrieved. These brave men had baked in the sun for *forty-one* days. Forty days would have been a very Biblical number, like the forty days of Jesus in the wilderness or the forty years of the Israelites wandering in the wilderness.

Forty was a symbol of testing, so forty-one was a testing plus one. The first black soldiers to fight a major battle were about to return from the wilderness. Although their spirits rose on May 27, like smoke from cannons, it was now the second week of July, and their bodies could be redeemed.

Levi jammed a hand into his pocket, making sure he still had the item he found on the battlefield. Strolling back to the Union lines, he paused to remove his hat and wipe away the sweat streaming into his eyes. It was like walking across a desert, and he baked inside his heavy, blue uniform. He took a sip from his canteen, tied a bandana around his head, poured water on his hat, and drew the cool cloth down over his head, trudging on.

When he finally reached the cool of the willow forest, he found Madame Cailloux and Mademoiselle Minetta standing beneath the shade of a tree. As they saw him approach, they held on to each other.

Levi couldn't tell whether Madame Cailloux was terrified, hopeful, or both. He stepped before them, afraid to speak until spoken to. He looked down at his shoes.

"Well...?" Mademoiselle Minetta stepped forward.

"I got somethin'." Levi reached into his pocket and fumbled a bit, before pulling out a gold ring. The hand it was attached to had turned to jelly, but gold lasted longer than human flesh.

He held it out for Madame Cailloux to inspect.

She took the ring and put it in the center of her palm, staring at it for the longest time. Then her hand started shaking, and so did the rest of her body. Levi rushed forward to help catch her before she collapsed like a tent.

He and Mademoiselle Minetta helped her to find a seat on a nearby stump, where a cannonball had blasted apart a living tree.

Madame Cailloux squeezed the ring in her palm, placed her free hand to her forehead, and began crying like he had never seen a body cry before. Levi even had to fight back the tears—and he never wept. As a lump formed in his throat, he turned away so the women wouldn't see the shame of his tears, his eyes stinging like fire.

But the two women weren't paying him any heed anyway. They were too busy crying themselves sick as Madame Cailloux rocked back and forth, clutching the ring that had once been on the hand of her fallen husband.

50

New Orleans
Wednesday, July 29, 1863

Felicie could not believe her eyes. Thousands of people lined New Orleans as the funeral procession snaked its way through the streets. It was a hot, steamy day—ordinary weather for New Orleans in July, but it was anything but a typical day. How often do so many people come out for a fallen black hero—the blackest man in New Orleans?

Granted, most people standing along the *banquettes* were those of color, but there were still many white faces. What's more, the Federals had agreed to fly the American flag at half-mast for an entire month. Most impressive of all, General Banks had endorsed this massive outpouring of grief and respect.

For a black soldier!

Felicie and Minetta had accompanied André's remains back to New Orleans on the steamboat *Old Essex*, arriving in the city on July 25th—four days ago. Upon disembarking, her first surprise was that most of the women of color wore black crepe rosettes on their dresses—in honor of André.

For the next four days, his body lay in state in a closed casket in the Urquhart Street hall for the Friends of the Order. A soldier maintained vigil over the coffin at all times. A U.S. flag was draped over the casket, and his sword, belt, uniform coat, and cap were laid on top.

Jean Louis sat across from Felicie in the carriage that slowly moved through New Orleans, drawn by two black horses. Next to Jean Louis were his fiancé, Minetta, and Eugene, and sitting on either side of Felicie, leaning into her and clutching her arm, were Odile and Athalie. Felicie's mother and brother rode in a separate carriage just behind them, along with Father Maistre.

Eugene had finally accepted the fact that his father wore a Yankee uniform. In fact, he had even come to embrace it and wished the war would last long enough for him to enlist. Odile put up a brave front, but Felicie was most worried about Athalie. Her oldest girl had barely spoken after she heard the news of her father's death; the only time she ever seemed to talk was to express fear that Felicie was going to die soon. Her youngest, Odile, appeared happy, but who knew what went on beneath the surface.

Fretting about her girls was actually a healthy sign since she had been so consumed by grief recently that she'd almost forgotten she had children. But now that she worried about them, they were in her mind every day, which was good.

As the carriage continued past Congo Square, Felicie studied the sheet of paper in her hands—a copy of the poem written by the abolitionist poet George H. Boker. It was entitled "The Black Captain."

He just lay where he fell,
Soddening in a fervid summer's sun,
Guarded by an enemy's hissing shell,
Rotting beneath the sound of Rebels' guns

Forty consecutive days,
In sight of his own tent,
And the remnant of his regiment.

Jean Louis tried to keep this poem away from her with all its talk of rotting and soddening. But she'd found a copy posted on a telegraph pole and kept it with her at all times.

He just lay where he fell
And now the ground was theirs,
Around his mellowed corpse, heavens tell,
How his comrades for freedom swear.
Forty consecutive nights
The advance password went,
Captain Cailloux of the black regiment.

She stared out the carriage window, thankful her eyes were concealed by her black veil. She didn't want people examining her face, looking for signs of what death could do to a widow. Her veil was her cocoon, protection for her private grief. She leaned back, listening to the sound of somber music. The 42nd Massachusetts Regiment band had agreed to play dirges. An all-white band.

Is this for real? Felicie closed her eyes.

She would never speak to André again, at least in this life, and she had a hard time believing it. She kept expecting him to turn up at any moment. Whenever she saw a horse, she expected to see him mounted upon it, reaching to lift her up. She let the tears flow freely, knowing the veil would hide them. Felicie suffered greatly with her fifth wound.

"Behold, I shew you a mystery; we shall not all sleep, but we
shall all be changed, in a moment, in the twinkling of an eye,
at the last trump: for the trumpet shall sound, and the dead

shall be raised incorruptible, and we shall be changed. For this corruptible must put on incorruption, and this mortal must put on immortality."

Those were the words from the Requiem Mass that meant the most to Felicie—the idea that André's body, ravaged by insects, birds, and the sun for forty-one days, would rise again incorruptible. Father Maistre had said the Mass, but because he was still under the penalty of the interdict, no other priests could help. He was assisted at the gravesite by two black soldiers.

Was this really happening?

"I call on everyone here today to offer themselves as martyrs to the cause of justice and freedom," Father Maistre had said in his eulogy. "I call on everyone here to offer themselves as Captain Cailloux has done so nobly. He is our martyr. He is our American Spartacus."

Moving down Esplanade Avenue, people from the various black male and female mutual aid societies lined the *banquette* for over a mile. Many waved American flags, which would have been unheard of one year earlier. The day when the Federals arrived in New Orleans seemed a century ago.

At last, the hearse and the carriages pulled into the Bienville Street Cemetery, where the crowd spontaneously began to sing.

> *"The Lord, He thought He'd make a man.*
> *These bones goin' to rise again.*
> *Made him outta mud and a handful of sand.*
> *These bones goin' to rise again.*
> *I knowed it, indeed I knowed it, brother, I knowed it.*
> *These bones goin' to rise again."*

Eight black soldiers, Levi among them, carried the casket to the mausoleum.

"Thought He'd make a woman too.
Didn't know exactly what to do.
Took a rib from Adam' side,
Made Miss Eve for to be his bride."

It was like walking through an oven as Felicie passed among the tombs with Jean Louis and Minetta holding her up on either side. As eight men slid the coffin into the aboveground tomb, the sounds of wood scraping against brick would forever be etched in her memory.

"Serpent coiled around a chink.
At Miss Eve his eye, he winked.
First, she took a little pull,
Then she filled an apron full.
Adam took a little slice.
Smacked his lips and say 'twas nice."

One of the soldiers began to barricade the tomb, sealing André from Felicie, one brick at a time. Before he could put the last few bricks in place, she moved forward and inserted her hand into the tomb, touching the coffin one last time. Then she stepped back and watched as the final pieces were slid into place.

"The Lord He spoke with a ponderous voice.
Shook the world to its very joist.
'Stole my apples, I believe.'
'No, My Lord; I 'spect it was Eve.'
'Out of this garden, you must git.
Earn your livin' by your sweat.'
He put an angel at the door.
Told 'em never come there no more.

"Of this tale, there is no more.

Eve ate the apple and Adam the core.
The Lawd, He thought He'd make a man.
These bones goin' to rise again.
Made him outta mud and a handful of sand.
These bones goin' to rise again.
I knowed it, indeed I knowed it, brother, I knowed it.
These bones goin' to rise again."

...

A woman riding sidesaddle appeared in the distance, just a white speck against a field of swaying grass. The horse trotted as if it had all the time in the world. As the lady came closer, the man could see she was dressed all in white, like a bride. White dress, white shoes, white hat, white gloves, white umbrella, and a white veil concealing her face.

The man was dressed in a blue uniform with captain's bars on his shoulders, gold buttons, an ostrich feather sticking from his hat, and a curved sword at his side. The lady pulled up beside him, and they sat that way, just looking at each other for the longest time before either of them uttered a word.

Finally, he spoke. "It took you long enough to get here."

The woman laughed from behind her veil. "Have you been waiting all this time?"

"Every day."

"There are days here?"

"And nights." He leaned over and raised the veil from her face—the corners of his lips lifting into a gentle smile. "Just as I remembered."

"You hadn't forgotten my face?" Her eyes lit up with wonder.

"No. Had you forgotten mine?"

"It was hard to remember." She studied every one of his features, memorizing every detail as if for the first time.

"I'll forgive you for that."

They smiled, each leaning from their horses to meet in the middle with a kiss. Then, they turned their horses and raced across the unbroken ground of Eden, which lay unguarded once again.

EPILOGUE

André Cailloux died as the first black hero of the American Civil War. His grave can be found in New Orleans' Bienville Cemetery, known today as St. Louis Cemetery Number 2.

Felicie Cailloux suffered economic hardship after André was killed. Some friends intervened with General Nathaniel Banks because Andre was still owed back pay. However, the work on her behalf was to no avail. In 1867, she was denied the pension because of a clerical error. She died of a stroke on September 16, 1873.

John Crowder was buried in a pauper's grave, and his mother, Martha Ann Stars, had to make her case to receive her son's pension from the United States government. In 1874, the Pension Office agreed to pay her one hundred dollars per year.

Father Claude Maistre was eventually evicted from St. Rose de Lima Church. However, he soon began building a new church—Holy Name of Jesus. His schism with the Church ended when Archbishop

Odin died in 1870 and was succeeded by one of Maistre's friends. Father Claude Maistre passed away in 1875 at age 55.

Bricktop Jackson murdered her lover **John Miller** when he tried to thrash her with a whip. She grabbed the whip from his good hand, and when he tried to smash her with his iron ball, she yanked the chain on his arm and pulled him across the room, then proceeded to stab him to death.

Union General Nathaniel Banks continued to disparage black officers after the siege of Port Hudson. He wrote to President Lincoln, saying that black officers were "unsuited for this duty" and blamed them for the conflicts between black and white officers. Cailloux's 1st Regiment was left off of the list of regiments permitted to inscribe "Port Hudson" on their regimental flags.

DOUG PETERSON'S
CIVIL WAR SERIES

Check out Book 1 of the Civil War series:

The Lincoln League is the story of John Scobell, the first African-American spy for the U.S. Intelligence Service during the Civil War. It's also the story of his wife, Peg, as she spies in Richmond, the heart of the Confederacy. This thrilling novel also tells of the little-known Lincoln League, an extensive network of African-American spies operating right under the noses of Southern masters. Based on a true story.

Sample an excerpt from *The Lincoln League*, which you can find after the Acknowledgments.

AUTHOR'S NOTES

Before there was *Glory*, there was the story of the 1st and 3rd Louisiana Native Guards.

The movie *Glory* depicts the famous 54th Massachusetts Infantry Unit, one of the first all-black units in the American Civil War—a regiment immortalized for its assault on Fort Wagner on July 18, 1863. However, two months earlier, the 1st and 3rd Louisiana Native Guards attacked Port Hudson just north of New Orleans. I based the battle scene in *The Dixie Devil* on several accounts of the Siege of Port Hudson.

The Dixie Devil is also based on the true story of André and Felicie Cailloux, and I include many real-life characters within their story—among them, Father Maistre, Bishop Odin, Colonel Stafford, and Generals Butler, Banks, and Dwight.

The story of John H. Crowder, the sixteen-year-old lieutenant, is also true. I based his scenes on the document, *The Civil War Through the Eyes of a Sixteen-Year-Old Black Officer: The Letters of John H. Crowder of the 1st Louisiana Native Guards*. Crowder really did have an ongoing battle with Captain Alcide Lewis and Lieutenant Moss— two men who spread malicious lies to his mother and others.

Although black officers did challenge the segregation of blacks in separate streetcars (Star Cars), I should point out that there is no evidence that John Crowder was one of the officers who challenged the practice. His scene with the streetcars is fictional.

The family histories of André and Felicie Cailloux are based on reality, including the legacy of Felicie's mother as a concubine of a white man. André and Felicie were devout Catholics, who wanted to form a legitimate family. That is why André adopted Felicie's firstborn, Jean Louis, who worked as a carpenter and joined the military after his father died. Most other details about Jean Louis, such as his passion for photography and his love interests, are fictional. Minetta and Coralie are also fictional.

André did boast that he was the blackest man in New Orleans. In addition, the storyline about his involvement with the Louisiana Native Guards is based on history, but the subplot involving the murder of Roussel Pinard is fictional. Roussel is a fictional character, as are Colleen McCarthy and the Montforts.

However, the Live Oak Boys, the prostitute Mary Jane "Bricktop" Jackson, and her lover, John Miller, were actual figures in the New Orleans underworld. Although a man with a chain and ball attached to his amputated arm sounds like a fictional character, I did not make him up. Also, Bricktop Jackson did beat one man to death and kill another with her two-bladed knife. It wasn't until her third murder that she was arrested, but she was acquitted when the coroner concluded that the victim, stabbed a dozen times, had died of heart disease. While awaiting trial in prison, she met John Miller, the man with the chain and ball for an arm, working as a prison turnkey.

Note: Bricktop Jackson killed Miller on December 5, 1861, well before the events in *The Dixie Devil*. But I couldn't resist including such characters in the novel, so I let Miller live a little bit longer for the story's sake.

Much of the plotline with Father Maistre was true: his friendship with the Caillouxs, his decision to baptize slaves and list them in the registry next to whites, his protection of escaped slaves, and his conflict with Bishop Odin. The primary fictional element in his story was the blackmail—although he really did flee from Thuisy, France, because of his run-in with the law over money. (The details are not known.) Money was his Achilles Heel, and he caused controversy in several American churches because of accusations of financial impropriety.

The Mystick Crewe of Comus was the earliest crew in New Orleans before the Civil War, and I came across a 19th-Century book that described their theme each year during Mardi Gras. *Paradise Lost* was their theme a couple of years before the Civil War, and they paraded in devil masks. Therefore, in honor of John Milton's epic poem, *Paradise Lost*, I scattered certain phrases from the poem throughout *The Dixie Devil*.

I used dozens of resources in writing *The Dixie Devil*, but I should highlight my greatest source: *A Black Patriot and a White Priest: André Cailloux and Claude Paschal Maistre in Civil War New Orleans*, by Stephen J. Ochs. Other key resources included:

- *Black Soldiers in Blue: African American Troops in the Civil War Era*, edited by John David Smith, The University of North Carolina Press, 2002.
- *Black Union Soldiers in the Civil War*, by Hondon B. Hargrove, McFarland & Company, Inc., 1988.
- *The Civil War in Louisiana*, by John D. Winters, Louisiana State University Press, 1963.
- *Creole: The History and Legacy of Louisiana's Free People of Color*, edited by Sybil Klein, Louisiana State University Press, 2000.
- *Fabulous New Orleans*, by Lyle Saxon, Pelican Publishing Company, 2004.
- *The French Quarter: An Informal History of the New Orleans Underworld*, by Herbert Asbury, Basic Books, 2008.

- *General Butler in New Orleans*, by James Parton, Mason Brothers, 1864.
- *A History of the Negro Troops in the War of the Rebellion 1861-1865*, by George Washington Williams, Fordham University Press, 2012 (originally published in 1887 by Harper & Brothers).
- *The Holy Bible Containing the Old and New Testaments in the Authorized King James Version*, Good Counsel Publishers, 1960.
- *The Louisiana Native Guards: The Black Military Experience During the Civil War*, by James G. Hollandsworth, Jr., Louisiana State University Press, 1998.
- *The Negro in the Civil War*, by Benjamin Quarles, Da Capo Press, 1953.
- *The Negro's Civil War: How American Blacks Felt and Acted During the War for the Union*, by James M. McPherson, Vintage Books, 1965.
- *New Orleans: A Pictorial History*, by Leonard V. Huber, Bonanza Books, 1971.
- *Revolution, Romanticism, and the Afro-Creole Protest Tradition in Louisiana 1718-1868*, by Caryn Cosse Bell, Louisiana State University Press, 1997.
- *When the Devil Came Down to Dixie: Ben Butler in New Orleans*, by Chester G. Hearn, Louisiana State University Press, 1997.

ACKNOWLEDGMENTS

The Dixie Devil is about a forgotten slice of Civil War history, but it's also the love story of André and Felicie Cailloux. So, it's fitting that I begin by acknowledging the love of my life, Nancy. When we married in 1976, the pastor prayed that we would "love each other even more in fifty years." Well, we are closing in on fifty, and the pastor's words have proven true.

My gratitude also goes to our two sons, Jason and Michael, whom we love greatly—and also love to spend time with, talking about books, movies, and television shows. This novel is dedicated to their wonderful wives, Kristen Peterson and Ingrid Romero.

In addition, I thank the many people who read early drafts of *The Dixie Devil* and provided invaluable feedback—my wife, Nancy, as well as Vern Fein, Heath and Cavan Morber, Kathy Gullang, Ric Peterson, and my mom, Irene (who is nearing a milestone of her own —her 100th birthday). It's a joy to meet regularly with Vern to talk about writing, for he gives me a regular boost of encouragement. I get additional encouragement from my church family at Cornerstone Fellowship and my prayer partner, Scott Irwin.

A special thanks to the professionals who helped to make this possible—to Dinah Armstead, Ph.D., a language and diversity scholar and director of Culture Speak International, L.L.C. Dinah helped me make sure I have the French phrases correct. If any errors appear, I accept responsibility because it's probably a phrase that I neglected to run past her eagle eye.

In addition, thanks to Kim Hough for her masterful editing job; to Hannah Linder and Catherine Posey for the book's polished interior design; and to Vincent Davis II and Conor Franklin for their incredible marketing guidance. Once again, Kirk DouPonce provided a beautiful cover design that has made my books stand out visually.

I pray that my retelling of these incredible, true stories can match Kirk's powerful visuals. Thanks for exploring this forgotten corner of American history.

Doug Peterson

THE LINCOLN LEAGUE
EXCERPT

Richmond, Virginia
June 23, 1861

"Don't go," said Peg.

"I gotta," said her husband, John.

"It's a white man's war."

"It's our war, too."

"Don't believe it."

Peg and John Scobell stood at arm's-length from each other, just outside the servants' door of the Atwater house. They boarded in an attic room of the three-story home, which was tall and narrow with a V-shaped roof that shot to the sky like a church steeple. Peg wiped away a bead of perspiration from under her right eye. It was early morning but already hot as blazes without even the hint of a breeze.

John adjusted the pack on his back. "I'm goin' North to fight. I can't just sit idle durin' this war."

"Stay with me. For the first time, we're free."

"And I'm free to fight."

Master McQueen had just set them free, and now John wanted to leave her for a war. *It wasn't fair.*

Peg hooked an arm in John's. "You actually think the Yanks are gonna put a gun in your hands?"

"They will if I'm gonna fight for 'em."

"They'll put you in the front line to block the cannonballs. And what's gonna stop the Rebels from snagging you before you even get North?"

"I'll make it through the lines."

"Choose me instead of the war."

"It's not a choice between you and this fight."

"It is."

John's haversack was stuffed with food, and he carried a hunting knife hidden beneath his shirt. But his most unique weapon was a pencil and paper hidden in a pocket that Peg had sewn inside the cuff of his pants. John said that if he couldn't fight in the war, he would gather information for the North. But to Peg, spying sounded just as dangerous as shooting a gun, maybe more so.

"What do I tell people?" she asked.

"Tell 'em I'm goin' to Fredericksburg for work and that I'm bringin' you there when I got enough money."

Peg wondered if people would believe such a story. She buried her face in his chest. "I ain't lettin' you go."

John stood a head taller than her, and he put his lips to her hair. "I *gotta* go."

"You ain't leavin'."

Those were the very words her mama had used when her papa bought his own freedom and left the family high and dry. She was ten years old at the time, but she had a stark memory of being in their small cabin with her mama screaming that he couldn't leave them, and she kept pounding on his chest, like some crazed person pounding on a locked door. Her father shoved her small mother aside, like he was pushing aside a wild child, and he charged out the door without so much as a backward glance at Peg or her younger brother,

Shadrack. "You ain't leavin'!" Peg's mother screamed at the door, but she didn't even try to chase him down. Peg never saw her papa again.

And now this.

"You ain't goin'," she repeated to John.

"It's a matter of honor."

"Then honor me."

John leaned in and gave her a long kiss. Pulling away, he stared at her hard, as if he were printing her image in his mind like one of those daguerreotype photographs. With daguerreotypes, you had to hold a pose for what seemed like forever while the camera's eye memorized every living part of your body. Peg held her pose, staring back at him without a smile.

John said he wanted to say goodbye right there by the house, but she wouldn't let him. She hiked alongside him all the way through town, still trying to convince him to stay, although she knew by now it was a losing battle.

"Now in those times many shall rise up against the king of the South," John declared, as they moved toward the edge of the city. He recited this passage from the Book of Daniel to her almost daily. It was as if he was trying to convince her that he was being sent on a Biblical mission, like Moses or Joshua, and she shouldn't stand in his way.

"So the king of the North shall come and build a siege mound, and take a fortified city; and the forces of the South shall not withstand him. Even his choice troops shall have no strength to resist. But he who comes against him shall do according to his own will, and no one shall stand against him. He shall stand in the Glorious Land with destruction in his power."

John's eyes lit up whenever he spoke those words.

"Let me go with you, laddie." She tightened her hold on his arm when they stopped at the very edge of Richmond. "Laddie" and "lassie" were terms of affection that they often used—words picked up from their Scottish master, Dugall McQueen.

"Too dangerous, lassie," he said.

"If it's too dangerous for me, then it's too dangerous for you."

He didn't respond. They had reached a path leading north into the woods, for John told her he was planning to take a less-traveled route, skirting any Confederates along the way.

"I'll come back soon, when this is over, Peg. It's gonna be a short war."

Peg was suddenly so angry that she was tempted to punish him with cold silence. But she didn't. She held on to his arm, twisting the fabric of his sleeve in her hands. She didn't want to cry, but she couldn't help herself.

"Please. Choose me, John." She had also vowed she wouldn't beg. "Choose me, please."

Silence was his answer.

So she gathered herself and tried to command his loyalty. "I expect you back here in no time."

"Very soon, my lassie," he said.

He gave her one more kiss—good and long, so the daguerreotype had plenty of time to process.